THE IDIOT PLAYED *Rachmaninov*

MICHAEL BROWN

Hodder & Stoughton
LONDON SYDNEY AUCKLAND TORONTO

British Library Cataloguing in Publication Data
Brown, Michael, *1948–*
The idiot played Rachmaninov.
I. Title
823[F]

ISBN 0-340-48563-9

First published in Great Britain 1989

Published by Hodder and Stoughton,
a division of Hodder and Stoughton Ltd,
Mill Road, Dunton Green, Sevenoaks, Kent TN13 2YA.
Editorial Office: 47 Bedford Square, London WC1B 3DP.

Typeset by Hewer Text Composition Services, Edinburgh.
Printed in Great Britain by Biddles Ltd, Guildford and King's Lynn.

"I never enjoy going into that room. When I look into their eyes I see that whatever's going on in there, it isn't nothing."

ROBERT NIXON
Templeton Hospital for the Intellectually Handicapped.

". . . all knowledge of reality starts from experience and ends in it. Propositions arrived at by purely logical means are completely empty of reality."

ALBERT EINSTEIN

Preface

Truth really is stranger than fiction. The people of Westland are living proof of the saying. The bizarre is commonplace in their history, along with rugged individuality, resourcefulness, personal courage and practical humour. Their men made themselves famous for these qualities in World War II.

While my plot is fiction, many of the minor incidents, particularly the anecdotes, are either commonplace or taken from specific real events: the 'flatfoot shuffle', the chopping contests inside hotels, the connection between Stanley Graham and Nazi Germany, the extra-curricular activities of the reporter from *Stern* magazine, and many others. I have related the facts of one-off events as accurately as possible. Where I have invented anecdotes, I have kept within the spirit and character of Westland. Here's the point: no stunt or prank described in this book is beyond the provoked Westlander. If a totalitarian regime ever did take on Westland, I believe it would encounter psychological resistance out of all proportion to the size of the population. Let alone the armed resistance.

The spectacular 'bulldogging', catching wild deer by dropping on them out of a helicopter, has so often been performed in Westland that it no longer raises eyebrows there.

The water-tank episode is based on an incident in South Westland's Haast Pass when I lived there as a child. I still remember the shattering, mind-numbing noise. My mother thought Armageddon had come.

A big tree could be used to rip out a security fence in the way described. The incident is invented, though precisely the kind of anti-authority prank of which the Westlanders are capable.

In theory, the electrical petrol bomb would work; in practice it would be so unstable that only the most insane, or someone bent on suicide, would attempt to put it together.

The chemistry of the thorium stills is correct. There is thorium in Westland, but whether in sufficient quantities to lead to thorium moonshining is debatable.

The detail of Fentaz, the deer tranquilliser, is correct, including its effects on humans. My description of the effects of a mixture of Fentaz, Aminazin, Triffazin and Heliperidol contains some guesswork: the effect of the combination could well be very different from the sum of the individual effects. I don't often meet people who're partial to the concoction.

Which may all be incidental anyway because the story is really about the nature of mind.

With warmest thanks to Winston Cassels, Lin Forbes, Thomas Rochford, Ken Doig, David Byford, Lt Col Brian Hewitt, Ray French, Ralf Unger, Ian Dando, Squadron Leader Brian Phillips, Pilot Officer Martin Allen, Alan Fricker, Jenny McPhee, Tony Mooar, Avril and Douglas Brown, Jack Fergusson, Lyndsay Head, David Snale, James Scott, and Inspector Graham Clewer.

Some of the background material has come from Leslie Hobb's *The Wild West Coast*.

M.B.

We the people of Westland province invite the government to consider the children's story of *The Little Red Hen.*

It begins:

One day, the little red hen found a grain of wheat.
'Who will help me plant this grain of wheat?' she asked.
'Not I,' said the pig.
'Not I,' said the goose.
'Not I,' said the duck.
'Not I,' said the cat . . .

It ends:

'Who will help me eat the bread?' she asked.
'I will!' said the pig.
'I will!' said the goose.
'I will!' said the duck.
'I will!' said the cat.
'No,' said the little red hen. 'I will eat it myself.'

And she did.

It seems that the pig, after decades of neglect of Westland, has discovered the value of the radioactive element thorium in our beaches. But we of Westland are determined that not one grain of our thorium sands will be eaten by the pig, the goose, the duck, or the cat.

We have already demonstrated something of our determination. Believe us, that was a mere token.

Signed: 

Prelude

They say that Rosa Driscoll was an *idiote savante.* A wise idiot.

At Frazer Creek in South Westland they know there was more to Rosa than that, but they don't like to talk about it. Oh, sure, in the pub over a couple of handles of Westland Dry, they'll tell you what happened. They'll probably even pay for the drinks – now that it's over they can all afford it down there – but you'll notice there's one part of the story they keep side-stepping. Or maybe they'll touch on it in passing. If they like you. That kind of thing isn't handed out to just anybody.

And you can forget about trying to find her. Half the world is sniffing the trail for Rosa, wanting to apologise for the other half. But even in Westland so few know where Rosa and Mal are that you could fit all their tongues in a pickle jar.

No, your best bet is to keep your ears open at the Frazer Creek pub. And if you must open your mouth as well, take it easy – these Westlanders are touchy as hell about Rosa Driscoll's memory. And they're sensitive about their fat wallets too. The minerals of thorium have been on *their* beaches for anything up to 25,000 years; the fact that the price of thorium went from an obscure basement into orbit overnight was *their* good luck and nobody else's. Don't question it if you want to go on having a civilised beer and finding out what really happened. Even at the best of times you have to tread carefully with Westlanders. They're what the Welsh are to the British, but ten times more so. On top of that, they're individualists. They just don't behave like anyone else. Take the war, for example: they gave the Germans trouble out of all proportion to their numbers, and that was only slightly more than they gave the Allies.

They won't start with the thorium.

After they've sized you up they'll probably point you across the room through the smoke and the clatter and chatter to the piano, which stands on a platform by the dance floor.

The piano gleams with polish, meticulously cared for. There's a bowl of fresh spring flowers on top – and an ornately framed photograph of Rosa Driscoll, who's standing next to a children's slide. In the background there's a playing field with crooked manuka rugby posts and a Tinytown country grandstand. Rosa's large brown eyes look out of the photograph, inspecting you in a pleasantly interested kind of way. She's slender and fragile under a flounce of matted black hair. European features, but high, sculptured cheekbones that would grace the most striking of the Ngati-porou. The cheeks themselves are hollow; hers is the kind of haunting beauty that reminds you of the Third World. In this shot she looks perfectly happy, somehow quite at ease standing there with her doll, which is partly obscured by the edge of the photo.

She's a familiar sight now of course: the television news-clips have been shown so many times since the election that her image is on everyone's mind like footprints after the tide.

So you make your way back through the pub tables, and sit without saying anything, just prop your elbow and lift your glass – this isn't the moment to be spouting your own opinions. The locals will cogitate a while. One opens a new pack of cigarettes and extends it to you. Your host makes windows in the condensation on the jug and looks through at the bubbles rising.

'Funny thing about Rosa,' he says. 'Animals couldn't stand her. She drove them crazy.'

The attic was all but empty.

A broken chandelier hung from one of the beams. Daylight made colours in the remaining crystal, but cobwebs wrapped the colours back to white. Cracks between the floorboards set out for a single point at infinity, only to founder in the dust under the window. A new web rounded the corner of the window and a shadow moved beneath. The window was small, the glass quartered by leaden cross-hairs, and the outside world looked in, shutting its unseen eye. Sunlight angled through into the attic, burnishing the floor dust in a neat, creeping rhombus.

A toy piano with only two legs leaned drunkenly in the dust. The black keys were false, mere patches of paint over the white keys. At some time, white enamel had been slapped over the original blue exterior, leaving it with a colour like that of the glacier above the village.

A sound came: bare feet on the stairs. Timbers creaked.

Then there was a hand, holding a limp Raggedy-Ann doll that grinned like an imbecile at the ceiling. A waft of dust fell off a joist in the corner. Rosa Driscoll's head came almost up to the join of the kauri beams, and she stood so still that she could have been part of the attic.

Something was different about the attic. She looked around carefully to see if anything unexpected was lying in the far corners and she held the doll so that she could look too. Sometimes Rosa's mother hid presents if it was going to be her birthday; but no, it wouldn't be that because her mother didn't like coming up to the attic any more.

Nothing. The doll stopped looking. Rosa tried to think why she had come. From where she stood, she could see down the hill to the playing field and the grandstand. Closer to the house, a zephyr touched the tree tops. Inside, a dust mote sparkled in the sunlight near the toy piano.

A strange feeling came over Rosa. The floor seemed to be gliding sideways. The attic was drifting in some great pocket. Downstairs had gone away, disappearing behind her feet as she climbed the stairs.

Something touched her where her lowest ribs met in the middle. It was like being breathless or scared, though she hadn't run here and she couldn't remember if she was scared about anything. Her skin began to prickle, the way her arms did when she took a cardigan out of the basket of dry washing. Soon her skin was tingling all over, and cold, and she couldn't move her feet. Something was going to happen. Something frightening was going to happen.

'Stop it, Miska,' she said to the doll. The words emerged oddly, thickly, as if spoken by a child familiar with the vowels and consonants of another language altogether.

'It's not me,' Miska said, offended. She was also tingling all over.

A burning sensation began very low in Rosa's stomach at the same time as she heard the voices, jabbering and yammering and churning and then making the fire spread out and up through her body towards her head.

'Take it away!' she whispered.

'I can't,' Miska said, crossly, because she was burning inside too.

The burning reached Rosa's head.

She saw that the toy piano was really a grown-up piano. A bad girl was sitting in front of it and all the screaming and laughing and hammering voices were tumbling out of her hands through her fingers into the keys. Rosa opened her mouth to call out to make the bad girl stop, but couldn't work her throat. The bad girl shook her head violently anyway and kept playing, making the music go on and on and on, flowing over them, and Rosa and Miska clung to each other, making themselves like two stones nestling on the bottom of a river.

Then it stopped. Rosa opened her eyes.

The grown-up piano was a broken toy again and the bad girl had vanished.

In the pre-dawn, the herd was a mosaic of dark scales, shadow on shadow. A pulse of movement flitted from one deer to another, through ear and flank and tip of tail as if through a single entity. Ground mist sucked at their feet, a shallow lake that was luminescent under the last stars.

The lead hind lifted a foreleg out of the grey lake, then replaced it.

Close by, the black bush breathed, listening to the first call of Pipiwharauroa, the shining cuckoo, the bush ventriloquist, the bandit and changeling. It lays its eggs in the nests of other song birds which raise their new, strange offspring while the old merge into the forest floor. Half a season early, a call was already the full summer cry, twice a clear ascending note, once a curlicue, twice a falling musical sigh. Pee . . . pee . . . wharau . . . roa . . . Pee . . . pee . . . wharau . . . roa . . . roa . . . It came from all directions at once, out of the dark into the monochrome dawn, sharpening the outlines of the herd.

The herd browsed, dipping their heads into the mist in search of new blades. The master stag became visible by movement: a forward step, his antler rack tipped forward and sank. Two yearling males, spikers, not yet banished by the stag, moved among the outer animals. Their antlers were simple buds: soft and rounded with velvet, blunted Excaliburs bobbing on the surface of the lake. Amongst the herd there was always one head held high, ears in a taut, high 'V', jaws ruminating. As that head dropped, another would rise to take its place.

A hind thick with fawn lay on her side in the mist.

Colours crept into the morning. High overhead, the first peak flared white-gold. The snow fields of the high plateaux became the roof of the world. The glacier hung sparkling from the snows down into the South Westland bush, a blanket flung violently into the narrow space between the mountain tops and the sea.

The deer turned tawny red. The ground mist formed dips and hollows, rose into columns and thinned at the edges.

The pregnant hind had chosen her position well. She ranged with head and neck, lips wresting food out of the grey snakes that wound past her. She, of all the herd, was the most wary, her lips the first to still as something nudged the threshold of hearing. And even when the other hinds resumed grazing she wasn't satisfied. She rose, stood with head turned back over rump, nostrils wide, ears taut.

No sound.

One of the spikers investigated a pig rut. Within the rut was an unusual exposed root, a botanical oddity. The root had been attacked by a parasite and its end had formed, under the ground, in the shape of a flower. The Maori call it *puti puti o te pouri:* flower of darkness.

No smell.

The spiker snorted and turned to a small wineberry, stripping the best leaves from the top. His antler buds were already stained by juices from the scraping trees; later, the velvet would torment him until he thrashed in the pepperwoods and the mountain toatoas.

The hind's belly muscles rippled as she extended her senses

yet further. And back from the tip of one tendril came the electric warning.

Danger.

Even as she uttered the guttural bark, every head flashed up. Every face and pair of ears set simultaneously to a different direction. The pulse moved swiftly through the herd, turning a shoulder, flicking a tail, jostling a head and hoof, wheeling a body.

One

It was later than usual in the afternoon, so the cantankerous Friesian was glad enough to be relieved of her milk. She clonked a back hoof on the concrete a couple of times, then moodily contemplated the wall. Mal O'Hara, sitting on an upturned bucket, applied the Vaseline then settled his hands to the rhythm. Rich white jets rang into the bucket under the teats.

'Sooo, Dolly, sooo . . .' he murmured in case she was planning something.

The makeshift stall was against the outside of the barn, near the door. Up on a shelf inside the door, next to empty cans of gorse spray, were a tape player and a portable black and white television set. Both were turned on. The tape player scraped out chamber music for four strings, a combination that set Mal's teeth on edge but which kept Dolly civilised long enough to extract her rent.

The television set began the early evening news, fuzzy with the area's indifferent reception. A globe of the earth revolved on the screen then the newsreader's hound-dog face looked up from copy and spoke out to the hunched farmer and the flanks of the cow.

"Good evening. The government has confirmed that security for Westland's new thorium dredge has been turned over to the controversial counter-terrorist unit, the so-called Black-and-Greys. With the paramilitary unit already under fire for alleged breaches of human rights, the move has brought swift condemnation from Australia . . ."

Across the yard, the back door of the house flew open. An elderly man burst out onto the porch, shouting towards the barn.

'Mal, Mal! Turn on your telly, quick!' And rushed back into the house.

Malachy O'Hara went on milking. Only once did he give any

sign that he was listening to the item – a smirk, when an opposition politician declared that Westland had been thrown to the wolves by a regime without a leg to stand on.

A stranger would have been puzzled by O'Hara, unable to place him in any obvious pigeon-hole. He was in his mid-thirties, lean of stature, well muscled. His clothes fitted the farm much better than he did: a checked green bush shirt, dirty cords, unlaced gumboots and a shapeless green cloth hat over tangled black curls. His face was more that of a hard-bitten townie than a country cocky. A down-and-out townie at that, but with a brooding intelligence to the eyes. A five o'clock shadow of three days ago had bred and multiplied, adding to an air of disaffection with the world and with himself. His father had been known to refer to him, in the Frazer Creek pub, as a bum with a brain. But this was O'Hara senior's device for hiding his real worry – that O'Hara loins had brought forth a coward.

A wide, aerial shot of mountains and sea appeared on the television screen. A reporter's voice spoke over the pictures with an enthusiasm akin to the old Movietone Newsreels.

"Westland . . . the land of greenstone jade, gold, and thorium. Of mountain moonshine. Of deer and chamois, forestry and champion axemen, unemployment and, increasingly, poverty. But, most of all, this is a province of fierce individualism: the original settlers were a unique mix of nationalities, whose descendants have become famous for their scorn of authority and of laws they disagree with. And *that* is going to be the Black-and-Greys' greatest headache."

The milk zipped into the creamy contents of the bucket. The O'Haras' other Friesian, answering to Bird, chewed her cud patiently a few paces along the barn wall, waiting her turn. Overhead, cloud eased itself down the mountainside, neatly obscuring half the sky. This was a regular feature of the weather at the O'Hara farm: the back paddocks met the precipitous, bushed slopes the way a table meets a wall.

Mal's father, Oliver James O'Hara, appeared on the back porch again, danced in indecision and dashed back inside. Split rata was stacked chest-high on the porch, surrounded by the detritus of living: gumboots on unswept boards, wet-weather gear over the rail, a pair of trousers bleached and rotting in the sun. Stag heads, mounted on either side of the back door, stared across the yard in perpetual surprise.

The yard itself was littered with the paraphernalia of need and season: a rusty tractor, bits and pieces of machinery, a stack of whitebait nets by an empty dog kennel. A water-pump lay by a swampy stream, with trough and sacking board for straining gold traces out of the gravel. A long-expired Ford rusted on its axles against the fence; its windscreen was crazed and half a bale of hay spilled out an open door. Nearby, a battered Japanese motorbike leaned on its stand. Yellow sphagnum moss dried on trestles that stretched from the back porch to the barn. Underneath and about them ranged a dozen red Rhode Island hens searching the yard for titbits.

Dolly's tail whopped at a blowfly on her side, just above Mal's head. She turned her head, regarding him peevishly out of great, liquid eyes.

'Sooo, sooo, Dolly.' Keeping a hand on her as long as possible he brought the tape player closer, on the post next to her head. She tossed her head irritably to the front.

The whine of a helicopter squeezed through the scratches of chamber music. A small black speck appeared in the distance, low to the plain, close to the bush on the mountainside. The hens extended their necks, burring disapprovingly in the backs of their throats. Mal glanced at the approaching machine but went on milking.

The reporter appeared on the screen, trench-coated, for all the world a foreign correspondent in his own country. He was on a beach, scooping up coarse, dark sand and allowing it to fall through his fingers into the wind.

"Once, the Maori came to Westland's beaches for the greenstone. Then the Europeans came for the gold in these black sands. And when the gold was taken, the sand was once again just sand . . ." He stood, the beach stretching behind him. ". . . until the Manhattan incident: the discovery of a Libyan terrorist group with fifteen pounds of weapon-grade plutonium, sufficient for a crude atomic bomb. For years, the International Nuclear Commission had been urging a safer alternative to the plutonium breeder reactors. The Manhattan incident was the final straw, the catalyst for the swiftest, most widespread, most costly retooling in the history of technology – the change to the thorium breeding cycle, which is terrorist-proof. Overnight, that decision turned the thorium-laden beaches of South Westland into treasure troves that might have tempted even Henry Morgan to head for the South Pacific . . ."

Mal looked up appreciatively at the reporter.

The helicopter's whine became a pulsing thrum. Dolly stirred, Mal cursed and put his forehead and both hands on her flanks to calm her. A blue and white Hughes 500 swooped over the back field and settled. The engine noise faded and while the rotors still whirled, a figure emerged, striding across the grass and through the gate towards the barn. Beside him gambolled a Doberman pinscher.

The hens squawked outrage and scuttled under the moss trestles.

"For the New Zealand government the vast and sudden wealth here is a lifebelt thrown to a fast-sinking economy . . ."

'But first,' said a familiar voice, 'they've got to grab hold of it.'

Mal turned. As he did so, the man behind him swung his arm in a softball pitch. Mal's reflexes brought his arm up for the catch. But the ball was imaginary.

'Straight ball,' Ben O'Hara said.

'Strike,' Mal conceded.

With studied insouciance, his younger brother drew a hunting knife and extracted a stubby beer bottle from his pocket. The back of the blade popped the cap. Beside him the Doberman looked from one to the other eagerly, forelegs splayed, jaws ajar.

Dolly eyed the visitors balefully and rapped a hoof on the rail.

'Soooo, then, easy, easy girl.'

"It was six months ago," the reporter's voice said, "that a group of unknown Westlanders calling themselves the Little Red Hen first abandoned the legal channels of protest." The screen was filled with a grotesque, heat-contorted scrap hill – all that remained of the first thorium dredge. It had never lifted an ounce of thorium sand off the beach. Instead, the decades would feed it ounce by ounce to the sea.

'And all who sail in her,' Ben O'Hara said enthusiastically, raising his bottle to the screen.

Both men had the same build, the same swarthy complexion and dark, curly hair. But the resemblance ended there; one man could not have been mistaken for the other. On Mal there was the stamp of disillusionment, of ideals turned to puffballs. On Ben, from his fur-lined boots to the flying jacket on macho shoulders, was a boyish zest and eagerness.

After three helicopter crashes in five years Ben O'Hara still told people that any landing you walk away from is a good one. His love life had a similar history. And he tackled problems and obstacles the way a bull tiptoes through the daisies. But no one doubted *his* intestinal fortitude. His reputation for courage was sealed when he buzzed an army tank corps exercising with live ammunition near Lake Tekapo because he wanted to see if he could blow off their camouflage. His father had been known to refer to him, while drinking in the pub, as gutsy and self-made. However, this was O'Hara senior's device for stepping round his other worry – that O'Hara loins had also brought forth into the world a fool destined for a short stay. O'Hara senior suspected that some obscure law of nature had divided his genes with a hacksaw: all the brains to the older son, all the guts to the younger.

The reporter walked in from the side of the screen, hands in pockets, a bright-eyed Bogart.

"Even before the new dredge arrives it has been dubbed by the locals as Jonah of Arc, which may be an implied threat . . ."

'Doesn't miss much, does he?' Ben remarked.

Dolly lowed, lifted a hoof and took a swing at the bucket. Mal snatched it away just in time. 'Hamburger, that's what you are, walking hamburger!' he threatened her. He snapped off the chamber music, sloshed disinfectant over her teats and sent her away with a stinging slap on the rump. Next time she could bloody well wait.

'Well, what do you want?' he demanded.

Ben grinned, a rumpled grin like a Border collie. But it was also an uncomfortable, resentful grin. A memory came to Mal of the two of them side by side in the one-room school, Ben prodding his arm, moving it so he could see Mal's answers.

Mal shook his head at the younger man and turned away to pour from the bucket into a stainless-steel container. 'Oh no. Not this time. Enough is enough.'

'It's not for me,' Ben snapped. '*They* want it.'

'Bullshit. *You* want it Benjamin.'

'Don't call me that!'

The other Friesian plodded into the stall and waited to be milked. The Doberman turned to whuff interestedly at the hens ogling it from under the trestles.

'Stay Prince,' Ben ordered tersely.

'I don't want anything more to do with it.'

'But it's the specials! The Black-and-Greys! We never expected that.'

'I heard. And I don't want to know.'

'What do you want? You want me to get down on my knees? You can't just dump us like this. The others don't know what to do.'

'No. No way Ben. You started these boy-scout games. You finish them.'

Perversely, the younger man nodded. He relaxed. It was as if the course of the conversation had confirmed something, given him some kind of advantage. His grin re-emerged as he feigned a sudden thought and went to the barn entrance. He cast a searching eye around, strolled in and returned with a small cardboard box in his hand.

Mal stared as Ben removed a perished rubber band and opened the box. Inside were four hunting arrowheads, broadheads, each with four surgical steel vanes capable of causing massive internal bleeding and swift death.

'Still got 'em, eh?' Ben said lightly.

'Little bastard.'

A clumsy ploy, but effective. For generations the O'Haras of Westland had been hunters. More carcasses of deer, chamois, pig and possum had been humped down the mountains and through the O'Hara farm in the last century than all the rest of the farms and huts of the district put together. Hunting had been an unblemished tradition until Mal's seventeenth birthday. On his sixteenth, his father had presented him with a hunting bow, a set of arrows with field piles for practice and a stack of animal silhouettes to attach to straw bales. When Mal could put three arrows one after another through the heart of a silhouette stag from fifty paces, he would be allowed to go hunting with the bow.

Within the year, the teenager achieved the feat at seventy paces.

On his seventeenth birthday, he had taken gift wrappings off the box of hunting heads. In front of his assembled family he had picked one up, stared at its sleek edges, turned sickly white and dropped it. Since that time no threats, no cajoling nor clips over the ear had been able to persuade him to handle any weapons at all, let alone the bow.

Now Ben lifted one of the broadheads out of the cotton packing, and delicately rotated it by its base. After twenty years in the cotton, the edges still gleamed and light from the western sky flashed off each of the vanes in turn. He replaced it and looked at Mal with a speculative, mocking air. You see? his expression said. If you don't keep helping us, you'll be a coward, a chicken-livered yellow-belly.

'Jesus.' Mal ground his teeth. He stared at placid, patient Bird, waiting to be milked. Then at Ben.

Ben said nothing.

'Sodding little bugger, you still haven't got the point, have you? Look, look up there.' Mal waved his hand in the direction of the mountains now shrouded in cloud. 'What do you think that *is* up there? Vietnam? The Amazon? This country's too damn small for guerillas.'

'We've thought of that.' Irritated. 'There's no way they'll find the hide-out.'

'Have you thought of this then, little brother? It's going . . .'

'Don't talk down your nose to me.'

'. . . going to take just one hot-head like you to put a bullet through a special and we *all* lose. You and your boy scouts'll be dead just as soon as they can hunt you down. And the rest of the country will have the excuse it needs to stuff its conscience under the bed and back the government pirates. That what you want? Is that what you want?'

'Of course not.'

'No guns. Get rid of them.'

'No guns! Oh ho! That's good, coming from you.'

'You wanted my advice. You've got it. No guns. Don't even carry them empty.'

'If you think my people are going to go for that, you're crazy!'

'Are you their leader or aren't you? Christ Almighty, Benjamin. You might as well run up the white flag right now. Talk about a predisposition to losing!'

'Don't fucking talk *down* to me!'

'Shut up, Benjamin, I'm thinking.' Mal put down the billy and wandered around aimlessly, every now and then looking at the bush rising off the end of the back paddock. One of the more courageous hens minced across his path on its endless search for morsels, one large eye opening and closing on the Doberman. Bird waited, motionless, milk sacs full.

Mal looked again at the box of hunting heads, then went into the far back corner of the barn and contemplated the bow-hunting equipment that had lain unused for so long: fletching jig, bow square, spool, the quiver of cedar wood shafts. And the bow itself, which when strung ran its curves one into another like the body of a beautiful woman.

The toddler heard nothing at first. He was so absorbed in his game that he didn't feel the bite of the cold on his bare midriff and dirty feet. He slapped a crooked stick into a puddle, causing the inverted farm gate, the smokey-green trees and the sky below all to vanish in a storm. Then he permitted their shaky reappearance and did it to them all over again, creating and destroying them at will.

But the sound of engines penetrated. The stick paused. The jigsaw in the puddle sought its own solution and the manuka fence rails reassembled just in time for a series of metallic blue Land-rovers to flit along one of them, upside down.

In the lead Land-rover, the driver changed down for the crest of a rise, dropping the pitch of the smooth V8 engine. He glanced across the cab, but the commander was frowning, lost in thought.

Like the driver, Colin Renwick wore the safari-style bluish-grey uniform with its black boots, black beret, belt and epaulets. On the belt was a Smith and Wesson .357, a heavy weapon, but reliable. The men had initially been issued with Brownings which were choosy about firing in bad conditions; that was one of the first changes he'd made. His epaulets carried the silver crown and two pips of a Chief Superintendent. The police rankings were treated with considerable amusement by himself and his men, the central point of the hilarity being the gold bar on his own chest: the Commissioner's Commendation. The Commissioner's hands had trembled with poorly concealed rage as he pinned it on. Colin Renwick savoured the memory.

At forty-nine, the dour lines had advanced as far as the hairline had receded, though the eyes retained an incisive cunning and an acerbic wit. He had in fact begun his career as a genuine flatfoot, on the beat. Then, after what the records termed a resignation, he became a clerk, handing out dole money to people he took considerable care to avoid touching. That had lasted until the gorge rose in him and he upended his desk and walked out. Out of his job, his marriage, his family. Out of the country: within the month he'd been one of Tshombe's mercenaries in the Congo. Then, after ten years in Africa's trouble spots, he'd returned to join the Security Intelligence Service and risen swiftly through the ranks.

Now this. Officially, of course, he was once again a public servant. He even drew the pay-packet of a Chief Superintendent. That went into the bank along with his real pay-packet.

Out of his window, rimu trunks and oblique shafts of sunlit leaves flickered by. A hypnotic blur. He offered the driver a cigarette and chain-smoked. As the road began an elongated curve, most of the convoy became visible in the driver's mirror: eight Land-rovers, then the first of the army support trucks, a four-ton Mercedes.

A sign swept past. Colin straightened abruptly, 'Stop.'

Startled, the driver applied the brakes, watching the mirror. Behind them the convoy also came to a halt.

'Back up.'

The driver knew better than to argue. He leaned out, signalled his intention and the Land-rover purred backwards, compressing the front half of the convoy until the sign came back into view.

'Someone is rather too well informed.'

It was a professional-looking job, painted on a background of bluish-grey with a black border. It said in large letters: 'IT IS AN OFFENCE TO SHOOT AT THIS NOTICE.' In the bottom right-hand corner was what purported to be the issuing authority: '*By order* RENWICK'S SPECIALS.'

The sign was riddled with bullet holes.

Heads looked through from the back of the Land-rover. A door slammed, then another, and men appeared by the commander's window. Taking their cue from his grudging smile, many of them grinned. But a couple of men inspected the bush which pressed close on either side.

'It could be a trap, sir.'

'If it was a trap, your back would already be an imitation sieve,' Renwick said drily, noting with satisfaction the twitch in the man's shoulders. 'Use your head. If they wanted to put holes in us they'd have put up more than a rude note. Still, some cocky sod wants his stuffing removed. What's on the other side?'

Two men turned the sign. 'FRAZER CREEK 150 MILES,' it said. And under that was a stylised picture of a hen. The men looked to Renwick for another cue.

'Not much cock after all,' observed the 2-in-C, Ian Wilson. Colin suppressed a spasm of irritation.

'All right. Throw it into the trees, then catch us up.'

'Sir.'

He motioned with a hand and his Land-rover accelerated forward.

In the rear of the vehicle, men returned to their positions of boredom and discomfort, numbed by the hours of travel. Sophisticated as the new Land-rovers were, they hadn't been designed for restful journeys. Many of the men were hunched forward, heads drooping. One had his feet up on Renwick's personal crate, another had jammed his EWS rifle between seat and frame, and was using it as a head rest. The EWS was the new British army rifle, also brought in at Renwick's insistence. Lightweight, fully automatic, NATO standard 5.56mm ammunition, snug enough to ride easily with its owner in a cramped vehicle. As one European enthusiast put it, the EWS was 'Accurate enough to knock the eyebrows off a hedgehog at 600 metres, powerful enough to bring a bad man down.' And with a 30-round dump at 11 rounds a second, it was also guaranteed to bring the house down.

In each Land-rover there were nine men: an officer with two patrols of four men each. Plus Colin Renwick and Wilson. Seventy-four in all.

Behind the outer trappings of a police unit, the structure of the Black-and-Greys was similar to that of the British SAS, using modules of four: four men to a patrol, four patrols to a troop, four troops to a squadron. Like the SAS, the men addressed their officers as 'Boss', but the commander as 'Sir'. Of the meticulously selected personnel, two-thirds were either ex-New Zealand SAS or experienced mercenaries, the remainder were ex-police armed offenders squads, military intelligence or security intelligence. The lack of a written constitution and the morass of grey areas in the New Zealand statutes had allowed the creation of the paramilitary unit without a single word of new legislation. Such a force had been possible for decades, waiting only on a suitable rationale – such as the need to counter terrorism – and on the emergence of a national leader with enough secrets known, favours owed, and determination to stay in office.

Behind Renwick was an army- and intelligence-trained force, with the autonomy of the police in peacetime, and with the resources of army, police and the SIS at its beck and call. An elite, superbly equipped and perfectly legal private army in a western democracy.

The gnarled fingers feinted and probed, the knitting needles parried and harried in ritual combat, 29, 30, white over red, 31, 32 . . .

Edith Driscoll was content: a bag full of new wool, another multicoloured creation snug in her lap, and herself in her favourite seat at the playground on a fine spring morning. The sun stroked comfort into her old bones. Late jonquils and crocuses next to the seat nodded to the bees. Children travelled the slide like beads on a silver wire, up and over and down and around and up once more. To the old woman the shouts were barely distinguishable from the chirruping of the bush birds and the hum of the mower which poured green fountains into the breeze. The aroma of fresh-cut grass came to her, mingled pleasingly with the scents of the bush . . . 39, 40, red over white, 41, 42 . . . Yes. Content. As content as she could expect to be in an incomprehensible world.

On the slide, Rosa Driscoll lowered herself into a sitting position, tucking her blue cotton pinafore carefully under her. There was a small boy behind her and a girl on her way up the steps.

'Hurry up, Rosa!' Jimmy Hay was the same height, standing, as Rosa was sitting.

Busily, Rosa settled Miska in her lap, inched forward, let go, and swished down with a grin almost as wide as the doll's.

The boy came swiftly after.

'I'm going to beat you!' he challenged, then raced chuckling round the arm Rosa put in his way, heading for the foot of the steps. Rosa chased him but found the girl hot on her heels.

'Can I hold Miska?' Tui Jackson looked up at Rosa, reaching out a hand.

'Okay, you can hold her.'

'For two slides, shall I?' Tui was an opportunist.

'No. Just for one slide.'

A smile multiplied Edith Driscoll's wrinkles. Tui Jackson would get her two turns, but it would take persistence. Children gained the privilege on sufferance. Grown-ups, never . . . 65, 66 . . . Beside her the breeze rustled a corner of yesterday's newspaper. The headlines read 'NEW THORIUM DREDGE ON THE WAY GOVT WARNS SABOTEURS'. Further down was a picture of the first dredge: a burned-out wreck, a pile of twisted steel as big as the pub.

The mower came directly towards them down the middle of the rugby field, through the rye and cocksfoot and dandelions, and began a lazy sweep back towards the grandstand. On the motor Sid Mason winked and clucked his tongue at Rosa. Greetings to a child.

Mrs Driscoll sighed. For the men of Frazer Creek it was safer that way. For such as Rosa, physical beauty was barbed wire on a prison wall . . . 91, 92. Pearl. One, two . . . Hard to believe, looking at her now, the homely, lank-haired scrap of a child she'd been when she came to her and Tom. How long? Twenty-one years ago. Edith could still picture the sullen, skin-and-bone thing huddled in the corner of the Child Welfare rooms, thumb so far in the mouth that it made a lump in one cheek.

And she could still picture the face of the welfare officer.

'Mr and Mrs Driscoll, I can appreciate that at your age you want a child with a few years behind it, but I don't think you quite understand, she's a very disturbed little girl.' A baleful glance at the problem case in the corner. 'I mean have you seen how she responds to her name?' But even as she turned to utter it the child shrank even further into the corner, cheek to cheek with the doll.

'Stop, stop it,' Edith had hissed. Disturbed, yes. Pathetic, yes. And alone, like her and Tom. She and Tom had looked at each other then, and they'd not needed words. She had gone over to the wraith, crouching down. Close, but not too close. A name came from nowhere. Backwards out of Erewhon like the child.

'How would you like to be called Rosa?'

. . . 19, 20, red over white, 21, 22 . . . The child's memories had faded, but Erewhon's price was still being extracted: sometimes she wanted to take hold of Rosa and shake her just to make a laugh fall out, or to make her angry, or to make her cry. Tom had tried that once, out of frustration. He had tried to explain, 'I just wanted her to be more, more . . .' 'More what?' Edith had asked. 'More anything,' he'd replied in a dull kind of voice. But he had gone to his rest now and Edith knew she would be there with him but for Rosa.

'Give her back now,' Rosa demanded.

'I want another turn.'

'No.'

'You never share!'

'All right then.' Rosa gave in and the doll took another violent ride, its limbs flopping wildly. And again Edith Driscoll smiled. Miska was like King Alfred's axe – reputed to have survived the ages with the help of new heads and new handles. Like Rosa herself.

In the bush, a grey warbler trilled.

'You can't catch me, you can't catch me!' Jimmy Hay yelled from the top of the chute as Rosa came up after him. He waited, intoxicated by his own excitement, launching himself too late to avoid the tag.

Rosa seated herself and started down. As she slid, she began to tip sideways.

It happened so slowly that Mrs Driscoll was long moments realising something was wrong. Rosa appeared to have frozen, her hands hooked in mid-air, her eyes glassy. She spilled off the bottom of the chute, thumping onto the earth in a crumpled heap. Tui Jackson stood open-mouthed on top of the slide with Miska grinning hugely at the playground.

'Rosa!' Edith Driscoll cast the knitting aside and hobbled across the grass as fast as her aging limbs would allow. As she came closer, Rosa made an indecipherable sound and began to push herself up. For just a moment, the older woman was relieved. Then she saw that her daughter's face was distorted with terror.

Shocked, the old woman knelt and took hold of Rosa.

'Here, Rosa, it's all right, love. You're not hurt are you? It's okay now.' But Rosa cast about in wild-eyed panic, looking for the doll.

'Miska! Miska!'

Tui Jackson jumped as if someone had stuck a pin in her, slid down the chute and held out the doll gravely. Rosa clutched the doll to her chest, hunched over it and moaned. Edith Driscoll patted her hand anxiously.

'What's the matter, Rosie? What's wrong.'

'I had a bad dream.'

'Dream? What dream, Rosa? You're awake.'

Rosa looked up, blinking. The bright terror began to fade. After a moment she said, 'I can't remember.'

'There, you see? You're all right. You just had a fright. And you gave *me* one, you scamp.'

After a while, Rosa went back to playing, but not on the slide. She whirled the roundabout to a high speed, jumped on, clutching Miska, and between them they sent a frown and a huge grin whizzing round the perimeter of the field. On the slide, Jimmy Hay informed Tui Jackson, 'Once I had a bad dream. It came into my room and I shot it with my gun.'

On Moonlight Beach, the wreck of the first thorium dredge lay half in and half out of the water. Hard, dumping waves buried teeth in its side then scraped fingernails on the steep slope back to the sea. Each time, the corroding heap gave a tremor and became infinitesimally more like a sculpture created by the sea.

The wreck had company for the first time in many weeks. Men in civilian and army clothes moved about on the beach with measuring instruments and sheets of paper, or squatted on the black sand and drew diagrams and pointed. Driftwood lay along the high-tide line, a mass of roots twisted and tangled in fantastic whorls like a bed of snakes. Beyond it, amongst the flax and the ponga ferns that bordered Waikukupa Forest, soldiers carried long poles and rolls of mesh and barbed wire.

For two days, trucks wound out of the forest, laden with steel and perspex and electronic equipment for the new dredge.

Two

The desk-speaker issued a mellow tone, inviting rather than intrusive. The Prime Minister depressed a key. His answer was also a monotone and much more abrupt.

'Yes.'

'Brigadier Robson is here, sir.'

'Show him in.'

The panelled door opened, allowed a passage, closed discreetly.

'Take a seat, Ted. Read this.'

The head of the SIS took the proffered sheet of paper and allowed himself to be directed to an uncomfortable George III sofa. The PM, who preferred visitors not to be too relaxed in his personal office, returned to his work desk. He sat waiting, thumb and forefinger stroking his chin, looking out over Wellington harbour where pleasure boats twinkled in the breeze.

He'd had the personal office redecorated immediately on assuming office. It was now spindly Edwardian, reflecting the delicate touch with which the affairs of men must be handled. There was a Carlton House writing desk with satinwood crossbanding, silver blotter and inkwell; a fall-front bureau with silver tea service and a very rare three-bottle port madeira trolley; a skeleton clock in the likeness of York Minster, with gong and bell specially damped for his office; a bureau bookcase, which included on its shelves Ayn Rand's *The Fountainhead.*

His only concession to other periods was a miniature in Italian silk of Margaret Thatcher, the first leader of a western democracy with any inkling of how to run a cabinet in a predetermined direction.

The cabinet room, upstairs on the tenth floor, is known as the jewel in the crown of parliament buildings. Its daylight comes only from perspex panels in the ceiling. The walls are windowless, lined with shelf upon shelf of Statutes and Hansards, and perfectly circular – written and geometric testimony, in the PM's view, to the processes of democracy. When one inherited the nation, one also inherited that pinnacle of the democratic process, the cabinet; the one came with the other like a bride with a mother-in-law. Still, unlike mothers-in-law, the component parts of a cabinet could be rearranged. And politicians were remarkably similar to fleas in the way they could be trained: all one needed was a reliable information system.

He looked impatiently at the SIS man.

'Take your time, Ted.'

'Yes, sir. I'm familiar with it.'

'So is most of the country.'

'I believe the sub who let it through has resigned for reasons of ill health,' the Brigadier offered.

The PM made a gesture dismissive of shutting stable doors.

He rose from his deep-button swivel chair, unable to contain his wrath while sitting.

'What is it with these Westlanders?' he demanded. 'The Magna Carta of Westland? Delineating areas over which the government shall have no jurisdiction? The Magna Carta . . . ! From a bunch of raving lunatics who title themselves from a children's nursery rhyme? Tell me in God's name why the commentators are not laughing themselves silly? Never mind, never mind! The question was rhetorical.'

Robson knew better than to relax.

'Well?' demanded the PM. 'Let's have it.'

'I'm afraid it's too soon. We've still got no proof that there's anything more to this Red Hen business than an opportunist individual somewhere. Of course Renwick will assume the link with the saboteurs until – '

'Terrorists.'

'Terrorists, yes. He'll assume the link until we know otherwise, but equally there could be nothing in it. A oncer, from a nobody.'

The Prime Minister sighed. The problem with picking men for unswerving loyalty was that they very often had unswerving imaginations. He spelled it out, indicating the offending sheet of paper.

'I don't think you've quite got the picture. This Red Hen idiocy is potentially more damaging than the loss of the first dredge.' When the SIS man didn't answer, the PM strode to the window to gesture down at the parliament grounds. 'Use your memory, Ted. How many farmers stood in these grounds and roared their demand that I be installed as Prime Minister? A farming man for a farming country. How many?'

'Sixty thousand.' The SIS prediction had been half that.

'How many are there out there now?' the PM demanded sarcastically.

The Brigadier said nothing.

'And what do we have? We have the media seriously trumpeting opposition by a farm animal that's popular with pre-schoolers! And you tell me there could be nothing in it? Right now the Australian press thinks Father Christmas has come early in red feathers.'

This was an oblique rebuke and it extended the SIS man's silence. A poll conducted in Kings Cross, Sydney after the Gibson affair had revealed that the average Aussie Joe Blow wanted his navy to cruise an aircraft carrier off the New Zealand coast. And not because New Zealand had won another Test series on Australian soil – Gibson, a well known Australian journalist, had been beaten senseless and critically injured by assailants unknown while in New Zealand. The Australian press had been obsessed by the coincidence that at the time he'd been investigating allegations of brutality by the Black-and-Greys.

The Prime Minister saw that this had sunk in. He softened his rich baritone to its gentlest and most encouraging.

'Ted, you and I are old campaigners. We both know that the specials are best equipped to handle Westland efficiently.'

'Yes, sir.'

'I hope it's equally clear that the press is watching them like vultures. I don't need to remind you what's at stake.'

The Brigadier understood this only too well and tried to nod his head and shake it at the same time. If the Australians got their excuse to snip what remained of the CER trade agreement, the government would fall, thorium or no thorium. On the other hand, if the thorium didn't get out to the refinery the government would find itself at terminal velocity anyway.

'That puts Renwick into something of a pressure cooker.'

'Only until the local hot-heads give him an excuse, a *publicly acceptable* excuse, to clean up the problem efficiently.'

'Quite,' agreed the Brigadier.

The PM returned to his chair. The subtle resilience of the upholstery was calming. He nodded towards the paper still in the other's hand. 'Link or no link, I imagine the fellow behind that nonsense is the sort of character Renwick's people would enjoy a chat with.'

'Quite,' said the Brigadier.

'Thank you for coming, Ted.'

Three

'Go!'

Within the space of a tenth of a second, two axeheads sank into soft, white pine. The blades were so keen they penetrated three to four inches on the slant and the sound was no more than a soft 'chunk'. For three blows the assault seemed to make no difference, then the first fat chips floated cleanly out and onto the canvas on the floor of the Frazer Creek hotel.

The public bar throbbed with exhortations.

'Get into it, Finn!'

'Show us what you're made of, lad!'

'Placement, Floyd, placement!'

The blades looped, flashed and bit and looped again, working the bodies of the black-singleted axemen in a wave-like motion. At the tables, round the walls, up against the bar, men, women and children urged them on. The men's voices were loudest, the women and children's more penetrating. The very youngest children watched in silence, wide-eyed at the animal power and energy of the spectacle. One chip flew into the flames of the fire near Mal O'Hara. Another, with remarkable velocity, reached a table near the piano and demolished a glass of beer, bringing a shriek from the woman behind it and a surge of raucous laughter from around her. Many, particularly the farmers, were dressed in clothes with patches on patches and had little to spend but the laughter.

The axemen repositioned for the cross-cut, so evenly matched that the movements of their steel-capped boots might have been synchronised. The noise redoubled.

'Measure it out! Measure it out!'

'Timing! Don't lose your timing!'

'Put some weight into it, Finn; that's not a matchstick yer toppin'!' This last from a wizened bar-prop known to his drinking mates as Drop-kick.

The younger axeman, Finn, dwarfed his opponent in size. He was also the stronger, his strike-rate was higher than his opponent's and his lips were curled back with effort. Yet, it was the older man who began to pull ahead. The wrinkled faces at the bar nodded knowingly to each other: placement, placement – that was what separated the scratchmen from the also-rans.

Children climbed onto the bar to get a better view. The publican, Harry Withers, shifted peanut trays away from their feet without taking his eyes off the spectacle, while near him the bar television set flickered, unnoticed, with a picture of someone talking beside a map of Westland. Six men and two women poring over a book and a sheet of paper at the far end of the room turned to watch the outcome of the bout.

Finn, his back peppered by the curses of those who had laid money on him, raised his strike-rate to a ferocious level. But the wrinkled ones shook their heads at his tell-tale premature backward sway and at the erratic spurt of small chips. Moans roamed the bar.

'Yaah,' growled Floyd Smith as his axe swung for the last time. The top of the log jerked, spun through the roar of the crowd and crashed to the canvas. True to the art of winning with style, Smith reached unhurriedly for his tobacco pouch, seemingly unconcerned with his opponent's finishing efforts. Style came easily to Smith; he, after all, had driven the last of the great steam trains, bucking them through the gorges, drinking sweet tea – black tea because milk curdled in the heat and vibration – and, braced only by the thrumming soles of the feet, potting deer that gazed down from the bush.

The second log tumbled, the timekeeper called the seconds and the crowd paused, looking expectantly at Smith.

A lick of gum on tissue, a twirl of the cigarette, then an almost absent-minded nod to the publican.

With a rumble of approval, half the crowd moved towards the bar for the winner's shout. Wallets came from pockets, purses from handbags, settling debts; notes moved from hand to hand, grumble-greased. An enterprising ten-year-old collected from a series of disgruntled teenagers who had bet on size and strength. Mal O'Hara, declaring that he had been robbed, forked over ten dollars to Geoff Grimwood at the other end of the fireplace. Grimwood worked for the Department of Social Welfare, tracking down back-country recipients of the Domestic Purposes Benefit to report on who was sleeping with whom; he moved from remote settlement to shack to commune, smoking everyone's dope, writing down 'No problem here', and was seldom short of a warm bed.

Throughout the bar, the laughter and chatter and the rattle of glass and wood was returning to normal.

Mal found Ben in front of him. When Ben was out of his Hughes, he had the disconcerting knack of being somewhere without arriving. He pointed to the shapeless, unwashed hat on Mal's head, which had once been issued to Mal by an army quartermaster who would have called the MPs had Mal tried to return it in its present condition.

'That thing should be outside with the dogs.'

'Can't,' Mal said, inspecting his hat. 'She ain't been spayed yet.' He twirled the beer in the bottom of his glass. 'What do you want now?'

'Is that any way to talk to your brother?'

'What the hell do you want?'

'Nothing. Don't be so damn sensitive. I just want you to know that they think the sun shines out of your arse. They – '

'No!' Mal put his glass down. 'No, I don't want to hear it. I don't even want to be seen with you.' He made to move away, but came back, edging his brother away from the nearest group of drinkers. 'Anyone seen with you needs their head read. You think I haven't noticed what you're doing in here? You're recruiting, aren't you? Face to face in the public bar, stupid bugger . . . Look, pretty soon the specials are going to be here, right? Sooner or later they'll tag their first catch. And if you haven't developed a cell system by then, the specials are going to go through the lot of you like mutts at the dosing strip.'

'A what? Cell system?'

'To keep anonymous, for Christ's sake! So nobody knows everyone else.'

Ben blinked. 'That's a good idea, Mal.'

'Piss off. You're a bloody liability.'

'Anything you say, Mal.'

In the far corner, the six men and two women were back over

their book and paper. There was a free-drawn diagram on the paper and the text book was in front of the one answering questions. 'Don't even think about handling it without the mask,' he said. 'You get this stuff in your lungs and you'll be doing the cancer quickstep.'

In the middle of the room, Frazer Creek's mayor Tom Kidmann cleared his throat loudly, and welcomed them all to the Sunday chops.

'I find it incumbent on me . . .' Hoots and applause for this; Kidmann's great-grandfather had been mayor of Harihari. '. . . to congratulate Floyd on his fine win and suggest that he give thought to going up to Whataroa to take the Westland title off Billy Jones. To my way of thinking that would make him the national champion.'

The prolonged applause for this sally was interrupted by a single long buzz on the doorbell. Harry Withers turned out the bar lights.

'Take your partners for the flatfoot shuffle,' he intoned.

Without haste, more than a third of the patrons, including the children, picked up every glass, mug and jug containing alcoholic beverage and headed across the dance floor, past the piano and out the back door. Withers went to the front door, opening it just as the other closed.

'Gidday, John.'

'Gidday, Harry.' Frazer Creek's policeman walked in amongst the wood chips. At five feet and five inches, Constable John McPhail was reputed to be the shortest policeman ever to duck the height regulations. He was known variously as Short Stop McPhail, the Blue Shrimp, or, to those unwise enough to lend him money, the Copper Tub. Other Westland policemen thought nothing of joining patrons for Sunday drinks, but McPhail was something of a stickler for appearances – hence the flatfoot shuffle.

However, today was different. McPhail was clearly agitated and short of breath. By now, he would normally have ambled through the tables, past the sign which said, 'THE MANAGEMENT SINCERELY REGRETS THE LAW WHICH SAYS YOU CAN'T BRING YOUR KIDS IN HERE OR HAVE A CIVILISED DRINK ON A SUNDAY,' past the dart-board and pool-table observing that everything was in order. He stayed with the publican in the middle of the canvas. In spite of his preoccupation, he noticed that the group of men and women in the far corner had turned a piece of paper upside down. He knew this was done out of consideration for him and was touched.

'Harry . . .' He hesitated, unsure how to proceed. Several men materialised at his shoulder. '. . . Harry, about the specials. When do you suppose they're likely to get here?' He glanced significantly at the clock, which said 2p.m. Around him, several eyebrows jumped. Today!

Harry Withers got the hint.

'Five o'clock?'

'You sure it's that late?' asked McPhail.

'Four . . . ? Three thirty . . . ? Three – '

'Harry, you shouldn't go blabbing things like that,' McPhail said. 'You never know who's listening.'

'I'll try to be more careful,' Harry promised.

'Doesn't give me much time,' grumbled a weedy little man next to him. Tony Shadbolt, in dirty white shirt and a jacket that looked to be made from the skin of a mangy mule, was the owner, editor, reporter, copywriter, typesetter and printer of the weekly news sheet that gloried in the title *The South Westland Times*.

McPhail regarded Shadbolt gravely. 'Now see what you've done,' he reproved Withers.

Three o'clock. The time tripped around an otherwise silent bar.

The front door opened a few inches. People holding drinks peered round, saw McPhail still there and closed the door again hurriedly. McPhail looked pained. Ben, standing within discreet earshot of the policeman, felt eyes on him from the far corner – the man with the text book, questioning him – and he looked away quickly.

'Uh . . . where are they staying?' Shadbolt asked no one in particular, and with McPhail's help discovered like Withers that he knew the answer himself.

Shortly, the policeman completed his normal route across the room and out the back door. The patrons returned with their drinks through the front, to a bar so subdued that the sound of the television set was easily audible. The voice that emerged from it was deep and beautifully modulated. "Let me make this quite clear to those Westland authorities who would rather do irreparable damage to our economy than share the benefits of the thorium . . . we will *not* be held to ransom, we will *not* be threatened, we will *not* bow to the greed of the criminal elements attempting to take over the province."

The mayor, on the other side of Withers, was looking anxious.

'Uh . . . about this welcome. I'm not sure it's a good idea.'

'Of course it's a good idea.'

'But . . . the specials.'

'What can they do? You're the mayor!'

The bar began to empty. Smith and Finn disposed of the decapitated logs. The canvas was rolled up and the chips thrown on the fire. The free-drawn diagram from the corner joined the chips. Soon there was only Harry Withers, cleaning up, and then he went also, closing an inner door behind him.

Much later, someone came back into the bar and sat motionless at a table.

Colin Renwick swore under his breath. The words on the cardboard tacked to the lamppost on the main street read 'SPECIALS THIS WAY' and pointed up a side street. The driver double-checked his map, looked up with pursed lips and nodded. The convoy turned off up the short road to the rugby ground. There it halted again and this time the commander's expletive was less restrained.

Near the grandstand, attached to the side of a flat-backed Bedford, was a large banner which proclaimed 'WELCOME TO FRAZER CREEK'. Around it were several score people looking towards the convoy and applauding. Amongst them, a rag-tag brass band struck up 'Hail the Conquering Hero Comes'.

The driver looked at Renwick for instructions.

Renwick jerked his head and the convoy took the track round the rugby field, behind the grandstand to a gracious, two-storey house set back into the trees. The Land-rovers stopped around a circular rose garden and a moss-covered statuette of a cupid. The trucks pulled up on the front lawn. The house had once been a homestead, but years ago had fallen victim to the decline in farming fortunes. Faded lettering now declared 'MONA LEA GUEST-HOUSE'.

As the paramilitary and army men clambered stiffly from their vehicles, a matronly woman bustled out onto the entrance steps of the guest-house to gape at them.

'Here,' Nora Englefield crackled, when she found her voice. 'What are those trucks doing on my lawn?'

But everyone was looking across at the reception committee and the band. The band had switched to 'Calamity Jane'.

'Get those trucks off my lawn!'

Renwick glanced irritably in her direction, motioned Wilson towards her and went on looking at the band through narrowed eyes. Less than half the instruments were brass: the others were an assortment such as a banjo, a broomstick with bottlecaps, a washboard and a tea chest. The sound was painful to the musical ear – deliberately so; some of his men were muttering already and looking expectantly in his direction. But he took his time, studying particularly the genial figure holding the speech notes.

A black kitten with white paws came out of the guest-house door and rubbed its length along Nora Englefield's legs. Chief Inspector Wilson fronted up to the woman but kept his distance, because the smell of cheap sherry weakened the back of his knees. He was polite because with any luck he and Renwick would be fed from the guest-house kitchen rather than the mess.

'Mrs Englefield?'

'What?'

'You had a booking for Wilson.'

Mrs Englefield's mouth sagged open. The booking had been for two people. She stabbed a finger vaguely past him while he tried to convince her that they had brought more than a pup tent for the extras.

Renwick called in the squadron section leaders.

'Ranger belts and rifles. We're going to listen to a speech.'

The men were aghast. 'But sir, they're laughing at us. The bastards are taking the mickey.'

'Fall in behind the vehicles.'

'Here! If you lot think you're going to put tents up on my lawn you got another think coming!'

'Marker!'

Out at the grandstand, it was clear that the specials were going to come on out. The surprised and gleeful crowd speculated on the possible reasons and the organisers congratulated themselves on preparing for the eventuality. Tom Kidmann swallowed nervously, Jim Buchanan tested the microphone and the band switched to the tune 'Take Your Fingers Off It'.

'Here!' Englefield's voice carried across the grounds. 'Is this one of them government chit jobs? So I don't get paid for six months?'

'By the leff. Quiiick 'arch!'

Seventy-four Black-and-Greys marched out in three ranks, two paces between troops, officers to the side. Simultaneously the band lost its enthusiasm. In the ranger belts were radios, drop pouches, knives and Smith and Wessons. To each troop there were two recoilless Heckler and Koch 9mm machine guns with silencers. And most impressive of all, the EWS rifle. To Colin Renwick, the greatest practical asset of the EWS within New Zealand was its looks; back in the trucks he had stun grenades, CS triple chasers, Sakos with night-lights, even a pump-action Remington with a talent for opening doors by the hinges – but none of them could match the EWS for inspiring respect, especially in a backwater like Westland.

As the unit marched closer, what minuscule coordination the band possessed crept away, partly because the conductor was unable to keep his chin off his shoulder.

'Para . . . ade. Halt!' The booted feet crashed down with such precision that the conductor's baton jerked and died in mid-air.

'Ley . . . eff. Turn!'

When Wilson had the ranks perfectly arrayed, Renwick turned to the band and the crowd with an air of polite interest.

Someone nudged the mayor, who twitched, climbed up on the utility vehicle platform and stood wide-eyed behind the microphone. He felt an almost overpowering urge to check the time on his second watch, the one he kept in his pocket during the months of daylight saving.

He began well enough, because he thought of himself first and foremost as a performer. He welcomed the visitors with a fulsome smile, saying he was confident the local hospitality would reflect the eagerness with which the people of Frazer Creek had looked forward to their arrival. But he felt obliged to warn the guests about the discomforts and inconveniences that went with living in South Westland . . .

Here he made the mistake of looking up from his notes to see how the speech was going down. He noticed little things here and there: white knuckles round the stock of a machine gun, a boot shifted in a certain way on the grass, the curl of a lip, the chilling eyes of an officer with white sideburns. Suddenly he wanted to change the words, but he was now in lock-step with them.

'However, I'm certain the people of Frazer Creek . . . of Frazer Creek will endeavour to acquaint you with every possible . . . with . . . every possible hazard . . .' He felt his showmanship was draining away, flesh melting from the skull of a clown. Behind him he felt the crowd's smugness grow thin and brittle.

An aura of well-being settled over the parade ranks. The smart-cunt was coming unstuck. Glances of admiration followed Colin Renwick as he strolled over to the utility.

'Do go on, Your Worship.'

'Can't seem to read my own writing,' Kidmann mumbled.

'It could be the light,' Renwick suggested. 'Well, perhaps you'd do us the honour of inspecting the ranks.'

'Ah . . . I . . . Under the circumstances . . . Hardly appropriate.'

At a nod from Renwick, the nearest three officers walked to the vehicle. Renwick put out a hand and beckoned Kidmann with one finger. Kidmann's posture backed into the corner but his feet took him to the edge and down in front of the trio. The crowd gave an audible groan. 'Don't do it,' a few voices called out. But their mayor seemed hypnotised by Renwick. In the back of the crowd, Mal O'Hara was shaking his head slowly when he noticed something about one of the specials in the middle rank. A detail. Something his mind wouldn't let go.

Another nod from Renwick, a prearranged signal. The trio drew revolvers, pointing them upwards in front of them as they would escort swords. They arranged themselves around the mayor in a triangle, the weapons so close that his teeth ached. Renwick made a sign with his thumb. The three hammers clicked back and three parts of Kidmann's scalp tried to climb up the top and over the other side.

'Three,' Kidmann squeaked. 'Is that usual?'

'Haven't you done this before?' Renwick was surprised. The glances from his men were close to open worship.

Knowing that his only hope was in a brave face, Kidmann stepped forward. He was sweating even before they were lined up to inspect the first rank. Most in the crowd wanted to leave, but a perverse fascination kept them rooted to the spot, rather like watching a spider killing a fly and being unable to leave while the fly still struggled. The mayoral panache was taking a horrific beating.

But it was not yet dead.

Kidmann was still fighting the inevitable at the end of the first rank, so Renwick nodded the inspection party round into the second and motioned for the pace to slow down. There was to be no mercy.

In the back of the crowd, Mal O'Hara pulled his hat down over his forehead and bent his knees.

'Hey, Tom! One of them's in advertising!'

Frazer Creek's mayor jerked visibly. He took a deep breath as the priceless value of this information sank in. The heads of his escort wavered uncertainly as an electric silence settled over the assembly.

At first, he just stared furiously at the trousers of every man he passed, looking for the prize. But the actor in him was begging to get out, and the realisation that every man along the rank was trying to look at his own pants without a movement of the head brought real nonchalance to Kidmann's gait. He slowed the pace even further. He stopped opposite one man, forcing the escort to halt, waited until the constable's eyes had widened satisfactorily, then shook his head and moved on.

At the second man from the end, he halted, passing his gaze slowly down from the youthful, anguished face to the area below the belt. He shook his head gravely and looked around, concerned.

'We seem to have a problem here.'

The constable looked as though he had been sentenced to five years. His hand twitched desperately.

'Touch it . . .' Renwick said with deadly promise. '. . . and you'll clean the main street with a toothbrush.'

The twitching stopped.

Colin Renwick's neck muscles were trembling, his eyes over-bright. He looked round at the simmering crowd, the agonised specials, the army contingent watching from beside the grandstand, and at Mrs Englefield still in the doorway of the guest-house. Gradually, he forced a smile.

'I congratulate you on your powers of observation,' he said to Kidmann and motioned savagely to the escort. The revolvers dived into holsters. Kidmann was brought back to the front and the parade marched away.

The crowd, stunned by the unexpected victory, didn't applaud.

Mal found Ben beside him.

'Did you see his face?' Ben licked his lips thoughtfully. 'Didn't like it when it wasn't going his way, did he?'

'Pity there wasn't a camera,' Mal mused. But then he shook himself as if coming awake, glared at Ben, and went away over the grass with the rest of the crowd. Ben stared after him.

'You left the radio on,' Susan Withers said as she and Harry returned through the side door of the hotel. But Harry was still reliving the confrontation on the rugby field.

'. . . that guy with the white sideburns. Did you get a look at his eyes when Mal called out?'

'An officer?'

'Yeah, but not the chief wallah or the escort. This guy was just standing there. I wouldn't want to meet him in a dark alley.'

'Then don't. You left the radio on.'

Harry was already on his way up the stairs. 'Turn it off, will you, Sooz, if I don't get those finings into the brew I'll have to kiss this batch goodbye.' Harry Withers had two passions in life: chess and home-brewed beer. There was always a chess set in the bar, and there was always a bottle of carefully doctored brew under the counter, the latter being on-the-house for selected patrons who looked likely to use their fists to punctuate an argument. The critical ingredient was the ground-up roots of a local herb called Valerian. A bottle of the concoction was known from Hokitika to Haast Pass as a Zombie. Recipients were led gently to a mattress on the back porch.

In what had once been a bedroom for the children, he removed the airlocks from half-gallon jars containing the current brew and sniffed. Not bad. He always put in extra sugar to make the alcohol content impressive, though the drawback was that the little bottles turned into grenades if they weren't handled carefully.

He was just reaching for the brewer's finings, when he heard his wife running up the stairs. She burst in on him.

'Harry, quick!'

'What's the matter?'

'Come *on*!' She pulled on his arm. 'And keep quiet.'

He flapped his arm at the brew being exposed to the air, but caught up in her urgency allowed himself to be bustled back down the stairs and along the corridor where he could hear the radio still on the concert programme. With her finger on her lips, his wife pulled him through behind the bar.

It wasn't the radio.

The Withers knew nothing about the kind of music Rosa Driscoll was playing. They knew only that they were watching a pianist of extraordinary ability. More than that – it was as much as anything else the *look* of her that made the backs of their necks prickle. As if the most intense passions the Withers could remember were being brought back to them by the sight and sound of Rosa at the piano. The doll, Miska, was grinning at them from the far end of the keyboard, over the deft, flying hands and dancing fingers as the sound rolled through and through the empty public bar.

Rosa ended one work and without pause, or any sign of awareness that she had an audience, began the next. Rachmaninov's second piano concerto. The Withers knew neither title nor composer, but Susan Withers found herself remembering the death of her mother. An agonising, grim death. Her fingernails dug into her husband's arm and stayed there when the music changed, this time making her recall the time she found her two boys dousing a cat with petrol and preparing to strike a match; another change, and she recalled how Harry had made love to her on Gillespie's Beach and shouted over the noise of the waves asking her to marry him; and again when her daughter had called from Europe to say she was coming home. Change, and Susan was consumed by feelings of delight that made a desire to laugh bubble up inside.

Change.

'My Godfathers,' Harry whispered. 'This isn't possible.'

'Call Mrs Driscoll,' Susan said and shook his arm to make him move. 'Call Mrs Driscoll.'

While he was on the phone, Susan confirmed something. When she took her eyes off Rosa, the music didn't stir her to the same degree. The moment she looked at her again, the music furrowed right back into the things that made her want to shout or cry or smile. Yet there was nothing obvious about Rosa to explain why this should be so, only the utter absorption, the total concentration.

Rosa was still playing when Harry brought her mother in behind the bar. Mrs Driscoll hadn't understood a word of the phone call and was bewildered. The Withers kept looking at her as if she could tell them what was going on, but Edith Driscoll was a long way from being able to speak at all, let alone offer an explanation. She knew that in all of the years Rosa had been her daughter, she had never played the piano or shown interest in any instrument.

Change.

Erik Satie's '*Gnossiennes* One.' Like the Withers, Edith didn't recognise the music, but the poignancy and longing of it struck across the room and sprang tears down her cheeks.

Four

There was no door on the Hughes. The throb of the rotor was crisp and clear through the turbo whine. The Doberman pinscher and the two men peered down through the chin of the 500, Ben O'Hara's hands rode the controls. John Taylor held the gun, an Italian Marcheno adapted with locally engineered sleeves to fire beeper-drug-darts. The dog lolloped its tongue eagerly. The machine smelled more of dog than kerosene.

Taylor saw the deer first. 'There.'

'Damn! They're hot.'

A hundred and fifty feet below, the tussock flowed under a score of stags. They were like coloured pebbles in a stream, made to swoop and swerve by tricks of the light. But they had been in flight too many seconds, their body chemistry had altered. The drug would be useless.

Taylor laid aside the Marcheno, rubbing his hands with anticipation.

'It's late. Last chance,' he hinted, and clipped a coil of rope onto his belt. John Taylor was the best deer bulldogger in South Westland.

'Okay. Which one do you want?' Ben called.

'There. Eight pointer, forward right.'

The Hughes settled in behind a young stag of four to five years, antlers fat with velvet. Frenzied by terror, the animal no longer saw the herd. Briefly, urgently, it lunged from side to side, but exhaustion closed in until its body was running straight, disconnected from conscious mind.

Taylor climbed out onto the skid, blinking through the hair that beat about his eyes. Below him the muscles of the tawny back stretched and contracted, the neck muscles bulged, the antlers strained high. This was the moment of peak concentration, the time when he could smell the animal's fear before he smelled its body. He motioned with his left hand. Lower.

'You want the skid up its arse?' Ben complained.

The distance between Taylor and the stag fluctuated wildly as the animal moved over a rough patch. Changes of slope, distance, speed, the deer's movements, even alterations in the ground echo of the rotors – all information crowded in through Ben's eyes and ears and skin to become minute adjustments of the cyclic, the collective and the rudder. And another adjustment as Taylor hunched ready for the drop; in the pub unkind parallels were drawn between the way he made love to women and the way he caught deer.

The stag came to predictable ground.

Taylor dropped. He landed with his left side to the right of the stag's back, his hands to the base of the antlers and his feet to the ground. The feet thrust, his body twisted bringing the antlers round, and the stag was over and thrashing. A length of braided nylon came off Taylor's waist and looped round fore and hind legs, hobbling the animal. Frightened, bloodshot eyes stared, breath soughed in and out of the foam around the mouth. It tried to stand, tried again, then lay quiet, flanks pungent with sweat and urine.

Above, the Hughes began a very slow, tight circle. Ben scanned the flats, the tree-lines and up past the snow-line. Satisfied that no one was in sight, he sent the machine scudding sideways and down to a convenient mound. He and the Doberman bounded out, heading for Taylor with a second rope and a small black box. Within moments the stag was unhobbled, but tied by the antlers to the centre of the second line with a man at each end. The dog ranged on its heels and it took the stag two lunges to realise that it couldn't get at any of its captors.

After another careful look around them, O'Hara and Taylor ran the animal down the hill, away from the Hughes, into the trees.

They emerged without the stag or the rope. Ben kept watch, Taylor took the black box from him and set it into a natural crevasse in the top of a nearby outcrop of greywacke. He opened the leather casing at the top, revealing an automatic timing device and a large inset bulb and reflector aimed at the sky.

Then, all three were back in the helicopter and lifting away over the ridge.

The four specials stayed crouched, studying what lay ahead. They took their time about it because what they were looking at didn't make sense. In dense mountain bush, in the middle of nowhere was an old man and an equally old copper washtub. Flames licked in the firebox, smoke and steam rose into the foliage overhead.

The specials spread out with rifles and an HK at the ready and advanced across the moss, through the ferns, under the mountain beeches, their grey and black uniforms merging well with the shadows. The old man's back was turned to them and he seemed absorbed in feeding sticks into the fire. Soon they gave up crouching and walked upright, converging on him.

They stopped in a semi-circle.

'Whatchyou doin', Grandpa?'

The old man jumped up. 'By Jeez! You gimme a fright!' He looked scrawny but fit, his face pitted and scarred by a lifetime of outdoor work.

The sergeant looked at him speculatively. The other three poked in and under and behind things. It was less a clearing than a space between the trees with a trickle of water as an excuse for a stream. There were three large plastic containers with clear liquids in them and the tub itself contained what looked like dirty warm water. Upended, the old man's rucksack dropped a tin plate, a billy, several plastic rubbish bags and oddments of food. The sergeant went to one side of the clearing where the roots of a fallen tree had left a cavity, partially hidden by moss. Inside, resting on sand, was a square-shaped bottle.

Grinning, he brought it back.

'So if you got a fright, how come you hid the booze, Grandpa?'

'Gimme that.' Querulously.

'Uh, uh, naughty, naughty.' The sergeant held it away from the reaching hand and inspected it. Westland Gorse, Black Label. The best. He folded the stock of his HK, clipped the strap, uncorked the bottle and tipped back. As he swallowed, the old man's eyes watched the slop of liquid the way a cocker spaniel watches a bug. The bottle continued the round of dry specials.

The sergeant was still curious.

'What's your name?'

'McFadden. Herc McFadden.'

'Herc?'

'Hercules.'

'My, my.' The sergeant's eyebrows were impressed. 'So whatchyou doin' here?'

'Mindin' me own business,' snapped the old man without taking his eyes off the bottle. The specials hooted in mock fear. One used his foot to shift a gauze mask showing out of the front pocket of the pack.

'What's this for?'

'I've got a cold.' Nasally. 'Don't want to spread it about, do I?'

'Considerate, ain't he?'

'Come on, you old codger, tell us the big secret. What're you doin' with the tub?'

The old man looked abashed. 'I'm washing me clothes.'

'You're what!'

'I'm washing me clothes,' he snarled. 'The old lady won't 'ave me in the house till I wash me clothes.'

'Up here?' The sergeant was incredulous. 'Where do you live? You got a shack up here?' But the questions were lost in the laughter of his men. One walked around to the copper tub and tapped the housing.

'If I didn't know better, I'd say he was doin' a bit of moonshining.'

Another round of mirth.

'In this day and age?' 'My my, aren't we out of touch.' 'Yes, sir, lead me to the Hokonui Hooch.' 'Where's the coil, Grandpa?'

The para by the tub extended an index finger to the liquid warming in the tub. 'Hey, maybe it really is hooch.'

'Don't touch it,' the old man said hastily. 'It's a bit hot.'

'It's only warm.'

The para dipped the finger and brought it towards his lips. It didn't reach his lips because it started to hiss. He gave a yell, thrashed it about in the air and leapt into the stream, plunging his whole hand into the deepest part. The extra water increased the activity of the chemical at first, increasing his agony in proportion; he performed gymnastics round his immersed digit that brought near paralysis to his colleagues. Eventually the moving water washed the chemical away but when he brought the finger out a couple of minutes later, it was the same colour as his face.

'What in buggery have you got in there, you stupid old git?'

'It's bleach. I told yis not to touch it.'

'My fucking finger!'

'It's a bit on the strong side. But I *told* yis, me old lady won't let me in the house till they're clean. Me clothes.'

The para's comrades-in-arms were staggering about the clearing, holding their stomachs.

'I should put you in the tub, you stupid old fart!'

'Yeah? You and whose army?'

This provoked fresh howls from the audience.

Holding his wounded finger carefully out to one side, the para cracked the old man across the face, knocking him to the ground.

'Let's go,' the sergeant ordered in a weak voice. 'Give 'im his bottle back. Go on, give it to 'im. Crazy old coot probably needs it, don't you Grandpa?' He patted the old man fondly on the shoulder and led the others back towards the track. His shoulders shook and he kept repeating 'You and who's army?', and shaking his head.

In the clearing, Olly O'Hara regained his feet, holding his bottle in one shaking hand and adjusting his false teeth with the other. He said in a low, tremulous tone, 'Watch your lip, sonny. I can still thrash the likes of you with one hand tied behind me back.'

The two privates were not impressed by the beast they had to guard. Nor were they much impressed by the primitive beauty of its territory. Their boots scuffed in the heavy, black sand of Moonlight Beach, their SLRs drooped from weary shoulders and in spite of the midday heat their camouflage jackets were zipped to the top against marauding sandflies. It was a muggy, oppressive heat. It would soon sweat rain, and when it rained the mosquitoes would sing.

Behind them, the beast was feeding. All this first day, foot after foot, it had been eating Moonlight Beach. Bare steel and glass and bright yellow paint, squatting on treads twice the height of a bungalow. Its bucket chain ranged wide, tearing out sand and rocks from above and below the waterline with indiscriminate hunger. The sound of the chain alone would have been enough to deafen unprotected ears at close range, but on top of it came the sound from its belly: rocks entering the crushers were rendered down to sand, reducing the process of millions of years to a continuously shrieking instant.

The two stopped, turning to watch as the din multiplied in volume for a large, particularly stubborn boulder. Greenstone, New Zealand nephrite jade, now uneconomic to separate out. Soon, like the remaining gold, it would be just another waste product in a chemical soup at the thorium refinery across the mountains. Greenstone, gold and the thorium ore monazite had come down from the Alps together between ten and twenty-five thousand years ago, spreading out in vast cornucopian fans, covered by forests, worked at by rain and rivers and sea – and, each in its season, by man.

The beast disgorged its belly continuously onto a line of waiting trucks. Each of these, when full, joined the others by the security fence, which stretched a quarter of a mile, twelve feet high, topped with coiled barbed wire. Beyond it, others of the 2nd/1st Battalion detachment patrolled, also in twos. Beyond them, Waikukupa Forest rose away into murky wraiths of cloud.

A blue-grey Land-rover came out of the forest. It was admitted through the wire gate and an army officer met it on the sand, climbing aboard and handing out several pairs of ear-muffs. Colin Renwick was given an inspection of the army's beach security. Soldiers looked at him curiously wherever he went, some with resentment, some with respect. Further down the beach, past the contractors' huts, the remains of the first dredge were reduced by distance to a brown smudge by the oily sea.

The beast shrieked again.

'I'd like to put the bloody thing out of action myself!' one soldier roared at his colleague's ear-muff.

'What?'

The first made the mistake of taking a hand out of his pocket to pull aside the other's muff and shout again. He was bitten by a sandfly before his hand returned to cover. The two men continued their patrol, gazing sourly at the dumper waves and the pebbles leapfrogging in the froth.

Late at night, long after the dredge had been shut down, one of the guards by the wire heard a faint, humming sound very high overhead. It might have been a helicopter, but the eerie terrain played too many tricks with sound for him to do more than shrug and keep on walking. Some time later, a different guard saw a flicker of light out to sea. But that could have been a squid boat, or lightning on a distant front.

Five

'I can't,' Rosa said firmly.

The music teacher from Hokitika leaned back in his chair, exasperated. But after a glance at the expensively dressed city man beside him he tried again.

'Rosa, Professor Truman is a very important man. He's come a long way over the mountains just to hear you play the piano because he's heard what a good player you are. He has to go back soon and he'll be very disappointed if he can't hear you.'

'I *can't*.' The words were carefully enunciated in case he just hadn't heard her the first time. She was worried now, and sat with Miska cowed in her lap. Her mother was at a near table, her brows gathering resistance to the proceedings. Susan Withers watched from behind the bar.

'You mean you don't want to.'

'It wasn't me. I think it was that *bad* girl.'

Abruptly, the music teacher left his chair. His worn ripple soles squeaked across the dance floor to the piano where he stared down at the keyboard as if he could make it conjure without Rosa's hands. He had been here a week and in that time, she had played only twice, both times without warning. On the first occasion he had thought of her as his discovery. On the second, he had also known that there was nothing he could teach her. Those who can, do; those who cannot, teach only those who can learn by established methodology. He'd known then that he would need advice.

He put his right hand to the keys and ran off a couple of trills. He glanced sideways at the University of Canterbury's professor of music.

'When I heard her on Wednesday, her filigree work was clumsy. Her fingers were labouring to keep up. On Thursday, I'm telling you, it was flawless.'

The professor said nothing, resisting an impulse to look at his watch.

'I swear she had every note and phrase already there in her mind, perfect, but her fingers had to catch up.'

'It's *her* fault,' Rosa pouted at the piano stool.

'It's more than mechanical technique, she grasps the whole structure . . . she . . . she . . .' He wondered at his own unseemly urgency, but ploughed on. 'It's more than that. There's something about her presence when she plays; a . . . a . . . gestalt of the sight and sound of her that does something to you. I've never seen anything like it. I think it's unique.' A pause. 'You must think I'm raving.'

The professor sighed. 'Don't mistake me. It's just that I can't help you.'

'But you haven't heard – '

'I think that's the point, Mr Beaven. I wish I could have heard her. But even if I had, what could I do? You think the world should know about her, right? Well the world would be disappointed because she follows her own clock. The world's famous pianists all have one thing in common apart from the piano – they turn up for the performance.'

'I didn't mean that she should be another Horowitz,'

the teacher said curtly, fuming at the patronising tone. 'I just wanted . . . I just thought . . .'

'I'm sorry, but there's really nothing more I can do.' The professor picked up his coat and turned to Rosa, who was staring through the table top in front of her.

'Rosa?'

Rosa didn't look up.

'Rosa, I don't think the bad girl is so very bad. If she wants to play the piano again, you let her go ahead, eh?' But Rosa only scowled at her doll, suspicious of complicity. He shook his head and said, partly to himself, 'The world would run over her.'

'Thank you, professor,' Edith Driscoll spoke up warmly.

'Get her a piano.' And when Edith's face fell, 'Think of her body as the puppet and her mind as the puppeteer – the only string working is that of music. I have seen the effect of music on mentally retarded people at Templeton Hospital, Mrs Driscoll. Music can actually mend some of the broken strings.' He sighed, turning away, speaking almost to himself. 'Unfortunately, the power of music as a catalyst for synthesis is totally unrecognised these days.'

But when the patrons came in through the hotel doors that afternoon, there was a collection box on the bar labelled 'ROSA'S PIANO'.

Colin Renwick felt a quirk of disappointment when the message came through. The first sand convoy was safely through the Alps. Without a single incident. Not even a protest banner. The men had had high hopes of the Little Red Hen: it had smacked of real organisation – something to get the teeth into. Well, it was early days yet. Something would crop up, as it were. And the saboteurs who had disposed of the first dredge were still out there, presumably lining up for seconds.

As he worked through the existing SIS files, Mrs Englefield's black kitten pranced around the door, looked at him with high, bright eyes and scuttled mischievously about what was now his office.

The room had been the guest-house lounge. It still contained the conglomeration of furniture and fittings from throughout the century: a colonial fireplace with a carved, kauri mantel, brocade curtains about the bay window, a 'Blue Boy' framed on one wall with 'Highland Cattle' on the other, a roller-top writing desk, and a player piano in the corner with 'Remembrance' still in the roller and 'Robins Return' and 'Marche Militaire' on top.

He had removed the velvet sofa and easy-chairs to make way for an office desk and filing cabinets. Nevertheless, given that a certain amount of paperwork was inevitable, he found the room a comfortable place. The only real irritation was its preoccupation with time: a 400-day clock, a large and crudely made hour-glass on the mantel, and a pendulum clock in the hallway whose mechanism he could feel through the seat of his chair. He had already put a stop to the 400-day clock by jamming its brass balls, thus earning a memorably filthy look from Englefield.

Old bat. Every time she came in with the tea trolley she interfered with the curtains and turned the hour-glass.

The kitten skittered out from under the china cabinet, up and down the pedals of the player piano and over to the window where it attacked the curtains with white-tipped, black velvet paws. Colin picked up his beret from the table and flicked it, saucer-like, through the air. The kitten fled to the door and then provoked him from the other side, putting a paw underneath and batting an imaginary enemy. Colin chuckled. He retrieved the beret and dandled it up and down above the frantic paw.

Quickly overcome with the excitement, the kitten bounded off down the hallway. Colin sighed and returned to the cares of his desk.

The files. Two feet high and almost all worthless. In a province like Westland, a criterion as wide as 'Guilty or potentially guilty of anti-government acts' was like starting with only those skunks potentially guilty of making a smell.

An incident was needed. A starting point.

A seed.

The view through the window was more than pleasant, only partially blocked by the grandstand. Roofs of Frazer Creek nestled in the trees on the far side of the rugby field. The specials' own tent village had sprouted on the first night at the right-hand end of the field, including several marquees. Wisps of steam escaped through the vents at one end – the evening meal on the way. Every now and then Renwick heard a distant curse. The sandflies and mosquitoes always dined first.

As he watched, one of the officers went across to the grandstand. Specialist, Kevin Searle, walking round the structure and going in and out the only entrance. Colin's eyebrows rose. The grandstand! Well, perhaps it would be a suitable choice at that. A little ironic under the circumstances, but not without a degree of poetic appeal.

Ian Wilson came with a fat folder of print-outs.

'His Worship is outside and fretting.'

'Good, let him fret a little longer.' And it wouldn't do any harm to let Wilson wait as well. Everyone knew that if their commander ever slipped up, then his shoes would land on Wilson's feet. Not that Colin felt threatened. He objected to the man's horsy teeth more than his ambition.

'HQ have found out what happened to the local flatfoot,' Wilson said.

'Well?'

'Seems word came from the Commissioner's office, granting his application for compassionate leave for one year. Ten guesses where the application started out . . .'

'The Commissioner's office.'

'Right.'

'Surprise, surprise.' If HQ found something to pin on the Commissioner tomorrow, it wouldn't be too soon. Sourly, Colin flicked through the print-outs to find the one he wanted. He scanned, taking in only those portions likely to yield interesting results. Cit-file print-outs from Wanganui had improved by leaps and bounds with the addition of census data.

Malachy Vincent O'Hara. Citizen Base No. 08344836-30.
B/D: 20/8/50. LKA: RD4, Frazer Creek, South Westland. OC: farmer.

POL/Ref 0055-022-8344836-30; Pros Nil, Con Nil. Reg Weapons: nil. SS/Ref 0033-022-8344836-30: Benefit Payments Nil. IR/Ref 0046-022-8344836-30, default returns nil, pros Nil. PPT: A66-717-8344836-30 Stampadts: nil . . .

. . . Education: SC, UE, B.A. (Hons) (Pol. Sci.)

Pol Affil: Nil. Known Subv Org: Nil. Known anti-Govt agitation: Nil. Known Subv Act: Nil. University Political affil: Nil.

Misc. Affil: Hokitika Public Library card 7518, lapsed 22/3/76; Frazer Creek Rugby Club, lapsed 13/5/76; Frazer Creek Darts Club.

B/Acs: Westland Trusteebank 2443-803626051-00, P.O. 11-8211-0015558-30.

Bankruptcies: nil. HP agreements: nil.

Land ownership: nil.

Fishing License 0733202, Boat ownership: dinghy, motive power outboard. Opossum Trapper's License 07555; Whitebait stand FCCC WS43.

MOT/Ref 0019-022-8344836-31. MV: 19FOY Honda MB. Overdue WOF: Pros & Conv 07/03/68. Exceeding speed limit: Pros & Disch 14/11/75 . . .

. . . Married 02/11/73: Sally Elizabeth, nee James 0001-454-8341239-00, deceased 29/10/75. Children: Duncan Oliver 0001-022-8390334-00, deceased 29/10/75 Dougal Stephen 0001-022-8390335-00, deceased 29/10/75.

Father: Oliver Sean O'Hara 0001-022-8404276-30. Mother: Prereg, deceased.

Sib: Benjamin Donald 0001-002-8404183-35 . . .

Renwick handed the file back to Wilson.

'So much for Bigmouth; we've had more interesting profiles on the Salvation Army. But you could check out the brother; he's a "35".' It probably wouldn't help: half the population of Westland had refused to register for the citizen number. Initially. He tossed the print-out aside, picked up the next and scanned it even more quickly, knowing there would be nothing: 'Thomas Edward Joseph Kidmann. Citizen Base No 08267771-30 . . .'

'All right, show The Lord Mayor in.'

When Tom Kidmann stood in front of the commander's desk, Renwick didn't stand up. He asked Wilson to pour two glasses from a bottle of Seppelt on the cabinet.

'No, thank you,' Kidmann said stiffly.

The cork slid from the bottle with a discreet pop. The viscous liquid gurgled into the best guest-house crystal. One glass was placed firmly in Kidmann's hands and Renwick watched him, cradling his own, savouring the bouquet.

'Some of the best wines in the world come from the Barrossa. I do think there's a lot of sacred cow in the French wines, don't you? Good health. Take a seat.'

There was no seat.

'You can't intimidate me,' Kidmann said. He had meant to say, This is intimidation. He stepped forward and placed his glass firmly on Renwick's desk, intending to walk out. But Wilson was next to the doorway, imposing in full uniform and with pistol.

'Mr Kidmann, in their infinite wisdom, the local voters chose you as their civic leader. That being so, let me give you some advice to pass on to the men, women and children in your care. I am – '

'I hardly think – '

'Mr Kidmann,' Wilson reproved. 'You didn't interrupt the Chief Superintendent, did you?'

'I . . . I don't . . .'

'I thought not.'

Renwick continued pleasantly. 'Despite what the press says about them, Mr Kidmann, my men are quite civilised, in a manner of speaking. Just so long as nothing irritates them. Shall I *tell* you what irritates them, Mr Kidmann? Telephone operators who have difficulty finding a circuit; reversed signposts that are self-correcting after my men are gone; petrol station attendants who close down for the night when they see my men coming.' He leaned forward, his eyes boring into the mayor's. 'Bayonet tacks on the ground, Mr Kidmann; the dead possum that turned up in the men's laundry; windscreen wipers that magically curl up and hibernate in small boys' pockets. And in your store, Mr Kidmann, goods that jump in and out of stock depending on whether or not the customer is wearing a uniform.'

'I . . . I . . .' Kidmann's stomach made a noise like a passing stampede.

'For example, insect repellant which seems to have dematerialised from your shelves in large quantities. Now, my men have considered all this very carefully and have concluded that those who irritate them are probably working for a certain anti-government organisation.'

'I can't . . . You know very well that's not true . . . a general dislike, I mean it doesn't mean . . .'

'A bit tied up with our words, are we?'

'Dyslexics of the world untie,' Wilson said with concern.

'Know any Little Red Hens, Mr Kidmann?'

'No, no! This is absurd.'

The commander contemplated Kidmann's sweating brow and let the question hang. At times like this Colin always felt that a portion of him was standing apart and watching his own performance. It was never a pleasant experience. He watched even his best performances with distaste. It was the inexorability of it; the inevitability of each word and phrase and movement of a little finger, a path as certain as the next thump of the pendulum clock in the hall.

Kidmann was telling the truth, of course; the man would run a mile from such an association. But extracting information wasn't the purpose of this exercise anyway.

'Well, we'll say no more about it for now. But I do hope you'll pass on my friendly advice in the spirit intended.'

'You . . . You . . .'

'Yes, Mr Kidmann?'

When he had gone, Wilson observed, 'I thought the advent of the motor car had reduced inbreeding in the rural areas.'

They watched the crestfallen mayor walk away across the rugby field. It never ceased to astonish Renwick the public positions held by people who subconsciously expected to be humiliated in private. A momentary success. The results would be marginally beneficial.

'It won't all be that easy,' he mused to Wilson.

'If there are many more like him, it shouldn't be too difficult!'

'You miss the point.' Renwick indicated the topographical map pinned near the 'Highland Cattle'. 'What interests me is the high proportion of supposedly respectable individuals acting off their own bat to make life uncomfortable for us.'

'It'll take more than individuals to get near this dredge.'

'You underestimate their resourcefulness. Remember

Stanley Graham . . .' This referred to an incident near Hokitika in 1941. For twelve days, the Westland renegade held police and army at bay single-handed, killing seven men. German propaganda radio claimed that Adolf Hitler sent Graham a telegram: Hold the South Island. Sending another man to take the North Island.

Wilson wasn't convinced.

'I don't hear any red hens crowing. Rather more than one grain of sand is through the pass already.'

'I have a feeling, Ian. A feeling. Something down here is going to stretch us.'

Mrs Englefield came along the corridor pushing her trolley, singing 'Delilah' in a voice that only ever passed a true note by accident. The singing ceased as the trolley banged the door open. She swept in with the kitten frisking round her legs.

'Please knock when you come in.'

'Tea,' she declared as if they had been dirtying the carpet. She had started on the sherry earlier this afternoon.

'Put it on the desk, woman.'

They ate meals at the mess now. The woman's gastronomic atrocities were beyond belief. And the tea was little better; she slopped it out while murmuring endearments to the adoring kitten. Its name was Shadrach. Whenever Shadrach played too close to the two men's boots, she looked anxious.

As she left, she turned the hour-glass.

'Wait,' Renwick snapped. 'Why do you do that?'

'What?'

'Why, in God's name, do you turn the hour-glass, when you don't see it finish?'

'Hah!' She had been asked this before. 'My husband was a bum, that's what he was. Always had to rest. Rest, rest, rest, he spent his bleeding life on the sofa. Hardest thing 'e ever did in his life was join the Huddersfield Snail Watchers' Club.'

'What's that got to do with the hour-glass?'

'I got it made for 'is ashes. I like to keep the bastard moving.'

She went away, singing down the corridor. 'My, my, my, Delilah . . .'

'I knew there was a vicious streak in that woman,' Wilson said. 'That porridge . . .'

Colin snapped the hour-glass back the other way and stared at the ashes in it. He said, 'That's the most disgusting thing I've heard for a long time. The woman makes me sick.'

Oliver O'Hara used the blunt end of a kitchen fork as a lever and his other hand, around the neck of the bottle, as the fulcrum. The cap popped, spun, and was plucked out of the air by his bony hand and redirected into the rubbish sack by the sink. With the air of one who has proved that there is nothing to prove, he lounged back with his stubby of Westland Dry. The flesh under his left eye was streaked black and yellow, the aftermath of a bruise.

Fine foam swelled from the top of the stubby as he gave audience to a re-run of *McMillan and Wife*, starring Rock Hudson. His two favourite film stars were Rock Hudson and Marilyn Monroe; he kept an original 1953 centrefold of Monroe on his bedroom wall, the famous one in which all she had on was the radio.

'I'm leaving,' Mal said from the table. He was staring sourly at the contents of his plate: a fry-up of eggs, roast kumara and left-over shepherd's pie that looked like something out of the concrete mixer at the abattoir.

'Yeah,' grunted Olly into his stubby.

'Uh huh,' grunted Rock Hudson into the phone.

'I'm leaving!'

'What?'

'I'm going away. Up north. For good.'

The older man turned from the screen, gaping. Mal shrugged and pushed at a leathery egg.

'I suppose you think you're going to get away with it,' said Rock Hudson, checking the mechanism of his Beretta.

'What the blazes for? This is your place, here.'

'I have to get out on my own.'

Olly O'Hara came up out of the sofa onto the balls of his feet. Above him, on the wall, was his prize deer head, a twelve pointer taken up the Tatare twenty years earlier.

'You haven't got any money.'

'Ben wants help on a big order. I'll go after that.'

'You won't get a penny from me, not a penny.'

Another shrug. So who cares?

'What about me?' Suddenly pathetic.

'Hah.' Mal's hand waved at his father's fit figure.

'But why? Why, Mal?'

A prod at the mess on the plate. 'This is really disgusting.'

Olly shrewdly recognised this as an answer. He glanced at the photographs of Sally and the two boys on top of the bookshelves. But they had died a long time ago; if Mal was going to take off for that reason, he'd have done it before this. No. No, it was a smokescreen for something else. Mal had always expected to take over the farm. Now this, out of the blue.

The old man scrutinised his elder son.

'You're runnin' away from something.'

'Come on!'

'Yeah. You're runnin' away.'

'Don't talk bullshit.' Mal pushed his plate away and went to the fridge for a beer.

His father paced. Maybe Mal was scared the specials were going to follow up on him for calling out at the rugby grounds? No. A bit hair thin, that one. Not enough. But it had the right tang about it, somehow. Something smelt right, something. The old man's next thought was at once so terrible and exciting that it stopped him in his tracks.

'Here, Mal. It's something to do with the Little Red Hen, isn't it?'

'No. Lay off.'

'It is! It is! You know someone! You've got a contact!'

'No I don't.'

'Who is it? Who is it, Mal? I have to know.'

'Leave it alone, will you?'

'Please Mal, listen to me. You know how long I've been waiting for something like this.'

'No! You listen to me for a change! I don't know anything about the Hen, I don't know who they are, I don't *want* to know who they are.'

'You don't trust me. Is that it? Your own dad?'

'For God's sake! You've got your copper tub; you're already doing the government out of a mint. Isn't that enough for you?'

'Mal, I wouldn't tell a soul. Not a soul.'

'That's the problem!' Malachy shouted, waving his can. 'You never told a cop a damn thing in your life. But these aren't regular cops; you were *lucky* up there, can't you get that into your skull? Plain raspberry jam lucky because they didn't know what they were looking at. Next time, they will and you can bet your sweet life it's going to be a bit more than a smack around the chops when you play smart arse.'

'I can handle the likes of them.'

'Yeah? All right, maybe, just maybe, you'd keep your skin, seeing you're only a supplier and can't name any names. But suppose you do find out more. What happens if the specials twig that you've got some *real* information, eh? You think maybe they're going to give you a cup of tea and say "pretty please"? Or maybe you thought you could slip into the bush like the old days. Hell, you wouldn't even make it across the back yard! Now have you got the picture? If I did know something I wouldn't tell you. Got it? Got it?'

Silence. On the screen, Rock Hudson holstered his Beretta and slipped on his jacket.

'So that's why you're running away.' Quietly. 'You know somethin' and it's got you shit scared.'

Malachy O'Hara shook his head slowly. Rock Hudson headed for the door.

Olly shuffled his feet. 'An' you want to paint me with your big yellow brush, eh?'

Mal put his drink down. 'I don't believe this. You blind, bone-headed – '

'Shut up.' The old man threw himself back down on the sofa, spitting rage. 'Shut up and let me watch a *real* man.'

'He was gay. The rock had a soft centre.'

'Shut your lying, yellow mouth.'

As Rosa wheeled her bicycle across the yard, the empty billy clanked on the handlebars. The hens scattered. Dolly stared at her testily on the way back to the grass. Even placid, contented Bird, in the stall, swung her head. But Bird's cassette was in the player; Brahms's lullaby lilted about her head and she faced the front, blinking sleepily.

Mal looked up from the teats. His hands kept working and the milk squished rhythmically into the bucket.

'Hi, Rosa. Your mum not here?'

'No, she said I had to come all by myself from now on.'

'How about that.'

'Yes. I'm a grown-up woman now.'

Mal glanced at her quickly, and away with a jerky movement of his head. 'Yeah.'

'I didn't have to get off once. Even when I went in the potholes.'

'Good for you. But you won't go in the potholes with the milk, will you?'

'No-oo,' she grinned. Silly idea. And he laughed.

The wind blew her light cotton dress onto the mudguard, so she laid the bicycle flat on the ground, lifting Miska from the basket. She held the billy in one hand, forearm slightly flexed, more in the way of an adult than a child. Wind and late afternoon sun were to one side of her. Both played with the ends of her hair and the dress blew round her dusty, tanned legs.

She came a step closer. Mal kept his eyes off her. He wished she hadn't come alone. It was easier when her mother came.

Bird shifted and kept shifting restlessly, and Mal soothed her, surprised.

'Sooo . . . sooo, Birdy.'

'She must be thirsty,' Rosa said.

The cow swung her hindquarters, thumping the side of the stall.

'Hey, whoa Birdy baby, sooo, sooo, whaddayou playin' at?' He laid his forehead against her flank and she settled. 'Not like her to act up. Must be catching it off Dolly.'

'It's my turn.' Rosa always milked Bird.

'Uh, she seems a bit tetchy. Well, sure. I'll just settle her down first.' He turned up the Brahms and murmured to the cow, gentling her with his hands, then settling her back into the flow of milk.

'I hear you're a bit of a gun on the piano.'

Rosa smiled at the vision. Reminded of the bad girl, she raised a finger and shot her. Mal laughed again.

'Okay, there you go.'

Miska was placed against the wall to watch. Mal eased off the stool as Rosa slid on, reaching her hands for the familiar teats.

Bird bellowed and struck out blindly with a hoof. The first time, she connected with the bucket. It flew back into the yard, spreading its contents in a white curtain. The second strike was a haymaker and would have connected with Rosa had she not fallen back off the stool. The cow reared, still bellowing, crashed into one side of the stall, then lumbered away in fright.

Mal shouted obscenities after it and helped Rosa to her feet. 'You all right?'

She glared at him, but then, looking at the spilt milk, decided that the blame lay elsewhere.

'I think it was that bad girl again.'

'Bad girl? Bad . . . ? No, it's not . . . It was Bird's fault. Okay?'

'She doesn't like the bad girl.'

'No. Something got into her, that's all.' He stared at Dolly and Bird, both staring back from the paddock gate. Confounded animals. All that trouble for a bit of bleached mud in a bucket.

Rather than look at Rosa again, he inspected his hands. He could still feel where he had touched her. He kept his distance by filling her billy with the gleanings from Dolly. The hens were all under the moss trestles, except for a couple which broke cover to run under the back porch. He frowned at them, perplexed.

'You sure you're all right?' he asked.

'Bird doesn't like me any more, does she?' She placed the billy handle over the handlebars and stared wistfully after the cow. 'It's not fair. It was that bad girl.'

'She does. She likes you.' He was annoyed without knowing why. 'Bird likes you. More than anyone else. Okay?'

It was important to see her smile again before she left. He walked with her as she wheeled her bike back across the yard. Rosa's eyes had a faraway look to them and he tried different ways of talking her round. He told her the one about ducks having flat feet for stamping out forest fires and elephants having flat feet for stamping out burning ducks. No smile. He told her about the Dennehys across the way who had brought a wild piglet out of the Omoeroa, raised it as a pet, and now had a full-grown razorback boar that expected house privileges. No smile. Try again. He remembered that she had asked him to take her whitebaiting and promptly offered her the next trip. He would come and get her.

She nodded solemnly as she walked.

At the gate, she adjusted Miska's position in the basket and stepped across the pedals.

'Rosa . . . ?' He put a hand on her arm. 'It's all right. There's nothing for you to worry about. Is it the milk? Don't fret about it, it's only milk. It's nothing. It was my fault anyway.' But the arm under his hand had gone rigid from fingers to shoulder. Numb. It was like touching candlewax. He took his hand off, shocked and uneasy.

His chest thumped inside as she rode away looking puzzled and troubled. He called out to her to take care, though of what he couldn't have said.

Rosa didn't look back. She knew he was still out on the road watching her and that was all right. That was comforting. But she became absorbed in the ride: the splosh of milk in the billy, the squeak of the seat and the squidgy sound the tyres made on the tar seal, then the sawing of the cicadas in the gorse and the whisper of wind in her ear.

'You forgot to give him the money,' Miska scolded, moving so that Rosa could see the white envelope.

'You should have reminded me.'

'Edith will be cross.'

Rosa pedalled on.

A Land-rover passed her, but she hardly noticed the uniforms in the back nor the faces that looked hungrily back at her.

The fields narrowed out. The gorse clumped together hopefully, only to vanish as the road moved through the patch of bush before Frazer Creek. It was darker here under the totaras and the matais, but there was less wind and the sounds were so clear she thought she might hear a twig fall in the mountains if she listened hard enough. She heard a grey warbler. Close by, she saw and heard a silvereye, a tauhou; Tui Jackson had told her that if you saw a tauhou when the sun was near the horizon it meant you were going to meet a stranger.

'*No one* likes you,' Rosa informed Miska.

'Yes they do!'

'Don't.'

'Yes they do,' Miska insisted. 'They don't *care* about the painting.'

'What painting?'

'Look at the painting.'

There was a singing in Rosa's ears as she pedalled.

'The painting, the painting,' Miska said.

And there it was. On the wall at the end of the bed. It was a picture of a small girl holding up two cherries. She could see it above the mound her feet made in the blanket. The blanket was heavy and no matter how hard she tried she couldn't move. Her whole body was stiff. There were squirmy, sicky feelings in her stomach, but she couldn't move even her little finger.

The mattress was down on one side because there was someone sitting on the bed. She couldn't see who it was, she couldn't even take her eyes off the painting.

'If you don't help me,' said the man she couldn't see, 'you'll be a nasty, selfish, mean little girl and no one will ever like you . . .'

She was never allowed to take the painting down. She hated the painting but it was always there.

'. . . And you don't want that, do you?'

If she made herself really stiff, and concentrated, the picture might fall off the nail.

'Really, no one likes you except me. But we've got something special, haven't we, Princess? Our little secret.'

If she shut her eyes, she wouldn't see it.

'Now be a good, good Princess . . .'

No. I don't like it. I don't like it.

'. . . Don't make any noise, that's it, no noise or we'll have to play hide-and-seek in the cupboard.'

Rosa's eyes sprang open.

I don't want to, don't want to want to want to . . .

The trees were bent over here, against the sky. Someone had

been making a whining, mewing sound. The back of her head hurt and lay on something rough. The road. Her hands hurt. She sat up and looked at the grazes on them, then at the bicycle and Miska lying nearby. The billy top had come off and even as she watched it, it stopped rolling and the last milk drained off the side of the tar seal onto the gravel.

The flesh between index finger and thumb connected with the grip of the bow. Caressing, closing carefully, so that when the draw came there would be no torque to distort the loosed flight; closing slowly as the flesh remembered how to melt with the counterpoised tensions. The learning came quickly. The bow was a masterpiece that Mal had never really forgotten, a finely tuned instrument with limbs of laminated fibreglass and Canadian rock maple that would draw for him like a singer gathering breath for the first note.

He plucked a cedar shaft from the quiver, turned it between thumb and fingertip so that the turkey-feathers rotated. Two white and one yellow. When the yellow was outermost, he nocked the shaft, making the string sound two notes of slightly different frequency. At the other end of the shaft was a small tip, a practice field-pile.

He chose a target his mother had forbidden two decades ago: a gnarled wineberry about fifty paces away, at the end of the back porch. His mother had possessed an 'Oi, you!' capable of bringing down a mature teenager at a hundred paces.

A knot halfway up the trunk enticed him. It was in the centre of the shiny red bark, little higher than it had been twenty years ago.

The movements came quickly then. Standing side on, he raised the axis high, drew as it came down, held as the string creased his stubbled chin. The tip set, the arrow was gone. With a sharp *chunk*, it grew out of a point a foot above the knot and six inches to the left. The next was closer, above and to the right, the third a scant three inches from the knot.

He lowered the bow, trembling slightly with concentration.

For the next round, he waited until his mind was free of all distractions. Then the bow rose again and smoothly drew. Ah, and how it came back and back and back . . . The bow was an extension of his body. Bow, arrow, target, all one entity. Indivisible. Release in thoughtlessness, as a child drops a ripe fruit . . .

Six

The rugby field wasn't always mown by machine. Sometimes the Meers put a few hundred woolly lawnmowers on the field for a couple of days, partly because it gave them a change of feed, mostly because it was just a matter of opening the adjoining gate. The fact that Brent Meers opened the gate at sparrow fart could not be held against him because he was always up at that time anyway.

'Do you want the grass kept short, or don't you?' he asked the livid officer who found him in a distant field just before breakfast.

'Just get them out!' the officer grated. He had been asleep when the sheep moved in amongst the tents.

But the job was done by the time they returned. The specials were more particular about sheep dags than rugby players. 'Next time, we eat mutton,' they promised the farmer, who went away muttering about ingratitude.

To some, the episode was food for thought.

Three nights later, the entrance to the grounds was blocked by a truckload of pig manure. That was followed the same day by a letter with the Frazer Creek County Council letterhead, on paper stolen from the county office. It required the counter-terrorist unit to make adequate provision for their sewerage, or they would face court action.

A guardhouse was installed at the main entrance to the grounds. Anti-vehicle posts were dug in along the entrance through the children's playground.

All the same, the more adventurous teenagers found that they could get close without being seen by coming down through the bush beside the guest-house. Two of them crept into the unused woodshed one night, with trays loaded with old tin cans containing small quantities of water. The woodshed was made of ponga. The darkness of the cavities in the surface of ponga attracts sandflies and mosquitoes. With stagnant water inside, the woodshed became an insect Club Med.

Others used catapults from higher up, to loft missiles into the grounds, though this was not an outstanding success – only the most powerful catapults could reach the tents and the boys were unnerved by the thought that sooner or later they would find a deputation of specials waiting for them in the trees. They sent a few half-hearted stones onto the guest-house roof, telling themselves that Mrs Englefield deserved it for letting the specials use the place. But they found the sight of Nora Englefield in her nightgown, screaming blood-curdling threats under the moon, almost as unnerving as the thought of being caught by the specials.

'You've tested it for sound?'

'Yes sir. It's perfect.'

Colin Renwick nodded. It would be. The interior of the grandstand was completely enclosed by concrete, except for the door. The echoes of their voices shambled dully around the rough surfaces.

The space round the walls was almost empty. What little park equipment there was had been pushed forward under the lowest level of the seats that formed the sloping concrete ceiling. But there was a shelf with a sink against the back wall and Searle, intending to work in comfort, had taken advantage of it; he'd installed an electric jug, tea pot and cosy, with two easy-chairs nearby. There was even a peg, already hung with Searle's white coat. White. Another detail of Searle's method. What was the colour traditionally associated with his trade? Yes. Fuligin. Darker than black.

No windows.

The space in the centre was occupied by a canvas cubicle,

whose walls were anchored by the grandstand's four central pillars.

Renwick lifted a flap and went in.

It was a space within a space, with its own peculiarities of sound, giving the impression that whatever move you made, someone behind you was doing it also. A bare electric bulb protruded from its canvas ceiling, casting dirty yellow light onto a carpenter's bench that still had its vice. Underneath the bench was Searle's box of equipment.

The cubicle wasn't precisely a cube: one end was extended and narrowed to the door, which had been altered so that its upper and lower half swung independently like a stable door. Nothing of the interior of the grandstand could be seen from inside the canvas. Searle had done well.

'It'll do.'

'Rather delicious don't you think,' Searle grinned. 'Literally right under the public eye.'

'Not to mention their rear ends,' Colin said sourly, glancing up.

'Of course I won't be fully prepared until the next supply truck comes in.'

'It's a slow start anyway. But we should have some work for you in a couple of days. As of now, this is off limits to all but you, your assistants, Wilson and myself.'

'Yes, sir.'

There was a bilious taste in Colin's mouth. In this airless place, his aversion to Searle was magnified ten times. Kevin Searle, with distinguished white sideburns and iron-grey eyebrows, scrubbed his fingernails five times a day; he would have scrubbed them just before this inspection. And still he reminded Colin of a blowfly that settles onto the skin without warning. The man disgusted him, the more so that he needed such careful handling. But he was the best there was, having developed a method that, as far as Colin knew, was unique. It brought in the results. Whatever handling Searle needed, he would get.

Outside, the sun was brilliant, briefly blinding both of them.

'I may need . . .'

'Listen,' Renwick said.

Someone was playing a piano. Expertly. He peered around and as his eyes adjusted to the light, looked up the hill. It was coming from a large white house a hundred yards away. Well, well; so there was someone civilised in this God-forsaken backwater after all. The discovery gave him a burst of warmth that tempted him to go closer, through the children's playground.

A series of cascading notes came to an end and a new piece of music began. First, a driving base, then, over the top, a searing melody. He knew the piece well, his wife having played Chopin's 'Prelude 24' many times in distant days. But he was intrigued by the savageness of the interpretation. Anger, bitterness, a barbaric harshness he had never before associated with the piece.

'Something wrong, sir?'

'Quiet.'

He stood stock still. Extraordinary. One could almost imagine the suffering and nobility of the composer. But no, no . . . really, the pianist was taking far too much liberty with the piece. It was too emotive. Too much. Way over the top. Quite uncomfortable in a way.

It ended.

Searle was looking at him strangely.

'This grass badly needs mowing,' Renwick said, swishing a polished boot in the long blades. 'You've still got the mower under there, haven't you? Good. Get one of your assistants to resurrect it. The place looks sloppy.'

There was no sound from the house on the hill now. He went back to his office, where Nora Englefield's kitten Shadrach came and batted its paw under the door again. He teased it to a frenzy.

Seven

Mal watched stolidly as Ben and John Taylor trotted the hind into the trees, came out without it, and hid a black leather box in the tussock while the Doberman frisked the tree-line. When they ran for the Hughes, Mal stopped Ben with a hand on the chest.

'Explain.'

'Not now.'

'*Right* now.'

'You want us to get caught?'

'Caught? What the hell do you mean caught? I thought I was helping you bag deer for Hanrahan.'

'You just did. I'll explain on the way back. Let's go.' Ben shoved his way past.

'On second thoughts, don't explain,' Mal shouted after him. He checked the surrounding peaks and ridges to get his bearings, eyeing the nearest slope to the plains.

'I wouldn't do that,' Ben called back. 'You'll be bushed overnight and there's a nor'-wester on the way.'

'Let him go,' Taylor said beside him. 'The committee's not going to like this.'

'You thinking of telling them?'

'No.'

The Hughes wound up to full revs, waiting while Mal returned. On the way he stopped to pick a mountain lily. He took his time, sniffing it ostentatiously. Then he climbed in.

'Funny. Very funny,' Ben said. But his mood was buoyant. As the machine tilted and the mountain slid away to their left he spoke over his shoulder. 'You'll like this. The light in the black box is to help us find the same spot at night and the deer is cover for the run to the ships.'

In his astonishment, Mal side-stepped the fact that he didn't want to hear about it.

'*Your* people are doing that? As well?'

'Yep. The Little Red Hen is running the whole show now.'

'Jesus, you're crazy. One mistake and the whole lot goes.'

'We've thought of that. Nobody from one operation sees anybody – '

'No, no. Leave me out of it. I must have been crazy coming along on this.'

'He doesn't want to know,' Taylor muttered pointedly.

'Suit yourself. No skin off my nose. That's not why I brought you along anyway.'

Nothing more was said as they skimmed south. Mal simmered in the back and the Doberman slobbered over him, enjoying the extra company. Taylor dipped into a magazine that showed a multicoloured trio of women at play on pink satin sheets. A Korean tourist had once told Taylor about the aphrodisiac qualities of a glass of blood from antlers in velvet. Taylor never did things by halves; after six glasses he developed needs New Zealand was incapable of satisfying and had to catch the next flight to Kings Cross, Sydney. A reporter freelancing for *Stern* had once hired him to demonstrate the various methods of capturing deer. The reporter was so taken with the net-gun and its possibilities, he'd then hired a camera crew as well, along with two women tourists from Franz Joseph hotel to run naked across mountain glades while being captured by helicopter net-guns.

They came down on a ridge high above the coast, on a shoulder off the line of sight of Frazer Creek.

When the rotors stopped moving, the only sounds were the tick of the cooling motor, and music from the cassette radio in Taylor's duffel-bag. Taylor pulled out a nearly full bottle of Westland Gorse. Ben reached over, took it, and swallowed reverently.

'Help yourself,' Taylor said sarcastically.

'Don't mind if I did.' Ben offered it to Mal, who refused.

'What now? What have we stopped here for?'

The cassette radio murmured and Ben turned it up. Through the static, a rich, baritone voice. "I must say I find it tiresome that certain sections of the media continue to perpetuate this myth that elite equates with sinister. How many reports of human rights abuses in Westland have there been so far . . . ? Precisely. And I suggest to you that no one is better capable of bringing these terrorists to justice, these mad dogs who seem hell-bent on preventing the country from using something they do not have the resources to use themselves. This is one case of dog in the manger that would be funny if it weren't so potentially disastrous."

Ben snorted.

Taylor said, 'Has it occurred to you that after tonight, they're going to put one and one together and come up with the whole damn two hundred?'

'So? It's got to be sooner or later.'

Mal pushed his door open and jumped out. But Ben grabbed binoculars and intercepted him in front of the Hughes.

'You started what I'm going to show you. You're responsible for it! Got that? And you're going to see it if I have to ram your peepers into the eyepiece.'

He kept the glasses long enough to make three quick sightings himself. They were long range, so he lay down in the tussock to steady the instrument with his elbows. First, something up by the glacier. Second, out at Moonlight Beach. Third, a stretch of the main road below, visible in spite of the bush because it lined up with their ridge. He nodded, satisfied, and handed the glasses to Mal, who took them with no grace. A dark dot became a vehicle, a van of some sort, parked by the side of the road. Two figures moved around in front of it and appeared to be looking under the bonnet.

'We're following your instructions to the tee. We're going to take out . . .' He broke off because Mal had dropped the glasses.

'What's the matter now?'

'Shut up.'

'What?'

'I said shuddup!' Mal rose and strode two paces down the ridge then turned. 'What does it take? A fucking sledgehammer? You're a walking disaster area, Benjamin. I don't *like* cowboys and Indians. I don't want any part of it. I'm going away, all right? Up north. Starting again, and nothing, nothing is going to get in the way. Got that?'

'You po-faced hypocrite. All the kudos but none of the danger, huh? Christ, I bet you'd shake hands with yourself if you condescended to let your right hand know where your left was.'

'If you get the old man into something he can't handle I'll put you in hospital.'

A prod became a push, became a shove, and then the two were wrestling and rolling down the ridge, trading punches as they went. They finished with Ben sitting dazed, scratched by thorns, against a matagouri, and with Mal standing a few feet away nursing a split lip.

'Takes you back, doesn't it?' said Ben, grinning and panting. Without moving from that position, he mimed a softball throw, twisting the fingers. A curve ball.

Mal ignored it contemptuously, spat blood and tramped away towards the tree-line.

'You can't dodge it,' Ben yelled. 'You're *in* it, big brother.'

In the helicopter, Taylor glanced at them in disgust and went back to his girlie magazine.

On Saturday nights it was their table. They had squatters' rights, consolidated by between fifteen and thirty years of devoted occupancy. For them the old saying was literally true: between them they had passed enough ale through their systems to fill the Hokitika swimming pool.

After the first jug they addressed each other only as Dipstick, Drop-kick and Fucknuckle.

'Listen, *Drop-kick*, I'm tellin' you, it's the Frog bomb tests.'

'French bomb tests! Jesus, *Dipstick*, you talk a load of crap. There's nothing knocking the whitebait back 'cept too many hundred-percenters on the river.'

Dipstick took special care with the scorn of the reply because he was an accomplished hundred-percenter himself, an expert at putting a net across the entire width of the river at the critical point of the tide and then getting away with the catch before the upriver baiters brought their fists downriver.

He was also an accomplished drinker. He once held the Westland record of thirty-nine imperial pints and he had been the recipient of more bottles of Harry Withers' doctored brew than anyone in South Westland. Twelve Zombies, no less. He boasted that when he died they would have to beat his kidneys to death with a stick. He had a wife up Granity way, who kept a recording of his voice to keep the kids in line.

Their arguing voices were as much part of the pub as the smoke and the chatter, the clack of pool balls and the throb of the three-piece band next to the piano. A viscous 'Moon River' poured from the saxophone across the pocket-handkerchief dance floor where teenagers wriggled, the middle-aged swayed, and an elderly couple waltzed cheek to cheek.

Near one end of the dance floor, Rosa Driscoll played knucklebones. She and three children squatted on the carpet where they had been sent because of the din the pieces made on the table tops. Brenda Mason went through 'ones' and 'twos' deftly, tossing all five pieces, catching as many as possible on the backs of outstretched fingers, then tossing one of those caught while picking up those that had fallen off. At 'threes' she missed.

'My turn,' Rosa said with satisfaction. In no time her hand was dancing through 'gathers'.

'That's not fair because you've got big hands.'

'It is so fair.' Tui Jackson had already heard Rosa's defence of this charge and presented it for her. She spread the fingers of Rosa's hand. 'There's bigger holes, so they fall through more.'

'So it's the same then,' Rosa capped off. She went swiftly through 'snatch'. But when she got to 'through the needle' she hesitated. She needed to use her left hand as well, the one holding Miska. This shouldn't have been a problem; she could have put Miska straight into her lap or given her to one of the others. But she didn't. Ignoring pleas from the other three, she kneeled up, leaned over Tui and tapped the arm of Mal O'Hara sitting at the nearest table.

'Mal? Mal.'

'Gidday, Rosa.'

'You can hold Miska.' She held it out as one confers an honour.

'I can?'

'But just for a short time.' And she went back to knucklebones.

Word went round. Rosa Driscoll had given her doll to an adult. Guess who?

Mal found himself the centre of attention. Grinning faces, mostly, but there was also an element of envy in some of the men. Mrs Driscoll wore a thoughtful expression, and Sharlene Rassmussen looked sideways at him from the other end of the pool-table. Carefully, he sat the doll in his lap where it could beam between the glasses at his amused drinking mates.

'You had this problem for long, Mal?' they asked.

'Suits you. What do you call her?'

'Don't worry, Mal, your secret is safe with us.'

He spread his hands modestly. 'Some of us have got it, some haven't.' When Tom Hay went for his round, Mal ordered one extra, pointing at the doll, '. . . for my free-loading friend here.'

But Miska didn't see the round arrive. Rosa's attention was so much on where she had left Miska that she dropped a vital knucklebone. She presented at Mal's side, holding out her hand, and the doll was transferred without a word. After she returned to the game, one of the dancers told the children to move their hands further away before they got them flattened. They shuffled a few inches and continued to play.

In the centre of the room, the argument was ripening.

'Now look here . . . look . . . stoopid bas'ids. The Frogs wanna see us go down the tube, right? An' . . . an' . . . lemme finish . . . the bait an' the orange roughy an' the tuna all cut out in the same year, didn' they?'

'Sure, Dipstick, sure,' Drop-kick sneered. 'I s'pose the Frenchies planted an agent in the tuna, eh?' Drop-kick was a retired fisherman who remembered when fishermen scratched the boom to raise a breeze and poured wine to leeward when coming across the bar in a storm.

Dipstick was losing ground and knew it. And if there was anything Dipstick hated most, it was losing. He had once done thirty days for an assault on a judge at the dog trials after a ewe attacked his dog. When a white-haired man of about fifty-five years walked past their table, Dipstick rose unsteadily.

'Hey! You, Moa.'

'Not you again.' Moa donned a look of contempt. He had made his name by successfully hoaxing city experts with footprints in the likeness of the extinct giant moa. Years later, he had come out of the Fiordland wilderness raving that he had heard the booming of the kakapo and wondered why no one took any notice.

'You, you don't talk nothin' but bullshit,' Dipstick enunciated. 'Always did. Always will.'

'Right. Outside.' Moa put his jugs down on Dipstick's table and led the way through the door, which carried a large poster of a hen.

Harry Withers didn't bother with Doctor Zombie. Moa would drag Dipstick round to the back porch mattress himself. Harry was from a long line of expert publicans, stretching back to the gold rush. It was his great-great-aunt who could at a moment's notice sweep every piece of glassware under the counter and order some of the roughest and hardest men in the world down on their knees; when the officers of the constabulary burst in, she would be reading from Revelations. It was Harry himself who developed the Kumara Economic Theory in the great depression: if a stranger spends a pound at a pub, the owner then spends that pound at the next pub and that owner at the next and so on, the one pound note slaking thirst and increasing till-turnover throughout the town.

The only real interest in the scrap came from a small boy who followed the two men to the door, miming uppercuts with his fists.

He didn't get to see it, because it didn't take place. No sooner had the two gone through the doorway than they were on their way back in, Dipstick looking like a startled, sober rabbit. But what really brought the bar to attention was the way the pair peeled off to either side of the door.

Patrols Alpha to Golf, nearly half of the specials, walked in to a frozen silence. The last note of the saxophone hung in the air. Drinks stopped halfway to the mouth, a dart player posed for a sketch and the pool player was oblivious to the fate of the eight ball. For a moment, knucklebones clicked, then that sound ceased also. Susan Withers looked about for the children in the room. Two had hold of their parents' drinks.

The Black-and-Greys were in full uniform, with buttoned-down pistols.

Harry Withers resumed drying a glass as he eyed the weapons. 'You have to bring those things in here?'

Boots tromped through the tables towards him, stopping at the bar. They were here to exercise the elbow.

Harry tried again.

'Wouldn't you boys be better off drinking in your mess? Friendlier atmosphere.'

For this he was rewarded with a display worthy of a commercial for toothpaste. A twenty-dollar note slapped down on the counter.

'This is a public bar. That's my money. Good enough for you?'

The Withers had seen a few things in their time, but a pride of uniformed policemen demanding to be served in a bar full of minors was new. In a hostile bar at that. Harry took his eyes on a trip: from the green note on the counter, to the inspector stationed at the door, to the clock on the wall. In a moment of odd perception, he noticed that Tom Kidmann's expression was vacant, almost lifeless.

'What's yours then?' Withers said.

The draught hoses began to flow. As the first specials pushed outwards with their jugs looking for places to sit, a spontaneous migration took place. First one table near the bar, then all tables opposite that end of the bar emptied of locals who took their drinks to the other end, filling up the empty chairs. The specials had little choice but to accept the separate zone, which took up a quarter of the bar.

'And behave yourselves,' Withers muttered. 'Or I'll call the cops.'

Two women began to make for the door, but they were intercepted by a third woman, who hissed something at them. They returned to their seats.

Kingi Hastings started it off. It was a simple thing, the tone of his voice rather than the wisecrack itself, a fragment of cheer that was for the people round him, only for friends. Only for the people he liked. Very soon everyone got the idea, and the sounds of Saturday night at the Frazer Creek pub returned – with that subtle difference. It was as if the room had shrunk by a quarter. The homely atmosphere stopped where the specials began as surely as if the smoke haze had been cut off with a knife.

The specials put up their own show, laughing uproariously at their own jokes; but that palled. They might as well have been back at their own mess. What they had come for lay across that invisible barrier. Feminine company had been so denied them in Westland that every now and then a busload of girls had to be brought over for them from Christchurch. Two of the girls on the last bus went to a doctor afterwards, complaining of repetitive strain injury and trying to claim from the Accident Compensation Commission on the grounds that the injury was work-related. When the case went to court it was postponed because the air-conditioning couldn't cope.

Two paces across the barrier were a couple of girls down from Whataroa. Both were dressed as punks from the sharpened tip of their Mohawk hair to the acid holes in the mini-skirts. But neither was anaemic and there was no doubt about their gender. One in particular exuded an interest in grazing her hormones on the wide open range. She was facing the specials. While her companion sat in profile to the paramilitary men and giggled behind one hand, she absent-mindedly allowed her knees to drift apart under the table.

The specials most affected were those sitting in a wedge-shaped area of the same angle as the girl's thighs. One, transferred recently from artillery, remarked that if the girl lay on her side the elevation would be seventy-five degrees. There was no calling out, just hands and eyebrows poised to beckon. But somehow the upper half of the girl never seemed to look their way. Still chatting to her friend, she wriggled, settled lower in her chair and took a long sip at a concoction with green and red cherries.

Four specials stood simultaneously, took their chairs through the dividing line and sat down at the girl's table.

All six were together for about three seconds. That's how long it took the two girls to gather their purses and stand, looking as if they had just seen a particularly hairy and repulsive spider. They left through the door beyond the piano.

The saxophonist whispered to the other two musicians and they played a familiar rag. No one sang the words, but everyone knew them anyway: '*Take your fingers off it, don't you dare touch it, you know it don't belo-o-ong to you.*'

As Renwick listened to Wilson's summary, he toyed with the brass poker he used as a paperweight. No decent paperweights. Another pebble in a mountain of irritations.

'Malachy O'Hara,' Wilson said. 'We've found a mention of him in a feature article promoting decentralised government; but he's one of a big list and the article is seventeen years old.'

'Great,' Colin grunted.

'His brother's no better. Checks out as a "35", bent a few flying regulations, a fistful of speeding tickets, but that's all. Uses a chopper to catch wild deer for the farms . . .'

'Wonderful.'

'Lima patrol found Gillespie's Beach with a lot of holes in it; but I looked that up – Gillespie's still has recoverable gold. There's a couple of hermits down there taking it out. Must be busy; there's a lot of holes.'

He handed the reports over. Colin picked out the file on Ben and threw the others down without looking at them.

'If you were Charlie, Ian, about to have a crack at the dredge, you would presumably be interested in knowing the whereabouts of army and special patrols throughout the operation, would you not?'

'Agreed.'

'How would you go about it?'

Wilson eyed the report still in the commander's hands. 'Helicopters? Well, ideally, yes. But are they capable of that much cooperation? We've got to remember where we are, you know.'

'I know precisely where I am and I don't care for your tone.'

'No offence intended.'

'Apology accepted,' Renwick said drily. 'You're forgetting that the whole labour movement started in Westland; their ability to organise depends on how worked up they are. But we've been through this. Failing anything better, we'll work on the helicopter angle. Get me a read-out on helicopter operators between Haast and Hokitika. Again looking for resistance to legislation.'

'Hah,' Wilson said cynically as he went.

Renwick watched him go. Something would have to be done about Ian Wilson. But the man had a point. They would find, yet again, that so many had breached regulations the information would be next to impossible to interpret. The aggressive individualism of the Westlanders meant that their responses, movements and associations just didn't follow expected patterns. They often didn't follow patterns, period.

He leaned on the window sill.

One solid lead. One. It was all he asked. It was all he usually needed.

He would set in motion the usual time-consuming procedures. He had to, in case the more direct methods failed. But just identifying potential informers could take weeks, establishing them, months. Plants, in this closed community, would take elaborate planning and months or more to get results. Not that he had months. The politics were too tight. His masters were impatient already.

And yet there should have been some pointers by now. Gleanings of gossip, scraps of tapped conversation pointing to a leader. Where were they? Now that the thorium was getting to the refinery, some of his men were openly siding with Wilson, speculating that the resistance had fizzed with their arrival. Even that the Little Red Hen was a myth penned by an individual now wetting his pants under a bed somewhere.

Perhaps.

But there was something out there in the houses and hills and sandflies. Something much more threatening than the wearisome petty harassment. Something for him, personally. He sensed it as surely as if he could smell it. Charlie was out there all right. And Charlie was always a fisherman. Sooner or later he would dangle a hook to be swallowed whole, the line to be teased and worked along until it was time to pull Charlie in. Soon, Renwick knew, this hook would lie with the others in the walls of his innards.

He turned. Wilson had returned, had been talking to him. Behind him, Nora Englefield was dusting the cabinet and vases.

'What?'

'I said the supply truck is going to be delayed. The driver parked it on a hill in Hokitika and someone took the brakes off while he – '

'Wait,' Renwick snapped. 'Mrs Englefield, I told you not to come in without knocking!'

'I did. If you kept your ears clean you'd have heard, wouldn't you?'

'Get out. Go on. I don't want you in here.'

'Well just so long as you're *sure*. As long as you know what you *want*.' She pressed thick lips into a thin line and made for the door. On the way past the mantel she twisted the hour-glass.

Colin surged across the room.

'For heaven's sake woman, take the bloody thing with you. Go on, take it out . . .' Finding the brass poker still in his hands he threw it into the coal scuttle so as to take hold of the hour-glass. But he couldn't move it. Its base was screwed to the wall behind.

He took his hands off it, aware that something was very wrong. Nora Englefield's face was stricken with horror, eyes fixed on the coal scuttle, and retrospectively, Renwick heard a squeak and a hissing sound. When he drew the poker from the scuttle, Shadrach was on the end of it sighing his last sigh. Colin lost colour, steadying himself with one hand on the mantel while Mrs Englefield went away down the corridor alternately screaming and gagging.

'Good God,' Wilson said, looking down at the dead kitten. 'A black kitten in a coal scuttle.'

Eight

One by one, the computer-controlled systems of the thorium dredge were shut down for the evening. There was a slow throbbing, a gasping of hydraulics during the system checks, then the beast of Moonlight Beach was asleep.

The last truck waddled to the assembly area to complete the convoy: sixteen Cummins V8 Fords, each with 18 gears for the long haul up through Westland, over the Lewis, down into Canterbury to the refinery. The escort vehicles fell in: two Land-rovers with soldiers, one with a patrol of specials who would stay with the convoy as far as the pass. Guards unshackled the gate. Each truck, laden with twenty tons of sand and pulverised rock, moved out onto the track. Then the ponderous metal snake wound into Waikukupa Forest towards the main road.

The wind died. The sun melted on the wave-tips. The forest became a vast bear rug, rumpled beside the fire the soldiers made of driftwood. Around the flames, they drank hot, sweet tea, listening to the sea mutter to the gathering gloom.

The soldiers' hands moved constantly in the steam, brushing and slapping at their faces, necks and wrists. One man picked a dark speck off the back of his hand, gave it its full pedigree then ground it to a smudge.

'Three supply trips and no repellant,' he snarled. 'Those fuckwits in ordnance don't know what the word means.'

'You'd think the store would have some.'

'Storekeeper's probably shit hisself handing it over to the specials.'

They heard the nearest duty guards passing along the fence: a crunch of boots on coarse sand. Down the beach, a generator woke with a lurch and hummed; lights came on in the contractor's huts and in tents beyond. At the water's edge, the waves lay down and sighed on the pebbles.

'Play us a tune, Edwards.'

The thin-faced youth with hands hidden mandarin style in his sleeves was reluctant. But at a nod from the lieutenant, he produced a mouth organ and played 'Black Matai': 'What are you singing, black matai, black matai? There's snow in the tops and the rain's falling down. What are you singing, east wind in the matai? Your love's left the station, she's gone to the town . . . she's gone to the town . . . to the town . . .'

A voice boomed, amplified, out of the bush.

'Evening boys.'

The mouth organ squeaked and died with its lips on. For a moment, nothing moved, then the sergeant, a Vietnam veteran, fanned with his hand. The men dropped behind their driftwood seats, snatching at their SLRs. The lieutenant rattled words into his radio mike. The two nearest duty guards had not waited for orders; fear had already winged them over the high-tide line of driftwood in a single bound and they lay against it fumbling with safety catches. The mouth organist's lips were dry, his eyes wide and scared, his young face white in the light of the fire.

'It's the dredge they're after, isn't it?' he whispered to the nearest man.

'Shut it,' the lieutenant hissed.

By the far tents, the security siren swooped into its first oscillation.

The amplified voice began again. But this time, because it was trying to make words through incoherent laughter, it wasn't intelligible. There were other gleeful sounds in the background, male and female. Finally a different voice took over.

'Well done, lads. Glad to see you're awake. Now look, we've gathered you here tonight to welcome you to our beach and we want you to make yourselves right at home. Feel free to swim in the rip tide any time you like.'

The ring of soldiers erupted. Half a dozen took the first running steps towards the nearest gate, looking pleadingly back at the lieutenant. But the sergeant pointed out that it was nearly dark and the officer ordered them to spread out along the line of driftwood. Lights raced towards them along the beach. The voice continued.

'By the way lads, sorry about the convoy. But you know how it is with sand these days.'

Every soldier's eye turned to the approximate place the convoy had disappeared into the bush.

'Oh my great giddy aunt,' said the lieutenant.

'Paaaawk pok pok pok,' cackled the voice from the trees. 'Paaaawk pok pok pok.'

The radio was squawking in the officer's hands. Frazer Creek

HQ talking to the beach commander. Renwick: 'Where in hell is that convoy, Captain? If you've let it leave in the dark, I'll have your pips.'

'My giddy aunt,' breathed the lieutenant.

Well after dark, the lights of the search party swung onto the convoy's rear escort vehicle, on the track that wound around the forest swamp. It was slewed across the track, blocking pursuit, on its side with the bonnet hanging open, crowbar holes in the radiator core and the sump, and the radio mike ripped out.

The search party heard voices. They deployed into the bush and closed in on the area beyond.

Their torch beams found the convoy personnel, escort and drivers. The hands of all thirty had been fastened with that most effective, simple physical restraint yet invented: standard police-issue nylon strip cuffs, which once fastened can only be cut off. All hands were cuffed around a heavy rope encircling the buttresses of a puketea. Among the thirty were the four escort specials of Kilo patrol. They were naked except for the distinctive black and grey jackets, covered with sandfly and mosquito bites and quiet with the murderous rage that is beyond hysteria.

All their firearms and knives lay on the ground a few feet away, intact.

'Photographs,' one muttered to the rescuers. 'The bastards took photographs.'

The other escort Land-rovers were in a similar condition to the first, but off the track. And the sixteen sand-laden trucks had gone.

It took another hour and a half to find them. They were parked in a neat line along one side of the main road, well to the south of the Karangarua. The patrol that came across them approached cautiously because one truck engine was screaming in neutral. It kept on in mechanical agony even after the ignition was cut, and the fuel line had to be closed off. The patrol leader sniffed the fuel. It had been spiked with kerosene. He checked the entire line of trucks, groaning at what ignorant bastards were capable of doing to beautiful pieces of machinery.

Every one had been burnt out, haemorrhaging through the top of the pistons.

In the face of sabotage on that scale, the other discovery seemed only a detail at first. But it raised questions that wouldn't go away.

'Gone? What does he mean, gone?' Colin stared at the radio. The comms operator repeated the question into the mike.

'The sand is gone. All of it. We checked every truck; there's only a few bits blowing about in the trays.'

'Must have been dropped on the way.'

'Didn't see any sign of it.'

The operator looked to the commander for instructions. Renwick took the microphone slowly. If they had disabled the trucks, why bother to dump the sand? Take it? No. They could hardly bowl up to the refinery with it. In any case no one in their right mind would try transporting 320 tons of sand in secret. Not possible. That meant it had been dumped. Which also didn't make sense.

He thumbed the switch.

'Find it. Forget the trucks. I want to know what happened to the sand.'

'In words of one syllable, Hayes, convince me that it was possible for you to be taken without so much as touching your safety catches.' Renwick's head moved in a manner that made Sergeant Donovan Hayes expect the click and hum of internal gears. Hayes was a frightened, angry man. In some places on his insect-ravaged skin, there were welts on top of welts. But that was now the least of his worries.

'No warning, sir. The tree was down immediately round the bend. The moment we stopped they had their rifles trained on us and a light in our eyes. We couldn't see a thing, sir, couldn't move a finger. It was the same for the rear escort. The bastards must have measured it all out and had people strung out all along the trees. Sir, I'd like to volunteer for the search par – '

'Spare me the histrionics. Describe Charlie.'

'We only saw one or two. Bush shirts, boots . . . Balaclavas.'

'No faces.'

'No sir.'

That confirmed one thing. They were dealing with at least some two-headers; people they had probably all seen openly on the main street.

'Describe the rest of their clothes.'

'Cords, jeans, nothing out of the ordinary. There were some women, sir.'

'They spoke?'

'No sir, but . . . ah . . .' Hayes formed his hands in vague cup shapes.

'Never mind. I don't need anatomy lessons. Describe their firearms.'

Hayes and his three colleagues all blanched simultaneously. One shifted his feet.

'Ah . . .'

'Well? Get on with it.'

'It was hard to tell. The light was in our eyes.'

'You didn't actually see any arms, then.'

The four looked at each other for help, but found none.

'You're holding on to something. Don't piss me about!'

Hayes took a breath. 'There were bows and arrows.'

The grandfather clock slow-marched in the hallway. Wilson, standing next to Renwick, wondered for an instant if these elite of New Zealand's armed forces could possibly be indulging in a joke. He dismissed the notion. Then a thought occurred to him and to the commander at the same time. They glanced at each other. Renwick leaned forward, bestowing on the men a smile that reminded Hayes of the way a mongoose smiles at snakes.

'The photographs. You said they took photographs. Now think very carefully. Could the bows and arrows have been in the photographs?'

Hayes looked ill.

'They did it deliberate like. Two with the bows and arrows came out in front of the lights. And . . .'

'And . . .'

'And they put on fancy kind of green jackets . . .' Hayes began to mumble. 'With wide fringes round . . . ah . . . here and round here.'

'Holy Mother of God,' Renwick said. There was another

silence, in which the commander seemed to be staring into the distance. Then he snapped back with the suddenness of an electric shock, issuing orders to Wilson.

'Suspend the search for the sand. Get the major here, I want every spare army man for this. Split our patrols. Two specials to three army men. Only specials to enter buildings. As of now we are on a house-to-house looking for a darkroom with developing equipment. Locals are to be given the impression that we are in hot pursuit of terrorists. Start with Frazer Creek then move out on a grid search. Every shack and hut, everything with a roof.'

'The whole district? What about HQ?'

'HQ will clear this one,' Renwick said grimly, reaching for the phone.

The searchers were swift. In the smaller dwellings, the shacks and huts, they were in and out and gone in little more than a minute. Too many buildings to search, too little time to spare. Families were rousted from sleep and held in one room, listening to the boots and flinging doors within their own walls. The curious thing was that every man, woman and older child held at gunpoint that night would remember it in all its detail, as vividly as if they were describing it from a photograph. They would recall inconsequential details: the exact position of a toy on the floor, the movement of a spider on the ceiling, the rattle of a loose pane in the night breeze.

The youngest children would remember it as a dream because it seemed unrelated to their waking life. Some, slightly older, experienced a delayed reaction; terrified wails often came from houses when the specials had already moved on to the next.

There was very little violence. The political risks of such an operation without the declaration of a state of emergency were so thoroughly impressed on the specials that they held their thirst for retribution in check, but individual specials prayed that they would come across at least one local considerate enough to put a foot wrong for them.

Colin Renwick discovered an unexpected disadvantage of spreading his force so thinly.

It happened first at Steve Nolan's place. The searching special found no developing equipment, but he did spot a balaclava on a nail on the back door. He grabbed it and ran back to the front room, waving it as he burst in.

'Gotcha,' crowed the special holding the Nolans at gunpoint.

'What? What're you talking about?' Nolan advanced on them in his confusion.

'Resisting arrest,' said the one holding the balaclava and tried to hit Nolan's spine through his stomach. They took him away out of sight of the houses and beat him very carefully with a length of shower hose, then raced him to the comms tent on the rugby field.

Five more locals were brought in for the same reason before it was realised that balaclavas have more uses in the country than bank robbery and the hijacking of convoys. In every case, the balaclavas had not been hidden. The locals were taken home by stony-faced men and left without apology. It taught the district residents that at least the lower ranks of the specials were mostly townies with little knowledge of the country and even less of Westland.

When Ben O'Hara came in over Hanrahan's deer farm close to midnight, there were lights speeding along the road towards him. It wasn't a surprise: he had known all along that this was one night when very few people would be immune. All the same, his stomach was knotted and his heart pounding as he dropped towards the holding pens.

He came down quickly, half hoping to have the hind out of the net before all the confusion started. But the lights were sweeping in the gate already, and from the air he could see the gaunt figure of Hanrahan turning this way and that, uncertain of what to do.

'Don't do anything different,' Ben muttered and descended until the back of the netted deer was touching ground. Hanrahan took the hint and moved forward under the chin of the Hughes. But as he reached for the strop, two Land-rovers shuddered to a stop and armed men deployed round the helicopter, rifles trained on all three men. Hands waved the machine down.

Ben swore; with its back grounded the hind would struggle to stand and would tangle its feet in the net. Hanrahan came away to argue with the specials and point to the deer, so Ben risked lifting a few inches. Taylor's forehead broke out in a sweat. But Hanrahan returned, waving. Ben dropped and the deer was released.

The two flyers emerged with hands high, to a ring of men aching for them to do otherwise. Rifle snouts motioned them face down in the mud of the holding paddock while the Hughes was searched. Out of the corner of his eye, Ben saw the hind high-step a few yards, stare at the Land-rovers' lights, then glide away into the darkness. He heard Hanrahan open his mouth without being asked, and close it on a grunt of pain. Then there was silence except for sounds of clambering in the Hughes and voices calling back and forth on the Land-rover RTs.

The rifle muzzles returned O'Hara and Taylor to their feet.

'This shotgun has been fired.'

'What's this all about?'

'I'm asking the questions. What was it fired at?'

'Have a look at the dart hole in the hind. That's all it can fire, the gun's been adapted. Look at the sleeves.'

'Why so late?'

'It might have been a stag we caught. You let a stag go in the daytime and he'll have the fences down. The dark keeps 'em calm.'

'These?'

'That's the drug for the dart. That's the antidote. Have a look at the other hole in the deer. Watch out! That's Fentaz – don't get it on your skin, that stuff'll put you in hospital.'

The special put the bottle gingerly back in the box, then picked up a different box, a black one, leather-bound. He opened it, revealing the light and the timing device.

'This?'

'We're experimenting. At some frequencies the flashing light hypnotises the deer like rabbits. Gets you in for a clean plug before they get too hot for the drug.'

The Land-rover radios squawked again; at their slightly different distances from the men, one sounded like an echo of the other. One of the army men went to them and came back.

'We're behind,' he informed Ben's questioner. The sergeant gave Ben a long, calculating stare and noted down the helicopter's details: 'Westland Recovery ZM-HBB.' Then, after a search of the farmhouse, the outhouses and the pens, they were on their way to the gate, leaving Ben, Taylor, Hanrahan and his wife and teenage sons standing in the starlit paddock. The hind's liquid-pool eyes watched them from the furthest corner of the pen.

It was some time before Hanrahan spoke.

'Come in. We could all use a drop of something.'

'Yeah,' Ben said shakily, uncorking Taylor's bottle of Gorse.

Early next morning, when the Land-rover patrols were still boiling dust off the side roads, Mal O'Hara came into Frazer Creek for supplies. None of the Land-rovers slowed for him or anyone else. None deviated from a path straight down the middle of the road, and twice he had to ride his motorbike into the grass. In the village itself, a Land-rover rounded the church corner at speed, forcing him to brake and slew to a stop. He sent an expletive after it, but there was no reaction on the set faces watching him out the back.

The two that went through the O'Hara farm buildings during the night had recognised him from the rugby ground welcome committee. So they had put extra time and care into the search, anticipating the pleasures that would come from finding whatever they were looking for. They had gone away disappointed; but such relief had then flooded the old man's face that Mal had become suspicious.

'Here, you got something on the property?' Mal had demanded.

'What's it to you?' Olly O'Hara had sneered.

So Mal had conducted his own search, turning the old man's room upside down, going through the barn by torch-light, eventually finding ten gallon drums of mineral acid and caustic soda under a sack. And he'd taken hold of his father and rattled him like a toy.

'What do you think you're doin' keeping that stuff here, eh? Eh?'

'It's a bit heavy, ain't it? I'm takin' it up a bit at a time because I don't know anyone who's man enough to take it up for me, do I? Keep your shirt on! There's no problem, the stupid bastards don't know what it's for.'

'But I'm livin' here. I'm livin' here! You didn't ask me!'

'You'd have said no, wouldn't yer?'

'Too flamin' right, I'm sayin' no.' He had taken the containers outside into the dark then, emptied them on the ground and painted over the labels. The next two hours had been spent in shouting. Far from being contrite, the old man had stepped up his demands that Mal put him in touch with the Little Red Hen. There hadn't been much sleep on the O'Hara farm in the night.

There were few people to be seen in Frazer Creek.

Mal parked his bike by the front steps of the store, where there was a small knot of residents, including children who never let go their parents' hands. They talked closely and looked about a lot with their eyes. They knew little more than he did. The grapevine had been severely hampered, because the specials had shut down the telephone exchange during the search. Several had tried, without success, to find Tony Shadbolt to get more information; but Sally Shadbolt didn't know where he was and said she didn't care, and the newspaper office was empty, the lock broken during the search. So far, there'd been nothing on the radio. The only solid information wasn't connected with the search at all; according to Ken Hastings, Nora Englefield had withdrawn her life savings from the post office and taken a trip over to Christchurch without telling anyone why.

In the store, between the hardware shelves and the groceries, Mal came across Rosa and Edith Driscoll. The overnight search had left Edith with a breathlessness that wouldn't ease; she had become frail suddenly, as if the frailty had been there in her bones waiting. But Rosa was the opposite: constantly on the move, unable to keep her feet still.

'Are you going to take me whitebaiting tomorrow?' she asked Mal, having learned that the word 'today' makes adults feel pestered.

'Ahh, I don't know, Rosa.' Mal was uncomfortable in the presence of her mother.

'You said you were going to take me,' Rosa pressed.

'Ah, sure, yeah, if that's all right,' he mumbled, glancing at Edith.

But the aging woman was looking at him with warm eyes. She said, 'You don't have to explain anything, Mal O'Hara.'

'There's nothing *to* explain,' he said hotly, when Rosa was out of earshot at the delicatessen cabinet.

'She can't go on depending on me.' Edith Driscoll touched his wrist with a cold finger and looked at him so directly that he couldn't miss the pleading before he dropped his eyes.

When Rosa returned, she placed her doll in Mal's trolley and informed him that he was allowed to take Miska for a ride. He slowed on the way to the counter, forcing Rosa to go ahead, wanting to say to her mother, I'm leaving soon. I'm leaving, I'm going away up north to start again. But he couldn't bring the words to his lips.

At the counter, Tom Kidmann looked at the passenger sitting in Mal's trolley on a pile of TV dinners, and raised eloquent eyebrows.

'Don't knock it till you've tried it,' Mal growled testily.

Colin Renwick's voice dropped acid into the phone.

'Yes, fifty yards on either side, from the beach to the main road. That's your problem and I'll solve it for you – bring in logging crews from the east coast and Nelson. Yes . . . yes . . . are you by any chance under the impression that this is an order . . . ? Good, good, am I what?'

He covered the phone with his hand and said in wonder to Wilson, 'He wants to know if I'm aware it's a national park.'

'So young, so soon promoted to his level of incompetence,' Wilson sighed.

'Have them here by tomorrow night,' Renwick said into the phone, then put it down, looking at the map on the wall. There was no question of holding back the convoys until the track was cleared, but with the all important lead still eluding them he had to plan ahead. A mosquito piped in his ear and he flapped it away; a blowfly would sound like that if it flew fast enough.

Two patrol leaders loped past the window, the one in front holding a newspaper. He was on his feet as they knocked and entered, and he and Wilson knew from their faces that there was little point in continuing the search for the developing equipment.

'Already?'

'Someone has worked fast.'

The local news sheet, *The South Westland Times*, was placed in front of Renwick. At the top of the front page was the headline: 'NO SLEEP FOR SANDMEN'.

The bulk of the page was taken up by three photographs. In one, a Land-rover lay on its side with broken radio dangling. The second, taken from high up, showed a line of empty trucks stretching into the dark. But by far the greatest space was devoted to the top photograph. In the background of the shot was a row of men tied to a tree, including the four wearing only the jacket of the specials. In the middle and foregrounds were two men, each with a bow and quiver of arrows. One wore an expression that was clearly, in spite of the balaclava, a cocky grin. The other, in the foreground, had his back to the camera, his head hidden by a jacket hood which carried on it a small picture of a hen. The jacket was encircled in two places by broad fringes in the style of Robin Hood.

Colin reached for the phone, saw that his hand was in danger of shaking and brought it back. Time. He needed time to think.

'Just give the word, sir. We'll find the newspaper guy.'

'How did he do it?' Wilson was puzzled. 'We've had someone watching his office.'

There was no way to stop it now. Charlie would have couriers from Bluff to Cape Reinga before nightfall. Copies to Australia might be intercepted, but in the long run it was a waste of time. Somehow he had to find a way of turning this fiasco around before the first copies reached the network media. He had to have his lead. The two men before him were waiting for a decision, waiting for him to pluck something out of the air. Wilson was watching him too, inscrutable. Ambitious Wilson. Colin's gaze went to the map, as if there might be a clue there.

There was a knock on the door, and eventually Wilson answered it. After a moment's incredulity he opened the door wide for the others to see for themselves.

'Morning gents. Tony Shadbolt, *Westland Times*.'

There was no response. The four uniformed men seemed set in a tableau.

'May I come in? Oh, I see you've got a copy already. That was quick. I'm going to be doing a special follow-up edition and I'd appreciate a comment from you about the hijacking.' He took a reporter's pad and pencil out of the front pocket of his moth-eaten jacket. His pencil always showed from the top of the pocket to remind the world of his shorthand abilities. Surprised by the staring faces, he said cheerfully, 'I haven't come at a bad time, have I?'

'I don't believe this,' Wilson murmured.

'No, Mr Shadbolt,' Colin Renwick said slowly. 'Not a bad time at all. I believe we may be able to accommodate you.'

'Thank you. First off, can I ask you – '

'I'm sure you won't mind if I ask you a question first. You printed this in Hokitika?'

'That's right. You're well informed. I haven't had zinc plates for years.'

Colin spoke warmly. 'Worth the trouble for a scoop like this, I'm sure. An admirable effort. You must have been up very early indeed to do it in time.'

'Yep.' Shadbolt looked modest.

The postures of the four uniformed men in the room underwent a subtle change. All the tension faded out of Colin Renwick's face. He smiled, though there was a hint of sadness to the smile; it was a familiar path that stretched ahead now, overhung with bitter-sweet fruit.

'Ask and you shall receive,' Wilson muttered, astounded as ever by Renwick's knack of pulling his head out of the lion's mouth just before the jaws closed.

A worry teased Shadbolt's forehead.

'Someone slipped the photos under the door,' he said anxiously.

'Of course, of course. Excuse me a moment.' Renwick turned to the two patrol leaders. 'Find Inspector Searle would you, and ask him to step over to his office.'

'Yes, sir,' they said in unison, and left.

Colin rose, shepherding Shadbolt towards the door.

'Well, Mr Shadbolt, let's go for a ride while we chat. A shame to waste such a beautiful morning. After you.'

'You seem to be taking all this very well,' Shadbolt said as they moved outside. This was hardly the terse 'No comment' he'd been expecting. Visions of a second sccop in twenty-four hours came to him. It just showed how much times had changed. His great-grandfather had run Hokitika's *West Coast Times* in the days when outraged readers went visiting the editor with a horsewhip; his hardy ancestor had mounted his own horsewhip on the wall behind his desk and used it to educate such visitors about the freedom of the press.

With Wilson and two new uniformed men, they boarded a covered Land-rover and sat in the rear seats as it rolled smoothly out of the rugby grounds.

'First, Chief Superintendent, what's your comment on the method of the hijacking? You know: taking from the rich to give to the poor.'

'Let me begin, Mr Shadbolt, by quoting another fictional character. Not Robin Hood, but Sherlock Holmes. This comes from *The Copper Beeches*: "It is my belief, Watson, founded upon my experience, that the lowest . . ." Are you getting this? ". . . that the lowest and vilest alleys of London do not present a more dreadful record of sin than does the smiling and beautiful face of the countryside." '

Shadbolt's pencil scribbled furiously. Good stuff. Let the city dailies eat their hearts out.

'Cold, isn't it?' Colin observed.

'Doesn't bother me.'

The two men with them closed the rear flap and returned to sit between the rear and the front of the vehicle.

'Any more comment on the style of the hijackers?'

'No, Mr Shadbolt. And that was nothing to do with the hijacking. That was merely an observation that Sir Arthur Conan Doyle had a well-developed respect for isolated buildings in the country, because of all the unpleasantness that could go on inside them without anyone hearing what was going on.'

'I see.' A frown. 'Sorry, lost your drift there . . .'

'He was wrong, because precisely the same effect can be achieved with buildings in close proximity to others. All you need is good sound-proofing. But then Doyle never realised that society's greatest horror takes place constantly right under everyone's noses anyway, city *and* country. The worst strappados and bastinados, the worst abacinations and defenestrations, are those performed on the mind, within the respectability of that iron maiden holy of holies, the family.' He noticed the newspaperman's bafflement. 'Excuse me. A slight digression from the subject.'

'Which is?'

'Why, the suffering that man inflicts on man.'

Shadbolt licked his lips and resumed scribbling.

The Land-rover stopped, backed up, stopped again. The back flap was raised to reveal a tent-like enclosure, lit by an electric light, leading to a carpenter's bench. Three men were standing near the entrance looking interestedly at Shadbolt.

'Where's this?' Shadbolt blinked, disoriented by a tent space with night-lighting in the middle of the day.

'I wanted to show you what I meant about sound-proofing.'

'Oh. But I don't see that this has anything to do with the hijacking.'

'But it has. Indeed it has. Here, try it for yourself.' He motioned with his hand and two of the men came forward to help the puzzled Shadbolt down. 'Smith and Jones and Brown here will help you. They'll ask you how you knew the photographs were going to turn up in the early hours and you can answer as loudly as you like.'

Blood drained from Shadbolt's face. Gently, Smith plucked the newspaperman's Eversharp and his pad of notes from nerveless fingers and when Shadbolt looked at Smith's eyes he swayed on buckling knees.

'Free press,' he gasped at Renwick watching him sadly from the Land-rover. 'Prime Minister guaranteed . . . free press in Westland . . . What charge . . . ?'

Colin held up a weary hand to hold the closing of the upper door. 'I hope you're not really that naive, Mr Shadbolt. Dealing with your esteemed mayor is as much as I can stomach.' He nodded to the man at the door, but held up his hand yet again. 'Another fictional character, Mr Shadbolt. Graham Greene's Captain Segura. "One never tortures except by a kind of mutual agreement. It is an instinctive matter on both sides." I think your side of the contract was in being too greedy for a scoop.'

The grandstand door closed. The Land-rover rolled forward a couple of paces and stopped for Renwick and Wilson to disembark.

'As I said,' Wilson remarked. 'Inbreeding.'

Wilson strolled, Colin walked heavily back towards the guest-house.

They paused to listen, but there was no sound to be heard from the grandstand. The day was absurdly quiet, Colin thought, and his ears sought a sound to focus on. He looked up at the white house on the hill, half-hoping, half-afraid that he would hear the music.

Delta patrol found the sand, or what was left of it, almost on Frazer Creek's doorstep, at the end of a four-wheel track branching off the road to the glacier.

The Land-rover nosed to the end of the track, which stopped abruptly against a fallen tree, about where the map indicated it should end. The area had already been inspected once and the patrol might have turned and gone if it hadn't been for the heavy-vehicle tracks that disappeared under the tree.

On the other side, the four men found an unmarked loop in the branch road: hardly more than a muddy sweep of cleared scrub, criss-crossed and scoured by the wheels of many trucks. Even then, they only saw the sand when they went to the very end of the loop.

The sand had been dumped onto a rock shelf forty feet down. There was a good deal missing, and from the boot and shovel marks and the impressions left by various back-packs it was obvious how it had been removed. Sand trails led into the trees as far as damp, coarse sand takes to drop off boots. The boot prints led only to the labyrinth of trails that went in every direction through the bush.

A sign had been left in the sand.

'I will eat it myself,' said the Little Red Hen.
And she did.

Later, Renwick and Wilson stood in the drizzle, looking down at the remains of the convoy's load. Wilson pointed to a single wheel-mark at the edge of the dumped sand; somewhere out in the South Westland bush a wheelbarrow full of beach sand was being pushed along a trail.

Wilson made a guestimate.

'Even if you allow 80 pounds a load, they must have had at least five hundred loads out of here on their backs.'

'And what do you deduce from that?'

'Charlie has built himself a thorium refinery up there somewhere and found a way to hide it. And . . .' He had the grace to look uncomfortable. '. . . he's got a better organisation than I thought.'

'What we also deduce, Wilson, is that we have lost the first set and the umpire neglected to tell us that the rules for this little game had been changed.'

Nine

Whenever the Prime Minister was angry, he flicked his Adam's apple, a habit that survived from distant school days. The action produced a hollow thud that he once used to irritate a detested geography teacher at Auckland Grammar.

He made the Brigadier wait while he scanned the photograph again. The intercom toned and spoke to him; he picked up the phone and listened, giving monosyllabic acknowledgments at lengthy intervals. When he replaced the receiver and regarded the SIS man, the pupils of his eyes were cold and bright.

'The *Dominion* has printed it, the Australians have it, *Time* is sniffing for its front cover. It's being touted as the news photograph of the year.'

The Brigadier swallowed. He couldn't shake the impression

that a momentary lapse of attention would cost him something vital to what was left of his well-being.

The PM's words came at him across the photograph like a silk whip.

'And you don't yet have a single arrest.'

'Renwick has his first suspect.'

'One.'

'One is often enough, with Renwick's methods. And there's the sand. The DSIR are checking that.'

'I'll be surprised if they don't find Renwick's head stuck in it.'

'But, sir, the restraints on him are enormous. On top of that, he's now having to cope with his own men; this hijacking seems designed not only for the media, but to deliberately mock and belittle his men. And him. As he said in his report, the terrorists appear to be deliberately provoking overreaction, with the presumed initial aim of triggering Australia to cancel CER, and the ultimate aim of bringing down the government.'

The Prime Minister considered this. He had come straight from a quiet lunch at Bacchus; at his age digestion required not only a good wine but a civilised interval of time before resuming the rigours of office. He sat back and clasped his hands across his complaining stomach, comforting himself that he wasn't setting a precedent in placing the entire armed forces at the disposal of the police in Westland. Peter Fraser had done that in 1941 to dispose of the renegade Stanley Graham.

'Tell me about Renwick.'

'He's the best we have. The best field commander in the country.'

'There was a question mark about his stability.'

The Brigadier blinked. The PM absorbed every obscure detail that crossed his desk. 'But that was a domestic incident. And we're talking more than two decades here. I know the dates coincide, but the resignation from the police force was over a disagreement with his superiors . . . on a matter, incidentally, which drew him to our recruiters in the first place. I have no doubts about him at all. If it's humanly possible, he'll do it. Forgive my forthrightness, sir, but I believe you're underestimating the difficulties he faces down there.'

'I thought he could deliver results under pressure.'

'There's pressure and pressure. He has barely any more freedom than the regulars.'

'Now you listen to me, and listen carefully. Frazer Creek is about to become a goldfish bowl. There'll be more reporters there inside twenty-four hours than you can shake a writ at. Australia is standing over the CER agreement with the slasher. We're holding the voters, but only just.' He nodded at the photograph. 'This kind of media manipulation is so damaging that if we have another loss, we *could* go under. If I invoke open censorship, we *could* still go under because this imagery is already out there doing its work. But most importantly, if Renwick allows his men to give vent to their wounded feelings we *will* certainly go under. He must, I repeat must, deal with the terrorists, but in a manner that will stand public scrutiny. Do I make myself clear?'

'Quite, sir.' The SIS man had not missed the more subtle stress on the word 'we'.

'I believe the appropriate phrase is "quiet efficiency", is it not?'

The Brigadier nodded gloomily.

'As for the leader . . .' The PM paused to look out across the harbour. Whitecaps. Infernal Wellington wind. '. . . Put it this way, Ted. I appear to have had a bad dream, about the fellow behind this Red Hen outfit. I dreamed that he was arrested and allowed to stroll onto a public dock with a keg of gunpowder under his arm.'

Ten

When the first Australian television news crew rolled into Frazer Creek, it stopped off at the office of the *South Westland Times*, hoping for a few pointers from the local in the business.

There was a sign on the door: 'GONE UP GLACIER ROAD ALL DAY.' They took the sign at its word, travelled the road without finding Shadbolt, and went on instead to Waikukupa Forest.

Later the same morning, an independent New Zealand crew took the same bait and drove up the road in a hired Hiace with all their gear. On a remote bend, they were stopped by four men dressed in bush shirts, cords and boots, and wearing balaclavas. The four dug the CP camera out of its case, smashed the lens and ripped film out of two magazines. Then they used their knuckles to help explain how glad they were to see the crew.

'Who told you to come over here makin' up bullshit about the coast, eh?' 'If there's anything I can't stand it's a townie bullshit artist.' 'I'll tell you something for free, Stickynose: Westlanders don't like townie press coming pokin' around in other people's business, right? So just get on your horse and ride out. If you're still around this afternoon you'll be dog tucker. Got that?'

'Got it,' mumbled the reporter, holding his ribs and nursing a split lip.

The shaken crew promptly reported the incident to the nearest police, in fact the only police. An inspector sat them down one at a time in the prefab guardhouse at the edge of the rugby field and studiously took down their statements. Could they describe the type of cloth of the shirts, the size of the checks and whether or not the boots were made out of leather? Yes, it would be investigated, though with the present workload, it might take some time to produce results. Sign here, please. Sure, stick around, but stay in town here where you can call on us if you get in trouble; and mind how you go, some of these local hayseeds play it rough. See you.

Wellington sent Renwick four more special patrols, two more infantry platoons for the beach, and an air-force detachment of six Iroquois helicopters. He came close to raising Cain over the Iroquois. They were the same machines that had laboured through Vietnam: antiquated, and sluggish at high altitude – rather like the incumbent minister of defence.

And they sent him an expert on thorium refining.

Much against his wishes, the expert was given his orientation on one of the aerial patrols, a tour of the entire region west of the main divide from north of the Okarito Lagoon to south of Jacobs Creek. All the way, in the thudding Iroquois, he felt airsick. His plea that he would see nothing of any possible use was answered by the pilot with 'Orders is orders. Lie back and enjoy it.' So the scientist, who knew that fear of flying is a perfectly logical phenomenon if you considered enough psychological parameters, endured the flight over snow-capped ridges, endless rolling expanses of bush, over a drowned kahikatea forest, lagoons, beaches and lakes. At a low angle, the lakes reflected their surroundings like mirrors; but high overhead, he could see ancient black tree trunks in the depths, tangled together like the fibrous pupil of a massive eye. At such times he closed his own eyes and pressed his forehead on the cold perspex.

But he did, after all, see something useful. The pilot drew attention to a wisp of smoke coming out of the trees, which thinned out even as the Iroquois swerved towards it. The pilot thrashed the tops with his down-draught, but the canopy was too thick to see anything more.

'That's the fifth time in two days,' the pilot said. But he complained, 'Could be anything. The bush is riddled with huts, bivvies, shacks, you name it. All sorts of weird characters hole up in there, even in winter. Don't know how I'm supposed to tell them apart from up here.'

The scientist's eyes narrowed thoughtfully. He brought out a notebook and began a flow diagram, but his psychological parameters forced a postponement of the attempt.

He was much more at home back at Frazer Creek, lecturing Renwick's officers and senior men from the army and air-force detachments. He rather wished the tent walls would stop moving, but with a makeshift blackboard behind him, he quite enjoyed himself.

'You have a problem, gentlemen. You may not be looking for a single refinery at all. The international markets are paying astronomical money even for low-purity thorium oxide. What that means is that the refining process could be carried out with very simple equipment.'

'Such as?'

'Well . . .' The scientist mumbled to himself for a moment and made markings on the board that meant nothing to the officers. They drew increasingly impatient, so he spoke his thoughts aloud.

'Some kind of hopper to keep the sand and the caustic soda at 140 degrees minimum . . . water supply to dissolve the trisodium phosphate . . . a filter, no, decanting would be simpler still, or just tip the liquid on the ground if you don't want the excess caustic soda. Hmm. Mineral acid into the hopper to dissolve the rare earth and thorium hydroxides . . . pour it all out, then back in through a filter to remove gangue . . . add a base to precipitate out the pure thorium oxide . . . Hmm.'

He faced the officers, surprised.

'It's far simpler than I thought. All you need is a filter, a heatable hopper and another container of equal volume, and the chemicals are available almost everywhere. In fact with a little less purity, you could get away with just the hopper. And the water supply of course.'

'That's all?' Renwick said. 'One heatable hopper?'

The scientist enjoyed the discomfiture of the non-professionals who had charged ahead without first consulting an expert; he was of the generation that believed scientists to be the highest evolved species of man.

Renwick noticed a sudden change of expression in one of the inspectors.

'What's the matter with you?'

'I've just remembered something. Wadlow said his patrol came across a crazy old man halfway up a mountain with a washtub. An old copper tub. Said he was washing his clothes in it.'

The room rang with laughter.

'It *is* possible,' said the scientist, intrigued. 'As long as you coated the copper with something. A silicone spray would do it.'

'Now *there*'s rot-gut for you!'

'Wait a minute,' Renwick objected. 'The refined stuff is radioactive. What about handling?'

'Thorium is only the starting point of the breeder cycle. It's principally an alpha emitter, the particles are slow and heavy. They travel only eight centimetres in air and are most unlikely to penetrate the skin. But the particles would cause cellular damage and cancers in the lungs. An operator would need to use a breathing mask of some sort.'

'That's *it.*' The inspector was excited. 'It stuck in Wadlow's mind because he found a gauze mask!'

The room rocked with enjoyment.

'God help us. All the old moonshiners have climbed out of their beds and gone back into the hills.'

'They must think they've all passed over to the great still in the sky.'

'Get me a copper kettle,' sang an air-force pilot. 'Get me a copper coil.'

'So you could store the stuff in ordinary glass?'

'Certainly.'

The officers liked this even more. 'I can see it now, the comeback of the Hokonui quart.' 'Now you too can glow in the dark.' There was a sense of expectancy among them, a feeling that a tide in the affairs of men was about to turn.

They waited on Renwick, who was frowning in concentration.

'Illicit alcohol production beat the enforcement authorities because neither production nor distribution was centralised. But thorium has to go overseas, which presupposes a bottleneck . . . Which lends itself rather nicely to association with an already established illegal organisation.' He rose, stared at the map, turned to the officers with a glint in his eye. 'Gentlemen, I think it's time to indulge in the romance of busting a few moonshiners.'

Behind Annie's Peak, on a secluded shelf in steep and heavily bushed slopes, the collection began. Two score of Westlanders came out of the trees in ones and twos, bowed under heavily laden packs. Some were well past retirement age and carried as little as forty pounds; some, in their physical peak, staggered in with three times that amount. Which made the older ones remember when they thought little of humping deer carcasses out of the tops. A few of the young ones stayed bent for a while after they dropped their loads, provoking remarks about greed and the soft, modern generation. Half a dozen women came with their own loads, scorning all offers to carry their bags the rest of the way along the shelf.

At one end of the shelf was an empty fibreglass hopper with sling hooks for a helicopter. Beside it was a small, black, leather-bound box.

It was almost time. Most kept their packs intact until the last moment and talked in soft voices, always listening. In the bush the ear picks up danger before the eye. One or two began to remove their load from the packs: a heavy, greyish-white powder sealed in two or three layers of impermeable plastic, usually Frazer County rubbish bags. The weighty preserving jars had been done away with a few weeks earlier when the collection system was streamlined.

The Collector stepped out from the trees. He wore a balaclava, a gauze mask over his mouth, and a pair of gloves that went up to his armpits. He carried a long stick and a duffel-bag. He opened the duffel-bag revealing hand scales, a calculator and rolls of used banknotes. There was little repartee; his garb made him too distant, too strange.

'Okay, let's be having you.'

One by one, the sellers donned their own masks and brought their sacks forward. Each was opened and looked at, a sample spread on the rubber glove and worked between thumb and finger, the whole sack weighed on the scales, the money counted, the load eased gently into one section of the hopper so as to raise the minimum amount of the dangerous dust.

'Eighty-two pounds – 738 dollars.'

'What're you talking about? That's 85 per cent pure, easy!'

'If it's more than 75 I'm a busted ass. You want a better price, use a filter. Don't waste my time. Next. Okay, yep, grade one . . . 96 pounds – you've got 1,104 dollars, so call me Father Christmas and don't spend it all at once. Next . . .'

He looked suspiciously at one sweating face, then probed the powder with his stick. It encountered something and the gloved hand dived in, coming out with a lump of concrete that looked like a piece broken off a firebox.

'Fuck off,' he said in a bored tone. The culprit repacked his powder, emitting a string of fluent expletives, and departed. Those who got caught cheating sold nothing till the next collection. That was the rule.

When the bad girl went up to the attic to play the piano, Rosa sometimes followed her up the stairs. She was afraid of her and never tried to stop her or take Miska from her. She kept doggedly behind, so as not to lose sight of Miska.

But Rosa always stopped at the attic doorway, because the bad girl thought the attic belonged to her. The bad girl wouldn't share. The bad girl did scary things. Like today at the deer farm; Rosa had wanted to bottlefeed the pet fawns like her classmates, but the bad girl had come and scared the fawns away so nobody could feed them.

In the attic, the bad girl wasn't content with just playing the piano. First she might curl up on the floor and hold the sides of her head and scream. When this happened Rosa would hear footsteps coming to punish the bad girl; but it would turn out to be Edith, who would stop in sight of the attic, shake her head and go away again. Edith was scared of the attic now. Then the girl would go to the piano and make screaming music, making Miska listen too.

Or she would screw up her face and say horrible things out of a screwed-up mouth like grown-ups did when they were really, really mad, and then she would make the piano mad too. Or she would walk around in a nasty way, with hot squirmy feelings in places where Rosa felt only stony numbness, but acting as if she liked it; and she would go and make hot squirmy things come out of the piano. Or, worst of all, she would laugh. Oh how she laughed. Deep down and loud so that Rosa would know that the footsteps *must* come to punish the bad girl. When they didn't, Rosa would get just a little mad, which made the bad girl laugh even louder, which, in turn, made Rosa scared again while the bad girl and the piano laughed together.

This time, as Rosa watched from the attic doorway, she felt very small like Thumbelina, watching the bad girl from a walnut-shell boat that was spinning round and round over the plug-hole as the water sucked away.

So for the first time, she ran away downstairs, leaving Miska alone with the bad girl.

Later, shivering, she found Miska had been returned to her.

'You're not to talk to that bad girl ever ever ever again,' she told Miska.

'Well I want to,' Miska said resentfully.

But Rosa knew what to do. She took a kitchen stool to the hall cupboard and poked around in the top shelves until she found what she wanted. It was a rug hook, many balls of wool of different colours, and a rectangle of webbing with a little wool already sewn into one corner. Edith and Tom had given it to her on her twelfth birthday, but after a single evening's work she had abandoned it.

She set to work clearing the webbing, with Edith's unstitcher. Tui Jackson arrived to play and stayed to watch. When the webbing was ready to begin again, Rosa found a crayon to draw the outline but hesitated.

'Can you draw a little girl feeding a fawn with a bottle?' she asked Tui.

'Yes,' Tui said, grabbing it. 'I can.' But Rosa didn't like the result. She scowled and rubbed it out with a cloth, then tried Edith. She had to repeat her request because Edith was rocking herself and dreaming again.

'Can you draw a little girl feeding a fawn with a bottle?'

'You draw it, love,' Edith said.

And Rosa did.

Eleven

The package had been posted from Harihari, just twenty-five kilometres to the north; which entitled it to a separate, though unremarkable, opening procedure. But when the control senior put his ear to it, he heard a sound that made his ear curl back against his scalp.

Ticking.

In a trice it was out near the side fence, underneath the paddling pool Nora Englefield had bought for her grandchildren.

For an hour, nothing happened.

Normally at this point the bomb specialists would have detonated a small charge next to it. But the bomb squad, like the rest of the specials, were bored and frustrated by all the restraints. A diverting challenge like this was too good to miss. The other factor Colin Renwick considered was that the package was addressed to him. But before making the decision, he donned a kevlar jacket and went out to look at the object, treading gently on the grass, peeling back the paddling pool to spill the water, squatting on his haunches to inspect it.

If it was a bomb, it was a small one: almost cubic, barely four inches to a side, though easily big enough to take his head off if it was full of plastic. The plain brown wrapping paper was tied with string in the old-fashioned way. 'Chief Superintendent Colin Renwick, Mona Lea Guest-house, Frazer Creek,' the address said. Blue fountain-pen ink. An immature but unmistakably feminine hand.

'All right, open it,' he ordered. And straw bales were stacked in a wall, with spaces for probes.

While Colin waited, a Land-rover backed hard up to the grandstand entrance, then drove twenty yards to a wooden prefab building, backing hard against that door also. A second vehicle came around the rugby-field track and backed up to the grandstand. The first prisoner exchange was complete. Shadbolt would be held in the prefab until his information checked out, then he would be shipped out over the pass to a special camp in Canterbury.

Two Iroquois warmed up in the sun, took a patrol aboard, and lumbered away over the bush: squat dragonflies whose growl could be heard long after they faded into the distance. The moonshine flights, as they were now called, had located and destroyed two copper-tub thorium stills but had yet to capture a moonshiner.

Another Australian television crew turned up at the barrier by the guardhouse and was told, politely, that all news releases had to come from the Commissioner's office in Wellington. The crew took pictures of the tent- and prefab-filled grounds from where they stood.

The outer, cardboard layer of the package came apart easily. The inner part proved more difficult; it was a hinged, sprung box that took ten minutes of cajoling with the probes. After a wait, one man went forward. The relaxation in his shoulders was a signal for disappointment. No bomb. The waiting men strolled forward to look at the contents of the box. They burst into laughter and a smattering of applause. Heads turned in Colin Renwick's direction. The bomb-squad inspector brought the package to him.

'Been reading my private mail, then?' Colin growled.

'You're a lucky swine, sir.'

'Flattery will get you nowhere. Hop it.'

It was a watch. Rather, it was a high-precision, presentation time-piece of superb craftsmanship. Roman numerals on a jade backing, border as black as ebony, and a face of pearly grey-blue. The note was in the same feminine hand as the address:

> Fate has placed us on opposite sides so there is no hope for more between us than this token. Please accept it and remember when you look at it that there was one whose words could not adequately speak for her heart.

Unsigned.

'Good God,' Wilson said, next to his elbow. 'An anonymous admirer. Someone needs a better optometrist.'

'You'll be hearing from my lawyer,' Colin said. But he noticed that the swathe of grinning faces now extended all the way to the guardhouse and that irritated him. He turned the watch over. The backing was a different metal from the rest of the housing. No inscription. He handed the watch to Wilson. 'Get the bomb boys to take the back off and check it for bugs. The wording of the note could be ambiguous.'

Wilson pretended to be crestfallen. 'That's looking the gift horse a bit in the mouth, isn't it?'

'Greeks, Wilson. And Westlanders bearing gifts.'

But when he returned to his office, Renwick read the note three times again before allowing paperwork to summon him back to his desk: on top of the pile, a communiqué from the Commissioner's office, rerouting an enquiry from the Ombudsman acting on behalf of one Sally Shadbolt re missing husband. Could Renwick shed any light? Damn them; he was a field commander and shouldn't have to deal with this kind of nonsense on top of everything else.

Next, a report from one of the logging crews clearing the Waikukupa track. Its grab machinery had been sabotaged during the lunch break, the guards had given chase. No one captured. As usual. Another report from a patrol on the Gillespie's Beach road: suspected Charlie spotted and chased into the bush, warning shots ignored, no one captured. More holes in the beach. The latest terrorist sign, 'IT IS AN OFFENCE TO SHOOT AT THIS NOTICE', had been brought in for analysis, identical to the others except for the distance referred to on the back. 'FRAZER CREEK 60 MILES'. Each one they found was a bit closer. This time the patrol had seen it planted. They'd got close enough to shout a warning to halt, and to fire over the heads of the group that dodged into the trees. No one captured.

A deputation of patrol leaders presented at Colin's door.

'It's impossible, sir. Charlie has cottoned on that if they leave their guns at home we're only shooting over their heads. They love it. The bastards are playing with us.'

'We even had one lot come back out to give us the fingers.'

'Bit of lead in the ear would fix it pretty good, sir.'

'Sir, I'm having a problem keeping my men under control.'

'There's an easy way to solve *that* problem,' Renwick grunted, making the last speaker wince. 'Now you pass this on to anyone else who can't see beyond their own noses. Anyone who can't control themselves and stuffs up the procedure is out. No hearing, or enquiries, they'll be down the road with nothing. We cannot take the risk of a suspect by-passing Searle and the detention camp and turning up in front of a television camera with anything more than a bruised shin. Clear?'

Silence.

'If warning shots aren't working, don't use them. Use your

legs. And from now on I want every shot fired accounted for in a written report.'

'Just like bleeding flatfoots, sir.'

'Put a toe wrong and you *will* be, Hicks. You think I enjoy this? You think I enjoy being made to look like an idiot? I promise you, sooner or later Charlie will give us an excuse for our day of reckoning. He'll overstep the mark.'

'That's what they're waiting for *us* to do, sir!'

'Precisely. And by heaven if we haven't got the discipline to win that sort of waiting game, we shouldn't be in the job. Now get the hell out of here and next time come back with a way of bagging these slippery bastards for Searle without putting holes in them. And with their tongues in good working order.'

They went.

Colin picked up the handwritten note, but dropped it quickly when the bomb-squad inspector returned with the watch.

'Clean as a whistle,' he grinned. 'The men are asking if you'll tell them what brand of deodorant you use.'

'Fly spray. Now buzz off.'

For an hour the watch lay by the drinks cabinet. During that time he gazed at the note yet again, not reading it, but looking right through it. Eventually he strapped on the watch, surprised and gratified by its warmth against his flesh. A thought occurred to him, directing his eyes to the window; and in the same moment he heard the piano. He went to the window and opened it wide, listening raptly, knowing that it came from the white house on the hill. Satie's '*Gnossiennes* One'. Haunting, exquisite; of longing, and unrequited love.

Searle came out of the grandstand, into his field of vision, like an insect crawling onto a clean photograph. Colin could see immediately that something was wrong. That much was obvious from the extra briskness of the walk, the anxious incline of Searle's head, the worried face that presented at the door.

'I'm terribly sorry, sir, but there's a problem with the patient.'

'Well?'

'Perhaps if you have a look . . .'

'Is that absolutely necessary?' Renwick's mouth soured.

'Certainly preferable, sir. I'm afraid there's been a slip-up.'

The white house was silent again as the two strode across the grass to the grandstand, and for that Colin was thankful. As they passed close to the grandstand's side wall, Renwick stopped suddenly, staring at a picture that had been painted on the concrete. The paint was fresh. A cartoon, created no doubt by one of the bored, off-duty men. It depicted a red hen lying in the dust with its tongue hanging out and its feathers in disarray. Above it stood a triumphant, rampant rooster.

'What the devil is that doing there? How long's it been there?'

'A few days, sir.'

'Get rid of it. It's hardly the place, is it? Or shall we bring in O'Hara to tell the world about our advertising again?'

'I'll get someone to go over it with white paint, sir. I should have thought of that.'

'All right, now let's get this over with.'

Searle led the way under the lower half of the door to the grandstand, into the yellow-green light of the canvas room. He shut the door behind him. Stainless-steel instruments hung on a rope across one canvas wall. There was a strong smell of disinfectant. Searle's two assistants stood waiting near the carpenter's bench, Jones looking downcast. On the bench was a slightly built man, his thin limbs spread-eagled by four clamps. He was naked, covered in sweat and shivering convulsively.

'Sorry to keep you waiting, Peter,' Searle said. 'Be a good boy and show the commander your legs.'

At the sound of Searle's voice, Peter Talbot of Whataroa went rigid, his muscles in spasm. His eyeballs rolled and he strained against the clamps, trying to curl into a foetal position. The backs of both knees were purple and black.

'Do keep still, Peter, there's a good lad, or we'll have to take another sample.'

'No, no-o-o . . .' whimpered Talbot.

Renwick jerked his head savagely in the direction of the canvas flap. He lifted it, leading Searle into the darker limbo between the canvas and the concrete.

'I can do without your bedside manner when I'm here,' Renwick hissed.

'Of course, sir. I'm sorry.'

'All right. The legs. Don't tell me, let me guess. Jones got over-zealous.'

'You mustn't blame him sir, he's a bit inexperienced. It's my responsibility. I shouldn't have taken a break at that particular time.'

'A couple of bruises we can live with. But if he does it again, he's out. Also, keep it to yourself; I've only just now been telling the section leaders to be careful with prisoners, partly because you're the only one who knows what he's doing.'

'Of course. I feel terrible. It's so amateurish.'

Renwick clapped a reassuring hand on the man's shoulder, though it made his skin crawl. 'If everyone was as reliable as you, Searle, the job would be a lot easier. Just see it doesn't happen again.'

Relief flooded Searle's face.

'Now give me progress.'

'Well, the prognosis isn't good. We're still at the ground floor and they've got a refinement of the three-man cell that's going to be tough. I'd stake my reputation that each man only sees faces on the same level as himself.'

'Damnation.'

'Still, in a province like this, I'm hoping for vertical recognition anyway, voices, that sort of thing. We need more patients, sir. Moonshiners. Anybody. And something else. I don't think we're dealing with a normal vertical structure. This one has been told there's no leader.'

'Insurrection by committee? Idealistic claptrap. Unofficial or otherwise, there is *always* a leader. You'll get a different story as soon as we get our hands on someone on a higher rung.'

'I'm sure you're right, sir. What shall I do with Talbot?'

'Is there anything more on him?'

'More detail, certainly. You never know what inconsequential detail will turn out to be useful later. But I'd much prefer fresh material, sir.'

'You'll get it.'

Searle took his white coat off a hook by the sink and slid into it. There was a stethoscope in the front pocket. A stainless-steel utensil was soaking in hot water in the sink behind him.

Renwick turned abruptly on his heel, moved swiftly through

the canvas flap and made for the door. But as he went, Talbot raised his head and called out to him in a broken voice.

'Please, please, not again. Don't leave me alone with him. I've told him everything I know. If I knew anything, don't you think I'd tell you? But I don't, I don't. Please.'

Colin reached the door.

'Please, please! Dear God, there's nothing worse than this!'

Colin stopped. After a moment, he turned and went back to the carpenter's bench where he looked down at Talbot as if the man were lying in the bottom of a distant valley. When he spoke, his voice was dry as dust.

'But there is, Mr Talbot. There is. There's something much much worse than this. Be thankful you'll never know what it is.'

Talbot met Colin Renwick's eyes. His jaw sagged.

'My God,' he whispered, and momentarily he stopped shivering.

As Colin left, the astonished and much-interested gazes of Searle and the two assistants followed him to the door.

Outside, the music was waiting for him. He had known somehow that it would be; he remembered now that he'd heard it drumming in the back of his mind even as he spoke to Talbot. Chopin's 'Prelude 24' again. An abrupt change of mood, though welcome in its own way because it overshadowed Talbot's first noises, which writhed like needle-thin snakes through the grandstand wall next to him.

He found his feet taking him across the grass towards the playground and the road up the hill.

A voice called from behind and he turned. Wilson.

'What?'

'The hunting-bow registrations have come through. There's only one local name. Malachy O'Hara.'

'Date?'

'Twenty years ago. Signed by his father.'

'You came out to tell me that?'

'You going somewhere? You're not armed. Shall I get you an escort?'

'What am I? A prisoner?'

After a pause, Wilson said, 'Just asking.'

Renwick turned on his heel and continued on through the swings and slide and roundabout, onto the road up the hill. It was unusually hot. A haze clung to everything, even to the shingle at Renwick's feet. It affected his ability to focus. He stumbled on the stones as the slope increased and it seemed as if the haze shimmered in time to the turbulence of the music. Again, the interpretation was far too free, much much too emotive. Where was the dignity and subtlety of the piece? He sweated, loosed the neck button of his jacket, but fastened it again. If it weren't so hot, he could think more clearly.

The notes cascaded in his head. But when he stood at the gate, it occurred to him that the piano had been silent for some time. He shook his head and blinked and waited until he had restored full command of his senses. Then he knocked.

The door was open, but no one came.

He knocked again. No answer. On the top step he could see right through to the lounge.

After a third knock, his feet took him inside, where he listened to the sounds of the house. One step followed the next until he stood stiffly in the lounge, almost at attention, wondering vaguely where the piano was. Why had she stopped playing? What was he doing here, uninvited in a strange house? In a strange but homely room: soft furnishings, a deep fluffy rug, a framed photograph of an elderly man, a cane rocking chair of the sort that creaks beyond all oil and reason. On top of the table was a rug webbing with a home-made pattern just begun: someone's legs and the feet of an animal.

He went to the window and looked down at the grandstand, the guest-house, at the rugby field where all the tents and prefabs sat like dirty, McCahon rectangles on a bright green canvas. Why was he up here? A leader of men was supposed to be able to choose his course of action.

A door opened and closed somewhere. Feet moved in a hallway. It was, he thought, rather like being caught with the hand in the biscuit tin. An old woman appeared in the lounge doorway. At the sight of him, she reeled and clutched at the centre of her chest, panting.

'Mrs Driscoll? Please don't be alarmed. I knocked but there was no answer.'

'You've already searched here. We haven't done anything!'

'No, no, of course not.' Colin snatched off his black beret. 'I heard the music. There was no answer when I knocked. The door was open. I'm sorry to alarm you.'

Her wide eyes went to the crowns on his epaulets.

'I'm Colin Renwick, Mrs Driscoll. I'm not here on police business. I heard the piano.'

'The music? You came for the music?'

'Yes.'

'*You're* interested in Rosa's music?' Uncomprehending.

'Yes, I . . . wondered if I could meet her.'

'She's retarded.' Sharply.

'I heard that. But the music. It's so . . . It's extraordinary. I wanted to meet her, to see for myself.'

'She's only a child. She's upset. She's always upset after she plays. You'll scare her.'

'Mrs Driscoll, I doubt if anyone who can play music like that could possibly be scared of me.'

They weighed each other up.

'She's not here.'

'But she was playing just a few minutes ago.'

'When she's upset she does her rug, or she goes to the graveyard. That's where she is. Visiting her dad.'

'I'm sorry. I didn't know.'

He followed the flick of her eyes and went to the bay window. A distant figure was emerging from a path at the bottom of the trees. Black hair, bright blue dress, bare feet padding in the dust and grass, and something floppy held in the hand.

Twelve

When Mal rapped his portion of Wiener schnitzel with a fork, it snapped in three pieces.

'Was this an act of God?' he demanded. 'Or do you really think it's supposed to be cooked like this?'

'What's wrong with it? A little carbon is good for the system.' Olly O'Hara crunched and chewed steadily. But in his state of dentistry this was tantamount to hard labour. 'If you got a girlfriend, we wouldn't have to eat muck like this, would we?'

'In this day and age? Don't count on it.' The last woman Mal thought twice about had informed him that men were just as capable as women at mindless, repetitive, demeaning work.

'That Sharlene Rassmussen's got the glad eye out for you, you know. She looks like she could be a real goer in the kitchen, not to mention in the sack, eh boy.'

'You need help with your tie?' Mal looked dangerous.

But Olly's grin remained intact. Sharlene Rassmussen had a figure that could have shown Marilyn Monroe an inch or two in the right places and the thought of having her round the house was more than appealing. His grin was like a shifting of the continental plates and almost as difficult to deflect.

But it could be done.

'I'm leaving, remember.'

Olly changed to a fork for the gravy, in which he had entombed most of the crumbs. Every now and then he glanced up at Mal, taking in the restlessness that showed in the flexing of the shoulders.

'Jim Dennehy reckons they've cleared the Waikukupa track halfway back to the beach already. Like a plucked chicken both sides. Heh, heh, get that – like a – '

'I got it,' Mal assured him.

'Says one of the logging crews is from Whataroa.'

'Uh huh.'

'Went up to Nelson to volunteer and gave Nelson addresses.'

'Yeah.'

'Now the government is putting them up in a fancy Whataroa motel.' Olly waited in vain for the beauty of this arrangement to register with Mal.

'That right.'

'Yes! That's right!' The old man leapt to his feet and stamped around. 'You knew, didn't you? You know every damn thing that's going on, but do you tell me? Hell no. Your old man might catch a cold if he knows what's going on, right? Mal, Mal, you know how I handled those buggers up the hill!' His memory of the encounter with the specials round the copper tub had kept up with inflation; in a year he would remember that he had planned the whole thing; in two, the specials would have run in terror from him, ploughing through nettle and bush lawyer and charged by stags cleverly attracted by his mating calls.

'This is getting . . .'

'What gives you the right to hold out on me?'

'. . . to be like a broken record.'

'What gives you the right to keep me out of the action? Your own father! That's what I want to know.'

'You can't leave it alone, can you? You're like Ben's Doberman. Once you get the teeth in you need a bloody bucket of cold water over you!'

'Am I a baby, or what? You know what's happened to you? *You're* older than *me*, you know that? Your gut is a dried arrangement.' His teeth champed between gears. 'Have you looked in the mirror, lately? Had a real close look? Or are you too yellow even to see yourself for what you are?'

Mal stood up, still holding his plate, but staring down at it. He dropped it; it split neatly across the middle and congealed gravy sagged through onto the formica.

'Jesus,' he muttered. 'I look after your neck and this is the thanks I get. Why do I bother?'

'*Don't* bother!' Olly's mouth frothed into overdrive. In this state he usually ignored bends in the road. 'If you're leavin' you can just fuck off now, for all I care! Go on, see if I care!'

Much later, when empty cans of Westland Dry lay about them, the old man said by way of a peace offering, 'Did you hear what Ben told those townie coppers? That he catches his deer after dark. Not bad, eh? But he's takin' a chance, silly bugger. If they find out he's pullin' their tit, they might think he's got something to hide, eh?' Halfway through, he suddenly lightened his tone and finished speaking without looking Mal in the eye.

Mal looked at him, puzzled.

Later, Mal took a pictorial feature out of an old Australian *Penthouse*, the issue with frames from a low-budget blue movie purporting to star Marilyn Monroe before she became respectable and famous, and he pinned it across his father's poster of her. Then he went into the bathroom and stared at his reflection in the mirror.

The duty special at the entrance to the rugby ground became suspicious when the media contingent vanished. He was accustomed to a continuous stream of reporters, photographers and cameramen taking pictures from the barrier arm, pestering him to admit them, or to contact control for them, or asking him damn fool questions like what he thought of Westland. Individually they came and went, his expression of boredom never faltered – until they all disappeared at the same time. One moment they were there, the next they were jumping into vehicles and driving away, turning left into the main road.

He called control.

Control sent the standby patrol out to investigate.

The patrol found the media jostling with a crowd of amused but mystified locals around the church notice-board. All the usual public notices had been covered by one large poster: a photograph showing two cheerful specials leaning on a farm gate. On the gate post was a tin box printed with '5.56 mm ball'. Standard NATO issue. EWS ammunition. A ribbon encircled the box, topped by a fancy bow and attached by a string to a large card, which carried the message: 'COURTESY OF THE LITTLE RED HEN'.

One of the specials gaped at the men in the photograph.

'That's Fitzy and Harris,' he said to the patrol leader. 'What's going on?'

'I don't know, but I'm sure as hell going to find out.'

They ripped the poster off the board and took it back to control. Control took it to Colin Renwick, who promptly ordered the recall of the moonshine patrol carrying Kevin Fitzgerald and Mark Harris.

'It's got to be a fake,' Wilson said.

'And a good one.'

'But why? Seems a bit obscure. And why the gate?'

'I have a bad feeling,' Renwick muttered.

The telephone clamoured. A priority call from Wellington.

'Renwick. Yes . . . Yes . . . It's just in front of me now.' Throughout the next ten minutes of shouting he kept his cycs on the poster. When he put the receiver down he turned to Wilson.

'Gate Pa.'

'Gate . . . Good God!' Wilson's inscrutability slipped.

'. . . and the *Gallery* journos have twigged. Good Lord above, Charlie thinks this is a spectator sport!'

'I thought the *Gallery* reporters were safe.'

'Safe, my eye! Who's going to stop them giving free history lessons to their Australian friends?' Both men fell silent, trying to sort legend from fact, both knowing that the distinction would make little difference to the public. As little as trying to draw a distinction between a fake photograph and a real one.

The battle for Gate Pa, 1864, was arguably the most glorious Maori victory in the history of the Maori-European wars. Fewer than 250 Ngaiterangi warriors, armed with obsolete muskets, shotguns and long-handled tomahawks, defeated 2,000 of Her Majesty's finest.

Tales emerged of nobility and chivalry that would have drawn astonished acclaim from the knights of the round table. Even before the battle, when the soldiers landed in the harbour, the chief Rawiri Tuaia sent General Cameron a note to inform him that a road had been built all the way to the pa fortifications 'so that the soldiers would not be too weary to fight'. Another letter detailed for the general solemn rules of battle: civilians would be left unharmed, captured soldiers would be disarmed and handed over to the authorities, armed soldiers who lost courage and fled to a house of God would be left in peace, the wounded would be treated with kindness. Psychologically the Maori won before the battle began. And they kept their self-imposed rules. A woman, Heni Pore, became a legend in her own right by bringing water to a dying British officer, tending him all night. A warrior returned the sword of a wounded soldier, hilt first. Chief Rawiri Puhirake strode up and down openly on the parapets during the bombardment of the pa, calling down to the British gunners, '*Tena tena e mahi i to mahi.*' Do what you must. Do your work. And it's said that when the soldiers ran short of supplies, the Maori of Gate Pa offered to give them weapons and ammunition so they could keep fighting.

Fitzgerald and Harris returned from the moonshine flight, very worried men. They were double-marched to Renwick's office, stood to attention and confronted with the poster.

'It's a fake, sir! That box wasn't on the gate post.'

'That much we worked out for ourselves.'

'The bastard! He said he was freelancing for *Woman's Weekly*, friendly as hell.'

'I take it you didn't know the photographer.'

'No, sir. Sir, Maybe they could slap a "D" notice on this?' Helpfully eager.

'God help me . . . get out of my sight, both of you. Go to control and make out a description. And get them to send it to the flatfoots. Go on, get out.'

When the two stricken men had gone, the telephone burred again. Another priority call. The conversation was, if anything, even more terse than the last, though this time Renwick took over its direction. And its conclusion.

'Surprise, surprise,' he told Wilson drily. 'They want results. They want them quickly.'

'You astonish me,' Wilson said.

It occurred to Colin that Wilson's ability to observe him inoffensively for long periods was highly offensive.

'No results from blue flight?'

'No.'

'We'd better look at the problem first-hand.' He studied the map, chose the area with the greatest concentration of red-tipped pins. 'We'll go with green flight.'

The Iroquois took them sou'-sou'-west, over bush-clad ranges that sparkled in the wake of a departed front. They followed the contours, maintaining maximum speed and minimum profile, just above the bush, leaving a wake in the tops. For three-quarters of an hour they thudded monotonously down the western side of the Alps, almost to the maximum range of the 214ST.

A few civilian helicopters were out, like insects hunting for pollen. Wilson trained the glasses on one skimming a mountain tarn. Westland Recovery ZM-HBB.

'Keep popping up, these O'Haras,' he observed.

But Renwick was gazing into the target area, lying just ahead.

He knew they might get nothing. The moonshiners were getting smarter, avoiding days with weather conditions that would hang their smoke in the air. But there would always be some, like Shadbolt, with more greed than sense.

The descent team rechecked its lines. Renwick ran them through a strip-assemble of their weapons. The fastest man stripped his EWS in 12 seconds, assembled in 20, including firing check. Not bad. The slowest did a 15, 26. Too slow. Do it again. Go! Keep 'em busy, keep 'em bushy-tailed; the military panacea would not cure the frustration, but it did relieve some of the symptoms. In part, however, the exercise was to keep Renwick occupied; like many qualified pilots, he made heavy weather of being a passenger.

The team played Euchre with a pack belonging to Kevin Longman, the slowest at stripping his weapon. In the field he always kept a pack in his left breast pocket because he had once dreamed that playing cards had stopped a bullet meant for his heart and that the last card holed had been the joker. This last detail of the dream so appealed to his team mates that his pack had become something of a Black-and-Grey mascot. He always shuffled and cut the pack before patrol.

The Iroquois tilted sharply.

'Stand by.' The pilot caught Renwick's eye and pointed.

Smoke. The merest wisp, hardly more than a cigarette's puff over green crepe, its near invisibility indicating probable effort to conceal. And at a lower altitude. Good. If – and it was a big if with these noise buckets – if they hadn't been heard already, they now had a minuscule edge.

The crack of the engine softened as the Iroquois tipped forward and built air speed, delaying by a few seconds the harder, carrying sounds. The descent crew attached rope eyes to the RAD pins. The aircrew ran the doors open, flooding the interior with the pungency of the bush. Longman scooped up the cards, shuffled, cut, offered them around for a lucky touch. Many accepted, a few declined. Under the present restrictions, they weren't going to see any real action.

The floor tilted hard back and pressed up under their seats.

'There!'

And there it was, the problem laid out for Renwick at a single glance. A glance was all he had: a single glimpse of a figure sprinting across a sparse patch of bush. Renwick found the descent team leader beside him, sighting along an EWS.

'Pow,' the man said.

The fugitive disappeared under the heavy bush mantle, heading for a well-prepared bolt-hole no doubt.

Point made.

As the floor levelled, the pilot shouted. The descent crew dropped away, rappelling down like spiders on silk. When they had gone, Renwick and Wilson followed, Wilson's gangly form like the spider known to children as a Daddy-long-legs. Long familiarity with the drop had never dulled Colin's awareness of the pilot's release mechanism, there in case the machine itself came under attack.

On the ground there was a moment of disorientation: the change of light levels, the tossing mantle, the soft, sodden undergrowth. Danger check, cover check, hand signal to pilot. The machine crabbed away overhead. Somewhere there was swift movement through the undergrowth, fading. Then there was only the hiss of a fire and the sound of a liquid bubbling. Renwick and Wilson holstered their side-arms and walked through to the miniature refinery, the 'still', the moonshiner's testament to kiwi ingenuity.

The firebox under the copper tub was open, filled with sticks and burning well. To minimise smoke: small, dry sticks of rata, kamahi or leatherwood. A viscous liquid boiled in the tub. There were ten county council rubbish bags filled with sand, two plastic containers with clear liquids and a filter adapted from a concrete shingle screen.

The refined thorium oxide was hidden in another rubbish bag, below a false layer of moss under the firewood stack. Renwick paraded the sensor of the flight geiger counter near the bag. It stayed nearly quiescent until the bag was opened, then the needle leapt across the scale and the random clicks became a steady buzz.

'Hokonui hooch never had a punch like that,' Wilson said.

Footsteps heralded the return of the descent crew, empty handed.

'We need dogs that can do the drop,' Kevin Longman growled. And for this rancorous wisdom he was detailed to do the spanner-drop, which entailed staying behind long enough to lob a grenade between the tub and the bag of thorium oxide. By the time he caught up with the rest, the grey-white powder had settled over the remains of the copper tub, the kindling firewood, the bags of sand, and the foliage round the clearing.

Mal took Rosa Driscoll part of the way on his motorbike: down Rockinghorse Road, onto a four-wheel track through the bush until the mud became axle-deep. From there they went by foot, carrying their gear to a tributary of the Frazer River where half a dozen runabouts wait for their owners in varying states of buoyancy. Mal's aluminium dinghy had been overturned by the last flash flood and had to be emptied and sluiced free of algae and brown water stains. But the outboard motor, taken from a plastic bag in the undergrowth, started on the first pull.

Cautious for submerged logs, they pushed out into the Frazer, heading downstream for the mouth. On board was a box of tools, a fold of patch netting, a plastic bucket and a lunch box. And Mal's bow, with a quiver of arrows; Rosa had found him sending arrows one after another into the knot hole on the wineberry, and extracted a promise to teach her how to shoot.

Rosa moved awkwardly at first. She sat in the bow seat with Miska beside her, gripping the gunwales tight, knuckles white, mouth nervously open as if also planning to hang on with her teeth.

'This is your first time in a boat?' Mal asked as he opened the throttle.

'Once I went in a very big boat with a swimming pool on it. And there was a man with a sword and lady dancing with a tiara.'

'Sure, sure,' Mal grinned. 'Just ease up with the hands before you break off bits of my boat.'

She relaxed quickly as she found she could move a little without upsetting the balance of the craft. After that, she watched about her with a keen eye: the occasional bough passing overhead, the flash of a sacred kingfisher, two elegant long-legged birds that, side by side, dipped courteous beaks to their own reflections in the water, then jacked themselves away with wings in perfect unison.

'Blue herons,' Mal said.

'I know.'

'Sometimes we get a white pair drop in from Okarito.'

'I've been to Okarito.'

She became adventurous, dipping fingertips in the water that chuckled under the bow, delighting in the contrast between the slow speed of the water and the swift passage of the trees on the bank.

A vision, Mal O'Hara thought. And was troubled by a sense of unreality. She was a vision out of a picture book, in mulberry T-shirt, Roman sandals and tight, bright new jeans. The breeze blew thick hair about her fine-boned cheeks and when Mal looked once, they were the cheeks of a disturbingly beautiful woman; when he looked again, she was a child; and once, while seeing her only with his side vision, he even fancied that it was an old woman sitting in the bow of his dinghy. As if she was never quite in focus. As if a quiet snap of the fingers was all it would take to cause a subtle realignment.

She bent over the bow to show Miska the water and he took

his gaze away abruptly and checked the fuel level. He watched the water slowing for the tide turn, watched a submerged log with only a small portion showing above the surface, and a lonely wattle on the bank, surrounded by native bush, growing in a spineless, inverted U.

A couple of hundred yards from the mouth they came to his stand: a jetty-like construction with vertical slides for the nets and screens and with feet that tiptoed on the feet of its reflection. A corrugated-iron shelter for the nets and tools squatted on the bank. So near the mouth, the bank was really a gently sloped beach of shingle and sand, lightly salted with round, marble-whitened rocks. A sand spit lay between stand and the sea, but Rosa and Mal could see spume lifting into the air and hear the boom of the waves on the bar.

The tide peaked. Mal brought the nets and screens from the shelter, slotting them into the sand like deep drawers side by side. Rosa brought him two screens, surprising him with her easy balance on the plank leading to the platform.

When the whitebait came, they crouched together on the plank as he showed her what to look for: the silver undulations, the flit of shadows on the sunlit bottom. He gathered a clutch of white rocks and dropped them into the water, making the tiny fish even easier to spot as they flowed along the screens and into the first net. That net was raised. The effervescent, flickering, silver and white stream poured into the bucket. Mal picked out a single whitebait by its tail, put it between Rosa and the sky, and twisted it this way and that so she could see the prismatic colours the sun painted in their bodies. The sea breeze pushed her T-shirt round her breasts.

'I'll show Miska.' She took the tiny transparent fish and clomped off down the plank towards the doll, which grinned in a chair of sand.

'Hold your horses. If you make a racket, they'll head out and around.'

'Oh.' Crestfallen.

'It's okay. Really.'

'I'll go very quietly.' She went down the plank like an apprentice burglar, while he watched her, entranced.

Overhead, cloud scudded smartly in from the sea, loose as a

fleece thrown on the sorting board. Shadows and sunlight ran braiding across the sand and flax.

They lunched high on the beach where the breeze discouraged the sandflies. And they lunched well: not for nothing had Edith Driscoll spent year after patient year teaching the skills that she saw as her daughter's only chance of a normal life. With this particular excursion looming, she had taken Rosa by bus to Hokitika to buy the tightest, sexiest jeans in town. On the way back, she had mentally rehearsed instructing her daughter in the ways of men; but she fell into dreaming again and believed that she had given the instruction already.

Mal sat back in a tortuously shaped driftwood, allowing his taste buds to worship the bacon and egg pie at their leisure. When he complimented Rosa she glowed with such open pleasure that he laughed in delight. After a while he scooped up a double handful of sand, opened a gap between the hands and watched a well form in the top of the sand as it sucked away from underneath.

'There's a lot of people are running round like idiots about this stuff, Rosa.'

'It's got thorium in it,' she said smugly.

But when the black sand had all run away he crouched with furrowed brow, drawing patterns with a stick.

'Yellow,' he muttered.

'Pardon?'

'They think I'm yellow.'

She wriggled over and touched his forearm, inspecting the skin, and smiled a brilliant smile.

'That's silly. You're not yellow!'

A snort of laughter burst out through the scowl and her next words also caught him completely unawares.

'Are you *very* sad, sometimes?'

In some confusion, he searched her eyes but could see no hint of the origin of this insight. There seemed nothing to focus on, nothing reachable in her to latch on to. But then, when he placed a hand on her shoulder, he saw a flash of such glittering intensity in her that he was startled. For a moment, nothing else existed for him. He leaned forward, brushed his lips against hers, closing his eyes.

She was utterly still. The lips were cold wax.

He drew back with a small cry, glimpsing the flick of the tail end of her fear. She was herself again, relaxed, gazing at the river. She had blotted it out.

It had not happened.

He walked down to the beach, picked up a stone, and hurled it with all his force at the nearest rock; it ricocheted out over the river and hit the water just as the echo smacked back from the valley wall. The stupidity of his own reaction compounded his confusion, but when he glanced back at her she seemed only mildly interested. He imagined himself going back to her and trying to find out what made her tick. But that meant questions like Who are you? What are you? And the thought of her likely reply made him curse. Instead, he went to the water's edge to splash cold water on his face.

By mid-afternoon the bucket was full. The sandflies began a concerted attack. Rosa strode up and down slapping at exposed skin, cheerful as the sunrise, though Mal noticed that she now kept Miska with her wherever she went. One-handed she helped pack away the nets, and drag the dinghy down through the clinging wet sand.

As they set off back upstream to the tributary, the breeze blew fresh in their faces and they left the insects behind. He noticed that her balance had improved to the point that she moved around the dinghy with confidence. She remembered the bow and arrows, still under the thwarts wrapped in an old tarpaulin. With one hand, she unwrapped the canvas sufficiently to see the weapon, then rewrapped it and returned to her seat without comment.

Mal ached somewhere he couldn't identify.

'Did the sandflies bite Miska?'

'No,' she grinned.

'You must have been feeding her vitamin B, then.'

'No, of course not.' She chuckled, shyly mocking. And a little of the morning's magic returned. Rosa picked individual whitebait from the bucket and held them sparkling in front of Miska, who was still clutched in one hand. Once, her fingers brushed him after she delved in the lunch box, and the touch radiated through him.

Then, she half stood, holding out a whitebait to him, pretending that she was offering up a snack. But in the same instant Mal swerved to avoid a branch on its way to the sea. As her other hand went to the gunwale for support, the doll vanished over the side. Rosa shrieked, stepped off the boat after the doll, and immediately began to sink.

For an instant, shock paralysed Mal. Her terror became his. He shouted something, he didn't know what, and spun the dinghy with the throttle wide open. The circle completed, he reached down for a hand just under the surface, hauled on it, changed his grip to her collar as her head emerged, craning, gasping for Miska. She thrashed, unaware of Mal's shouts or of the dinghy. It was impossible to bring her in over the side, so he dragged her to the stern. But one heave on the struggling woman put the port corner briefly under water. He let her fall back and with grip clamped on her upper arm, panted and swore with fluent urgency as he worked out his options.

There was only the bow.

'Miska!' she screamed.

'Rosa. Shut up! Listen, get in the boat first!'

But she was fighting him off, completely beyond reason. The doll was out of her sight, almost submerged a few yards away. He became rough with her in his fear, swearing viciously, dragging her along the side so that the boat spun precariously beneath him. At the bow, he tried once and failed. He slapped her, turned her to face away from him, and growling with effort hauled her in backwards with a hand under her chin.

The moment she was on, she scrambled to her knees, wild of eye, spotted the doll and headed for it.

'Oh no you don't.' He pushed her back down into the bilges. She fought back, demented, and he was appalled by her strength and the volume of her shrieks. He adjusted his grip, kneeling on her and twisting her arm behind her back. From then on he worked one-handed: wrapping the cord on the spindle, starting up, steering round again to where the doll was floating. It was face up, smiling its red cotton smile through water to the sky, a patchy smile now, the dye like smeared lipstick.

He plucked the sodden lump out and thrust it down in front of her.

The shrieks cut off as if with a knife.

He released her. She gathered the doll in with a long, drawn-out moan of reaction and pain while he put his fist against his forehead and forced his breath out through his teeth. He watched warily as she crept out of the bottom of the boat and resumed her place in the bow. She was dripping wet. Her T-shirt was torn, and so thin it hid almost nothing. He took his gaze away with an angry jerk of his head. They were still drifting.

'Jesus Christ, what kind of doll is worth that?'

'Miska doesn't want you to hold her any more.'

'Great! You tell Miska that's just fine by me.'

He turned the craft and it pushed upstream again, with both of them in sullen silence. It occurred to Mal that it was the first time he had seen her angry. Well, fine. He hoped she was enjoying it. The silence lasted twenty minutes, then he noticed that she was starting to wince and move her feet about. Soon she was rubbing her thighs, obviously in pain.

'Well, what's the matter now?'

'They're too tight!' The jeans were shrinking as they dried.

'They're new?'

'Yes.'

'Hell.' Mal remembered some drunken fool up north dying after he went to sleep in the bath with new jeans on. 'Well, bugger it, you'll have to take them off, won't you?'

Rosa thought about this. 'I don't want to.'

'Why me? Why me? All right, suit yourself. Just don't tell anyone I told you to take your pants off.'

In two more minutes, she was writhing with pain and emitting little moans.

'I can't feel my foot.'

'Don't be so damned stupid. Take them off before we have to cut them off.'

'Miska says I'm not allowed.' Her feet were turning an unhealthy blue.

'Take them off! Or I'll take 'em off for you.'

She looked at him sharply, considered the threat. She undid the belt, then struggled with the jeans.

'I can't.'

'Ye flaming gods and little fishes!' Mal took the engine back to idle, ordered her to hang on to the bow, peeled the jeans off her and flung them into the bilges. The rest of the journey to the tributary he spent glaring at the river on one side or the other.

The Kakapotahi deer farmer was puzzled. In the last hour of touring the farm, the two Black-and-Greys had asked no questions about people. Only about deer. The senior officer had professed a curiosity about deer in the light of the boom in deer farming. The farmer had no reason to disbelieve it, but he still had difficulty reconciling the personal interest with the impersonal uniforms, the military-style jackets, the black berets and the pistol on the 2IC's hip.

However, Chris Doig's visitors were pleasant and courteous. They weren't in the least put out when he steered them clear of the fawning paddock, where hinds gave lusty, guttural barks, trying to keep track of playful offspring. In fact the two officers followed him rather like the attentive, obliging students Lincoln College kept sending over. But without the pimples. And a vast improvement on the average loopy tourist whose mental development had stopped at *Bambi*.

Doig was flattered. As long as they kept asking intelligent questions he was happy to oblige with the answers and the tour.

Colin Renwick, strolling easily, hands clasped behind back, took an interest in two paddocks in particular: one an enormous scrub-covered field with three hundred hinds scattered across it; another, much smaller, with eight mature stags. A couple of the stags were 400 pounds' weight on the hoof, in prime condition, with glossy summer coats.

'Why aren't there more stags?' he wanted to know. 'Come the rut, that's a lot of hinds out there.'

Again, the farmer was gratified. For once, a townie who could talk about the rut without looking like a booby out of water. 'You're dead right. I'm getting twice that number in. But maybe not for the reason you think. Physically, they could maybe manage it, but the problem is psychological.'

'Get away.'

'No kidding. They need the competition.'

'Gets them raring to go?'

'Too right. These aren't your namby-pamby domestics, you know. These here are wild animals . . .' He gestured grandly towards the stags. 'Survival of the fittest and all that. You put one of these beauties in with too many hinds and he'll walk around in a circle bellowing for the competition to come on out.' The stags in question were quite still, statuesque, grouped in an effortless artistic arrangement as if a powerful hand had placed them just so. Watching the humans watching them. Colin found the combination of colours before him – the tawny red of the deer on Erin green grass, set against the pure white peaks behind – exquisitely beautiful. A tableau inviting his own hand to reach out and touch.

'They don't look too competitive yet.'

'Come back in the roar. Pretty close now. We put 'em in the biggest, roughest paddock we've got and they go to it. Hell of a performance. They'll turn half the paddock to mud, spray themselves with urine, and bellow – you haven't seen or heard anything like it. I've seen the top stags lose a hundred pounds' weight in a few weeks.'

'Must be difficult getting them to adjust from the wild.'

'You got it. You've got to be a mite careful bringing them in. Any rough handling and they're venison.'

'I can imagine. That'll be why you let them orient to the new territory after dark.'

'Right, right. And in daylight the stags'd go the fences.'

'Direct by chopper the best way?'

'Not by choice. I prefer to road them in, in a darkened trailer. Smoother transition.'

'But if you caught them by chopper in the dark anyway, it would be more direct to bring them straight in, surely.'

'In the dark? Not a chance. Not a hope in hell of catching them.'

'But I heard you could get them with a flashing light. A bit like rabbits.'

'Haw! Someone's been pullin' your Aunt Mamie. I mean the deer just aren't out in the open to . . .' He stopped, looked with narrowed eyes from Renwick to Wilson and back. A look of disillusionment and disgust came over him. 'Aaah fuck. You been pumpin' me dry. I shoulda known. Have I landed some poor bastard in lumber?'

Renwick didn't answer.

'Where I come from, if you got a question you ask it straight.'

'Where I come from, you wouldn't have answered it.'

'You might have something there. Now piss off! And don't drop your guts near my fawn paddock.'

Wilson's eyes flashed. He came a step forward, but Renwick stopped him with a look and a motion of the head. As the specials drove off the property, he extended his country courtesy by getting the driver to close the gate. And he gave a sardonic wave to the distant, mute figure of Chris Doig.

'The smart arse tumbled too soon,' Wilson complained. 'But at least we know Ben O'Hara's got something to hide.'

'Thin, too thin. Why is it so damn tenuous?'

'Do we bring him in for a chat anyway?'

'Yes.'

Wilson made the call.

But two minutes later, as they passed the junction with Rockinghorse Road, they saw Malachy O'Hara, approaching on a motorbike. He had a shivering woman passenger on the back who never lifted her face from his shoulder. O'Hara was without trousers and his face looked ready to give birth to forked lightning.

'Like I say. The name O'Hara keeps ringing like a supermarket cash register. Let's get him in as well.' Wilson grinned. 'Want to throw in indecent exposure?'

'No . . .' The commander was frowning into the distance. 'Wait.'

'What's the matter?'

'Cancel the pull on his brother.'

'What? What the hell for?'

'Don't question my orders! Cancel it! You go too far, Wilson.'

Wilson's eyes widened. In all the time they had worked together, Renwick had never pulled rank in such a manner; he was becoming unpredictable lately. The driver was watching them on the quiet, startled. It was verging on the irrational, Wilson thought. But if that meant Renwick being removed all the sooner, well and good. Just so long as he didn't take anyone else down with him. Like yours truly.

Wilson caught the driver's eye, accepted the microphone, and called, countermanding his own order. After a while, Renwick's expression returned to normal. He spoke pleasantly, as if the incident had not occurred.

'I have a feeling, Ian, a feeling. I think the O'Haras merit some rather careful time and motion study before we pull them in for a chat.'

An hour after sunrise the following morning, a pair of army men with high-power binoculars were stationed in the bush a few hundred yards uphill from the O'Hara farm. As morning cloud came briefly down the mountainside, the two moved with it. Staying off the trails while keeping in sight of the house was difficult to do at all, and impossible to do in comfort; to observe a particular arrival or departure often required hanging out of a sodden tree or standing on a rotten log likely to collapse without warning.

At seven thirty, two cows came from the south paddock and stood by the barn. One of them manured the wall.

At eight, the observers recorded the arrival of a salesman on the back porch who seemed to be asking for something rather than trying to sell. He and the old man disappeared inside, but soon reappeared. The salesman drove off. After that one of the observers donned a pair of headphones and nodded to the other. These days, the SIS labs were turning out bugs that looked like dress pins, with microphone and transmitter in the head and with the rest of the pin as the aerial. The relays were the size of a matchbox and one now lay under the O'Haras' back porch.

One of the cows stamped a foot. The other lowed.

The observer with the headphones grinned and handed them to his colleague. The voices were clear in spite of background crackling.

'. . . *not* milking her and that's *final*.'

'Whaddaya want? A whip and a chair?'

'Do it yourself, you lazy old fart.'

After a while the binoculars picked up the old man stomping across the yard, scattering hens on the way to the barn.

A similar pair of observers set up near Ben O'Hara's hut, which lay between Frazer Creek and the glacier. And Renwick personally installed a couple of specials in a discreet camp two thousand feet up, on a ridge with a line of sight to the helicopter on Ben O'Hara's front lawn, across the valley to the O'Hara farm, plus a clear view in all directions north, west and south.

Around twilight, when the birdsong was melting back into the bush, Renwick saw Rosa Driscoll again, without at first realising that it was the second time in a few hours. He would have missed her and driven past the Frazer Creek graveyard, except that his eye was caught by the china-blue dress she'd worn when he visited her home. He told the driver to halt further along, by the church, refused the escort and walked alone back along the graveyard fence-line.

But he came to a standstill before he reached the gate. Now that the chance to meet her had presented itself, he would have to let it go. He could hardly accost her at her father's graveside. It wouldn't be long before one of the media swarm found him, and he didn't care to contemplate what a paper like *Dominion* would do with the caption beneath the photograph. Damn the PM; what was the use of clamping down on 95 per cent of the media while allowing publications like that to say what they wanted? Too much sacred kowtowing altogether.

She was on the far side of the graveyard, facing away from him, amongst gravestones that were new and shone with the fast-fading light. Somewhere, a night bosun piped. 'Pee . . . pee . . . wharau . . . roa . . . roa.'

Nearer to him was a stone made of Westland jade, the colour beneath its lustre deepening swiftly to black. Across the fence from him were the oldest of the graves, dating back to the gold rush. One, out on its own, was surrounded by dead grass. It said simply 'THOMAS HICKS.' Colin Renwick had heard the story. Hicks, a child of the gold-rush bar-rooms, had killed his wife and three children in a fit of depression when he couldn't pay his gambling debts. He was hanged by a lynch mob. Even now, four generations later, her family's descendants gave the Almighty a helping hand by spraying insecticide round the grave. But it was said that the men who attached the noose were those he owed money. In Westland, a man pays his gambling debts before any other.

She held something out from her – a doll – set it down on the ground and stood back. She appeared to be talking to it. He wished she would turn around.

Suddenly he was rocked by a feeling of déjà vu. Something familiar, something uncomfortably close to him was happening here. Yet he could not possibly have seen this woman looking at her father's grave before now.

Turn around, he urged silently.

But wait. The motorbike . . . riding with Malachy O'Hara . . . The woman whose face he hadn't seen. Her? Yes, the more he thought about it, the more he knew it must be her. How could she demean herself by riding around with a yokel who wore no trousers in public? Immediately, another and much more disturbing feeling overrode the first. And it astonished him. Jealousy? For a supposedly retarded woman he still hadn't met?

Turn.

Sensing his presence, she did turn.

They looked at each other over fifty yards of headstones.

How very beautiful she was. How delicately fragile. And somehow noble, though that could well be the light, which was beginning to play tricks with his eyes. The woman was hypnotising him, damn it. Mentally retarded? No. This woman could in no way be mentally retarded. Suddenly he drew in his breath, glancing down at the gift watch. The luminous strips on the hands were already glowing for the evening. Her?

He found his fingers gripped too tightly over the fence rail. She was still looking at him. Or was she staring into space? Damn light!

The feeling of déjà vu intensified, perhaps because she reminded him of his ex-wife. His ex-wife had played the piano also, and she'd had Rosa Driscoll's kind of dark-haired good looks. Originally. Until she got sick and withdrew her affections. And turned his daughter against him. Frigid bitch. How she had laughed at him when he wanted to lie close and shut his eyes and rest his head on her breast. Laughed at him! The memory kindled the burning even now. Women were incapable of affection. Women had taken his simple need and fashioned it into a demon that had mewed and gibbered in his nights and made him do things . . . do things . . .

No. He would not think about it. For him of all people it was impossible to undo what had been done back then. Impossible, now, even to make amends; God, in His overly-lauded wisdom, had chosen to make an exception of him, allowing him to sow, then denying him the reaper.

Rosa Driscoll turned away and sat down on the graveyard grass. In doing so, she sank completely from his sight. For some reason this made his stomach churn. He wanted to call out, No, no, get up. Stand up. Look at me, let me see you.

A reporter's car swept past, slowed and turned and came back.

Colin walked back towards the Land-rover, where his driver was watching him covertly in the mirror.

INTERMEZZO

All day the hind waited, in a thicket of kanuka and beech. She was alone, though she could hear the breathing of others of the herd. Sometimes there was the sound of a hoof placed, a leaf expertly parted from a stem. Far away up the mountain, a stag thrashed antlers in pepperwood.

The hind's time was close.

But she was sick, her swollen hide patchy and dull. Her eyes stared, her tongue lolled in silent agony, and she could not take nourishment even from the young fuchsia next to her. She had been in labour two and a half hours. Her waters had broken and the back legs of the fawn protruded. Even so, the hind remained standing until she sensed that one final effort would bring about the birth, then she dropped to her side and convulsed.

The fawn was alive, wet, black in the first moments after birth. The dying hind severed the cord. She attempted to eat the sac and placenta, to keep predators from the birthplace and to help the process of identification. But she failed. She tried to lick her fawn, to dry it, again helping identification. In this also, she failed. Soon she laid her head back on the moss, her eyes glazing.

The fawn struggled to its feet. It stood over its mother's body, one hoof next to the swollen milkbags. It listened to the drip of water, the brush of leaf on leaf, the distant tap of a hoof. It smelled the body and the bush and the earth, all of which was its mother.

Fear came.

'Meengk!' it cried in distress. 'Meengk! Meengk!'

Thirteen

There's a pause in the telling. A round arrives: a jug, a gin and tonic, a couple of Gorse and sodas. Your host takes a cigarette off his lower lip and leans forward, fixing you with his eye. The others are watching you also.

'You believe what you read in the newspapers?' he demands.

'Most of the time,' you say.

'Well don't. No pub riot ever started just because a woman sits at the piano and tickles the ivories.'

Rosa Driscoll was the trigger, not the finger that pulled it.

The inhabitants of Frazer Creek district suffered the random, lightning searches, the invasions of privacy in their own homes, the jokes about inbreeding and thicks-in-the-sticks, the loud main-street speculation on the sexual habits of women who refused the specials' advances. Isolated women were raped. Carefully. No bruises, no witnesses. Men and teenagers showing less than craven humility to the searchers were worked over by specials who knew how not to leave marks. No bruises, no witnesses.

More thorium stills were destroyed by grenade, poisoning the forest.

The specials in their turn dreamed of the day they would be permitted to extract retribution from their tormentors. Many dreamed it quite literally, some of the more susceptible men waking the camp, shouting from their night fevers about women who discussed manure when they walked by, about boys who urinated on their parked Land-rovers. About the greasy-pig event at the local fair, in which the pig was painted grey with black trim before application of the horse fat. About the press article that appeared on the community notice-board reporting research by the Victorian Department of Agriculture, which had revealed that in dealing with pigs a certain standard of manners and etiquette is required.

There was the local remake of the rooster and hen cartoon the commander had ordered removed from the grandstand wall. The local version appeared on the side wall of the post office. Like the first, it showed the rooster standing over the hen, but this time it was sagging in a vital part and a bored-looking hen was tapping its feathers in the dust, saying, 'We'll let you know. Next!'

After that piece of plagiarism, the specials abandoned what little remained of their main-street graces. Unless there was a camera present, they ignored queues, said please only with shirt crumpled in their fists and walked three abreast on the pavement. A youth, egged on by friends to stand his ground, was sent reeling into the street with a cuff that rang in his ears for a week.

Steam. In a kettle whose lid and spout had been sealed on both sides.

In the pub that Saturday night, everyone knew something was going to happen. The chatter, the thump of darts, the click of pool balls, the swish of ale – all seemed muted and shallow as if they were a façade. The music of the three-piece band slithered weakly on an almost deserted dance floor. Conversations, arguments, jokes, were conducted with shoulders forward and heads down.

'What's going on?' people asked each other. No one knew and yet everyone knew.

One of the specials reached back from his table and took the poster of the hen off the back of the door, dropping it to the boards. No one spoke about it. No one challenged him.

'I don't like it,' Harry Withers muttered to Sue, words he had last uttered when the Epitaph Riders dropped in for a convention.

An Australian TV crew came in, disgruntled by three days of shooting with only wallpaper pictures to show for it. They were so surprised to find the special patrols drinking in the pub they went straight back out to bring in their camera. On their return, the undertones of the atmosphere sank in and they subsided into one corner. There they toasted the Australian columnist who described New Zealand beer as 'A flat, warm slop which when drunk becomes a vicious, gaseous, bubbling emetic clawing at the tripes like a famished rat, bringing on cold sweats, shuddering and a ringing in the ears.'

The specials could have told them about really dodgy beer.

In part, the specials were back in the pub this Saturday night out of a sense of fair play. During the week, one of their supply trucks had dropped off one more crate of beer than was marked on the docket. Not a mistake that bothered anyone until the extra crate made its presence felt on a hot afternoon. The contents had been replaced with another golden liquid, recharged with CO2 capsules and professionally recapped. Beer doesn't taste the same the second time round. The specials had decided that because there was no hope in that particular hell of nailing the culprit, the beer would have to be freely and generously replaced at the one source available in the village.

The first specials up to the bar had explained the logic of this to Harry Withers in straightforward terms. And Harry had no difficulty with the concept at all. He didn't have to have explained to him the cost efficiency of free beer for the specials as insurance against some drunken louts coming back in the night to dent his hotel.

The villagers were less understanding. It was one thing to adjust to uniformed cops drinking in a bar full of minors. It was quite another to have them free-loading the drinks. If Dipstick, for example, had been asked what cops were for, he would have answered 'To stop you drinking.'

At the table that straddled the line between specials and locals, Dipstick, Drop-kick and Fucknuckle were talking. More to the point, they were not arguing. To Harry Withers' alarm, they started to agree with each other. Behind the bar, he wiped his brow. 'Run upstairs and bring down some Zombies, will you Sooz? Better bring a crate.'

The specials talked with each other while cruising their eyes around the contours of the local women, particularly Rosa Driscoll and Sharlene Rassmussen.

Sharlene spotted Mal O'Hara alone at a table and extricated herself from the advances of Ken Hastings, the post master. She adjusted her clothing to give more air to her most negotiable assets and headed for Mal's table.

'You owe me a drink,' she declared, settling into a chair opposite him.

He looked at her morosely at first, but then more agreeably. 'Fancy me forgetting that.'

'Double Gorse, rocks and breakers,' she ordered, scooting her empty glass across the table.

Amongst the specials, Sergeant Donovan Hayes poured from jug to glass, considered that an inch of head was too much and extracted a top-up from Withers. Tony Hanrahan threw a dart and cursed as it clashed on the wires and stuck in the floor. Down in the space between the tables and the dance floor, Rosa's knucklebones game was deteriorating. Since her arrival she had become distracted and listless and in the end she gave up the game and took her doll to her mother's table.

'Miska's sick.'

'Is she? Does she want to go home?'

'No.' Uncertainly, Rosa sat. One of her mother's friends brought her a drink but she left it untouched.

A young man came to Mal O'Hara's table. Alan Meers from Harihari.

'Hey Mal, got a sec?'

'Yeah?' O'Hara saw Alan through an image of Sharlene Rassmussen's cleavage.

'Ah, alone.' Conspiratorial.

'You don't say,' Mal said sourly. But the Meers boy wouldn't go away, so Sharlene shrugged and took herself back to the bar to wait. The boy took her place, became even more secretive and didn't whisper until he had brought a hand casually up between his mouth and the specials.

'I want to join.'

'Yeah? Join what.'

The teenager was taken aback. 'You know . . .'

'Listen sonny, this'll take less time if you give me a hint.'

The boy flushed scarlet and his shoulders squirmed in agitation. He went to borrow a pen, visited the toilets and came back with a scrap of toilet paper folded to the size of a five cent coin. On it was a stick drawing of a hen.

Mal crushed the paper in his hand.

'Who told you to ask me?'

'Ah, word just kind of got round.'

'Well the word is wrong, sonny. You just send it right back where it came from.'

'So who do I ask?'

'I don't know what you're talking about.'

Crestfallen, the boy apologised and went away.

Sharlene began a comeback, only to see Ben O'Hara slide into the chair in front of Mal. At the sight of his brother, Mal jumped and came close to knocking over his drink. Ben moved the drink further away.

'They want your help again.'

'Get lost, Ben.' Mal looked towards the bar and Sharlene who pouted at him.

'I'll tell you what they want, Mal. The problem is in the final move. It's our last card, so we have to be certain it's going to work. It's got to push the specials over the top; but they know we're after that now. They're so damn disciplined . . .'

'Doesn't anything penetrate your tiny skull? I'm finished with all that and I'm finished with you and I told you to push off.'

'Well, have it your own way. As long as you're happy for word to get round that you abandoned us halfway through a campaign that you started, and that you're a gutless, yellow-bellied, jelly-kneed son of a bitch who couldn't even find the balls to point young Meers in the right direction.'

Mal went white, sagging where he sat.

'Conscience bothering you, Mal?'

'You put him up to it, didn't you?'

'What we need, brother, is a way of suddenly boosting the level of small-time resistance, they've got to be driven crazy just before we play. We need a way to bring in everyone who's still just talking about it in armchairs – like you. Nice, ain't it?'

Mal stood, gaping down at Ben in disbelief. Then he walked through the tables to the back exit. One of the band's seamless ribbons followed him outside where it wriggled and died as the door closed on it. He wandered out to the far side of the car park, walking in circles on the shingle and holding his face with a clawed hand, hearing the moths on the glass of the door and the night birds in the bush.

As he went back in and through the tables, he avoided looking at Rosa Driscoll. Ben was waiting for him. Impassive. Confident.

'Tell me something, dearest Benjamin. Does your glorious leader know of my existence? Or are you taking all the credit?'

'He knows. Believe me, he knows.'

'Well you can tell him this really is the last time, because I'm away in three days and he can bet his sweet life I won't be leaving a forwarding address.' Ben waited. Mal tossed the rest of his drink into the back of his throat. When he continued his voice was like the bitter July wind that comes down off the snows.

'What you need is a living symbol – not the Red Hen – a two-legged, walking, breathing, human symbol.'

'Like what?'

'Like the one that's sitting at the table over there. With the doll.'

'What in blazes are you talking about? She's backward, you idiot.'

'Think about it. Think about her and Westland. She's beautiful. She's cut off from the world. She's got almost no voice, but you've heard how powerful her feelings are when she plays the piano? See, she's looking at it now. And look . . .' The bitterness swelled with self-loathing. 'Look at how the specials are eyeing her natural resources.'

Ben's eyes were narrowed with concentration. His lips moved silently.

'. . . I haven't finished. One more thing you need. Sitting back there. Waiting for you.'

The Australian television crew.

'Oh man,' Ben breathed. For the next two minutes he thought it through much as he would mull over the value of a new hind. He went away then, leaving the room, only to return ten minutes later. Sharlene Rassmussen was back with Mal and was sitting at the angle most advantageous to displaying her wares. Mal caught Ben's arm as he went past on the way to the Australians' table.

'Am I to deduce from this that your Lord and Master has given it the green light?' His words were slurred.

'You could say that.' Ben's eyes were contemptuous.

'What's goin' on? What're you two talking about?' Sharlene demanded irritably.

'Why don't you just flop them right out on the table and let him take his pick?' Ben told her as he departed.

For the next twenty minutes, he drank with the Australians in the corner.

There was only one couple left on the dance floor. At the end of the number, the dance band gave up the struggle. A dart game finished and no more began. Dipstick and his two companions fell to drinking in complete silence. A Zombie appeared in front of each of them. The three men left them unopened, each wondering why his heart was behaving like a jack hammer. Dipstick blew his nose, a sound like a flushing toilet.

The last surge of self-conscious laughter squelched away, leaving only a flat murmur. Susan Withers whispered something to Harry, looking at the phone, but he shook his head at her and spread his hands. The senior special conferred with another officer, then disappeared out the front door at speed.

'What's goin' on, mate?' the Australian reporter asked the nearest drinker, but the answer was a shrug. Beats me. The reporter whispered to his cameraman and sound recordist. The cameraman went through a colour balance then propped the instrument on his shoulder and took an unobtrusive wide pan, connecting the uniformed specials with the locals. And he took a leisurely zoom of Rosa Driscoll, cuddling and soothing her doll.

What happened next was far beyond what the reporter, Ben, Mal or any one individual in the room could possibly have anticipated. Rosa Driscoll walked through the tables, placed her doll carefully at the treble end of the keyboard, and began to play.

'Prelude 24.' Every eye in the hotel was riveted on her. For the first few seconds not a limb moved. At the crescendo of the second ascending run, a visible start went through the Westlanders, as if through a single body. When the melody switched to the bass, the hair lifted on the backs of the necks of every Westlander and uniformed special in the hotel. At the start of the final crescendo, a terrified toddler began to wail on his mother's knee. At the table on the border between the locals and the specials, Dipstick pushed his glass away from him.

'Oh . . .' he murmured to the glass. '. . . you fucking swine.'

And with that, he and his two companions launched themselves at the nearest uniforms, bellowing, punching, swinging chairs.

The pandemonium that followed was on a scale that hadn't been seen in a West Coast pub since the gold rush. Those with children rushed them out the exit and rushed right back in as the two sides fell upon each other like opposing breakers. Women waded in with beer jugs and high heels, oblivious of the fact that the Black-and-Greys were in no mood to apply their punches according to the sex of the target.

The villagers outnumbered the specials two to one. But the specials were trained in the less than gentlemanly arts of street fighting. Alicia Nolan, the matronly store assistant, stood on the bar, cackling and swinging the draught hose and nozzle. Kingi Hastings swung a table, destroying it on a special who should have been a tank in World War II and thereafter he used one of the table's legs. Sheila Buchanan and Hetti Nolan formed a devastating partnership confronting specials with a full glass and an empty jug. Harry Withers sat behind the bar with a new cigarette in his mouth, trying to strike a match on a beer-soaked matchbox.

It was bloody, it was glorious, and the locals knew they were taking part in a fracas that would go straight into Westland's folklore. It was understood by both sides to be as inevitable and as good for the soul as the sun coming up in the morning. That may have been one reason for a curious aspect of the battle: not a single special used his pistol, or even drew one from its holster. But it mustn't be thought that it was a clean fight, or that it owed anything to the Marquess of Queensberry. Far from it. The riot in the Frazer Creek Hotel was conducted in deadly, joyous earnest.

It came to an end with two pistol shots.

Colin Renwick and Ian Wilson stood in the doorway. Smoke

curled from the barrel of Renwick's Smith and Wesson. Plaster drifted down from bullet holes in the ceiling onto groaning, sprawled bodies, on broken furniture and splintered glass. Peter Hanson from Karangarua took a last swing with a chair, missed, sagged to his knees and collapsed. Someone rolled out from under a broken table and lay still. Others huddled, nursing wounds or broken limbs. Women who had fought with savage joy on their faces now burst into tears. And this was a signal for those standing to begin looking after those who were not.

Icy with rage, Colin Renwick walked further into the room, polished boots crunching on glass, pistol at the ready. Some of the specials still vertical looked down strangely at their buttoned holsters. Renwick's gaze swept the bar: over the debris, over Ben O'Hara sitting dazed against the wall, his brother Mal standing unhurt further away, over the clock, 10.16, the television camera with its tiny red light, the piano and its empty stool. And from there to the open exit door where children wailed and peered into the gloom, trying to see their parents.

The Australian television crew left the village at well over the speed limit with a prickling sensation on the backs of their necks. And with good reason. Forty miles north, another car passed them at even higher speed. Five more miles and they were flagged down by two men waving petrol containers. There wasn't much choice; a car blocked the road. The two men multiplied by two, all in bush shirts and jeans, and the three television men were dragged out.

'Dog tucker,' one of the attackers said. Then they beat the television men unconscious.

But that turned out to be a tactical error. A search of the station wagon turned up not a single can of film, not a trace of celluloid; and the Australians were no longer in any condition to assist with enquiries. The attackers didn't dare use the radio: Charlie was listening these days and the problem was too specific for existing codes. In the end, deducing that the camera must store the pictures electronically, they destroyed its internal wiring and threw the remains into the swamp down the bank.

Then they accelerated away back south, leaving three badly shaken but very determined Australians to resume their journey to the nearest international airport with a cassette of moving pictures still taped into the back-seat springs.

Shortly after midnight, and at a much slower speed, a convoy of cars and Land-rovers droned north with wounded from the hotel. The convoy was later to be dubbed by *Truth* as the column of agony, and thereafter was referred to by Westlanders as the agony column. The levity became acceptable because, in spite of the high number of casualties, in spite of the biggest drain on bloodbanks in Westland's history, in the end there was not a single death from the riot in the Frazer Creek pub. The other statistics would plump about like dissatisfied pillows for a while, but the record would show that sixty-three were treated in Westland hospitals, fourteen being admitted. Six, with serious injuries, were flown by helicopter directly across the mountains to the base hospital at Christchurch. Four of those did a stretch in the intensive care unit, one of them literally. In all, there were seventy-two casualties, twenty-seven of them Black-and-Greys.

Dawn revealed the wreckage: furniture, glass, clothing and dark stains, out across the hotel car park and into the main street. The morning breeze blew bits of paper round and toppled a sheet of broken window hanging from its putty.

A patrol found a work of graffiti on the church fence: 'FOR ROSA', in luminous green letters three feet high. A work party was sent to paint it over and found photographers waiting for them. Threatened with arrest, the photographers moved down to the Post Office where the same sign had just appeared on the wall adjoining the rooster and hen cartoon.

The work party returned to the rugby field.

Other signs went up on the gates of several private homes. 'BED AND BREAKFAST, SPECIAL MEDIA RATES.'

The media contingent doubled in size by mid-afternoon and became a circus, trotting its hooves in and out of every driveway. Reporters from the Sunday papers took the bit between the teeth with eye-witness accounts of such lyrical and poetic form that much of the copy went straight to print, completely by-passing the fabrication departments. These heroic accounts were all different. But then coherent, verifiable copy was hard come by: the mayor was in hospital, plaster and shock, the police commander referred all enquiries to the Commissioner in Wellington, and the publican was a nutter who kept telling reporters that it was possible for pawns to win a game of chess.

Some were surprised by the lack of visible tension between the two sides. Some were lulled by it. One report quoted an unnamed authoritative source who hoped that the bloodletting had eased tensions and that a lasting peace might now ensue in this picturesque corner of New Zealand. A Wellington regional reporter stood in front of his camera in pouring rain and talked to it about the air having cleared.

By late afternoon the Driscoll house was under siege. Here, the media sensed, lay the real story if it could just be made to sit up and perform for them. Edith Driscoll went out the back door to the shed. The stampeding of feet, the fusillade of shutters and the shouts put her into such a state of trembling she had to be helped to her own back door.

It was Rosa they really wanted. And while they caught not a single glimpse of her, there was no shortage of material for the sound recordists. All afternoon, the white house on the hill was a music box. For four hours, a great variety of music poured from the attic window. At first it was unexpectedly light and carefree. There was the joyful finale of the Waldstein Sonata; a serene Schubert sonata, and Schumann's love-filled Kreisleriana, played with such authoritative delicacy that even the most hardened journalists on the road fell silent.

'She's retarded? That can't be for real. Who is she?' they asked the locals standing further back on the road. With some deliberation, a sawmiller from Whataroa removed a stalk of grass from his mouth and answered them.

'She's Rosa.'

This response was recorded as a drop of authentic colour from the sticks.

'Maybe she'll play it again,' someone said, referring to the catalyst that wrecked the pub.

'What was it?' three reporters said, pens poised.

No one knew. But everyone thought she would get round to it because the mood of her music was falling as the sun dipped to the horizon. She brought out Mozart's sleeping volcano from under sunny fields, the brooding anger of Beethoven's 'Appassionata', the undercurrents of hatred in Tchaikovsky.

Then it came again. 'Prelude 24'.

'That's it,' the locals said. 'That's the one.'

Not being able to see her, the reporters were perplexed as to how the music could possibly have set off a riot. But the only consistent element in all the eye-witness accounts was that it had.

'Chopin,' mused one reporter to a colleague when it had been recorded. 'There's an angle there. What do you bet she's angling for the Nazi thing? Resistance to occupation. Warsaw Concerto. Charge of the light cavalry against the German Panzers.'

'Where the hell have you been?'

'Pre-flight inspection,' Wilson said steadily.

'Look at this.' Renwick swished his boot in dandelions and rye and browntop up beyond his ankles. 'The best known patch of grass in the country and it looks like the back yard of a brothel. I told Searle to get it done.'

'He told me. The mower was missing a part – '

'He told *you*? Why?'

'Why not? I guess he didn't want to bother you.'

Further argument was cut off as a pair of Iroquois changed pitch for take-off. The wind blast freed a few late seedheads, whipping them past the two men, then the machines were slapping overhead. The moonshine flights went in twos now, risking the greater noise for the advantage of dropping men on both sides of the thorium stills. So far the results had been marginal to say the least. All they had to show for sixty paired flights was a single moonshiner, surprisingly, a young man, barely out of his teens. He'd known only the time and place of the next collection in his area – and that information was obsolete the moment word spread of his disappearance. The problem remained, if somewhat better defined: how to catch enough moonshiners, uninjured, to ensure eventually finding one with a collection too imminent for his or her disappearance to stop it taking place.

The Iroquois shrank away to the south-east, blending with the distant bush.

As the two men resumed their walk across the field, the duty inspector came running towards them.

'Sir. The film. Bates missed it all right. It's on ITV from Oz.'

The control centre was now in the room opposite Renwick's office. He and Wilson strode in to find the entire staff watching the television set. The screen showed the Driscoll woman walking through the sea of hotel patrons and the voiceover carried an Australian twang.

". . . for that reason widely regarded by Westlanders as a symbol of their opposition to oppression. But the music she played here in this remote country hotel appeared to be some kind of signal to the patrons . . ."

The picture stayed on the pianist and the crowd without a single edit until a few seconds after the battle began. Then as the chaos was reaching its full height, the picture disappeared, leaving the newsreader like a startled rabbit. He picked up a studio phone, listened, replaced it.

"We apologise for the technical problem there. And . . . moving on to the next story . . . The theft of the radioactive substance cobalt sixty from Christchurch Hospital's radiology unit is worrying . . ."

A computer operator turned the sound down.

'Too late,' Renwick said softly.

The duty inspector switched the set quickly through the two state-run channels. Nothing. He switched it off. With the exception of Wilson, the entire complement of the control room fixed their gazes on Renwick. Wilson wandered around without expression, looking at objects as if they held some intrinsic interest.

What did they want this time? Colin thought. A rabbit out of the hat? A short-order miracle?

One of the radio operators wasn't listening to his set. The telephone tap dancer had completely removed his headphones and Colin could hear the tinny rattle of someone's conversation from across the room.

'Pull yourselves together,' he snapped at them all. 'So Charlie cons a little sympathy out of the civvies. How much will that count when we've nailed the bastards and shown the public that they're greedy little graspers like anyone else? Zilch! The public is eternally malleable and infinitely ductile, and don't you forget it. Get on with it. Keep your eyes and ears open – sooner or later some little thing that you hear or see is going to tip the balance. Carry on. Nothing that matters has changed.'

'What about the woman?' the control senior asked.

When Colin completed his instructions, he left and stood alone for a moment in the corridor. A second fiasco. With only groundwork results to offset it. Within hours, he could be replaced. Who? Wilson probably. Or Mitchell or Pomare, both panting in the wings in Wellington. It would be so unfair. He had done the real work, the preparation. He needed more time. In another week, the track through the Waikukupa Forest would be ambush-proof, and every day narrowed down the probable location of Charlie's hide-out – somewhere within a twenty-mile radius of the glacier. Time. Time. Carry on. Play to the whistle.

His forehead felt clammy. He'd been off-colour for a couple of days. He looked down at his wrist-watch, deriving wry comfort from the sight. Even if nothing else was clear, today had at least made him understand the wording of the note that came with the watch.

Another ripple of nausea.

Faintly he heard Mrs Englefield's hideous singing voice coming from the back of the house. 'So before I break down the door, forgive me Delilah, I just can't take any more. My, my, my, Delilah . . .' He'd not seen the old bat for weeks, let alone got any tea out of her, in fact she hadn't uttered so much as a single word to him since the kitten died. She probably didn't know the meaning of the word 'accident'.

He trod down the corridor. He would ask her if she had anything for settling the stomach and maybe he could buttonhole her and explain. She had to see that he wasn't the kind of person who would run a poker through a kitten on purpose. She could not be allowed to go on thinking like that.

When he reached the kitchen, she was no longer there but her two grandchildren were: a three-year-old boy and a baby he had heard addressed as Boglet. While Colin stood in the doorway, the boy belted the baby over the head but then carelessly left his leg within reach. The baby picked it up like a ham and sank its tooth into it.

Colin squatted on his haunches as the boy wound up a force 10 howl.

'Here little chap, you – '

The howl erupted, making all further attempt at communication a waste of time. Nora Englefield appeared on the back doorstep, staring at the commander with an expression at once accusing and unreachably remote. To Colin's astonishment and alarm, a prickling sensation began behind his eyes. He stood and turned back down the corridor, only to find Wilson there. Watching him.

Wilson said something.

'What?'

Wilson's lips moved again. There was a peculiar look on his face.

'Wait, I can't hear a thing with this brat squalling.' Renwick closed the door on the scene and the two men retreated towards the front of the house. 'What is it?'

'I think Searle has just proved that he'll never be replaced by a computer. He's got the name of the leader.'

Sharlene Rassmussen grimaced with pain, sat up in bed and bent her left little toe upwards. Cramp. She coaxed the muscle into relaxing, then lay back, a little dazed.

'Hey boy, you kept the wraps on that one for a while.'

'Yeah.' Mal was a little sheepish, a little smug. He twisted round and nuzzled his face between her legs.

'You don't want to keep things all bottled up like that, Mal.'

'Whaddaya mean?' His voice was muffled.

'You know . . . bottled up. It's bad for the nerves.'

Mal's head surfaced, frowning. 'Lay off, will you?'

She pinched his bottom while he retrieved a pillow from the floor, but he ignored the assault and lay back with his hands behind his head, gazing at the ceiling. Sharlene pulled up the blanket, sighed and combed her fingers through the hair on his chest. Body carpet. She liked body carpet. Men without chest hair made her think of slugs. She sighed again, traced circles round a particularly long, thick hair, grasped it firmly and yanked it out.

'Ow! What'd you do that for?'

'To help you remember my name.'

'What?'

'Go on, what's my name?' A knowing laugh.

'What are you on about, Sharlene?'

'*I* only play the ukulele.'

'Oh.' Silence. 'Did I . . . ? Did I . . . ? When I was . . . ?'

A shrug.

'Jeez. Sorry Sharl. Hit the nail right on the thumb, didn't I?'

'It happens.' Sharlene shrugged again as one who is used to life's little backhanders. What really hurt was that the competition was mentally retarded. If Rosa *was* mentally retarded. There were a few people beginning to wonder about that. But hell, Mal was still leaving up north in the morning; they were both going to lose the bum anyway. Funny that she had thought she could get him to stay. Hilarious. A tear came to the corner of her eye and she got rid of it on the corner of the pillow without him seeing.

Mal looked so disgruntled that she patted him on the arm. Sharlene Rassmussen was incapable of staying aloof from the chinks men revealed in bed.

'You got a nice hammer, Mal. You going to take me home now?'

'Now?' Mal peered at the clock.

Sharlene sat up matter-of-factly and found her T-shirt, which said No Dice across the chest. If he didn't understand why she had to go home then there was no hope at all.

'Now, Mal.'

'A drink first? Coffee?'

'No thanks. Unless your dad's waiting outside the door with one.' But she said it disarmingly. The old man had been at her with drinks and cigarettes and all the high faluting manners right through dinner – if you could call it dinner – apologising for his cooking and saying how things had been a bit crook lately without a woman round the place. She was surprised the old man didn't buy her flowers and chocolates. And then scarpering off to his room; he might as well have played a trumpet and laid a red carpet down the hall to Mal's bed. Came on a bit strong did the old feller. But he knew he was saying it for her. Crafty old bugger. What the heck? Two votes out of three wasn't enough anyway.

Outside on the main road, an engine changed gear. The shabby curtain flared with light, flared again.

Mal sat up.

'Who the hell's calling at this hour?'

More than one vehicle. Land-rovers. They skidded to a halt in the shingle outside the front door at the same time as boots rattled on the back porch.

'Shit, what's happening?' Mal leapt out of bed, reaching for his cords. But he didn't get a chance to put them on. The back door burst open. Boots pounded in the tiny hall, another door crashed, then the bedroom door leapt at the adjoining wall, revealing two men in black and grey uniforms, one down on a knee. A pistol and a machine gun were trained on the bed.

'Freeze!'

Mal missed the aptness of this instruction. 'What the fuck do you think you're doing?'

'Shut up. Hands up.' The rude end of an HK winked for emphasis. Mal raised his hands slowly and felt Sharlene shrinking against him.

'You, get up . . . No, not you, gorgeous. You look fine just where you are.'

Mal snatched up his cords, was propelled along to the living room, thrust to the floor and handcuffed. With a querulous cry of protest, Oliver O'Hara was dropped in a heap beside him. The old man spat something and a boot was placed on his face. A warning.

The room came apart round them. The contents of the cupboards spewed onto the floor. Drawers flew out of their housing and overturned. Cutlery clashed and spread. But it was the bookcase that interested them most, Mal saw. Every book had its pages fanned before being discarded. The searchers grew increasingly frustrated. RT noises came constantly through the open front door. Once, Mal heard the name Rassmussen. While the search of paper continued, he heard the name mentioned again, inside the house. Something about a reputation. And shortly afterwards, the sounds in the bedroom began.

'Animals,' Mal snarled, rolling onto his side.

A boot sank into his stomach. Shortly he was half-dragged, half-carried out into the slivering night wind and thrown over the tailboard of a Land-rover.

The ride was a disorienting limbo. Sound, touch, smell, all seemed disconnected and fragmentary: boots, rifle oil, the drone of the engine, the glows of cigarettes which caused spectral visages to appear and vanish above him. His head bounced on the rough flooring when his neck muscles tired. He tried rolling onto his upper back, but a boot dissuaded him.

'Where are you taking me? This is a mistake.'

But they pretended he hadn't spoken.

'What's the charge? What am I charged with?'

He hadn't spoken.

Psychology, he told himself quickly. Must be part of the psychology, like the time chosen to arrest him. This thought gave him an anchor, which he used to slow up the discombobulation of his senses.

The vehicle stopped, went into reverse. Moving on grass, Mal decided. It stopped again. A bag came down over his head and he was pulled over the tailboard and down into a cold place. A dead space. Even through the sack he felt that he was surrounded by an impermeable membrane. He tried to touch something with his shoulders, anything, to enable the tactile sense to fill the holes in his mind. But they held him still and the sack filled with the smell of his own fear.

Still nothing was said. They made no human sound.

Something snicked behind him, his hands were freed, then held. He was laid out on a rough wooden surface with a trough in the centre that reminded him of the benches at his old school woodwork class. The sack was stifling him. He wanted to shout out that he couldn't breathe. His trousers were removed, his arms and legs spread-eagled and clamped. He felt a whimper trying to rise into his throat and quelled it. Dry, his throat was dry. But he thought they wanted him to ask for water and wouldn't give them the satisfaction. He only allowed his lips to move inside the sack. Water. Water.

The sack came off. Brilliant yellow light poured down, roasting in his eye sockets.

When he could see out of slits below his eyelids he tossed his head around trying to see who was near him, but there was no one. Pillars. Canvas. Odd instruments on a rope, some with metallic straps, some with probe-like extensions. He heard something beyond the canvas. A splash of water. Hands being washed: a sound so ordinary that it was comforting. He strained to hear every drop of water.

A doctor lifted the canvas aside and came to him. White coat and stethoscope. Distinguished-looking. And pleasantly surprised to see him.

'Hello Mal. I'm so glad you've come. A lot of people leave it too late and can't be treated. You know how it is. Now I just want you to relax and we'll have it out in no time.'

Fourteen

New life was injected into the nation's graffiti industry. 'FOR ROSA' appeared on government buildings and vehicles, on private fences and supermarket windows, on statues and bridges and roads and even on trees, where a knife was often used to encase the phrase in a heart. Eventually it became as endemic as the Kilroy slogan after World War II, and the variation 'ROSA WAS HERE' took off on a second wave of spray-paint.

No one organised it. No one needed to. As a symbol, Rosa tapped something universal; her passionate, wordless image was translatable to any cause espoused by those who feel themselves to be downtrodden by a more powerful, more articulate 'them'.

A score of organisations promptly adopted her as their mentor, including the self-styled Rastafarians of the east cape who conferred upon Rosa a *whanau* and honorary Maori blood. An article in the prestigious *NZ Farmer* declared that Rosa Driscoll symbolised the pain of the long-suffering farmers who had put the PM into power on a free enterprise platform, never realising just how free the enterprise would be, and how land would be concentrated in fewer and fewer hands.

'Rosa,' the article trumpeted, 'speaks from the heart about the use and abuse of absolute power. The Prime Minister would do well to take note that those who are stifled in one direction will find another way to express their anger. He appears not to have learned the one certain lesson of history – that those who abuse power, lose power. He appears not to realise that society is a single entity: when he stabs part of it, he will eventually feel the blade himself.' The following morning the editor surveyed the site of his head office, where someone had carelessly dropped a match, and went into retirement.

In Westland, the petty harassment of the specials, the army and the outsider regular police, trebled overnight.

No government property was safely left unguarded. Official vehicles were a favourite target, particularly for invasion by sugar cube or kerosene. Women prone to wearing boiler suits rediscovered the feminine knitting needle, the steel variety, which could be sharpened, hidden between seams in the suits and slipped into tyres.

Sabotage of food and drink developed its own band of adherents. Working on the premise 'You are what you eat', the chemicals of choice were those likely to cause spectacular plumbing difficulties. Take-away bar owners kept salt-shakers of ground-up laxative tablets for specials unwise enough to get hungry between official meals. At cafés, plates appeared at the same time as uniformed customers, containing a new 'downer' version of Alice B. Toklas cookies. It was even risky for the army and special camps to use county water supplies; so much so that a few camps switched to plumbing their own water from mountain streams, until someone released a powerful diuretic above the intake for the camp at Gunns.

Youths, calling themselves 'nark-sharks', used their parents' welding or soldering equipment to make spoilers: two six-inch nails, each sharpened at both ends, bent almost to right angles and welded together at the bend. When thrown, they always came to rest with one spike pointing upwards. For deployment of spoilers, nark-sharks worked in pairs: one would watch for a patrol vehicle from a hidden spot on a curve in the road and signal its approach to the accomplice beyond the curve, who would lay a line of spoilers and head for the hills. A risky occupation. They weren't as familiar with the bush as, say, the moonshiners. They couldn't move both fast and quietly. Many found enraged and very fit specials hot on their heels a couple of minutes after the deed. The youths were known to the specials as 'brats'; every patrol carried a rubber hose and specials began a chain of linking marks round their belts. Each mark corresponded to a 'brat spanking'.

No bruises. No witnesses.

A Karamea couple, both made redundant from government jobs on the same day, planned a variation on a trick from an American movie – a scheme that was to them so glorious in concept it rekindled their love life and they spent the first day of unemployment working through the Kama Sutra. Then they set off on a second honeymoon tour of Westland with half a dozen 30-yard wire strops and half a dozen sets of licence plates salvaged off the abandoned cars that lie about Westland.

It was superbly planned and executed and they almost got away with it. At each chosen town they waited, sometimes for more than a day, for an army or specials Land-rover to park just forward of a lamppost. Helped by spontaneous attacks of blindness in passing Westlanders, they then attached a wire strop, with a lot of slack, between the tow-bar and the lamppost. When the specials returned to their vehicle they would notice a car pulled to a stop just ahead, containing a couple having a row of theatrical proportions. Suddenly, the man would notice the specials, his eyes would widen, his lips mouth 'cops' and the car would take off on smoking tyres.

The couple left government-owned rear axles attached to lampposts in Karamea, Westport, Greymouth, Hokatika and Frazer Creek. But in Frazer Creek they made an error of judgment in attaching the strop to a lamppost with a rotten base. When the time came, the post snapped like a matchstick, blacked out the town, and the couple found an intact Land-rover bearing down on them with two smoking specials visible through the windscreen. The couple survived the on-the-spot enquiry, which established that they knew nothing about the Little Red Hen. They ended up kept in food, clothing and shelter by the government without having to work for it.

In the Frazer Creek district, normally law-abiding citizens laid quiet siege to the police headquarters. Obscure and ancient typewriters tapped out hate mail posted to individual officers as their names became known. One mail sack reached the Frazer Creek headquarters containing, along with the men's personal mail, a long-dead, dismembered and badly addressed possum.

Two specials, not caring for scented love letters, left cuts and bruises on the next nark-sharks to fall into their hands. Within half an hour of the parents' parading the boys' injuries for the media, the two specials were sacked and on their way over the mountains, leaving their colleagues close to mutiny. The potential insurrection was quelled by the section leaders, who were first quelled by Renwick.

'The next one to play into their hands, I'll hold for prosecution,' he hissed at them.

'How are we supposed to – '

'Call me sir, damn you.'

'Sir, the men can't be expected . . .'

'What are you? Undisciplined riff-raff or the elite of the special services? The men can and will control themselves with petty saboteurs! You can and will control yourselves with everyone who comes into your hands until Charlie oversteps the mark and firm action on our part gains public respect-ability. Clear?'

'Yes, sir.'

'If any of your men disobey me, I'll fire their officers as well. Clear?'

'Yes, sir.'

'Our time will come. Dismissed.'

The sacking of the two specials didn't satisfy the father of one of the beaten nark-sharks. His lust for vengeance led him to connect together four normally obscure and disparate facts. The guest-house was too heavily guarded to get near in person; the road leading to the rugby ground pointed exactly at the guest-house across the field; the top rail of the crash bars on his ute projected higher than the front of the bonnet; and in his back yard was a corrugated-iron water tank ten feet across – as old and leaky as a busload of bowlers returning from the Buller tournament.

Delivery time was set for four thirty a.m.

He placed a dozen rocks in the tank and at the bottom end of the road balanced the tank on its side, on the bonnet and crash bars of the ute. Then he leaned out the open door to see where he was going, eased out the clutch and pushed the accelerator to the floor.

The ute was doing seventy miles an hour by the time it passed through the barrier by the guard's booth. Halfway across the field he stabbed the brakes, parted company with the tank and wheeled away between the crooked rugby posts through the play area to the hill road, mowing down a clump of shrubs to get past the barrier posts.

The tank, with rocks driven to hysteria inside, roared at high speed past the grandstand towards the guest-house, this noise alone causing an instant laundry problem in some tents. But the din was multiplied by the guards themselves who, thinking that it was some kind of rolling bomb, pumped bullets into it in an effort to blow it up before it reached its target. In the guest-house, Mrs Englefield, certain that Armageddon had come, slipped out of bed onto her knees and prayed for forgiveness.

The tank ran out of momentum in the rose bushes a few yards from the house.

Nora Englefield, never having given or taken anything on tick, bowed her head again and asked if the forgiveness could be held over.

The next sign proclaiming the offence of shooting at this notice went up ten kilometres from Frazer Creek.

Jimmy Hay achieved what no adult could have done. His inconspicuous size allowed him to wander unobserved from the swings to the grandstand without being noticed. He climbed right up to the top where he heard a faint and vaguely disturbing sound. He looked around, puzzled, and finally located the source. The sound was coming from a quarter-inch gap between the top step and the back wall and when he put his ear to the gap the noise became very disturbing indeed. He scrambled down and ran bawling across the grass, with a guard giving him the hurry-up from behind.

'There's a tyrannosaurus rex eating people under the grandstand,' he told his mother.

'Yes, Jimmy,' his mother said.

'Here he is again.'

The spotter located the origin of the hum and raised his glasses. His colleague grunted disinterestedly, flipping the next page of a survivalist magazine. The Hughes 500D wafted down the upper reaches of the glacier.

'What's he up to?'

The other glanced up from a photograph of an American military chaplain blessing a nuclear missile. 'Tourist run.'

'Not unless he's taken to picking loopies out of the bush. And in this weather he'd set them down on top for a shufti . . . He's pulling up.'

The blue and white machine drifted sideways from the glacier half a mile up from the face and hovered above the trees a few hundred yards from the ice. There, for ten seconds, it was as still as a hoverfly, as if fixed to the earth by invisible struts.

The second spotter left his magazine and reached under the bivouac, bringing out a map. He spread it in front of him, rotating it to match with the lie of the valley below.

'Don't move even your little finger,' a voice said behind them.

They took the instruction literally.

'Now lads, very . . . Touch that and you're a porcupine . . . good boy. Slowly now, up on your knees, hands up, turn around.'

Half a dozen arrows were trained on their chests, bows drawn by figures in balaclavas, bowstrings creasing rough black wool. Both specials looked down at their pistols and back at the bows, faces agonised.

'Galling, ain't it? Enough to put you right off your breakfast. Drop your ranger belts. No? You got five seconds . . . four . . . three . . . two . . .'

Hands fumbled at broad buckles. The black ranger belts fell. One of them had two marks scratched into the leather.

'Been doin' a bit of brat-spanking, 'ave we?'

The two specials looked drawn about the gills.

'Let me put a splint in 'is leg,' pleaded one of the archers.

'Don't be stupid. You want to hand them everything on a plate?' A turn of the head. 'Did you bring the can?'

'Yeah.'

'Okay.' The first speaker turned back to the specials. 'You two can drop your shirts.'

Forty yards back into the trees, two more figures in balaclavas watched. Both were agitated.

'It's too much of a risk!'

'We've got to take it. Anyway, he only opened the map, he couldn't have had time to locate it. Even if he remembers the general area, it's just about impossible to find the entrance.'

'What about Ben?'

'So he hovers for a moment, so what?'

'But why take the chance?'

'What choice have we got? Kill them? Give Renwick what he's waiting for? He'll unleash the dogs and Joe Bloggs will say we had it coming.'

'Hold them till it's over.'

'Crap. What's the difference to Renwick? Like the Cackling One said, it's not over till we get them to do it to us *without* the excuse.'

The other made a sound halfway between a laugh and a groan. 'Brings a whole new meaning to turning the other cheek, doesn't it? Bring some friends please and kill a few of us as brutally as possible. In front of the assembled media if it's not too much trouble. R.S.V.P. Sometimes I wonder if our clucking leader has been into the magic mushrooms.'

'He's not been wrong yet.'

'Maybe you're right.' A sigh. 'I still think we should check with the committee about these two.'

'Sure, go ahead. I'll build the fire, you wave the blanket. Or do you want to use the specials' radio?'

On the edge of the ridge, the two specials lay on the ground, bare-chested. They were told to stand and did so. The glitter in their eyes became murderous as the captor with the spray-can exchanged it for a camera and took photographs. The two men were handcuffed with ratchet strips taken from their bivouac, then led away down the ridge. In the early evening, they were pushed out of the bush onto the main road just south of Frazer Creek.

They tried to make it to the rugby field without being noticed. But with their chests and backs spray-painted with iridescent roosters in advanced states of impotence that proved difficult.

In the bush bordering Moonlight Beach, the regular army patrol came across a coil of wire. No ordinary wire, this was nearly an inch in diameter, thick enough to haul a tree. One of the Waikukupa track logging crews was close by, it was probably theirs. The patrol called beach control to call the logging crew.

'Yeah. That'll be ours,' the reply came. 'Leave it there, will you? No one's going to pinch it.'

The patrol continued through the trees near the beach.

Fifteen

Rosa knew it was coming the instant it left the attic and started down the stairs.

She was in the lounge, working on her rug. She hooked one row at a time, left to right and back again, which entailed constant changes of colour and made the picture fill from the bottom like rainbow water in a pot. She was up past the girl's knees and the belly of the fawn. Through and up, twirl and slide; through and up, twirl and slide; through and up . . . a rhythm now so familiar that her hands and fingers often took over the task. Unasked. No matter how hard she concentrated, she couldn't fill her head with just hook and wool and rug all the time.

That was the danger. Nasty, nasty things were out there somewhere, hunting for her. At night they waited for her to come out from under the blanket so they could see her and pounce on her. But she had made a hole in the blanket and breathed through it all night, sometimes afraid in her half-sleep that she had made the hole too big and that they would get her when she breathed in. During the day, they waited for breaches in her concentration.

On the stairs, jabbering.

She had been seen.

The rug hook fell as she snatched up Miska, the chair crashed and she was swinging the back door before her mother found voice.

'Rosa? Rosa? What are you doing? Are you making a cup of tea?'

But Rosa was running her bike down the path and through the gate, scooting it frantically downhill before she mounted. She didn't see the photographers and heard nothing of the fury of the camera shutters and the calling out.

Halfway down the hill, the back of her head felt the thing come out the door to see where she was going. It started after her.

'Tell it to go away,' she screamed at Miska in the basket.

'It won't,' Miska called.

Rosa whimpered, releasing the brakes and making the wind rush in her ears. That helped. But she hit loose shingle as the road levelled out and turned past the playground. She noticed as she fell that a swing was going backwards and forwards with no one on it and the roundabout was twirling with no one there. Then she was up and riding again, feeling no pain, only the creep of blood down one knee. The jabbering grew louder, shrilling higher.

'It's coming!' Miska cried out.

Rosa's head whirled round. And there it was, a colourless blob of distorted air gliding after her.

She bent over the handlebars, grunting with effort, thrusting with her knees until the wind buffeted in her ears again beating back the thing behind her. She passed the Post Office at full speed, passed the faces that turned and stared on the steps of the store, passed the open road sign to the north. The first fat drops of rain splattered on her face and the back of her hands. Lantern-jawed clouds rushed in from the north and the wind they brought added to Rosa's protective mantle of sound.

The rain became a welcome downpour, slashing through the trees, flashing on the road that went through the bush, over bridges, past a ditch where frogs gaped on the bank, by paddocks with bright golden gorse where cattle watched her with astonished eyes as she pedalled by. Her lungs were raw, her legs were powered by rubber bands that wanted to snap.

Still it hung behind her shoulder, shrilling higher and higher through the rain and wind.

Her speed dropped back. She felt every flop and lollop of the wind as it became too tired to help her, every stone under the tyres conspiring to hold her back. Miska began to cry, and the sound rubbed on the tyres, wasting precious momentum.

A rise slowed her further. At the very top, next to a bank of exposed clay, there was suddenly no speed at all. Rasping for breath, she dismounted. The bike crashed onto its side, back wheel turning. She sank down in the clay, curled up, closed her eyes and began to spin round and round.

The jabbering became a voice.

'All I want,' the voice said, 'is for you to be nice to me. Your mother can't be nice to me any more so if you don't help me I'll have to find another woman. But I'm an honourable man, and . . . You don't know what that means yet, do you Princess? What it means is I can only be with one woman at a time so I would have to leave your mother. That would break up the family and it would all be your fault.'

'I don't want to,' she whined. He smelt hot and sweaty which put squirmy feelings in her and made it hard for her to breathe. The sheet was too heavy, crushing down so that she couldn't move. The girl with the cherries was smiling out of the painting on the wall. One night he had told her to try to smile like that; she had tried because he said it would make him feel good, but she hadn't done it right and he'd got mad instead.

Somewhere a piano was playing.

If she kept her eyes shut really tight, she wouldn't see his face, or his hand. But not too tight; it mustn't be as tight as all her other muscles or it would make cracks and she would see through them.

'Your friends think you're ugly. That's why they don't like you. Except me, sweetie-hon. Nobody loves you as much as me. We've got something special, haven't we? It's our secret and we won't tell anyone because no one would understand. Isn't it just the nicest thing? Be nice. Nice.'

She could hear the fear in his voice. When he was scared, he threatened her with the cupboard. Christmas at Gran's. Christmas at Gran's.

'If you tell anyone, you'll be a nasty, selfish little girl that no one would ever love any more. You'd be a bad girl, and you know what happens to bad girls, don't you? Bad girls go in the cupboard.'

Threepences and sixpences in the pudding! Special ones. Grandma says only special ones can go in the pudding. The ordinary ones are poison. She swaps them.

'If you tell anyone, they wouldn't believe you anyway. But they might, yes, they might believe you and then your mother would leave and that would leave just you and me. There . . . there . . . isn't that nice?'

If it's me that finds the half-crown, everyone will clap and laugh and Grandma will let me serve up the ice-cream and sprinkle the hundreds and thousands and give me an extra helping. But . . . But . . . But Daddy will say he's proud of his little girl. He'll say I deserve a big hug. He'll give me a cuddle . . .

'Now what are you doing that for? Stop it. I thought you were a nice girl . . . Shhh . . . Shhh . . . that's better. Mustn't wake the bed bugs, eh? That's my girl, my little Princess. I know, you be the Princess from Snow White, lying on the deathbed after you've had the poisoned apple. Okay, now I'm the handsome Prince riding through the forest and I see you lying there in the glade . . .'

And mercifully she is no longer in the bed. She's standing by a woman who's playing the piano. And she's waiting for the nod. Waiting for the nod. She always has to turn the page of music when the woman nods. The woman's dark skin is pallored by her sickness, her voice is husky, bitter like lemon rind. She speaks while she plays the dabbledy music.

'You horny little monster. You Satan's morsel. I saw the way you were looking at that magazine. No wonder you get him upset.'

She nods. Turn the page.

'Mummy, you're like a talking book because you tell me when to turn the page. Isn't that funny?' She bursts into anxious laughter. The piano stops abruptly.

'Stop that! Oh, it's easy for you to laugh, isn't it, you little vixen? Think you've got him round your little finger, don't you? Got it all over me, haven't you? Well don't laugh on my time, baby face.'

The white fingers run on the keys. Dabbledy dabbledy dabbledy dabble . . .

Nod. Turn the page.

Mercifully, her mother and the piano are gone.

Turn, turn over and curl round the hand, trap it by kissing it. Yes, the Princess kisses the hand of Prince. He'll like that. If I do that maybe he'll forget about . . .

'Now the frog.'

'I don't want to.'

'But the Princess *always* has to kiss the frog or it won't turn into a prince.'

'I don't want to.'

'Now what are you doing? Stop that crying. Only *bad* girls cry. If you don't stop, it'll have to be the cupboard. *Bad* girls play hide-and-seek in the cupboard.'

No, no.

'And this time I'll shut the door.'

No, no, no, no, don't shut the door shut the door shut door shut the shut the shut door no no . . .

'Are you all right? Christ, what a racket. She's nuts! Hey, what's the matter with you? Quieten down, will you, we haven't laid a finger on you. We're not going to hurt you.'

Rosa opened her eyes.

'Rosa Driscoll?'

Uniformed men. Two of them crouching beside her. Another two further back by a Land-rover.

'Must be her. There's the doll. Hell, she's a mess.' The two helped her to her feet, gently, a little afraid of her, even reassuring her and fetching her doll the moment she sought it. Very slowly her stunned expression gave way to puzzlement.

'I had a bad dream.'

'That right? Well you can tell the commander all about it. He wants a word with you.'

The rain thundered on the guest-house roof, making conversation difficult even in Colin Renwick's office on the ground floor. There was little wind outside; the water fell in vertical relentless sheets, flattening the long grass in the rugby field. Even the blades of the Iroquois seemed to droop for no other reason than the rain. Almost nothing could be seen of the town and nothing at all of the surrounding hills. There was no question of aerial searches in these conditions.

The din eased. The psychologist's hands were raised in horror.

'An hour? You brought me all this way and you want me to do it in an hour?'

'Things have changed.' Renwick looked at his watch. 'Right now the press are baying at the gate. A score of news agencies is hounding the Commissioner's office wanting to know why I'm holding a mentally retarded woman in custody.' There had also been hot messages between the Commissioner's office and the Wellington office of the SIS.

'But it can't be done!'

'She's faking and I – '

'If you're so sure, why do you need me?'

'As I was saying . . . She's faking it and I want proof.'

The psychologist laughed, an edgy nervous laugh that quivered in his heavy jowls. His forehead was unusually high and the skin taut and shining like a peeled egg. 'Absurd. Even under ideal conditions, all you get from a mind jockey is a subjective judgment. And you want testing and evaluation done in less than an hour? With a presumably uncooperative subject? That eliminates the Peabody test, the Stanford Binet, the – '

'It doesn't have to stand up in court. Just give me the best you can, I have to know. I have to be sure in my own mind.'

'Why me? From what I hear you have your own specialists for extracting information – and with a somewhat more flexible code of ethics.'

'Have a care, Hillock,' Renwick hissed.

'Look, why don't we just forget I came. I'll forget the time wasted and I'll still owe you, right? How's that?'

'That's enough!' Colin rose. 'Enough of this nonsense. We're running out of time. I'm calling in your account *now*. One way or the other.'

'Fat lot of choice I've got. This is unofficial, right?'

'Of course.'

'Well, I suppose there are one or two ways . . . I could try making her angry.'

'How? I don't want her touched.'

'Please! My methods are a little different from yours, Chief Superintendent! I meant verbal shock techniques. Make her angry. "Have you been raped yet?" That sort of thing. The responses can reveal a lot.'

'All right, all right. Good. All I need is for you to spot one flaw. Come with me.'

He took Hillock out of the office and upstairs where the din of the rain was twice as bad. In the upper corridor was an open door, guarded by a uniformed special lounging in a kitchen chair. It seemed to Renwick that the special rose from the chair with slowness bordering on insolence, but he let it go, preferring to watch the psychologist's first reaction to the sight of Rosa Driscoll.

'Did you do that to her?' the psychologist shouted above the rain.

'She hasn't been touched. She was riding in the rain, fell in some mud. What do you think we are, Hillock?'

The former guest-room had been stripped of all but a plum-red Chesterfield chair and a wash basin. Bare, the room was clinically bright: white ceiling and bare cream walls and ancient linoleum, faded except for a rectangle where a mat had once kept the chill from bare feet. Rosa was huddled in the corner, rocking her doll. One side of her clothes, face and hair was caked in dried mud. Hearing the voices, she glanced up, saw the pyschologist, but kept on rocking. There were crayon drawings round her feet, including one of a mouth, defined by two curved lines for the lips with two sets of jagged lines for the teeth. The teeth were heavily blacked in. She was humming, low-toned, in her throat.

'Why's the door open?'

'She asked us to leave it open.'

'She asked . . . ? And you . . .'

'It seemed a reasonable request.' Drily.

Hillock looked back in at Rosa. 'If it's an act, it's a good one.'

'Of course it is. They've had a long time to get it right. There's some meticulous long-term planning by a lot of people behind this. A little too convenient, don't you think, that her child welfare records can't be found? Anyway, she's been a bit too clever for her own good.'

'How's that?'

'Never mind. You don't need to know.'

Hillock shrugged. 'I'll need paper, more crayons and another chair.'

'You'll have them.' Renwick nodded to the guard.

As he watched the man saunter downstairs, the rain eased. The thunder on the roof dropped back to a mutter.

Mal O'Hara had a theory about pain. It had been with him ever since school when the biology teacher said that if you snipped here . . . and here . . . in the brain, you could enjoy a life, albeit a short one, without pain. So, while copying a cross-section of the brain down from the blackboard, Mal had formed his theory: control the mind and you control pain. Simple. As the biology teacher had also said: all great inventions are simple.

This first draft of his theory had lasted only until the next day when the biology teacher found him blowing up a condom on a gas tap. The teacher had stuffed his unkempt head in an unkempt locker and demonstrated the fibrous nature of cane by splintering one on his backside. On the first stroke, the pain declared that it wasn't going to be dismissed as imaginary without a fight, whereupon the pain and the theory flopped about in the darkness and pungency of locker 27 like two crows fighting over a stale sandwich.

The pain won.

The second draft occurred between the fifth and sixth strokes, a revelation that so overwhelmed him he hardly felt the sixth stroke and promptly took this to be proof of his discovery. If pain was real, then it could be treated as a solid object and put somewhere out of the way; it could, for instance, be wrapped up in brown paper and string and sent to wriggle uselessly in Peter Buchanan's locker on the bottom row. So, with the help of the constant supply of pain normal to a schoolboy, he had refined the technique over the years and considered himself to have graduated when he turned down a dentist's offer of anaesthetic – though his blind fear of needles may have played a part in that decision.

In the lull, in the yellow light and the green canvas shroud, he tried to remember his theory about pain. He succeeded in gathering in a few of its shreds, but then couldn't remember the shape of it and how the shreds should be rejoined. After a while the shreds seemed just to be bits of brown paper and string, drifting about, blown apart by the first white-hot bolts.

How long had he been here? Hours? Days?

There was a faint throbbing. He didn't know if it was a helicopter or something inside his head. Sweat residues stung the corners of his eyes. His vision was blurred. He could no longer focus on the weave of the canvas. The two helpers, Brown and Jones, were leaning on the canvas, on something hard behind it. They watched him without curiosity, waiting for Doctor Smith to return.

Cold. Cold from the sweat. At least put a towel over me.

'Cold,' he croaked.

Brown and Jones didn't move or speak.

Technique, part of the technique.

He knew what Smith's technique was now. He had figured out why it worked, why it had blown away his childhood defences like chaff on the wind. His only human communication was with Smith. Doctor Smith was the only source of comfort in a black pit in which Doctor Smith was the only source of pain. The doctor murmured to him, soothing his agony with his voice, smoothing his brow with one hand while administering hideous pain with the other. The giving of pain and the giving of healing intertwined. The double helix of snakes strangling the staff. It was the deliberate crossing of fundamental drives, the excruciation of the mind.

His mind was the dungeon, an oubliette into which the torturer descended by first excoriating the upper layers.

Anxiety rose. Where was Doctor Smith?

'When's he coming back?'

Brown and Jones said nothing.

With a scrape of canvas and a rustle of his white coat, Doctor Smith returned, looking apologetically down at Mal. With his right hand he stroked Mal's hair back and took Mal's limp hand and squeezed it reassuringly.

'I'm sorry to keep you waiting Mal.'

Mal O'Hara gagged without pulling away. There was nothing left in his stomach already. He stared directly and unblinking into the glaring light and tried again to remember his theory about pain.

'That's it from the school, sir. Tucker and Tree are still going through the house.'

'What grade is she in?' Colin Renwick looked down at the drawings and books.

'There's only one class. Kids are primer one up to beginning high school. And that's all I found out; the teacher clammed up tighter than a weasel's arse and the sprogs looked at me like I'm Dracula's brother only uglier. Poisonous little vipers wouldn't give me the time of day.'

'All right, all right, you're not the only one getting it. If you want to be the friendly cop on the corner, you're in the wrong outfit. This is all there is?'

'Yes, sir.'

'Less than other kids had?'

'Yes, sir, some of the kids' desks were chock-a-block. You want me to bring that teacher bitch in?'

'No. It's too late for anything but the big fish now and she's almost certainly a patsy. Driscoll wouldn't go to this trouble for someone in the know.'

He sifted through the pictures first.

Typical, he thought, of the sort of stereotyped child's painting an adult would do: transparent houses with stick figure occupants. Mother: a single line for the waist, a triangle for the skirt, disproportionately long thin fingers and a set of teeth that would have graced a shark. Hah! Now if that had been his former wife it would have been an accurate portrayal. Father: huge hands, head touching the ceiling, indicating dominance no doubt . . . Yes, yes, clever, very clever indeed. Perhaps Hillock should see this . . . Child: no facial features at all; just a blob with a couple of circles for ears and mess of brown for the hair.

The most recent painting still smelled of watercolour on newsprint. It was a little different. The figures were slightly more sophisticated: a girl with a crown like a row of fangs on her head, a robed male shape standing opposite holding a stick, a wand, in an oversized hand. Rosa Driscoll had a thing about hands, or was that part of the act as well? And this painting had a title: 'The Wicked Sorcerer.' The Wicked Sorcerer . . . wasn't there some kids' story about a sorcerer who turned a princess into stone? He couldn't remember. He'd lost touch with that sort of thing. Rosa Driscoll, on the other hand, would have been well schooled, so to speak.

Another recent painting. Typical of the others except that the male figure was drawn with explicit genitalia.

'That was up on the wall, sir.'

Colin sniffed. 'Anything goes in a classroom these days.'

'She's not getting enough of it, if you ask me, sir.'

'I didn't ask you,' Renwick flared. 'That'll be all.'

As the door closed, he flipped through the reading books.

Country library service: *The Ant That Sneezed*. A chain reaction: the ant sneezed, which made the mouse come out of the house, which made the cat very fat, which made the toad cross the road, which made the car swerve on the tar . . . and so on, leading to shipwrecks at sea and chaos in the land.

'Well, well,' Colin said softly. She must have kept it in her desk as a joke. Confident, very confident.

The phone burred.

'Renwick here. Yes, put him through . . .' He flicked through Rosa's writing exercise book while he spoke. 'Yes. I suppose you know the Commissioner has referred all questions on the Driscoll woman back here. I thought you'd sorted the bastard . . . It's the worst possible thing. Things are too damn delicate . . . Time? We're *that* close to cracking it down here and you tell me it'll take time . . . ? I don't care . . . Someone up there has got to front up!'

The conversation ended quickly and he slammed the phone into its cradle.

He put a hand over his stomach. More nausea. If it was still with him tomorrow, he would see the army MO.

The first pages of the exercise book were filled with three- or four-sentence stories: 'After lunsh we went to the swiming hole. Kevin Doig dropped his watch in the water. It woodint go any more. It was fun.' Many such stories were followed by a gold star. Undoubtedly well deserved, Colin thought. One of the recent stories was considerably longer and copied from a reading book: 'The Great Big Enormous Turnip. Once upon a time an old man planted a little turnip and said "Grow, grow, little turnip, grow sweet. Grow, grow, little turnip, grow strong." And the turnip grew up sweet and strong and big and enormous. Then, one day, the old man came to pull it out . . .' The transcription continued through to the end in which the turnip came out of the ground only when the old man, the old woman, the granddaughter, the dog, cat and mouse came together in a communal effort.

Tolstoy, Renwick mulled. Alexei Tolstoy. Communal. Little Red Hen. Of course. Well, well, he said to himself again. She was quite a little jokester.

There was a knock on the door.

'Come.'

The psychologist entered, rubbing his hands together. 'Fascinating woman. Fascinating.'

'You've got it? Already?'

'No, not yet. I thought you'd like a progress report while I shake down a problem.'

'Hurry it up then.' Swiftly, irritably, Renwick brought him a chair and he sat on its outer edge.

'She presents as someone with not only mental retardation, but also severe emotional disturbance. Now here are the alternatives as I see them.' Hillock counted them off on his fingers. 'This could, as you say, be a completely conscious stance by a woman of adult intelligence – in fact she could be a very bright cookie indeed. In that respect of course, it could also be partly genuine in that deliberate conscious reversion to childhood, adopted for too long, could become part of her emotional framework . . .'

'Yes, yes, get on with it.'

'Three. Normal intelligence but with a genuine traumatic experience resulting in reversion from nubile adolescence to a safer infantile stage. In such cases you often get nymphet signals indicating a desperate need for nurture.'

'Out of the question. No one could have anticipated the thorium price hike more than a decade ago.'

'It could be the result of cerebral damage – selective damage to tissue. Her symptoms are also consistent with ingestion of some toxic substances. Then there's Huntington's chorea. And it's not beyond the bounds of possibility that she's quite genuine; I don't like the term '*idiot savant*' but there are well-documented cases of a very high, very specific functional intelligence within a low formal intelligence framework – '

'Wait.'

'Yes?'

'I sent you in there to choose between two possibilities. You come back with seven?'

'Please let me finish. If you want an opinion already, I would be tempted to consider the possibility of the *idiot savant* syndrome in an intelligent person *caused* by massive trauma . . .' He tickled himself thoughtfully under the chin. 'Of course there is a school of thought that holds the feats of an *idiot savant* to be mechanical, the product of a remarkable rote memory. But that model has been discredited because many *idiots savants* display sensitivity to the rules governing composition, implicit knowledge of structural rules in the generative sense – '

'Stop.' The commander came round the side of the table. He could see that the psychologist was laughing on the other side of his po-face. 'I don't think you quite understand me, Hillock. This is not a consultation by the couch. Either you use your skills my way or I'll close your account my way. Get back in there and find me evidence that she's faking or you can kiss goodbye to your career.'

'You'd do that?'

Renwick gave him a humourless smile.

'Oversimplification,' Hillock mumbled, cowed. 'And there's still the problem . . .'

'What problem!'

'She's presenting a stimulus response pattern I've never met before. I can't even tell if the stimulus is internal or external.'

'Talk English,' Renwick said dangerously.

'In the middle of a sentence – even in the middle of a word – she flinches and adopts an appeasement posture as if someone's going to hit her. All the time she seems to be listening to something, digging her fingernails into her palms. Each time she looks out the window.'

'Outside? Where outside?'

'That way. Towards the grandstand.'

There was a pause.

'Did she mention the grandstand?'

'No. Should she?'

'No.' Renwick stood. He put his hands in his pockets and walked around the room, looking at incidental objects: the scrolls on the player piano, the horizontal hour-glass with ash in both ends, the map on the wall which now showed a second and smaller red circle, also centred on Frazer Creek and the glacier. Knowing that the psychologist was observing his switch in mood, he went to the window and looked out across the field of tents. Another two Iroquois were winding up. The lower slopes were clear and the upper slopes were coming into view.

'Don't you think, Mr Hillock, that life is like being chained to a railway jigger? No matter how much you try, you can't change its direction, you can't get off, and you can't stop pumping the handle.'

'Why does it seem that way to you?'

Renwick spun and spat. 'Don't you *dare* try your couch tricks on me!'

'I . . . I'll go back and talk with Rosa again. Given the limited time, I think direct confrontation is the only realistic approach now.' But the police commander was staring at him.

'No.'

'No?'

'You've done enough. You can go.'

'Just like that?'

'You're right. It's a complex matter. One mustn't oversimplify.'

'But I should at least say goodbye to Rosa.'

'Tyson!' Footsteps in the hall. The front steps guard appeared in the door of the office. 'Constable Tyson here will see you to the gate, Mr Hillock. You won't say anything to the newshounds. Not even who you are. Thank you. I'm grateful. Goodbye.'

When the bemused psychologist had gone, Colin took the written note that had accompanied the watch and placed it next to Rosa's exercise book. At first glance, the flowing longhand of one seemed unrelated to the printing of the other. Not that he would have expected her to make it that easy anyway. It would take a handwriting expert.

The whining of the Iroquois outside became an authoritative thump and the first machine rose from the frantic grass. Ten to five. The decision could not be delayed much longer.

He called operations.

'Ask Searle to put the patient on hold in exactly three minutes . . . you heard me. Three minutes from now.'

He went out the door, locking it behind him. He'd had to get a new lock fitted, because the original key to the lounge had long since disappeared and no new key could be cut to fit. He'd not issued Wilson with a key. Wilson had his own office and one did not run an efficient security system by handing out duplicate keys.

In the upstairs corridor, Colin dismissed the guard.

Rosa was curled up in the same corner, still drawing on the floor. She glanced at him as he entered, then went back to her drawing. He sat quietly in the plum-red Chesterfield, aware that he was breathing faster than usual, watching her without speaking. She hadn't attempted to clean herself up, as an adult would do. Around her feet was a cluster of stick figures and houses similar to those he had just seen. More mouths with bared teeth. A superb performance, he thought. But every now and then she flinched as if to a stroke of pain and her eyes flicked through the window, an embellishment that surprised him. If they had found out about the grandstand, then this was not the time he would have chosen to reveal it. Still, it meshed nicely with the performance. A remarkable woman.

Three minutes.

There was no change in her demeanour, but the flinching stopped. Colin's eyes narrowed. A fluke.

'Let's stop playing games,' he said.

She glanced up, crayon in one hand, the doll in the other.

'You can drop the act now, Rosa. If that's really your name.'

Nothing discernible happened in her eyes. But Colin nodded to himself. Again, he could hardly expect it to be so easy. He smiled, sitting back and propping his chin in one hand. 'You're a first-rate actress, but I'm afraid the show is over. You've been rumbled. Exposed.'

'I have to go home now.' Suddenly, clutching the doll.

He grinned admiringly. The childish vowels and consonants were flawless. She probably didn't even think about them any more.

'But there's no point now. We know how you were recruited, who recruited you, why they saw you as an untouchable symbol. Power *and* omnipotence. Not granted to many, is it? Oh yes, Mal told us everything.'

'Mal has to go home too.'

Colin sighed. He would have preferred holding his reserve ace until he'd established the upper hand anyway. He noticed how thick the dust was on the floor and the window sill. As the specials took over each room, Englefield would abandon it. The thicker the dust, the longer the Black-and-Greys had been there: an hour-glass that couldn't be turned horizontal.

He leaned forward intently.

'The thing is, Rosa. I know about the watch.' He tapped it, smiling gently, watching her, aching to catch that first moment of relaxation, the opening of the gates.

She frowned at the watch.

'We are absolutely alone,' he added even more softly. 'No one else is listening. Nothing is being recorded. Just you and me. You can say what's on your mind and no harm will come to you.' Try as he might he could not shake the feeling that the situation was familiar. He knew the current theory, that déjà vu was no more than a short circuit of memory from the present event – a fraction of a second earlier. His mind was playing tricks on him, his brain felt fuzzy round the edges.

'Is Mal going home now?'

'You don't understand. Rosa, Rosa, I can get you out of this. It's become bigger than you, but if you trust me, I can help you side-step it. You can come out without a blemish and when it's all over, we can be together.'

'Are they taking him to hostible?'

'What are you doing? Why are you going on like this? Can't you see what I'm offering you? This is your only chance. It's *our* only chance!'

'I want to go home now.' Shrinking back from him into the corner.

'Stop. Stop.' Desperately searching her eyes. 'Rosa, you must trust me. It's not the way your note said, there *is* hope for more between us. Look, give me just the smallest sign, a nod . . . a sign . . . anything. It means . . . so much . . . Then you can let me take it from there.'

For just a moment, a look of faint puzzlement crept forward into her eyes. Then it dissipated from within. She shook her head abruptly. Her eyelids clamped down.

'You understood,' he breathed. 'Did you? Is this your way of telling me? Please, look at me, I need more.'

Her eyes remained shut tight and she shrank further away, curling round her doll. He leapt out of the chair, ripped the doll out of her arms and threw it behind him.

'In heaven's name, woman!'

She let out a piercing yell, launched herself up and tried to scramble round him. He blocked her.

'Stop that! There's no need . . .'

She kept screaming, flailing, trying to see the doll round him, as if afraid that it would not be there at the next glimpse. Then Wilson was at the door, panting.

'What in God's name are you doing? Not her. Anyone but her. They'll be listening to that at the gate.'

Dazed, Renwick let the distraught woman past. She snatched up her doll and backed weeping into the opposite corner.

'Goddamn woman took me by surprise. I didn't touch her.' He glared at her and Wilson looked from one to the other.

'Get anything out of her?'

'No.'

'They're gathering at the gate. Yokels are coming in from all over.'

'What about the press?' Renwick was getting his wits back.

'They've got her mother out there. Come evening, she'll be yapping in everyone's front living room. And the Chief called . . .' An undertone of relish crept into Wilson's voice. '. . . He says the Commissioner can't be contacted and that "No Comment" isn't good enough for this. Until further notice you've got to handle the press yourself.'

'Damn you to hell and back, Wilson.'

'I'm just passing on a message. You've got to let her go.'

'Are you telling me?' Renwick blazed. 'Or asking me.'

After a long pause, Wilson said, flint-eyed, 'I'm asking you.'

'You haven't finished, Wilson.'

Another pause. 'I'm asking you, sir.'

'All right, Wilson, I like the suggestion. Let her go. No. Give her an escort and go with it yourself. But get her cleaned up first, give her anything she wants. Then the kid gloves right to the door, apologise to her mother for inconvenience, routine enquiries. The works. Clear?'

'Yes.'

'Take a patrol with you and post two men at each door to keep the media out. Tell the media protective custody – threats against her life by locals opposed to the Red Hen movement.

You know what's needed. But you are not authorised to say anything else to the media. Clear?'

'Yes.'

'How clear?'

'Very clear, sir.'

'Good, Wilson, good.'

And when he returned to his office, he called operations again to tell Searle to resume treatment of the patient.

On the Waikukupa track, the logging crew closest to the beach knocked off for lunch. Within a couple of minutes the hum of machinery elsewhere in the forest was stilled also.

Following the latest security measures, the crew brought their flat-backed Bedford, their log skidder, their hauler and all other major equipment in around them before lighting up the tea cylinder. The foreman made the radio check with the other crews. He cast an eye up and down the track, now vastly widened by a swathe of tree stumps. A second man stood with him, holding a set of climbing spikes.

No one in sight. The two nodded to each other, and the one with the spikes slipped away into the forest.

Joe Karaitiana from Whataroa halted a few hundred yards downhill, at the foot of a massive kahikatea with a top that talked to the sea breeze at 180 feet. As he watched the trunk's arrow-straight thrust at the sky, three figures came out of the undergrowth to join him. The group spent some time talking, pointing downhill and up to a particular branch in the tree, and squatting on the bush floor to draw diagrams in the earth. But they also listened, because the beach patrols were close. Once, when they heard the twittering flight-call of a redpoll, they faded into the bushes like mice into grass.

When they emerged, Joe shrugged into the straps of a small back-pack and donned his instep and hand spikes. He addressed the kahikatea with his eyes and as he did so, his lips moved silently. For such a tree one first makes peace with its spirit. Then he sank the first two spikes, hand and foot into the patchwork bark, and began to climb.

Sixteen

A unified anti-government strategy has never been the strong point of Westland, the province where two schoolboys once put each other in hospital fighting about the best way to put the teacher's strap through a mincer. Not everyone understood the tactical necessity of keeping the specials alive and kicking. And one unemployed post office electrician came within a whisker of tipping the balanced scales.

Ivan Whiteman of Karangarua, known for his volcanic disposition and boils, made a small but fiendish petrol bomb. Later, when it had been reconstructed from the debris, Renwick described it to an impromptu press conference as the most inhumane, ghastly device it had ever been his misfortune to encounter.

It was a previously unknown mechanism, possibly the simplest electrically triggered bomb yet invented. As well as the petrol, it had just four components: a plastic bottle with a full width top and cap, a piece of whitebait netting, a ball-bearing, and a big capacitor, capable of standing freely on one end with both terminals at the other. The netting was made into a small cage and funnel, attached to one terminal, with the funnel pointing to the other terminal. The cage held the ball-bearing until such time as a bump, or acceleration, moved it into the funnel, where it would roll down to the other terminal completing the circuit with a high-voltage spark. This capacitor-funnel-ball-bearing arrangement was lowered into the plastic bottle, which was half-filled with petrol. With the lid of the plastic container screwed on, it bulged with the pressure of air and vaporising petrol.

He placed this device in the back of a specials' Land-rover parked in Frazer Creek and went on his way.

When the specials returned, they took off without first checking in the back. But their hurry was also what saved them.

The acceleration tipped the bomb out the back as the ball-bearing completed the circuit. Even so it made an inferno of the rear of the Land-rover and the two men dived out of the cab with clothes smoking. But in the end, the only injuries they could show Renwick and the cameras were singed hair and a couple of grazes.

And later, to Renwick's fury, the Commissioner's office slipped the media a DSIR report that 'dangerous' was the wrong way to describe the new petrol bomb. 'Suicidal' was much more accurate. No one in his right mind would consider trying to put one together.

Reports quickly followed that left no doubts about Whiteman's state of mind. He had a history of manic depression and paranoia. He was a loner – and had been since he told a neighbour, in front of his wife, that he hated to look at the mantel when he was stoking the fire. The neighbour told reporters how the bread knife, thrown by the wife, quivered in Whiteman's buttock while he ran around looking for his rifle. He never held jobs down for long because he couldn't wake in the morning; his best was two weeks, and then only because he wired the alarm clock across his wrists via an alternator.

In short, he was crazy. Not accountable for his actions.

Particularly seeing he was dead. There weren't many people in the district likely to have had access to big post office capacitors, so a patrol burst into his house four hours after the explosion, only to find his body on the kitchen floor. A round had entered under the chin and exited from the top of his head. An identical capacitor and plastic bottle were found in the ceiling.

Within the hour, Colin Renwick consented to the press conference, allowing himself to be placed in front of the still smoking Land-rover. With the tacit agreement of the New Zealand press, an Australian television reporter hijacked the direction of the conference; but at first, Renwick was in control.

'All I can say at this stage is that it wasn't suicide. You have to realise that we're dealing with people who think the rules of civilisation don't apply to them. The indications are that he was killed by his own people because he failed.'

'He failed?' The reporter glanced at the wreck.

'He failed in his attempt to kill my men.'

'By his own people, you mean the Red Hen organisation?'

'They're your words, not mine.'

'Can you say what these indications are?'

'And prejudice the investigation? No. Suffice to say that we're following a strong line of enquiry.' In fact, he thought, it could well have been a murder: Charlie might conceivably have been alarmed at how close Whiteman had come to swinging public opinion behind the specials.

'Will this incident have any bearing on your difficulties in catching the mountain thorium refiners?'

'It's too early to say. But keep in mind that the moonshiners are now thought to be directly linked to the terrorists.' In the background, he could see on his officers' faces a hint of the old admiration. It warmed him.

'Most people would see this single incident as a rather thin link, Chief Superintendent.'

'That's pure conjecture. If the investigation shows that there's no such link, well and good. But it would be quite inappropriate to comment now.'

'So you think there is a link.'

'Believe me, young man, I'm not thinking anything that you put in my mouth.'

'If I could ask you about Rosa Driscoll, sir. Is it correct that she was in custody without being charged with an offence?'

'Let me make this quite clear. Rosa Driscoll was *not* in custody while in our hands. Like many others associated with that unfortunate incident in the hotel, she was asked to come in to give her version of events. She did so. Voluntarily.' Out of the corner of his eye, he saw a movement of the reporter's little finger followed by a movement of the cameraman's hand on the lens. Close up.

'With respect, sir, you have a cordon round her house. She is denied access to the media. She is surely in custody.'

'Kindly do not twist my words. Now that she is at home, in danger from locals who believe her actions are harming Westlands, she is in *protective* custody. A very different matter.'

'Witnesses have told us that when she was brought in, she looked as if she had been roughed up.'

Renwick nodded curtly. 'You're referring to the fact that she was covered in mud. And wet.'

'Yes.'

Renwick gave an exaggerated sigh. 'With all the publicity this woman has had there are still people who don't realise that she's an emotionally disturbed woman who's been terribly used by unscrupulous factions. She was found, by my men, *in* that state in the countryside. It was self-inflicted.'

'You're saying that she's mentally ill? As opposed to retarded?'

'I'm saying only that Rosa Driscoll is in need of much more care than my men are qualified to give, but we can at least see to it that she comes to no physical harm from local thugs.'

'Can you comment on reports that teenagers have been beaten up by your men?'

'Arrant nonsense. There never has been evidence of such a thing happening and for you to make the assertion without producing evidence is betraying your bias.' Colin felt the beginnings of sweat on his brow.

'There are also rumours that the assaults on the media have been by specials in mufti.'

'Since when does Australian national television allow its reporters to dabble in unsubstantiated gossip? Obviously you're more interested in parading your own prejudices than in dealing with facts. I will not be used as a platform. This interview is over.'

He turned and walked away, but the reporter walked with him, the cameraman and sound recordist following.

'Can you comment on allegations of torture in a hidden interrogation centre?'

'I told you this interview is over!'

'Sir, do you deny that what's really happening here is the rape of a province by its own governing forces?'

'Continue obstructing me and I'll have you arrested!'

Several officers took a step forward, waiting for the order. The reporter halted. The camera continued to record the progress of the contingent of Black-and-Grey officers, up the street towards the rugby ground. Once striding across the grass, Renwick snarled to Wilson.

'The bastard set me up. I don't want him near me again!'

'He could do with a private lesson in manners,' Wadlow suggested, looking back over his shoulder.

'No! If we can't make an open arrest the Australians are untouchable. But we don't have to make it easy for them. No more interviews for them; no one is to pose for their photographers. No one is to help them in any way.' He forced himself to breathe more evenly. He could have contained it better by announcing that he had the suspected leader in custody. But what he gained on PR he would have lost on the flurry of people covering their tracks. No. He had made the right decision. Better to wait for the clean sweep. Anyway, once O'Hara had spilled over, the men wouldn't take kindly to even more media breathing down their necks during the mop-up.

When the time came, the media would need to be side-tracked. He owed it to the men.

O'Hara, the bastard, was holding on, making a fight of it. He couldn't hold out on Searle for ever, but the timing was going to be critical. If only one could freeze time selectively, stopping it here, while allowing it to run there. One might rule the world. Alongside Hans Christian Andersen.

And there was Rosa. Rosa.

Last night his dreams had been filled with her. In them, her eyelid had winked with the sign she denied him in the day. All the dream-long night she had winked; even when he lay with her, rested his head on her breast with her fingertips massaging comfort, closeness, and understanding into his scalp, her eyelid had closed and opened, closed and opened. And after a while it had changed into the eye of a red hen, closing and opening.

He kept his gaze on the white house on the hill as his boots swished through the grass.

'Renwick.' A hand touched his sleeve. It was Wilson, slowing him until they were well behind the others.

'Well?'

Wilson dropped his voice. In this flat hollow between bush

and buildings, the breeze played unpredictable tricks with sound. 'There is a way to justify using lead to bring in the moonshiners. And anyone else for that matter.'

Renwick stopped, weighing up Wilson's carefully composed expression, irritated by the man's habit of drawing his upper lip back to reveal yellow teeth.

'How?'

'I'm just passing on this suggestion of course. I wouldn't want it miscontrued.'

'No. You wouldn't.'

'The media won't be happy about bullet holes in the moonshiners unless we show them a few holes in, speaking hypothetically, say three or four of our own people.'

'Speaking hypothetically, how does your helpful friend suggest we persuade Charlie to do that little thing?'

'Charlie might choose an ambush from the trees. Not to kill, of course. My friend happens to have a contact . . . in Auckland . . . a crack shot . . . knows the bush.'

Now that it had been shaped by words, Colin was surprised at the distaste he felt. There were worse things. Much worse. Interesting timing, he thought. Just when they had their first substantial lead. Just when the kudos was about to start coming down the line from Wellington. Well, Ian Wilson, you're a lot hungrier than anyone thought. And you have just made a serious miscalculation.

'Your hypothetical friend must have thought about who was expendable.'

'He wasn't thinking of the lads who've been with us all along, of course. But there's a few weak links in, say, Foxtrot. No great loss. Might give the rest just what they need.'

'Get them going you mean?'

'Yes. Motivation.'

'Well, I'll have to give careful consideration to what you've just said.'

A flicker of alarm crossed Wilson's face. He looked about, sucking air through his teeth. 'There are no witnesses to this conversation.'

'True, Ian. True. You realise, of course, that Mal O'Hara may well solve all our problems, anyway?'

'I realise that,' Wilson said, clasping hands behind his back. 'Much the better alternative.'

And they went on towards the guest-house.

There was another package waiting for Colin at control. He recognised the handwriting and shade of ink from ten feet. And with the leap of adrenalin came the understanding.

This was the wink. This was her sign.

'Same procedure?' asked the senior.

'No.'

'The first could have been a dummy.'

'No. It's safe. Let's have it.'

Light of heart, he took it to his office and closed the door. He opened a Châteauneuf-du-Pape and sipped, watching the package in delicious anticipation. When he removed the wrappings there was another spring-loaded box. Inside the box was a second gift.

It was a pendant. Of a design new to him. He lifted it out by its gold chain and held it cupped in both hands. To his delight, it too felt warm to the touch, just like the watch. Most of it was a local variety of greenstone, translucent, with subtle interior patterns, elegantly shaped like a snake, rather as he pictured Cleopatra's asp. The tail was ingeniously turned in a loop to hold the chain. The head was wide, pierced by a single large eye made of an attractive, shining metal, which, when he turned it over, seemed a familiar shade to the metal used to back the watch.

The note said:

> If you hold the greenstone in direct sunlight you'll see that the patterns resemble the surface of the moon. As sun and moon cannot shine together, we cannot be one. But by both do I think of thee.

Unsigned.

Cannot? Cannot? He moaned, ground his knuckles against his forehead and drank more red wine, forgetting to let it breathe. After a while, he took off his black beret, slipped the chain over his head and dropped the snake down inside his uniform jacket where it nestled in the hairs between his chest muscles. He returned to the window, opening it to listen. Play, he urged, play. Because it was right that she should play. How could he make her understand? Anything was possible if she would only trust him.

That night, very late, he stood at an identical window one floor up in the guest-house.

The sun had been taken down and replaced by a brisk half-moon. Cloud spiders scampered on the bush. The white music box on the hill gleamed but still didn't play. The bush was quiet, he coud hear nothing of the night birds. Nor was there any sound from the rugby ground; the men were asleep with the weekend girls from Christchurch, the bus that had brought the girls was an empty shell, the luckless guards glided on the perimeters like shadows from a tomb.

Colin pulled his robe closer about him as he looked back into his quarters. Just as empty, just as silent, in spite of the girl sitting on the bed. In the gloom she was like a blob of putty against the sheets and the wall. And less use. As well as her other, manifold inadequacies she had no idea when to close her mouth and when to open it.

He prowled the edges of the room, two moist eyes following his progress.

'Get dressed,' he said.

The blob jumped at the sound. 'I don't understand what you want. You just tell me, okay? And we'll do it.'

'Just get dressed.' He saw, to his disgust, that even though he was looking at her, she made no attempt to cover herself or even pull her legs together.

'Look, you wanna lay your head on my tits some more? That's nuthin' to worry about. There's a lot of guys just want to curl up on a pair like these. Maybe you didn't notice the first time but these are real comfy tits. That's what you want, in'it? You just have to say!'

'I shouldn't have to spell it out,' he growled.

'What am I? A mind reader? Look . . .' She put her head on one side and smiled at him compassionately. Poor guy. She cupped her breasts and lifted them towards him, an offering. '. . . why don't we snuggle up and you can start with these and we play it by ear after that. I don't care what you want to put where as long as you don't hurt.'

'You don't even begin to understand,' Colin hissed.

'Oh, it's understanding you want,' she sniffed, hurt.

'Get up and get out.'

'Hey. I thought we didn't have to sleep on the bus!'

Colin felt himself trembling. He looked down at her without inclining his head. 'You filth. You unutterable, cheap, disgusting bag of filth. Get out of here . . .'

'Hey, mister, I don't have to take this crap.' Bitter tears welled as she looked around for her clothes. 'Lizzy says we don't have to take crap from anybody, doesn't matter who they think they are.'

'Christ!' In smouldering rage, Colin scooped up her clothes, wrenched open the door and threw them into the corridor. 'Tyson!' he yelled. 'Tyson!' And when the house guard arrived he found a weeping young woman struggling into her clothes. He escorted her towards the bus, but on the way they encountered a sympathetic special who had been left out and couldn't sleep, so she took his arm and went with him to his tent.

In his quarters, Colin looked around for his robe then realised that he had it on. He remade his bed, lay on it, reached for the radio and turned off the silence.

Something had changed. Something had been added to the left-hand side of the equation.

What, then, was the resultant change on the right?

O'Hara! Pay attention, O'Hara. If you heat the solution of complexes before adding the acid, will you get crystallisation . . . ? Not fast enough. You're a daydreamer, boy. All right, I'll give you a clue. Name the crystal you would expect under room-temperature conditions. Merciful heaven, boy, you weren't listening to that either? You don't know. You don't know. Well, I'll tell you something I don't know, O'Hara. I don't know why you bother coming to school. What I hope, O'Hara, is that you'll leave your body to medical science: the world's scruffiest and laziest genius challenges science even in death – world's top boffins mystified by the only brain in history to be afflicted with disuse atrophy from birth. What are you laughing for, Patterson? If you stopped using your brain I wouldn't notice the difference. All right, my fine, feather-brained friends, enough of this fiddle-faddle; my ear is cocked, I am composed, I await wisdom . . . open your beaks and tell me if this crystallisation is endothermic or exothermic?

The lull was a long one this time. Usually they were so short Mal could see the end coming. Usually it was like gliding across a lonely desert island to where mountainous grey waves waited for him, carrying bits of brown paper and string and topped with spume and sweet madness.

Alone. Even the two assistants had left his side.

Indifferent, dirty yellow light. The bulb was always swaying when he looked at it, though he had never seen anyone push it. Sometimes, he would feel the bulb burn a wider track across his eyelids and he would open his eyes quickly to catch them pushing it, but he was always too late. There would only be Doctor Smith, holding him so tenderly, so understandingly, murmuring his support in rhythms that exactly matched the rhythms of the voltage. Opposites, rising and falling hand in hand – I'm so sorry, Mal, but if we don't try to get it out now it'll be untreatable later. Yes it hurts, it hurts, doesn't it. Now I want you to really really try this time. I know, I know, Mal, you've been trying so hard, but it's a difficult one, eating away at your insides and you'll have to put everything into pushing it out. All of it. Every nasty little bit. Oh, Mal, I know, I know how much it must be hurting . . . Push, push, you know what we want to hear, push it out and we'll take good care of it. No one need ever know where it came from, it'll be our little secret.

Nurture, hand in hand with pain.

He squeezed his eyelids tightly, trying to force moisture out. They must go on thinking that he was still snivelling when Smith left him alone. They must not be allowed to guess that something had changed.

Unwittingly, they had provided him with the third and final draft of his cerebral thesis on pain. It had happened quite effortlessly, independently of his will – and theirs. At first he'd thought that the waves had finally tossed him into madness. At one of the highest peaks of pain, when Smith was bending down, looking sorrowfully into his eyes, he had found himself standing, floating – he didn't know which – a few feet away, watching Smith bending over someone who was jerking in the clamps.

Watching Smith bending over himself.

The second time it happened, he had known that Smith could be beaten.

The third time, the pain alone pulled the trigger. He was gone down the flick-barrel before Smith had even stroked his hair. After that he'd had to hold back an impulse to tell Smith about the scar on top of the man's scalp.

Another daydream, O'Hara? Right . . . I'm up to here with you, boy. If you must behave like a mindless gazawp, I'll punish you like one. Write out, a hundred times . . . I possess the only mind known to science to be detached from its brain. Have it on my bench in the morning.

Now, with residual pain binding his bones to the bench, he drifted, marvelling at the sounds he heard, sounds like the fall of crystal in an echo chamber. He heard a voice out of the dead space beyond the canvas.

'It's all right, he's unconscious.'

Who's unconscious? he wondered.

'Okay, explain.'

'I think he's a deliberate blind alley, sir. A patsy.'

'That's impossible! Are you saying the last one lied to you?'

'No sir, Meeking believed it, all right. But he was wrong.'

'I'm telling you it flies in the face of all the signs! He *has* to be our man.'

'The signs must have been planted deliberately, sir. I'm sorry, but I'd stake my reputation he's not the leader. I don't think he's part of the organisation at all.'

'Then what the blue tack blazes is he?'

'I don't know. Frankly, he's a puzzle. He seems to hate the Red Hens. And he's obsessed with leaving Westland. I've had it checked out. He was due to head out the morning we admitted him.'

A different voice.'There's been no sign of a change in Charlie's activities since we brought him in.'

'Damn, damn, damn. A fat lot of use that is. You've tried him on the Driscoll woman?'

'Yes, sir. There's nothing.'

'You told him she spilled?'

'Yes. He tried to laugh. He really believes she's genuine. Someone has done a very careful selling programme here before we even arrived.'

'Then it has to be the brother.'

'One thing about Mal, sir. He's besotted with Driscoll. And he's got a guilt complex. He seems to be a bit of a lad – forced himself on her when he took her whitebaiting.'

'He what!' Whispered.

This was followed by a silence. Mal felt an unpleasant pressure that filled the spaces round him, dimming their colours.

'His brother. What about his brother?'

'Still nothing, sir, but he hates him like poison.'

'Why?'

'It turns out that Mal is the yellow sheep of the family. His little brother has a habit of rubbing salt in the wound.'

This was followed by the sound of pacing. It stopped.

'All right, Wilson. Bring in the brother.'

Even when they sat him up near the tailboard where he could see his own moonlit gate, he didn't know if he was about to live or die. The patrol leader's voice spoke beside him.

'You've got four hours to rest up, get your things together and leave Frazer Creek. Another two to leave Westland. You move straight out, you don't talk to anyone on the way, got it?'

'You're letting me go?' Mal didn't understand.

'Those are my orders.' The face came closer. 'Actually, me and the boys here would love you to be late. Know what I mean?'

Mal began to climb over the tailboard, legs weak and shaking, tensed for a bullet or a blow. Instead, a voice asked if he needed a hand, and pushed him just hard enough to drop him into a mud-filled rut in front of the gate. He watched the Land-rover wheel and accelerate away and lowered his head to touch lips to the mud.

He set off for the house, stumbling on the dark, uneven drive. The moon had set, the dawn was still dreaming, his vision was blurred. Fog. Why let him go? It didn't make sense. Ben. Warn Ben.

A dark shape bobbed and grew before him and became his father. Mal allowed himself to be supported up the steps, but then cast off the help and lurched to the telephone.

He cranked it, asked for a number.

Four hundred yards away in the bush, the army observer with the headphones raised a thumb to his colleague, who spoke into his radio mike. At the rugby-field control centre, the comms operator turned to the officers.

'He's doing it the easy way.'

'By phone? You must have done a lobotomy on him, Searle.'

'It's shock,' Searle explained modestly.

Renwick clicked his fingers at the tap dancer, who was already cranking up the numbers. A party-line phone warbled out of a control-room speaker. Three shorts and a long. The exchange operator tried yet again. Three shorts and a long.

Click.

'Yeah?'

'Get out. They know. They're coming for you.'

In the control room, several men made hands into triumphant fists. Some tried to talk, but were silenced by a fierce movement of the commander's hand. As Ben came fully awake, they heard the whuff of a dog. That would be the Doberman.

'Jesus! How did . . . ? What did you tell – ?'

'I told them nothing! Apart from the misfortune of knowing you, I don't know a damn thing anyway, thank God.'

'Then what the fuck are you doing free? What – '

'I'm leaving. They've given me four hours to get out. Now get the hell into the bush.'

'You fucking idiot! You . . . Christ! I've got to get out . . .'

Renwick nodded sharply to the comms operator, who spoke one word into his mike. Go.

'. . . How long have I got, Mal? Quick, tell me . . .' There the voice broke off as a crash penetrated. A dog barked. Another crash and a shout; the bark turned to a slavering snarl followed by the report of a Smith and Wesson. The snarl became a whimper and died. More shouts, then commands at a lower tone.

Around the comms operator, cheers broke out and men clapped each other on the back.

'At last! At last!' Renwick pounded fist into hand. He grinned fiercely back at the congratulatory faces. 'Solid ground and downhill.'

Miles to the south, Mal O'Hara put the telephone down as if it were part of a falling dream.

'Too late.'

'That was Ben, wasn't it? They got Ben.' And the old man's cheeks sagged when Mal failed to deny it. There were bruises under both Olly's eyes and on his neck. 'All this time. I sort of knew it was him. I sort of knew. But I didn't ask him. I was scared to ask him.'

'Yeah.'

'Mal?'

'Yeah.'

'I didn't tell 'em nothing either.'

Seventeen

'Your guilt is established, Mr O'Hara. Your choice is simple. You can do this the easy way or the hard way. We'll want everything, of course: leader's name, location of the headquarters, structure of the organisation, and names right down to the last moonshiner. Everything you can dredge up, if you'll forgive the pun. Ah, and everything on Rosa Driscoll . . . Please, you won't get an Oscar nomination here; we know she's involved, but I'm fascinated to hear more detail. She was quite a project, wasn't she? We know a great deal about the rest as well, so don't bore Doctor Smith here with red herrings. Well, what's it going to be? I don't recommend the hard way. You would be screaming down every remote corridor of your mind looking for things to tell the doctor long after you finished being useful. You might not even recognise the corridors.'

Looking down at O'Hara the younger on the carpenter's bench, Colin pondered the frailty of the human body. Laid out like this, it was difficult to envisage protoplasm more pathetically vulnerable. Time to go. This place and Searle stirred up the nausea. And he was weary and needed sleep.

'Not even the courtesy of a reply, Mr O'Hara?'

'You killed Prince.'

'Prince? Ah, the dog. According to the patrol leader, your Prince leapt on the revolver, killing himself. Involuntary suicide.'

'A fat lot of choice he had.'

'Perhaps. But you do have a choice.' Unlike myself, he thought. If freedom is measured by availability of choice, my friend, then I am more a prisoner than you are lying there in the clamps. There are no branch lines on my track. The jigger I pump is a microcosm of the universe, a mechanical toy running down in Hades' waiting room.

'What have you done with Mal?'

Renwick looked at his gift watch. 'In three hours time, your brother will be on his way out of Westland. If he's sensible.'

'Hah! Oh, believe me, he'll be sensible. Mal will definitely be sensible.'

'Yes, we've heard about your sibling tiff.'

'Don't kill the bastard too quick.'

'Your own brother? You're talking about your own brother? You surprise me. You can't mean that.'

Ben laughed. His eyes glanced at the gift watch on Renwick's hand long enough to read the time.

'All right Mr O'Hara, you've delayed us long enough. I think you've made your choice. A pity. Let me return you to the capable hands of Doctor Smith here, a practitioner of mind and body who may not be able to spell Hippocratic but who runs an efficient ward.'

Searle said. 'We'll take very good care of you, Ben.'

Ben flinched at the sound. His belly muscles knotted and he shrank slightly against the restraints.

'What do we do with these, sir?' One of Searle's assistants pointed to a shotgun and small metal case next to the wall. Renwick opened the case and studied the contents. They made no sense to him. On impulse, he took the case back to the carpenter's bench, where O'Hara's cheeks were now like bleached coral.

'Satisfy my curiosity, Mr O'Hara. I seem to remember your telling one of my patrols that your adapted shotgun was harmless. Convince me. Start with this.'

'A dart.'

'Obviously. I mean how does it work?'

'Like a hypodermic. The plunger's momentum pushes the drug through.' He was shivering, eager enough to talk on inconsequential detail.

'This?' A wire trailing.

'Beeper aerial. Track the deer.'

'This.' Renwick unscrewed the stopper on a glass bottle. He tipped it slowly, obviously intending to wet a finger and sniff it. O'Hara stopped him.

'Don't do it. That's Fentaz. Skin contact will have you vomiting in ten minutes.'

Renwick returned the stopper and inclined his head, acknowledging a courtesy. He lifted another bottle and his eyebrows.

'Antidote. Nalorphine. Without it, you've got doped venison.'

Renwick nodded, handed the box and its contents back to the assistant and told him to stow them in the corner. Queasiness dragged on the base of his throat. He turned away along the canvas, but O'Hara's voice came after him.

'Don't leave me with this shithead.'

Renwick looked back. Ben's eyes were wide and white. Unimaginable imaginings. The man must have an imagination after all. Good – a surprisingly swift beginning. It would be an appealing irony, if the macho brother turned out to be the quick study.

'Your choice, as I said.'

'How can you do this?'

'I shouldn't tell you this, Mr O'Hara, but if it's any

consolation there is something worse than what Doctor Smith is going to do to you. Shall I tell you what the world's most horrific torture chamber is? The human family, Mr O'Hara, the much-sanctified human family. The same in essence as you are about to experience, but potentially much greater in degree.'

But O'Hara didn't understand. It looked as if the juices of terror were flooding already. Colin made his way to the door. Why did he always overstay this place? It was like a quicksand, sucking him down.

He was halted again at the door as Searle's hand plucked at his sleeve.

'Sir.' A conspiratorial whisper. 'This may not take long. He's into stage two already. Something of a surprise because I haven't touched him yet.'

'Yes. I can see that.' Renwick shook off the hand as if it were diseased, pushing blindly at the door. A finger touched his sleeve again.

'By the way sir, I can spell Hippocratic.'

'Yes. Yes, yes, yes . . . it was a tasteless ploy. I apologise.'

'Thank you, sir.'

Outside, he leaned against the grandstand wall and took long breaths, sucking oxygen deep into his lungs. This in turn made him briefly dizzy and he didn't see Wilson's arrival from the office.

'The Brigadier is on the phone. The Aussies have pulled a fast one on us with Driscoll.' If Wilson noticed that Renwick was looking ill, he didn't comment.

'Yes?'

'They've conned our Ombudsman into giving them an interview about the questions he'll be putting to the PM. Police harassment of an intellectually handicapped woman, illegal detention and so on. Every satellite dish in the country is turned to Channel Ten. We've got to lift the cordon.'

'We've got to, eh? Are you passing on an order or was it entirely your own idea?'

'Passing it on, sir.'

'From now on I take my orders direct. Not through a messenger boy.'

'Yes, sir.'

Colin nodded to himself, satisfied. The intervening night had brought to Wilson full comprehension of yesterday's miscalculation. He'd built himself a cage and he could run around in its corners until Colin worked out what to do with him.

Colin stood away from the wall and looked up at the white house. Trees hid the road beside it, but he could hear the murmur of the media pack and the growl of tyres on loose shingle as more vehicles arrived.

'All right. Lift the cordon. Very shortly, she'll have a cult without a foundation anyway.'

The climber stopped two-thirds of the way up the giant kahikatea tree, where he could see out over the bush canopy. He rested on a branch the thickness of his waist, then laid out his equipment: a hand catapult, a climber's karabiner, two spools of heavy-duty game-fishing line, and a sinker painted iridescent orange. He jammed the first spool on an instep spike, attached the line to the sinker and fitted the sinker into the elastic of the catapult. As he worked his side vision dwelt on the beach, wary for the flash of binoculars.

The catapult stretched, steadied, flapped at the air. The orange dot sped out over the canopy, plummeting into the trees near the beach, with the near-invisible line trailing behind.

A pause, this time checking the beach directly. No change. No sudden movements. The roar of the dredge never faltered.

The climber joined the paid-out section of the first spool to the beginning of the second, and dropped the second to unwind into the depths below him. There was now a single line from the distant sinker, around the trunk of the kahikatea, over the branch he stood on and down to the bush floor. With fingers maintaining a light tension on the line, he waited, like a fisherman waiting for the nibble.

Within a couple of minutes it came: a firm tug, a pause, then two more. And he passed the same message down the line to the ground. The line began to slide past him towards the ground, quickly at first, then steadily as more strain came on. Soon he saw what looked like segments of a brown creeper twisting and coiling towards him across the canopy. A snake with an ovular head encompassing a single eye – the loop at the beginning of a log-haul wire.

The camouflaged wire crept past the climber and, with his help, round the main trunk until it was almost back on itself. With the karabiner he completed the wire circuit of the trunk.

The wire, stretching like a supplejack vine across the roof of the bush, was securely fastened to the kahikatea. The climber's job was done. He cut the game line free and descended so rapidly his spikes made a tattoo on the soft bark.

Mal O'Hara pulled off the road into ferns that tickled the belly of the petrol tank, not knowing where and when he had made the decision or if he had made it at all. He couldn't remember riding the last half mile. He flicked out the stand, left the pack strapped to the carrier, left the engine running, reluctant to kill its reassuring thump for the few moments this would take. He trod up the hill, past the parked cars, past a Land-rover full of specials. Their eyes followed him without expression or recognition.

There was no one outside the Driscoll house. The gate was open, lying back against a long-neglected chrysanthemum bush. For a moment, he thought all was quiet, but the thought itself acted as a switch and a purr of voices tripped into being.

The back door was open. He knocked. Unseen behind him, two uniformed men suddenly leapt out of the front of the Land-rover, but hesitated there, staring after him.

No answer. Someone he didn't know was moving on the stairs.

He walked in, and saw Edith Driscoll alone in the kitchen. She was making a clumsy job of setting the cosy on a pot of tea. Her hands were pale parchment stretched over the veins. Her eyes were sunken, retreating from him.

'Have you finished taking pictures now?'

'It's Mal, Mrs Driscoll. I'm leaving. I came to see Rosa.'

'You said you were going to go away when you finished the pictures.'

'It's Mal. I'm not – '

'I don't want your money.'

'Where's Rosa, Mrs Driscoll? I've got to see Rosa.'

She blinked a slow blink, which changed her expression.

'They wanted her to do it again because the camera wasn't ready. But she wouldn't.' The hand twirled the pot three times. *Clockwise because that's the way the world goes round, my girl, and because I say so. Not too close to the stove or the leaves won't settle. Now, did you remember to turn the pot? Three times, Edith, don't forget.* Edith Driscoll kept turning the pot. Three, and three more. Inside, the brew gathered momentum and a little slopped out of the spout with the steam.

Mal left the kitchen, pushed his way past two reporters interviewing each other in the hall and climbed the stairs towards the hubbub of voices.

'How the devil did that happen?'

'Nobody told us you were taking the cordon off Driscoll, sir.'

'I thought you told him to catch a crow.'

'We did, sir!'

'I wonder where he got the guts. How long's he been in there?'

'Just a few seconds. And he left the engine running.'

Renwick studied the house, a pulse throbbing in his neck.

'Do we go in and get – ?'

'If he's after the media it's too late!' Renwick snapped. His eyes swivelled to Hicks. 'But I don't think he is. When he leaves on the motorbike, tell Wadlow.'

'Yes sir . . . Ah . . .'

'What?'

'We were just wondering, sir. If this guy is no use to us, why aren't we just shipping him over to the internment camp like the rest?'

'At no point in any of Arthur Conan Doyle's fifty-six short stories and four novels does Sherlock Holmes say "Elementary, my dear Watson." Does that help, Hicks?'

'I get the drift, sir.'

'Drift back to your post then, Hicks. If you question my orders again, it'll be you shipping out over the hill.'

'Yes, sir. Sorry, sir.'

The patrol leader trotted back across the playground.

'Interesting,' Wilson observed.

'Indeed,' Renwick agreed, coolly. Wilson had worked it out,

he knew. Wilson had become intensely interested in the risk being taken to satisfy a personal grudge. But Wilson would not question the risk; if he did, Colin might not take it. Wilson, for all his inscrutability, was becoming laughably easy to read.

The duty sergeant appeared, saluted with a snap that threatened to pop his elbow socket.

'Suh. There's some people at the gate want to see you.'

'Well?' Impatiently. The sergeant knew the rules better than anyone.

'These people want to congratulate you, suh.'

'Really?' Colin was suspicious. You couldn't trust anyone in this part of the world. 'I haven't got time. Who are these paragons, anyway?'

The sergeant read them from a slip of paper. 'Citizens for community standards and Protection of the Family. PROFAM, suh.'

'Tell them . . . sorry, no time, much appreciate their support, we do our best under trying circumstances.'

'Suh.'

Colin also rid himself of Wilson's company. He walked out to the goal posts, giving him a different view of the white house up the hill. The thought of Mal O'Hara in the same room as Rosa was disturbing. Trying to make some kind of snivelling apology, no doubt. An apology! The way some people expected to have their heavenly slates wiped clean with a request for forgiveness. Well he needn't have bothered, the debt collectors had the matter well in hand.

The clouds had lifted, after hunkering low all morning. It was a meteorological habit in these parts that they did look like the same clouds suddenly higher up, as if the sky were a piston suddenly pulled back, leaving the air anaemic, waiting for something to pour in and enrich it. That something was about to happen. He knew it so certainly that he felt Searle's imminent arrival seconds before the white-coated figure came hurrying out the back of the grandstand. Searle had never before neglected to remove the coat before venturing out.

His smile stretched before Colin. He had succeeded. It had been cracked.

'Well, Searle. I think you have news for me.'

'I do indeed, sir. He wants a deal.'

'A deal!' Some of Renwick's humour vanished. 'I don't want to know about a deal. Just tip him up and pour it out.'

But Searle's face glowed. His feet shuffled deprecatingly, bringing Renwick a thrill of anticipation.

'I think this deal might be worth listening to, sir. But we're going to have to be swift off the mark.'

The attic was a swelter of people and equipment: cameras, lenses, tripods, mixers, microphones, video recorders, glaring spotlights with disapproving vanes narrowing the beams down on the woman at the piano. Soft leather jackets, mandarin collars, pin tuck bodices, a cream two-piece. They manoeuvred subtly for position, exuding the mellow, deferential air the press pack reserves for someone not yet proved to be its inferior. The air was hot in the lights, and thick with dust that had not been disturbed for years.

Rosa's solemn eyes flitted from one moving mouth to another.

A bit further to your left, Rosa. Round this way, Rosa, face the window. The window . . . We've got problems with the light. That'll do, I guess. Yeah, great. Great. Can you hold the doll up a bit? Closer to the face. No, like this. What's its name, anyway? Nice doll.

Hey, if you've finished, could we have her over by the window? We've got a deadline coming up. Over by the window, love. This way. Okay. Uh, maybe if you raise your arms a bit. Like this. Excuse me. This is just a microphone, so we can hear what you say. I have to put it here. Can I undo this? Excuse me.

'Like Pinocchio,' someone near Mal observed in disgust. 'Why don't they just attach strings to her fingers and make her play like that?'

'Pinocchio turned out smarter than he looked,' another replied. 'I reckon the specials might have something. I think she's doing a Hollywood. A real kid would be crying by now.'

If she gets the urge, she's not going to announce it, is she? I don't know! Lord knows if she'll *ever* touch the piano again, but I sure as hell don't want to miss it. Okay, hang an MCU just in case. Roll if she even *looks* at the piano. Stay with her, take your time about going in, I want to see plenty of piano. Then if she really gets into it, track around for the doll through soft fingers – that's a hot one – then tilt for the BCU on the face. No crash movements. God! The whole damn thing without edits. No. Does it *look* as if she's going to stick around for the cut-ins? No, no. Irrelevant cut-aways over my dead body.

Someone noticed that there was no printed music on the piano and this set off a hunt. There seemed to be no printed music anywhere in the attic.

The BBC crew began filming other reporters. The media angle. Cameras took pictures of cameras. One lined up on a director moving Rosa's limbs about: better yet – pictures of media insensitivity. The reporter and photographer from *Woman's Weekly* looked at each other, shook their heads and left.

Over to your right, Rosa, I want to get a bit of natural light on your face. Am I speaking loudly enough for her? Does anybody know? Maybe she needs a cup of tea. Damn it, I can't get the piano in the same shot. Why don't we move the piano?

An Australian television reporter in a tailored avocado two-piece took Rosa firmly in hand and guided her back to the piano stool. She sat beside her, with a protective arm around her shoulders.

'Don't you take any notice of these guys, love. They're chauvinist wolves the lot of them.' This was greeted by a chorus of hoots and chuckles. So she raised two easy fingers to them all behind her back. 'Yeah and they fuck dogs too. You just play the piano when you want and not a moment before.'

To her surprise, Rosa accepted the sheltering arm by leaning even closer, nearly cheek to cheek. There were a couple of low whistles from behind, but Marlene Papps of Channel 10 was more than equal to the occasion. She didn't move her arm, even when Rosa whispered to her.

'It's the *bad* girl plays the piano.'

'Listen, honey, it doesn't bother me if you're a bad girl sometimes. But if you don't feel like being a bad girl then you just tell them all to sod off.'

'Hey, hey, watch it Marlene. What're you doing to us?'

'What did she say? Did she say she was a bad girl? Hey, I like that.'

'They won't shut the door, will they?' Rosa asked her.

'Not if you don't want, honey.'

Suddenly, Rosa straightened as if someone had tipped cold water down her back. She turned and looked directly at Mal O'Hara hovering in the attic doorway.

'Rosa, I'm sorry. I'm so sorry,' his lips murmured. 'I didn't know it would be like this.'

'Who's he?'

A few cameras swung, prattling shutters at him. He backed away down the steps with his hand in front of his face.

'Hey look, look at her hands. Jesus, she's going to do it! Roll it. Roll for Christ's sake!'

Marlene Papps leapt sideways off the piano stool.

Rosa's fingernails came out of her palms, leaving angry red crescents in the flesh. She placed the doll at the end of the keyboard, where it grinned as her left little finger played the first note of '*Gnossiennes* One,' grinned as the plaintive, melancholy music swelled through the attic, silencing everything but the hum of the recording machines.

Mal stumbled down the stairs. He had only a fleeting impression of Edith Driscoll still turning the pot, then he was out and running down the road, away from the melody gurgling out of the attic window. The motorbike engine had stopped. He thrashed the kick-start, bruising an ankle, revved high and took off down to the main street.

In the middle of a musical trill, Rosa stopped playing. After long seconds of silence, the attic filled with low, despairing moans from the television people. One contract director was photographed beating his forehead against an attic beam.

By the time Mal reached the open road to the north, his motorbike was travelling at well over the speed limit.

Just inside the tree-line at the beach, four men worked at high speed and in almost complete silence, though for sound cover they could hardly have improved on the scream of the thorium dredge. They attached a pulley well above head height in a small pigeonwood tree, passed a rope through it and pulled.

Above them, in the canopy, most of the slack came out of the brown-painted heavy-duty wire attached to the kahikatea. Its lazy coils became shallow, taut waves as its downhill end nosed into the glossy foliage of the pigeonwood. The pigeonwood bent uphill, bowing to the kahikatea, and the rope was lashed.

A redpoll twittered nearby. The men melted into the undergrowth, leaving nothing under the pigeonwood. A patrol passed through, noticing nothing. The men came back.

Into the eye of the wire they fastened the ends of five more lengths of wire, each of much smaller diameter, each only thirty yards long. A long metal hand with thin metal fingers. Next, the fingernails were attached – five karabiners.

The men kept looking at their watches and glancing uphill as if they expected someone to arrive. After a long time, when no one came, they stuffed the five new wires up out of sight in the pigeonwood and slipped back into the forest.

Half a mile up, they came to an ancient grave site: the remains of a rusty spiked fence, overgrown with moss and creepers, and a mould-covered gravestone. A couple, man and woman, were already there waiting for them – the woman with a radio and a set of earphones.

'What's going on?'

'Nothing,' the woman said savagely. 'Not a damn thing. He hasn't called.'

'Why the blazes not?'

'If he hasn't called, how would I know?'

'Call and check then.'

'What good would that do? You know the rules. No transmissions from the Cooler.'

'Would they know at the Cooler, anyway? How often does he check in?'

'How the hell would I know?'

A black fantail looped, chirruped and departed.

'Fuck Ben. I say we go ahead without him. If he's been caught, we could all be in shit creek hanging about here.'

'If he's been caught we'll be in shit creek anywhere, along with everyone in the Cooler. No, no way; we just get one crack at it; if we're going to pop the paras' little corks with this stunt, the timing with the media has to be bang on and Ben's the only one with the timing. I say we give him another half an hour.'

They waited, uncomfortable in the damp forest, crouched or pacing round the gravestone, which said in barely decipherable letters, 'EDWIN HAINES DIED 1898 LIVED FOR THE GOLD, DIED FOR THE LORD.'

EIGHTEEN

Ben went through the checks. Oil temperature rising, friction lock collective, friction lock cyclic, release trim, controls free . . . The smells were richer than he remembered, and sharper and more penetrating. Even the phantom odour of Prince remained in the kerosene fumes.

The shower, food and hot drinks had restored the colour to his complexion. Most of the physical pain had subsided to a dragging ache. The touch of the familiar controls calmed him. But the world had taken on the dimensions of a tunnel in which his judgment and chance had better dance superbly well. The checks, his glances at dials and gauges, were slowed to nearly half-speed; his thought processes presented themselves for inspection like samples of merchandise to the buyer. There could be no mistakes.

Doors secure.

Seat belts.

'Your seat belts done up?' Solicitous. Concerned for their well-being.

'Very funny. Get on with it.'

Wilson watched every move without a blink. He was in plain clothes, identical to those usually worn by John Taylor. Behind were two more specials, also in plain clothes: bush shirts, jeans, a rolled-up balaclava for one because his hair was too short and too well trimmed. HK machine guns lay on the floor at their feet, out of Ben's reach. The dart gun was back in its clip in the rear, the dart box in its compartment next to a rear seat.

'If you leave the dart gun out,' O'Hara had told them, 'they'll have it all figured out before the skids touch down.'

Oil temperature stabilised, pressure 130psi.

Ben fished in a side compartment. Not finding what he was after, he bent down, used two hands to rummage through the contents.

'What are you doing?' Wilson was on edge. The machine had been searched once on Renwick's orders, and a second time by himself – thoroughly, making certain there was nothing O'Hara could use to double-cross them. Unable to come up with a logical flaw in the plan, Wilson had had little choice but to accept it. He remained uneasy.

'My gloves,' Ben said. 'Someone's taken my gloves.'

'It's not cold.'

'Not down here it's not. I never fly without my gloves.'

'We're going north, you said. Low altitude.'

'I get nervous without them. I get hives.'

'For God's sake!'

'Wait. I've got some rubber gloves. They'll do. Pass me the dart box.'

One of the specials handed it to Wilson, who unstrapped it and inspected it for the third time. He lifted the foam plastic base under the darts and bottles, took out yellow dish gloves, and gave them to Ben. With their dusting of talcum powder on the inner surface they slipped on easily. Wilson returned the box to the rear.

'Let's go. Let's go.'

Revs 100 per cent. The collective rose, pitch coarsened. The Hughes whined, tipped on its toes and pirouetted into the air. The pole nudged forward and the clutter that was Ben's house became a dwindling, untidy patch in the bush, then vanished.

When the Hughes was twenty miles north of Frazer Creek, five Iroquois rolled in from the west over a shallow hill, swinging in behind. Three miles back, they were a cluster of green-brown dots, an irregular wedge rising and falling with the contours of the Westland plain.

Inside the lead Iroquois, the thwack of the blades was echoed by the heavy staccato of the other machines. Eight other men, two troops, sat around Renwick, their checks long done, heads bowed next to weapons, eyes open and staring in the manner of men going into battle. Kevin Longman offered his card pack for the lucky touch, and this time it did the rounds. He shuffled, cut one-handed, and the pack went into his breast pocket.

Colin Renwick kept his binoculars on the Hughes. The need for radio silence was unnerving. The tip of his tongue played with his mouth ulcers.

A seventh man came out of the bushes by the grave.

'The loggers are getting twitchy. They're talking about backing off if we can't give them a go-ahead double quick.'

'They can't *do* that!'

'You want to tell them yourself?'

The group conferred.

'Okay. Go back and keep them sweet. Tell 'em to make the first cut and stand by.'

In twenty minutes, the message reached the logging crew near the kahikatea. The chain saw howled and sank into the soft bark. In three minutes it howled again as its teeth found no more resistance and came out of the scarf cut. Its voice dropped to an idling burble. A hook sank into the wood and a piece the shape of a gigantic melon slice bounced on the moss, leaving the trunk with a Halloween grin.

Above, the tip of the kahikatea shivered. It had first looked out over the South Westland bush when the Maori came to take jade from the beaches and when Captain James Cook stood off the coast in the *Resolution* and dipped his goose quill to write in his journal that:

> The most mischevious animal here is the small black sandfly which are exceeding numerous and are so troublesome that they exceed everything of the kind I ever met with.

'Slow down. A hundred and five knots maximum!'

'Yeah.' Ben eased back slowly. 'I hope they're still there.'

'For your sake they'd better be.' Wilson's grin was devoid of humour.

From the west, the main north road came obliquely in to

dodge about under them. Wilson noticed that O'Hara's eyes were flitting constantly to the road.

'What're you doing?'

'Looking for a marker.'

But Wilson also saw that their pilot's hands were beginning to tremble at the controls. O'Hara's breath was shallow and occasionally caught in his throat, pulling a tremor into his cheeks. Wilson was not concerned for his own physical safety – with the help of the two behind him, they could have O'Hara out of the seat and himself at the controls in seconds – but for the mission to succeed, O'Hara had to remain where he was. The three watched him, their alarm and contempt growing. When all this was over, Westlanders would never again tolerate an O'Hara amongst them.

'Pull yourself together.'

'My nerves . . . Pass me my tranquilliser, will you?'

'Your what?'

'. . . tranquilliser. It's in the – '

'You fly this thing on tranquillisers?!'

'Yeah. You going to tell the cops? Pass me the dart box, for cryin' out loud!'

'The dart box?'

'Of course, the dart box. You think I leave it on the seat for the fucking aviation inspectors to find?'

Yet again, Wilson opened the box and under Ben's direction pulled out a bottle labelled Fentaz. He unscrewed the top, fanned the vapour towards his nostrils and moued with distaste.

'So what do you put in the deer?'

'Same stuff, but a lot more. I only have to wet my lips and I'm right. Rock steady.'

'All right. Don't overdo it.' He handed it over.

'It's good stuff. You want some?' Ben offered by waving the bottle back in Wilson's direction. It tipped. A dollop of the clear liquid sloshed on the policeman's upper thigh where his cords were tight across the flesh.

'Idiot!'

'Sorry.' He turned to look over the back. 'You want some?' And he thrust the bottle behind the central column, spraying the contents liberally across the thighs of both men in the rear. Three sets of hands grabbed him simultaneously. The snout of a Smith and Wesson pushed his temple.

'What the fuck do you think you're doing?'

'Put it away. If you want to stay alive, you're going to need me alive to tell you how.'

The barrel wavered. The three men investigated the wet patches on their legs, lifting cloth away from flesh. But there was no pain, no burning. It might as well have been water. They watched their pilot screw the top back on the stopper with his gloved hands. Steady hands. Wilson grabbed O'Hara's shirt up by his neck and squeezed, the pistol expressing a renewed interest in the contents of O'Hara's head.

'What is it? What have you done?'

Ben checked the main road as far ahead as possible, changing course slightly to allow for a place where the road deviated too far for a good view. Had he missed a section? No.

'Listen, boyos. In five minutes you're going to be sick as dogs. Pretty soon after that you'll be unconscious. And if you don't get the right medical attention inside an hour, you're pork.'

'He's bluffing! Cockamamy bluff!' But the special who said it was peeling down his trousers.

'Antidote.' Wilson snatched the second bottle from the box. 'This'll be an antidote!'

'Bright boy. That'll be why you're a bleeding officer. Problem is, you don't know how much to take. And that stuff is worse than the Fentaz if you don't get the dose exactly right. As it is, you're going to have to use the darts as hypodermics . . .'

'You treacherous little shit!' Wilson's cheeks sagged.

Ben smirked. 'That's a good one coming from you. You didn't think I fell for the free passage thing, did you?' But when he looked down at the road again, his smirk lost its humour. 'Well, maybe you're right at that.'

He reached for the radio.

Wilson grabbed his arm and raised the revolver. But Ben just looked at him and shook his head and the revolver fell away. He changed the frequency of the set, tumbling the numbers up the scale.

'Mama to Jack.'

'Eeeehah, hello Mama! Where in hella you been? You okay?'

'A bit of swine fever, Jack. Sorry about the delay. Why don't you go chop down a beanstalk?'

'Yes, sir, Mama!'

In the lead Iroquois, the air-force co-pilot glanced back at Colin Renwick, then took off his headphones.

'HQ, sir. They've picked up unauthorised UHF traffic. Coded. Shorter than a sparrow's fart. They couldn't get a range, but they've got one of the directions. It's from up this way . . . 037 to 040 degrees from HQ. You want to reply?'

'No. No transmissions.' Interesting. Probably significant, but without a code to go on it wasn't going to be any use to them. Colin used the glasses to pick out the distant speck; what interested him more right now was the path of the Hughes, the small but significant changes in direction. Something wasn't right. Apprehension gnawed, when there should be only anticipation.

Mentally he retraced all the steps, looking for a flaw. He checked the map, but it only confirmed that they were in the general area indicated by O'Hara before they set out. He looked down through the chin of the thudding craft to where the main road zagged lazily from left to right underneath. A thought occurred to him like a stab, checked, and thrust again. He tried to recall the conversation with Ben O'Hara under the grandstand. No. No. Ludicrous. For that, the man would have to count on dice loaded like a Mexican jumping bean.

Three men crouched under the pigeonwood tree, holding in their hands the loose ends of the five wires. They watched the backs of the out-wire guards grow smaller in the distance, rechecked the activity further along the beach, then crept out to the twelve-foot security fence.

Three wires were attached by their karabiners immediately, the following two after one man stood on another's shoulders. All five wires were spaced at even intervals up and down the central stanchion pipe of the fence. Those wires sagged back to the pigeonwood, to which the mother wire was bound by a rope.

The men fell flat, wriggling back to the trees. Two rose to run. One stayed by the pigeonwood, breathing hard, holding a small kindling axe. In the distance, the two guards came to a bend in the fence. There they met two more guards, turned about and began to return.

Uphill, the two runners burst out of the undergrowth by the kahikatea.

'Go for it!'

For the second time the chain saw flung a bright spray of sawdust into the forest gloom.

At the beach tree-line, the kindling axe rose and fell once, severing the rope that held the mother wire taut. With the release of the system from the pigeonwood, the five wire fingers tightened with a rattle and clang that travelled the entire length of the fence.

Beads of sweat popped out on Wilson's brow. He leaned forward and retched, filling the Hughes with an acrid smell.

'Already?' Ben was interested. 'Must have been that whiff you had first.' But Wilson's action set a sympathetic reaction going in the rear. 'That stuff is even stronger than I thought. I wish you'd park your tigers in the sick bags. Have some respect.'

'What do you want from us?'

'Information.' He laughed at that, but the irony was lost on Wilson.

'How do we know you'll give us the right quantity of antidote?'

'If you don't tell me, or if you feed me bullshit, I'll tip some Fentaz down your throat when you're unconscious. You'll have the honour of being the first police casualties. Get a medal. Posthumously. You've got rotten teeth, you know that?'

One of the specials in the rear slumped in his seat and crumpled sideways. Wilson retched again.

'You can't . . . not your policy . . . that would give Renwick the excuse to shoot on sight.'

'You haven't got it yet, have you? In a few minutes I'm

hoping he's going to be past waiting for an excuse. Now, this is what I want to know . . .'

'Another course change, sir. Sir, I think they're following the road!'

Renwick snatched the map back in front of him and located their position, glancing at features in the landscape flowing below. He rapped his finger on the paper, allowed two inches further north for the Hughes. Yes, the Hughes was above the road. Another two inches along the map in the same direction was a cross already pencilled on the road line. It had been there before they set out. Wadlow's men.

'It's a coincidence,' Renwick muttered. His eyes met those of the troop leader beside him.

'A fluke,' agreed the troop leader.

The commander stared out at the distant speck, rising and falling. Time, time. Decision time.

'Call!' His hand gripped the pilot's shoulder. 'Call them.'

'Break silence?'

'Quickly. Call Wilson by name only.'

The co-pilot's lips moved next to the helmet mike. Renwick's heart thudded with the rotors. The lips stopped.

'No answer, sir.'

'Again!'

No answer.

'Close in! Close in to two miles. Give me the headset.'

'HQ want you urgently on channel – '

'Tell HQ to wait! Give me the headset! Wilson, this is Renwick. Previous orders relating to transmission are suspended. Acknowledge, acknowledge.' The only reply was the hiss of atmospherics and the silent presence of the listeners in the other Iroquois. Renwick tore the headset off and looked at it. Word spread swiftly among the waiting men.

'Sir. The Hughes is speeding up.'

'Catch them! Full speed!'

'No way, sir. He's got twenty-five knots on these grunters.' The thump of the engine became crisp and deep, the deck tilted. 'No . . . wait . . . we're holding on . . . he's busting a gut doglegging.'

'Maximum speed. Force him down. Force the bastard down.'

'He's still following the road! What's he playing at?'

'Get me Wadlow, hurry up, man.' The headset went on again. 'Reception, this is Blue flight . . . Wadlow . . . You're still waiting for your guest . . . ? Drive, man, drive. South. There's a chopper rescue attempt almost on him. I want him alive, do you hear me? Yes, I said alive! Him and his brother. Move!'

The lieutenant was the first to see the top of the kahikatea begin its gliding arc towards the forest canopy. But it was the sergeant who made the connection with the fan of wires and the fence.

'Down!' he bellowed to the men running along the outside of the wire. 'Down, get down on your faces!' But against the dredge and the swooping siren he could not make himself understood in time.

The central stanchion popped its stays first – an oddly tinny sound. Then the two either side of it, and so on, faster and faster, becoming a toneless discord. The slowest men were catapulted by the fence mesh up into the trees as most of a quarter of a mile of security fence climbed up into the bush canopy.

Ben saw Mal's reception committee barrelling almost directly towards him up a long incline. An instant later he spotted the motorbike, almost vertically below, the two moments separated by a flicker. Blood roared in his head. He hauled the pole sideways, swooping into a braking curve, then ramming the collective down. The helicopter dropped out of the sky like a plastic bottle towards the road in front of Mal.

The Land-rover was topping the rise, cutting corners.

'Hit a brick wall, you bastards!' Mal yelled at them. The three others in the Hughes were unconscious. Wilson had toppled down into the perspex chin.

Fifty feet. He hauled on the collective, his cheeks dragging with G-forces. Thirty. It would be heavy, but then he wasn't going to be flying again, anyway. Fuel-pump off. Electrics off.

The Hughes slammed into the road, breaking a strut. The

rotor tore into the seal on the uphill side as Ben departed on the other. Then he was sprinting downhill towards the braking motorbike, on the wings of a high-pitched Land-rover whine and the swelling thunder of the Iroquois fleet. He pounced on Mal, screaming into his face, somehow noticing how stupid Mal's expression was, hauling him off the machine.

'Run! Run, you fucker. Into the bush or you're dead!'

Lungs sobbing for air, leaden feet crashing through the foliage, stumbling through supplejack, over rotten logs and fungal outgrowths, the canopy thrashing under the green and khaki prowlers. Amongst it all came a faint popping, inconsequential until a piece of branch shattered beside Ben, turning his forearm into a pin cushion. They plunged deeper into the womb-like bush, taking images with them like splinters from a nightmare.

Nineteen

The finest dust motes still drifted in the attic. Moonlight cast them in a tilted column, so bright that the piano keys were clearly visible as Rosa played.

There was one other in the attic. The Australian television reporter Marlene Papps sat cross-legged on the floorboards, afraid to disturb by even the smallest sound the notes of '*Gnossiennes*'. Rosa had played the piece again and again, merging end into beginning, end into beginning into end, changing the interpretation as imperceptibly as the shape of the moonprint creeping towards her across the floor. The sound became hypnotic – an entranceway to Marlene's private moonpool, from which she fished memories of a succession of lovers, women and men. Yes, men – pathetic creatures who demanded performance ratings before departing. And under the hold of the music she pictured Rosa walking towards a common moonpool by a different path, through a forest in which a tiger lay concealed, watching her approach.

When the piano finally stopped, neither woman moved. The cadences continued in Marlene's head for some time. She was astonished by a feeling of spatial disorientation, as if the attic were slipping sideways through the night. She was annoyed. She had let a bit of moonlight get to her, something she could have set up herself with an 800-watt redhead and a sheet of blue gel.

Rosa turned, not at all surprised to see Marlene. She wrapped arms around herself, suddenly feeling the cold.

'It's dark.'

'Sit down and talk to me,' Marlene said.

'But it's dark.'

'That's all right. It's nice up here. Sit with me and let's talk.'

Rosa looked doubtful, but she came, first switching on the stairlight and pushing the door open as wide as it would go.

'You've got a thing about doors, haven't you?' Marlene said. 'And the dark. And dolls, eh? This is the first time I've seen you away from the piano without her. What's her name?'

Rosa spun her head to look at the keyboard where she had left Miska. In a flurry of alarm she jumped up and snatched Miska off the keys. But after a moment she came back.

'I forgot.'

'I've got a doll too.'

'What's her name?'

'His. Androcles.'

'Oh. Mine is Miska.'

They heard Edith Driscoll walking about below. Every now and then she talked out loud, in an argumentative tone. Marlene asked Rosa if her mother had a visitor, but Rosa said no.

'Rosa, was that the bad girl playing the piano before?'

'Yes.'

'Tell me about her.'

'I don't want to talk about *her*.'

'It's all right. I know about bad girls.' And when a look of suspicion crossed Rosa's face, '*I'm* a bad girl, honey. Believe me, I *know*.'

Suspicion changed to surprise. 'You're not!'

Marlene put on a modest grin.

'But you don't get really really mad!' Rosa objected hotly.

'Mad? Angry? Is that . . . ? But I do, honey, I do. I get really really mad sometimes. You should – '

'But that bad girl she gets so mad she wants to smash and smash and smash everything up into tiny pieces and I have to stop her, so she plays the piano and I bet you . . .'

'Hey, hold on.'

'. . . don't laugh too loud like her and cry too loud and get sad and black all the time so the black cat got your tongue in front of other people? You don't do that!'

'Wait, wait on . . . you're stampeding me, honey. What's – '

'You're *not* a bad girl. Nobody is as bad as *her*.'

'You're pretty sure about that, aren't you? What does she get mad about?'

'Things, different things. I don't know.'

'Does she want to hurt someone?'

'Don't say that! Don't talk nasty! I don't want to talk about it! I want to go to bed now.'

'Honey, are you mad at me for talkin' about it?'

'No!' Rosa looked scared.

Marlene Papps found herself at a loss for words for the first time she could remember. She got to her feet in agitation and walked about, waving her hands, trying to pluck what she wanted out of the air, aware that Rosa was watching her, fascinated by this behavioural flair. She paused by the window, looking down at the shadow patchwork of Frazer Creek, wondering how many inhabitants had been outside, listening to the music.

Then she crouched down in front of Rosa. 'You know what? I think that bad girl is really a very, very clever lady.'

'Well, I told you, I don't want to talk about her.'

'But I don't think she knows why she gets mad.'

Rosa considered this.

'No. She doesn't.'

'But if she found out why, she'd stop wanting to smash up everything.'

'No she wouldn't! She doesn't want to find out! I want to go to bed.'

'. . . then she would go away.'
Silence.
Then, 'Go away?'
'And leave you alone.'
Silence.
'And never come back?'
'Never. Would you like me to do that for you?'
Rosa bit her tongue. She gave a cautious nod. Marlene Papps took hold of her hand. 'I'm going to take you to a special doctor who can make your bad girl get out of town . . . but first, Rosa, there's something I want you to do for me.'

Twenty

'Stand by.'

The doors of the Iroquois slid back. The marksman wedged himself in the frame, dangling a leg, the gun loose but ready. Behind him, the descent team attached their lines and crouched, keen-eyed, weapons tucked around them, lines neat. Colin Renwick and his new deputy, Mark Turner, looked over the marksman's shoulder. The double barrel dipped as the Iroquois tipped back, braking; the body of the marksman became heavy, then light. His eyes hunted the gaps between the trees. And found a target.

'There.'

The helicopter tilted again, swooping, levelling, holding.

The first barrel spat with a crack like a stock whip. A miss. The second barrel fired.

'Got 'im.'

In another two seconds the target was out of sight again, hidden by bush. But there was no disappointment in the helicopter. The machine hovered. The specials waited. In under a minute, the target walked back out into the open, clutching its side. It looked up at them, waved to make sure it had been seen, and sank, kneeling, sitting, lying.

'Word has got around,' Renwick observed to Turner. 'That's the beauty of having an intelligent quarry. Knowing that it needs the antidote, it can't wait to get caught.'

The Iroquois moved a few yards. The descent team dropped.

Colin reflected that it had taken him much too long to come to this solution. And even then it had taken Wilson's bungling stupidity to make it obvious. In fact he rather owed Wilson a vote of thanks: in a single mistake, Wilson had both removed himself as a threat to Renwick and provided the winner with a politically acceptable means of capturing Charlie. Not that the man didn't deserve his disgrace; allowing an unarmed pilot to knock out three fully armed passengers without leaving the controls required an astounding degree of incompetence. Wilson, in his hospital bed, didn't see it that way, of course, but Wellington did. Wilson had sown, Wilson had been reaped. Elegant. Poetic. And yet wasted on someone incapable of comprehending the justice of it, let alone the poetry. Such were the absurdities of an indifferent universe.

The first of the descent team appeared next to the quarry, then the others with weapons levelled. The quarry pushed its arms away from its body in a T shape.

'The same chemical as for deer?' Turner asked.

'Exactly the same and absolutely perfect for what we need. Fentanyl citrate and azaperone. Reduces the ability to move, but keeps them conscious.'

'Side effects?'

'The same as for deer, for all mammals I imagine. But it's hardly a problem because human body weight doesn't vary as much. We're only getting the overdose side effects on the really small ones: salivation, a bit of temperature fluctuation, erratic breathing. Searle loves it. They're nicely disoriented when they arrive and he can play doctor to his heart's content. The psychological effects on an informed enemy are fascinating. We've already done away with the beeper. I suspect we could even replace the drug with a placebo and still have them come looking for us.'

'Heh, then you'd have to give them a placebo antidote.'

'True.'

'Which Searle could threaten to withhold.'

Colin smiled thinly. 'You forget the susceptibility of the mind. You'd have them dying on you.'

Below, the descent team was clustered round the lying figure. Fifty yards away, a drift of nearly clear smoke came out of the trees to vanish in the cross-winds generated by the rotors.

'What about shock? I had an enquiry from field ambulance.'

'I've told them already. There's an anti-shock agent in the Fentaz. They should treat themselves for cold feet. I despair of them: they'd be quite happy for us to pump bullets into the moonshiners, rendering most of them worthless for interrogation – but they get twitchy about a humane method that leaves the quarry with no wounds, very little shock and a loose tongue.' He closed his eyes against a waft of pain.

Turner looked concerned. 'You've had that a few days, haven't you?'

'Some.'

'Let me jack up the MO to come over.'

'What the hell are we going to do?'

'It worked perfectly. I don't understand.'

'It didn't bloody work! It was supposed to make 'em mad. It was supposed to push them over the edge! Instead, Renwick's kept them under control by hunting the shiners down like fucking animals and telling the press what a kind humane fella he is!'

There was a gloomy silence, filled only by the burbling of the radio. Every man and woman round the table was swaddled in many layers of clothing. Most necks were scarved, some hands were gloved. Coffee mugs steamed in the murky light.

'You know what this means, don't you? It's only a matter of time before they're in here like robbers' dogs.'

'The shiners don't know where we are.'

'Don't know, my arse. That was the theory. But it's been going on too damn long. There's been too much contact between us and them. I bet half the shiners out there have figured it out just from the positions of the thorium collections.'

'If they don't know for sure, why would they tell?'

'Come off it. You want Ben and Mal to give you another bedtime story about Doctor Smith?'

'All right, all right. But they'd still have to find the entrance.'

'What about today's collection? Cancel?' Moa asked.

'I say no. None of today's group operate where the Iroquois have been in the past two days. And they'll be on their way.'

'Well? What do we do now?'

'You know what we've got to do,' said Short Stop McPhail.

'Christ! It's like cutting off our own hand.'

'This whole campaign has been refined insanity! Noddy and Big Ears ask Mr Plod to rip their arms off in front of Mr Reporter!'

'Please.' Short Stop looked pained. In his multiple layers the fat policeman looked like Tweedledee.

'The rest of it has worked,' Ben said. 'And bloody well.'

'Until now. Until now. Things have changed, or hasn't anyone noticed?' The speaker avoided looking at Mal. Mal wasn't listening anyway. Nor had he opened his mouth except to sip from his coffee mug. When the attention drifted away from him again, he looked from one to the other, trying to pick the leader. Ben? Moa? Floyd? Short Stop? Could be any of half a dozen.

Susan Withers rapped the table.

'What choice is there? Let's do it while we're still a going concern.'

They studied the map before them, on the table of rough-sawn planks with gaps that held stale scraps of food and gobbets of candlewax. The Tilley lamp on the rafter was silent. Light came into the hide-out through corrugated perspex panels in the ceiling. It was a peculiar light, a derivative of natural daylight, but distorted by something above the panels that give it a gloomy, ghost-grey cast. Somewhere, there was a tic of dripping water and occasionally a faraway rumbling.

The walls were windowless, a sweep of irregular planks and exposed studs. On one wall, a series of racks held building equipment, heavy-duty clothing, boots, bows with strings hanging loose and quivers of arrows with brightly coloured flights. A workbench took up a complete wall. Above, a shelf holding several cameras, a chess board and a pack of cards, a vase with a fresh Mount Cook lily, and the radio. Numbers danced on the screen of a small device the shape of a bedroom clock – a frequency scanner. A great deal of clothing hung on wire frames around a pot-bellied stove in the far corner: shirts, socks, bras, balaclavas. The stove was cold. It would not be lit until dark. A single kerosene heater glowed hopelessly in the middle of the room.

One wall was broken by a hatchway to a kitchen, where two people moved back and forth, cooking on kerosene burners. In another wall, doorways to bunkrooms. One of these was closed, but a squeaking sound from inside indicated at least two people who had found a way to keep warm.

The faraway rumbling was suddenly louder, like the sound of an earthquake. But there was no shaking, no movement at all, and no one round the table took any notice. Their voices kept on intertwining, tangling sententiously over the map.

Mal drifted back through three days.

Riding the motorbike.

The helicopter crashing in front of him. Humpty Dumpty on the road. The wild chicken emerges. Any landing you walk away from is a good one. And together they run through the trees. All the King's horses thunder by in a straight line overhead, their breath raking the bush. Running, running with a vice for a chest and leg irons for feet. Running, as neat round holes appear in the leaves and rotten wood shivers, anticipating their boots.

And down.

'Get up!' Ben shouted.

'Rest . . . Got to rest . . . They're not after me . . .'

'Get up! They'll be putting troops in here like carrot seeds!'

'Delusions . . . grandeur, Ben.'

And up. Shuffling, scarcely faster than a walk.

When evening came they risked crossing to the west of the main road, which would not be expected. They recrossed as the light faded, and climbed until darkness bedded them on moss, and wrapped them in fitful, exhausted sleep.

At dawn, Mal wanted to head up into the nearest pass to the east.

'You want to commit suicide?' Ben demanded. 'They'll have spotters there already.'

'They weren't after me until you dragged me into it. Christ, I almost made it! You're your brother's keeper all right, you're my bloody jailor!'

Ben was amazed. 'For someone who's supposed to be a genius, you're doin' okay as a congenital idiot. Bloody good disguise, Mal!'

They stayed together. For three days they crept south through the tortuous contours of the Alps, well below the bush line, taking six hours to avoid exposed ridges they might have crossed in one, avoiding all tracks but those used by deer. Mal found that he had slipped into the soundless heel-and-toe footfall he last used as a teenager.

On the first morning they heard a stag herald the roar, a piercing, rumbling bellow echoing down from a snow-quilted valley above. The first of the rut, pivot of the seasons. The same evening they heard another and saw it on the spur above. Its autumn mane was already shaggy on the swollen neck, feet planted, head thrown back, antler rack tilted at the sullen and bloody sky. It rumbled out a challenge and a series of grunts. Then down from white fields came a proud reply, and the two men pictured in their mind's eye the challenged one, high-stepping through the patchwork snow around his hinds. This was the red deer at its most magnificent. Generations of hunters and mountain men stirred in the two fugitives.

They came to the line of soldiers late on the second morning. A cough, a striking match, the tap of boot on stone, the glint of metal through the trees. Camouflage jacket against bark. It took two hours to establish that the line closed off a natural bottleneck in the journey south, it was planted all the way down a ridge with its toes in an impassable gorge.

'You bastard,' Mal whispered to his brother. 'You *are* the leader, aren't you? You've been stringing me along. What the hell am I doing sticking with you?'

The line was thin, but with no gaps: single men perched silently on rocks or tree roots, each one in sight of two others. Tired men. Bored men.

Some time later, two of the soldiers heard a soft, contented grunting; they heard the scrape of a trotter, a whiffling snout, a snort. High-pitched sounds, suggestive of a suckling pig.

One soldier looked up the ridge at his nearest colleague who mimed chewing on a well-padded bone. So he advanced into the bushes with his SLR held like a club. Thirty yards in, his ears told him that the grunts came from a particular clump of bushes. He crept round the bush. And gave his own grunt as a heavy branch came down on his neck and shoulder muscles. Hands caught him halfway, lowered him to the ground and searched his pockets.

'Nothing.'

'Just our luck,' Ben mouthed furiously. No food, no matches. He picked up the SLR.

In a few moments, the second soldier heard what he'd been waiting for. And then more than he'd been waiting for. First a heavy thump, an animal squeal of pain and rage, then a high-pitched, gasping expletive. He went into the bushes to investigate, and seconds later, in the space the soldiers should have occupied, the two brothers crossed the ridge.

That evening, Ben lured a real pig, a small tusker, to a similar and more permanent fate. He gutted the animal in front of Mal. Mal seemed not to notice; he made himself busy jamming an SLR round into the muzzle of the rifle and working the cartridge free. He sprinkled two-thirds of the powder on kamahi twigs, leaving the rest in the cartridge with a piece of wool torn from his shirt tail. He loaded the cartridge, fired under the densest foliage he could find, then rushed swearing out of the greenery with the smouldering piece of shirt in his fingers. The twigs flared up immediately. They roasted the thinnest possible strips of pork in the quickest possible time, gorging their bellies while listening for unwelcome company.

By moonrise they were five more miles to the south. By midnight, they could see the lights of Frazer Creek as a pale glow on the flat.

On the third day, Ben redoubled the care and slowed the pace. Twice he made Mal go ahead while he waited, hidden, to see if anyone followed. But the only danger was from overhead. The Iroquois swept at maximum speed and minimum height, hiding the sound in the folds of the terrain, appearing almost without warning. The two kept eyes out for foliage mature enough to resist the downdraft.

Finally they came to a stream flowing under a black matai, where they waited hidden and in complete silence for more than an hour before committing themselves.

'Let's go,' Ben grinned.

He stepped out across the stream. At the far edge he pushed through a cluster of karamu, dull red with old berries. Behind the bushes, one of the roots of the matai formed a natural frame for the entrance to a cave.

Mal followed him in, feeling his way blind for many yards, then colliding with him. The echo of the grunt was drawn out, suggesting that the cave had much further to go. Ben was groping about for something up high. Mal heard a matchbox rattle, then orange-yellow light flooded the cave and the flame was transferred to a candle in a tin-can reflector.

Mal could see no end to the cave. The floor remained uneven and unpredictable, but the width increased until they could scramble nearly upright, watching their shadows leap on the walls. A black wire looped along with them: an aerial. A diffuse glow appeared ahead as they turned the corner. First grey-white, then blue-white. It seemed to fill the end of the tunnel with no one part any brighter than any other.

Ben stopped again, reached behind a rock and came out with two sets of crampons.

'Here? Your headquarters are here?'

'Yep.'

'How do you hide a hide-out on the glacier?'

'Not *on* the glacier.'

'I don't believe it.'

'You won't, even when you see it. Get these on.' They stepped into the crampons, tightened the straps and clattered towards the ice. It looked to Mal like a sheer face.

Ben stopped.

'Hang on.'

'What?'

'The others don't know that you're a chicken rather than a hen. Best keep it that way, right?'

Mal reacted without thought. He leapt to grasp his brother's collar, his other fist swinging to strike. But the strike froze as he found the tip of Ben's knife pushing up into the soft flesh under his chin. The two stayed that way, gazes locked by the light of Ben's candle. Mal's fist lowered slowly.

'Why did you bother to rescue me?'

'We need you. We've got too much staked in your head to let you go now.'

'You know, that's about the only reason I could believe.'

Ben shrugged. Mal pushed him away.

The ice was not a sheer face, after all. The rock did butt straight onto the side of the glacier, but a fissure angled uphill from it, a crevasse showing bedrock fifty feet away. As they moved along it, a series of ice caves opened up to either side. In spite of his anger and new hunger, Mal crouched to watch the light play in the ice columns and the water dripping with its resonant echoes. Above, the light was blue and white, but as they moved on and the depth of the ice increased, the blue vanished and the white came through like cold charity.

Water trickled faster around them.

'Damn,' Ben said. 'It's raining. Hurry it up; in a moment it's going to get pretty noisy.' As he spoke, there was a rumbling which seemed to come from all directions at once.

'What is it?'

'The glacier gets its skates on in the wet. We're heading into a place where all the little sounds get magnified by the shape of the bedrock. It's one of the disadvantages of the neighbourhood.'

They came out in a natural amphitheatre between the side of the base of the glacier and the mountain rock: a space behind a natural lip, protected from the flow of ice. Overhead, the roof was ice, a great, upside-down slope of it. The floor was greywacke rock and the whole space of the cavern was big enough to hold a house.

Which it did. The construction was like that of a Park Board hut, but twice the size, with a chimney and transparent panels in the roof.

'Welcome to the Cooler,' Ben said.

They moved down onto the rock floor, and began to remove their crampons.

'Move and I'll take your heads off,' a voice informed them.

'It's rude to point, Johnno.'

'Ben . . . ! And Mal . . . !' John Taylor's face was one huge grin. He laid a shotgun down, grabbed Ben's hand and clapped Mal's shoulder. 'Renwick's had half the army out for you two. Wasn't to invite you to a party either. Mal, you're a bit of a celebrity, mate. You . . .'

The rest of the words were lost as the ice boomed. It was like all the earthquakes Mal had dreamed of, rolled into one vast sound so deeply pitched that the human body seemed to take part in the vibration. The showdown between the immovable object and the unstoppable force, faithfully transmitted by the ice. Mal reeled, clutching at the nearest rock for support, only to find, to his incredulity, that nothing was moving.

Ben and John Taylor were laughing. After a while he heard them.

'Always gets you like that the first time,' Taylor said.

'Suffering Jesus.' Mal's senses adjusted to the fact that it was possible to stand.

Then a door had opened in the side of the hideaway, with people and hands to welcome them in. Within minutes, they'd been eating fresh-baked bread with butter, a plate of hot beans and mugs of steaming chocolate. The last thing Mal had noticed as they led him to a bunk was the air of tension. He'd wanted to ask why, to know before he dared to rest, but his head touched the pillow and fell through into sleep.

Now he sat with them, listening to the arguing voices while the radio muttered in the background.

There was little progress to their arguments, he noticed. They seemed to be tripping over their own anxiety. Now and then they glanced at him, puzzled – by his silence perhaps. But they didn't press him to contribute. Which was itself puzzling. They were uncomfortable with him for a reason he couldn't fathom. Only once did the tension give way. The sounds from the couple in the bedroom were just increasing in frequency and intensity when the glacier spoke again. The thunderous roar resounded for a full minute, drowning all argument at the table then stopping as suddenly as it had started. Which allowed those at the table to hear a voice from the bedroom.

'Oh Hamish, Hamish, tell me that was you.'

'I think the earth moved for them,' Moa said enviously.

The radio gave the hourly bird call – the skirl and boom of the kakapo, once thought to be extinct. Moa turned up the news.

"In Westland, the counter-terrorist unit has made significant progress in its hunt for the Little Red Hen organisation. Two more arrests of the so-called moonshiners have brought the total to eight. A spokesman for the unit says they're now following a strong lead in narrowing down the location of the hide-out."

'Doesn't mean a thing,' Moa said.

'Damn them. Notice how they call us terrorists now and how our headquarters has become a hide-out.'

'They think we're about finished.'

"In the meantime, New Zealand's biggest manhunt since the search for Stanley Graham has failed to locate the leader of the terrorists – "

Ben switched it off.

'Waste of bloody time,' he growled. 'Why didn't we get a shortwave set in and get some news that tells us something we don't know.'

Twenty-One

The following day, a Saturday, a thirteen-ton outside-broadcast van cruised into Frazer Creek. With heavy-breathing pneumatics, it pulled up at the south wall of the pub. Behind it came two hired station wagons and a light furniture truck, all filled with equipment and people. The personnel began to unload: sound gear, light stands, in-house monitors, cameras. Thick cables were run out of the van and in through the windows of the bar. The pub's front door came off its hinges to allow passage to the biggest of three cameras.

Locals drifted in to watch. No OB van had ever been through Frazer Creek that anyone could remember, let alone set up for a show. Josie Meers remembered seeing one up in Hokitika, years back, when the producer of a show called *That's Country* hired locals to sit their bumpkins on bales and chew straw.

The outside of the van said 'PACIFICA BROADCASTING'. But the people giving the orders and doing all the talking to Harry Withers spoke with didgeridoo twangs. Another Australian, Marlene Papps, joined them briefly, only to return to the Driscolls' house.

The onlookers waited for Harry to come near.

'How you goin', Harry?'

'Gidday, Bill.'

'Busy, are ya?'

'Yeah. Am a bit pushed.'

'Find out about you, did they?'

'Maybe, maybe not . . .'

'Course, your private life is between you and them Sunday papers.'

'Look, I'm not supposed to say, right?'

'Ah. Sure, Harry. We can understand that.'

And they did. It meant that the Aussies were planning to produce Rosa Driscoll in person. Which also meant that someone had found a way to get her to perform on demand. That swanky blonde Australian reporter. Through the window the locals saw that very few of the tables and stools were being moved. Lights were being set up not just for the piano but the whole bar.

'When's it all happen, Harry?'

'Can't say, Jack. You know how it is . . . You coming in for an ale tonight? Could be a round or two on the house.'

'Yeah, might drop in for a couple at that.'

Westlanders will bet on anything that moves, or doesn't move, as long as the results carry a sporting uncertainty. Within minutes, the going rate was five to one that the specials would close down the production before it began. And there were side permutations on the specials' method of choice: a legal technicality, intimidation of a key broadcaster or by an open show of force, interference through one of the relay stations – though the bottom fell through the odds on this last one when it emerged that OB vans had their own recording facilities on board and would not have to depend on state-controlled equipment. Any lingering doubts on that score were settled when the crew began to assemble a satellite dish on the shingle outside the pub.

Another ripple went through the odds when onlookers noticed that two of the television men seemed to have no particular job but walking round the pub and the van with walkie-talkies in their hands.

An electronic news camera was plugged directly into a panel in the van's side.

Just after midday a Land-rover turned into the park. One of the guards lifted his walkie-talkie and spoke into it. Within five seconds the Australian producer was outside the van. He locked it behind him and waited, clipboard in hand while the news cameraman stood ready, watching the Land-rover full of specials watching him.

Inspector Turner left the Land-rover and walked towards the producer. A small red light on the news camera winked on. Turner stopped.

'Switch that thing off.'

The light stayed on.

Turner's glance followed the cables from the camera to the van to the satellite dish. He turned to the producer, placing himself so that the camera couldn't see his face.

'I'm going to give you just . . .' He stopped talking here because a microphone the size of a salami appeared next to his shoulder. At the same time, the producer shifted ground, bringing the officer's profile round to the camera. Turner moved again to counter the ploy, but this move allowed him to see through the window of the van to where several screens were filled with images of himself.

'You were going to give us something,' the Australian producer prompted him.

And the new deputy commander of the specials turned on his heel, returned to the Land-rover and was driven away.

The odds shifted again.

Edith Driscoll didn't leave the house any more because she kept seeing people and cameras even when there were none. She was even more confused when it came time to do the Saturday morning shopping, handing Rosa the groceries list then delivering a warning not to go outside. Marlene Papps offered to go. But Rosa wouldn't be stopped and the two left the house together with Edith watching through the kitchen window like a caged bird. As they went down the hill, Marlene kept looking up and down the road.

At the store counter, Tom Kidmann slipped two Mars Bars into Rosa's bag and nodded at the doll.

'One for your friend.'

'Marlene is my friend, too,' Rosa said hopefully.

Kidmann laughed and looked enquiringly at the reporter, but Marlene was by the door, looking out through the glass. He handed the bag to Rosa.

'Haven't seen your mum for days, Rosa. She usually drops in for a chat. Is everything all right?'

'Yes, thank you,' Rosa said politely. And she added, 'Sometimes Mum does funny things.'

'Does she?'

'Yes. She talks to my dad but he's buried in the cemetery now. Do you know where Mal is?'

Tom Kidmann mentally halved the total on the cash register, and handed over the resulting change. Lately he had become impulsively generous and unpredictably weepy. With a furtive glance at the Australian reporter, he mumbled to Rosa, 'Play your heart out tonight, Rosa. We're all with you. You show 'em. You show the bastards.'

'But *I'm* not going to do it . . .'

'Pull finger, Rosa.' Marlene was still peering out the door.

Rosa leaned closer and whispered conspiratorially. '. . . It's the bad girl. After she gets mad on the piano again, Marlene's going to make her go away.' Rosa stood for a moment longer, looking puzzled about something. Then she said goodbye and departed with Marlene.

'The bad girl,' Kidmann repeated to himself. And finding himself weepy again, he disappeared out the back, leaving the shop empty.

Outside, Marlene bustled Rosa back along the street.

'Where's Mal now?' Rosa asked.

'I still don't know, honey. I'm sorry.'

Further along, Rosa slipped a hand shyly into Marlene's. But the reporter removed it, placing it instead through the crook of her arm. 'Like this, honey. Best not to give people the wrong idea.'

When the knock came, Colin transferred an array of bottles, a set of pipettes and a book from his desk to his top drawer.

'Come.'

'Williams, sir. Field Ambulance.' The MO carried a surgery bag.

'Ah.'

'You wanted to see me.'

'Yes. Yes, so I did.' He rubbed his eyes.

'Perhaps if you tell me the symptoms . . .'

'Of course. Of course. Sorry. Not enough sleep.' He described the persistent nausea, the headaches, the mouth ulcers and inflamed gums. The lethargy and loss of hair.

'If you wouldn't mind stripping to your waist, sir.' Colin drew the curtains and removed his upper clothing, sitting on the edge of the desk. His shoulders felt somehow more rounded without the uniform. While the MO went through the checks, he kept his spine stiff.

'Deep breaths, sir.'

Colin scratched an itch on his chest. He could hear the indistinct mutter of a radio news programme through the wall from control. Everyone was obsessed with the news. As if they couldn't trust the reality it grew from. He was a little tired of the cynics and beginning to find the one about not counting your hens until they've been catched distinctly unamusing.

'Say ahhh . . . So you've almost got them, then,' the MO said conversationally.

'We hope so, Captain.' He scratched his left wrist. Confounded itch. 'Well, what's wrong with me?'

'I don't know, frankly. It could be a stress reaction.'

'Rubbish. I've had stress reactions. I get asthmatic.'

'Yes, well I'd like to see you have a blood test anyway. In the meantime, a course of iron wouldn't do you any harm. And a mild tranquilliser.'

'What? What are you trying to imply?'

'Imply? Nothing at all, sir.'

'I don't need a tranquilliser.'

'It's a standard prescription. Doesn't inhibit performance and it'll help you sleep if nothing else.'

'Take your blood sample, and find out what's really wrong with me.'

'I haven't the facilities, sir. You'll have to go up to Greymouth.'

'At a time like this? Out of the question. It'll have to wait until this whole thing has been cleared up. Thank you for coming, Captain, don't call me, I'll call you.'

He locked the door behind the MO, dressed, yanked the curtains back around the bay window so that the brass runners all slammed together. Last night he had dreamed that his track had begun to turn. The straight railway line had become a great circle, and the jigger was picking up speed.

He brought out the book, the pipettes and bottles from the top drawer. He opened the book *Soviet Corrective Psychiatry*, donned rubber gloves, then began to work, sucking precise amounts into the pipettes from bottles labelled Fentaz, Aminazin, Triffazin and Heliperidol. Each time, he held the liqud with a forefinger on top of the pipette, then released it in a trickling stream into a bottle with no label.

Twenty-Two

The Prime Minister was in no mood to waste time with preliminaries.

'Your Renwick has a remarkable talent for invoking Murphy's Law then finding an escape clause for himself! Tell me how he's going to wriggle out of this one.' He thrust the latest telex at the Brigadier. Communications between the New Zealand and Australian premiers was now via the media.

> With the Black-and-Greys now closing in on Westland's terrorists, an international row has flared over the Australian television production team in Frazer Creek. The Prime Minister has accused the Australian government of masterminding interference in our internal affairs, while his counterpart across the Tasman, Bob Chrighton, says any further molestation of Australian press going about what he calls its lawful activities will be the knife that severs what remains of trans-Tasman trade.

The Brigadier shook his head. 'On this one, Renwick's hands are tied, surely.'

'You're beginning to sound like a broken record.'

'If someone in uniform or a short haircut so much as looks at that van, his eyeballs are monitored in Australia. Renwick is waiting on direction from here, sir.'

'Just as he sat back and waited for the woman to achieve this ridiculous status. Damn it, do I have to do the man's spelling for him?'

'Prime Minister, the pressures on him . . . !'

'There are pressures and pressures – I hear he has a soft spot for the woman.'

The Brigadier digested the implications of this without comment. No such information had crossed his desk. Nor had the media caught wind of it. Ergo, someone was reporting direct to the PM from Frazer Creek. He knew he should not be surprised that there was someone watching the watchers, but it was unpleasant to have it confirmed in such a manner. There were civilised ways of going about these things.

The PM looked bleakly at the pile of papers on his desk, of which two-thirds was about Westland. On top, the latest copy of *Woman's Weekly* carried Rosa Driscoll as the cover girl. The syndicated Bromhead cartoon showed himself in a restaurant being served with a roast 'W' from a weathervane; the waitress was carrying a doll and a burning wick protruded from the 'W'.

Outside, a lone drunk wandered across parliament grounds from the cenotaph.

'Renwick has forty-eight hours to find the terrorists.'

'That may be all he needs. He's very close.'

'He'd better be. You have the same deadline.'

The Brigadier knew there was little point in protesting. The replacement would already have been primed. Well, Renwick should have it all in the bag within the time limit. But when this was over, there were a few people in his department who would need rationalising.

'Yes, Prime Minister.'

'And it would be most unfortunate if the Driscoll woman gave her performance tonight, don't you agree?'

Twenty-Three

On the shelf behind Annie's Peak, the Collector came out from the trees. He was nervous.

'Everyone here?'

'Ah, what about Smithy . . . ?' The moonshiners looked around. 'Nope, Smithy's to come.'

'Shit. Who saw him last?'

'I guess I did.'

'How long ago?'

'Can't be more than four hours. His tub's not far.'

Unhappily, the Collector looked up in the air, in the direction the ugly Iroquois would come if they came.

'All right, let's be having yer then. Make it snappy. This job gives me the shits . . .' He opened his satchel.

As the second moonshiner presented his bag for inspection, one of the old timers stood up and peered into the bushes. The others fielded this new tension immediately.

'What's the matter with you?'

'Listen.'

'Don't hear a damn thing.'

'You catch on quick,' the old moonshiner said, hoisting his pack. No birds, no rustlings. Nothing.

With swift and almost silent chaos, men snatched up their bags of refined thorium and their packs.

'Stop where you are!' shouted an amplified voice. A score of specials burst out of the uphill bushes in two ranks, the front ten with levelled shotguns.

Westlanders may occasionally have sold short on the first ten commandments, but they've always made up for this on the eleventh – though shalt not get caught. Every shiner in the glade dived for the downhill bushes, only to find another line of specials waiting with more shotguns. The adapted shotguns cracked, plunger darts buried their needles in backs and legs. One of the women went down with a dart in her calf muscle and sat staring at it as if it was something beyond her comprehension.

Thirteen were hit. Most pulled the darts out of themselves and crawled, ashen-faced, back onto the shelf to wait for the antidote while icy fingers flopped through their veins. Eight escaped, crashing away down a slope that might have killed them had they not been on the wings of the eleventh.

'Hey, look at this!' Two specials stood laughing over their prize captive. The Collector was face down on the grass near the hopper, groping miserably at his buttock, which sported a hypodermic dart. The troop leader stood over the captive and grinned down at him.

'You ain't gonna believe how pleased the commander'll be to see you.'

In fifteen minutes the Iroquois fleet was overhead, darkening the shelf. A line dropped out of one and Colin Renwick descended, followed by Kevin Searle with a small suitcase clipped to his belt.

'It's got to be brought forward.'

'There's no way it can be brought forward. We can't get hold of a delayed flash any earlier.'

'Where's Harvey? Why isn't he back?'

'Don't be so damn jumpy,' Ben rapped. 'What's ten minutes?'

'What about a distress flare? Fired on the way back out?'

'No way,' Moa growled. 'There's going to be a vapour trail back to the machine as it is. You'd be picking pieces of me out of Milford Sound.'

'So wait till you're further away.'

'With a flare? You can't hit a barn door at two paces with a flare. Anyway, if I'm going to be shot at, I'm not having anything like that aboard after petrol and LPG. It's enough of a risk turning the motor over, damn it. And yours truly isn't coming in for a second run, I can tell you.'

'For crying out loud! It's not safe *here* any more. Somebody make a decision.' Short Stop glared at Mal, hugging his greatcoat tighter round him; the Cooler seemed more like a freezer every minute.

Mal had worked out the meaning of these looks and glances. There was only one explanation that made any kind of sense, though even that one strained at the edges of his credibility. The sheer enormity of it kept him here in the midst of the bickering, unsure what to do. No response seemed adequate.

The radio gave the boom of the kakapo.

"At three o'clock, the national news. The Prime Minister has accused his Australian counterpart of aiding and abetting terrorism . . ." As the item progressed, Mal stood, moving nearer the radio as if to hear it more clearly. Ben's eyes followed him.

"Westland's police have confirmed that the alleged leader

of . . ." Ben's hand came out towards the switch. Mal's grip closed on it like a vice. ". . . the terrorists, Malachy O'Hara, is still at large in spite of the most intensive manhunt in New Zealand's history. He and his brother, also believed to be a key member of the terrorists, are now believed to have reached the gang's hide-out in the South Westland mountains.

"And still with Westland . . . the radioactive substance cobalt 60, stolen from Christchurch Hospital six week ago . . ."

'Anyone listening?' Mal said, choking on his words. 'Shall I turn it off now?'

He did so anyway.

Guilt. Writ large on all the dumb faces watching him. Half a dozen people came out of the bunkrooms leaving packs half filled and he watched the guilt sweep across their faces too. Now that it was out in the open, an icy calm came to him.

'That was how you got out so quickly,' he said to Ben. 'You told them . . . You told them I was your leader.'

'No. No, I didn't, you've got to believe me. They worked that out for themselves. I had to tell them I could lead them straight into the hide-out so I could get to you. It was the only way to save you.'

'They worked it out?' Mal's laugh was like a crow cawing. 'They worked it out?'

Ben wouldn't look him in the eye. But Moa did.

'It's true. You *were*.'

'I what?'

'You were the boss. You still are.'

'I must be going insane. I'm not hearing this.'

'You've got to understand, Mal. It was the perfect answer. We knew they were going to torture whoever they got their hands on. We knew some of us wouldn't be able to hold out. We had to have a leader, a figurehead, who didn't know he was the leader . . . something for the lips to say . . . so that . . .' He trailed off.

Susan Withers completed it.

'Mal, you weren't to know, so that when they finally got round to you, your . . . your innocence would free you. And all their time to that point would have been wasted. You were the obvious choice. You must see that.'

Mal was glassy-eyed.

Moa grinned bitterly. 'Trouble was, your baby brother nearly stuffed it up. Showed you a bit much. Let family squabbles get in the way, didn't you Ben?'

Ben was looking at Mal speculatively, tauntingly. Mal knew what was coming, but it was Moa who asked.

'The thing is, we need you right now. It was your idea that got things working for us in the first place. We need you to complete the job. You know why. We're nearly stuffed and we still haven't pushed them over the edge.'

A shiver passed through Mal.

'Is this where I'm supposed to thank you?' he asked. 'You chew people up, use the juices to fuel the cause, then spit them out, eh? And you complain about Big Brother in Wellington. He could learn a thing or two from you lot. You got yourselves into this, get yourselves out. And you know why? Because you used me and you didn't fucking say please.'

'Ah,' Ben said, 'I think I understand. It's just like what you did to Rosa, isn't it?' And his eyes said *To save your precious self-esteem.*

Mal shook his head violently. He hauled the nearest crampons and iceaxe from the rack and made for the door.

'Where do you think you're going?' Ben mocked. 'Frazer Creek? Say hi to Renwick for me.'

'You can't leave us like this, Mal,' Susan pleaded.

'Try me,' he snarled, and in a minute they heard his boots echoing in the cavern.

The rug hook performed a tight, elliptical orbit, taking on the next white strand of wool. It dived into the base webbing, through and up, paused for the twirl, slid back and out, leaving the strand anchored. Through and up, twirl and slide. Rosa paused, delighted with the vivid white of the milk in the picture. The milk was complete. The fawn was complete, even down to the speckles. The background was nearly done. But the girl holding the bottle still lacked arms. Ah, and she hadn't yet worked out what colour to put in the empty part of the bottle.

The hook began again, deft, flying in and out of the webbing, making it slide about on the table.

'What's the hurry?' Marlene wanted to know, chin propped on elbows.

'I just like doing it fast.'

'That girl. Is that you?'

'No. It's a girl. Any girl.'

'Can I have some tea, now?' Edith called petulantly from the divan, as if she had asked twenty times before.

'I'll get it,' Marlene offered.

'Can I have some *tea* now?'

'I'll get it right away, Mrs Driscoll. I'll get you some too, Rosa.' On the way to the kitchen, she checked that the doors were locked.

'Get me the *tea* now!' Although sitting, Edith's knuckles were clamped round her walking stick. Her knitting lay untouched beside her.

In five minutes, Marlene was back with three mugs, milk, sugar and a steaming pot on a tray. She stopped in the doorway, unnerved that nothing had changed. It was as if she had stepped out of a photograph then back into it – Rosa hunched feverishly over the rug, the old lady still and staring like death. Marlene poured. 'Here's your tea, Mrs Driscoll.'

'You're a good girl, Rosa.'

Marlene straightened. Outside, the sun was low over the roofs of Frazer Creek, shade stretched its fingers across the tree tops. Three more hours. Maybe she could get Rosa to cook the meal. She went back to the table. The doll had slipped sideways in its chair, so she reached over to straighten it.

'Don't!' Rosa said sharply.

'No? I was just – '

'I don't want you to touch her!'

'Oh. Sure. So who gets to touch Miska?'

'Nobody.'

'Not even Mal?'

'Nobody!'

Marlene squelched a pang of resentment, trod the room, stopped and came back. 'You were mad at me just now.'

The rug hook froze. 'No I wasn't.'

'I haven't seen you get mad before.'

'No I wasn't! I wasn't mad!' Rosa snapped.

'Hey, hey, it's all right, honey. I'm sorry. Of course, it was the bad girl. I just didn't see she was there.' Idiot, idiot! She would blow the whole damn thing if she overdid the helpful bit. Christ, she could kiss goodbye to Channel 10 if Rosa backed out tonight.

'So much noise,' Edith quavered. The look on her face made the back of Marlene's neck prickle. Marlene went to the back door and looked out, returned, paced about, picked up the phone and asked for the assigned number of the OB van.

When it was answered she dropped her voice.

'It's Marlene Papps. Is Vic there? Yes, put him on . . . Vic, can you get a camera up here? Nothing's happening. I want a crew up here and outside the door so nothing *keeps* happening . . . No . . . Call it feminine intuition, Vic, ever heard of that . . . ? Okay, God, five minutes. Okay, thanks a million, sweetie.'

She put the phone down, breathing deep.

There was a knock on the back door.

Marlene blanched, uttering an expletive she usually reserved for inadequate men.

'Don't answer it.'

'It's Tui,' Rosa said, recognising the knock. 'I'll get it.'

'No! Let me.' Marlene reached the door first. Tui Jackson was standing on the step like a stork, right foot in left hand. Rosa came up beside Marlene. 'Do you want to come to my house?' Tui said to her. 'My dad found a funny bit of tree root in the bush.'

'She can't,' Marlene said.

'I want to,' Rosa said and jumped down to join Tui.

'Wait, Rosa. It's not a good idea. What about tonight?'

'There's plenty of time. I want to go to Tui's place!' Rosa scowled.

Marlene swore again and glared at Tui. 'How far is your house, little girl?'

'It's there.' Tui pointed to the house next door.

'Oh, thank Christ. All right. But I'm coming with you. Let's make it quick.' Rosa remembered that she had forgotten Miska again and brought her from inside. Then Tui Jackson skipped up the path to the road and once out on the shingle, she and Rosa held hands.

The four men in balaclavas were out of the trees and among them so swiftly that Marlene barely comprehended the materialisation of her fears. A fist to her solar plexus dropped her to the road, where she struggled to haul breath into her lungs. With vision blurred by terror, she saw Rosa bundled away. Much later, she would remember again and again her last glimpse of Rosa's face as it vanished into the trees. How white it was. How drawn. Most of all, she would remember that Rosa made no sound at all.

Tui Jackson, untouched, burst into howls for her mother and pounded the last few yards to her home.

Mal's thoughts began to ambush him with tricks to make him stop and rest. The current trick was a desire to see if his tracks in the snow were straight. He remembered a fragment from his early twenties, when his born-again grandfather tried to press him into going with him to church. Imagine, his grandfather said, that there are two men out in the snow, both of them trying to make a straight set of tracks. The man who looks back at his own tracks and uses them as a guide will make a crooked path; but the man who sets his sight on a fixed point far ahead will have tracks straight as an arrow.

Mal didn't need to look at the snow behind. The sentinel rocks of Callery Saddle were dead ahead. He laughed, just to hear a human sound; but it came out brittle in the wide, white expanses and vanished like a cloud of ice crystals on the wind.

The crampons swung on his back, prodding him at each step. His hand was freezing round the iceaxe, his feet filling with lead. If he didn't get over the saddle and down to a lower altitude smartish, he could look forward to frostbite for company.

A helicopter passed high overhead, the sound crisp and clean off the snow. A civilian craft. A Bell. Not that he really cared any more. In fact he had rather invited a shaker and dice into this game by choosing Callery Saddle; he could have traversed further north, down the Gunn and up the Perth, and been certain of a clear pass.

Behind and below, the narrow Westland plain was haze-veiled. He spared it barely a glance; it held nothing more for him.

The snow had an even consistency, allowing him to rest some of his strength in the hypnotic rhythm of the step. Push and roll, heel and toe; each time, a puff of snow jumped on the wind stream. As he neared the pass, the wind gathered strength, rushing past him through the gap, pushing him more and more eagerly to where he wanted to go. The powder thinned out, lifting away from his boots in cunning wisps, exposing bare ice. The sun wrapped itself in a white greatcoat and gave no warmth.

Sometimes, he lowered his eyelids, walking in an orange, pulsing dark.

Opening his eyes after one such interlude, he saw an odd lump on top of one of the sentinel rocks. And as he drew closer, the shape became recognisably human; it grew a face that watched his approach.

Mal stopped beside the rock, leaning his shoulder against it. The view down into the Whataroa was stunningly beautiful with great blocks of dazzling white dropping away to a mountain tarn, then to the deep green bush. But sometimes the view was obscured, because the wind moaned by him carrying powder and dropping it as a fine mist.

'You nearly made it, Mal,' said the lump of rock.

'You're wrong, Ben. I *have* made it. You can't stop me this time.'

'*I'm* not going to stop you.'

Well back, on a shelf sheltered from the wind, the blades of Moa's helicopter turned slowly. Ben came down the rock closer to Mal to make himself heard more easily against the wind.

'There's something you have to know, Mal. They've got Rosa. They've taken her into the mountains.'

Mal kept looking down into the Whataroa.

'Where in the mountains?'

'They've got her in a hut.'

'Which one?'

'Mal . . . Mal . . . You know it's not as easy as that.'

Mal's lips curled back. He crashed his fist into the side of the rock and howled his rage. 'Jesus Christ, leave me alone!'

The last patrol crouched. Its leader signalled.

Ready.

Sixty keen-eyed men watched for Renwick's signal. But he made them wait: the army support unit was still moving into position on the ridge. He traversed the ridge with his binoculars to see if he could detect their movement. To his satisfaction he saw none.

Only he and Turner could see the bushes that hid the entrance to the Cooler. A light sun shower fell, hardly more than mist. It dampened the rocks in the streambed and gave sharply defined edges to the sunbeams that reached the bush floor. Behind him, a rifle butt showed here and there, a pair of crampons, a dulled boot, a blackened face.

A sound intruded: groaning. He made a furious signal. There was a thump and the groaning ceased.

An army officer wriggled through the bushes, tapped Renwick's arm and gave a thumbs-up. Army back-up ready. The army had strict orders not to come beyond the entrance unless called. They had pleaded to be in on the kill on the grounds that their mountain training made them the logical spearhead. Thin, considering that most of the specials were ex-army; in any case nothing, nothing could have persuaded the specials to relinquish the opportunity and the army knew it.

Turner was looking at him enquiringly. Still nursemaiding him.

Are you all right?

I'm fine.

He turned, jerked his head. The sunbeams flickered as three score men glided forward across the streambed.

'Your two and up three.' A five-dollar note slid across the table to feed kitty – a cluster of coins and notes next to an unopened brandy bottle. The bottle gleamed seductively in the light from the open door.

'He's at it again. Take him down, Wellsey.'

Sergeant Wells considered it, then plucked a five from his supply.

'And two more.'

A fan of cards fell on the tin sheet that surfaced the table. 'I'm out. Who dealt this shit?'

They were distracted by the woman's voice. Rosa Driscoll was sitting by the fireplace, looking at the flames and black billies on mounds of ash, talking to her doll. They went back to their game.

The hut was a forestry service construction of the old type, colloquially known as Dirty Dick's. It was true to its name and it was dingy. The one tiny window was cracked and layered with spider web, letting in almost nothing of the afternoon sun. Wide open, the door was little better. Candles were already spitting in reflectors made of old tin cans, giving enough light to make out the grime and grease of years, the bag of long shrivelled onions hanging from a rafter, the mice droppings in the spilt flour along the wall.

The bunks were torn sugar sacks hanging in four by two frames, scattered with loose pages of girlie magazines. A faded, out-of-date, topographical map of Mount Cook and Westland national parks was nailed to the wall, next to a magazine photograph of the old parliament buildings. Someone had scrawled a message on the photograph: If the government is the answer it must have been a bloody silly question. Another hand had applied an addendum: So why are you freeloading in a government hut?

The fireplace was made of round stones taken from a nearby creek. The smoke preferred to exit by the door rather than the chimney, not an unusual phenomenon in the old-style huts – the advantage being that it makes the huts unfit for sandflies and mosquitoes.

The three men at the table, and the fourth on guard outside, were resentful. The last radio message had recalled the second troop hidden around the clearing, but had ordered themselves to stay with the bait. And there had been no radio contact since. Which meant that Charlie's hide-out had been found, that they were being left out of the party, and that this trap had been a total waste of time. They were also bored. Their one diversion since arriving had been the discovery of a possum up an abandoned sluice pipe. Half a cup of white spirits and a match had brought it out of the pipe like a fireball out of a cannon.

Their weapons were slung on nails near the door.

As Rosa looked into the flames, a mouse rattled along the wall, turning into the fireplace and making a dash for freedom along the cold ash at the outer edge. It vanished through a crack in the mortar. Rosa kept rocking, murmuring to Miska.

'Two pair, ace high,' Foster said.

'Full house. Give us the IOU back.' Chuckling, Wells pulled kitty towards him and ripped up the note proffered by the disgusted Foster. Then he reached for the brandy bottle, bringing approving grunts from the others.

'Thought you'd never get round to it, Wellsey.'

'They've forgotten about us. Get the champagne glasses, Foz.'

Foster brought enamel mugs from the window sill as Wells slid the cork from the bottle. He noticed that the woman was no longer looking at the fireplace, but at them. He sat as Wells rubbed his hands in anticipation.

'How you havin' it? Straight, or by itself?'

'Make mine neat.'

Foster jerked his head in the direction of the fireplace. 'Must be your charmin' smile, Wellsey.'

The others looked at Rosa.

'Whatchyou starin' at?' Foster demanded.

Rosa didn't seem to hear. Foster shrugged and the men wet their lips reverently on the red-gold liquid. But after a while the staring from the fireplace irritated him.

'I said, whatchyou starin' at?'

No answer. The stare continued as the three men ran their eyes over her. Sergeant Wells took a nonchalant sip of brandy.

'You know what? I think this poker needs a bit of spicing up.'

Not long after the advance troop reached the opening to the cavern, the singing began. A tuneless, drunken voice quavered from the hide-out, quivering with discordant echoes. Bloody secret weapon, the men of the advance troop mouthed to each other. They backed out of sight, removed their crampons, preparing to go in. Colin Renwick pushed his way through.

'It's *her*,' he breathed to Turner. 'Englefield.'

'. . . Forgive me Delilah, I just can't take any more . . .'

The men grinned again. 'We should wait till she gets to the bit about breaking down the door.'

Renwick peered round the edge of the ice, trying to see the hide-out more clearly in the half-light. Suddenly he turned to his deputy.

'Does it bother you that the chimney is going? Pouring smoke up round the ice in broad daylight?'

'Shit.'

Swiftly, Hicks' troop fanned out into the rocks on the cavern floor, straining eyes for booby traps. Stone's men followed, then Williams', threading out to encircle the windowless structure, looking for hidden exits. Four men with HKs and full magazines stationed themselves opposite the door.

'No gas,' Renwick ordered. 'We go straight in.' Two men returned cans of CS triple chaser to their pouches.

Alpha patrol used a Remington to open the door.

Nora Englefield was sitting against the wall, in the middle of the biggest sherry binge of her life. When the dark shapes burst in with weapons levelled, she laughed in a careless, relieved way, holding out the flagon.

'Too late, me fine boyos,' she cackled, but tears of self-pity welled as the specials formed a semi-circle round her; she realised through the alcoholic haze that these men had been waiting a long time and she was all they had.

As the first boots connected, Renwick was pulling them off.

'Get off! Get away!' he bellowed.

They backed away very slowly, leaving her already unconscious. The men looked at Renwick in a strange manner, as if they didn't know him. He knew then that if they detected even the smallest crack in his own self-control, he would lose them.

'Throw some water over her. We need her tongue. Look for records, anything written, starting with the fire. Destroy nothing. Leave it like this for the photographers.'

He stalked the room while they did his bidding, using his presence to assert his authority, clamping down hard on his roiling nausea. He saw the frequency scanner with its numbers still dancing up and down the scale, the radio with its valves smashed, the rack of bows and arrows, still full. The huge poster of a Rhode Island hen. And a piece of paper tacked to a bunkroom door proclaiming: 'THE RED HEN AWARD FOR IMPECKABLE TIMING GOES TO . . . HAMISH AND SERENA.'

A chess board had been carefully arranged on the table. All of the black pieces, including the king, were boxed up in one corner by the white pawns. The pawns were the only white pieces on the board. Colin was irritated – more than anything else by the fact that the arrangement could not have been reached under chess rules. The irritation added to the fingers raking his stomach.

He watched a wad of papers come out of the pot-belly stove, in flames. They'd been thrust into the fire without being separated first. Stone opened up the wad.

'Sir! Have a look at this.'

The first sheet, blackened round the edges, showed a crude freehand outline of a beach, with indecipherable markings. Colin peeled it away and scrutinised the next. Then more, one by one; and they began to reveal a pattern.

Against the wall on the other side of the room, Sergeant Wadlow was slapping Nora Englefield's cheeks, attempting to wake her, when he noticed a piece of brown paper inside her coat. He let her head fall and inspected the paper. It had clearly been intended to wrap a parcel for the post, but had been rejected for use because of a mistake in the spelling. The addressee was Chief Superintendent Colin Renwick. Wadlow took a hard look at the woman, then brought the paper across the room towards the commander.

But at that moment, the officers turned up a slightly burned map that galvanised them to action.

It was the most carefully drawn of the maps, containing detail of individual rocks in the sea and patches of trees, even ponga ferns, that identified it as Moonlight Beach. There was even an outline of the dredge. But the marking that brought the reaction was a curved line, an open ellipse that ran in from the sea, passed at its tightest curvature close to the outline of the dredge, then returned to the sea.

Renwick spun on the nearest man.

'Wadlow. Top speed! Get back through the tunnel to the field radio. Tell them to call the beach. They're to expect an attack from the sea. From the sea. Have you got that? Go, go!'

Wadlow ran, stuffing the brown paper in his pocket to show the commander later.

'Choose a number,' Wells said loudly, as if she was deaf.

Rosa seemed unaware even of the cards in her hand. Her eyes drifted across the discards, the card fans, the kitty, the nearly empty brandy bottle, the tattooed arms. Dravitski's tattoo was a work of art – Hong Kong's finest tattooist had given him a three-coloured, fire-breathing dragon with a body that writhed when his muscles flexed. But Rosa's eyes didn't linger even on that. Her head was cocked on one side, as if listening for something.

'Choose a *number*, you dumb slut,' Foster growled.

Rosa blinked.

'Eight,' she said. And the men sighed with impatience, their eyes on her torn dress. Sergeant Wells leaned over, held his hand next to her cheek and delivered a slap that might have been affectionate if it had been softer. His lips over-articulated through a half grin.

'How many times do I have to tell you, sweetheart? One, two, three, four, or five. Say one of those.'

'Five.'

'That's my baby.'

Her cards were plucked from her fingers. Another five took their place and her fingers were closed round them.

'Dealer takes two . . . tum te too . . . whaddaya got?'

Three sets of cards tipped for the show.

'You too sweetheart. Hold 'em over. That's right. Well, well, two sixes. Too bad, you lose. Take off your other sock.'

'Jesus Wellsey, what're you doin' to us?'

'You're just a tease, ain't you serg?'

'Take it *off*, sweetheart.'

'Smart-ass bitch. That dumbo act is getting up my nose. Look how she's hangin' on to that doll.'

A silhouette appeared in the doorway. 'You buggers leave some for me.'

'Don't worry, Smitty. The rate Wellsey's dragging it out, we'll die of old age first.'

'Get back out and keep your eyes peeled,' Wells snapped. 'Or you won't even get a sniff.'

Smith left, banging the door shut. Rosa gave a long moan, half-standing. But the door fell back of its own accord.

'Now, sweetheart, sit down and take that sock off. You don't want to make us mad. You really don't want to make us mad. Look, I'll help you.' Wells reached down to Rosa's calf and yanked a leg up, cracking her shin on the table and nearly tipping her backwards off the form. The sock came off. 'You see? You really don't want to make me mad. I'm not nice when I get mad.'

'He's not,' agreed Dravitski. 'He's fucking diabolical.'

'Next hand. Deal.'

Foster scooped up the cards, split the pack and shuffled in an impressive arch fan, cutting one-handed. He dealt, spinning the cards out impatiently.

'Discards. Come on Wellsey. You're a bleedin' sadist, makin' us wait, you know that? You want us to do sumpin'll make us all go blind so you can 'ave 'er to yourself. I know your game.'

'The bad girl is coming,' Rosa said suddenly.

'Really? Friend of yours? I like her already. Discard, Rosie baby. Choose a number.'

Twenty-Four

Under Ben's knife, the white fungus took on the approximate shape and size of a bullet. It was the bright white of absolutely dry fungus, the type that grows on dead and dying beech trees.

The Maori, who came for the jade in the beaches, carried fire on their backs in carefully wrapped, glowing pieces of fungus. Into the base of the shaped fungus, Mal inserted the tip of an arrow. The prepared shaft then joined another, a reserve shaft, lying across a twig to avoid contact with the damp ground.

There was no time for more. The two lay still, listening to the easy mutter of voices as a patrol passed by further downhill.

Then there were several sounds at once. On the beach, a siren began to soar. The radio of the recently passed patrol chattered urgently. A voice gave an order and boots thumped away towards the beach. The dredge abruptly ceased its roar, the change so marked that for a while it was like a new noise making new demands on the ear.

'Goddamn! They've found out.' Ben stood to peer down at the beach. Three troop carriers raced down the sand from the huts near the gate. Men in civilian clothes clambered down the ladder from the dredge control room. In a frenzy, he hooked his fingers like claws, shaking them and digging fingernails into his temples.

The siren stopped.

From far away came the mosquito's hum of a helicopter. Only the highest frequency reached them, a pure, smooth sound, the rest filtered out by distance.

Mal dipped a knee to his bow, bending it, slipping the string into its notch. As the tension came on, the string thrummed softly. He took a fungus tipped arrow, fitted it to the string, held it loosely and closed his eyes. Concentrate. The bow. The shaft. The target. Bow, shaft, target. Bowshaftarget.

'Here we go, brother,' Ben whispered. 'This is where you join the race of men.'

The trucks halted round the dredge, soldiers poured from them, fanning out and throwing themselves onto the sand facing the water. The hum became a throbbing whine, a gnat over the ocean grew into a helicopter with a second gnat slung beneath.

'Weave Moa, weave you bastard,' Ben groaned. But the small Bell helicopter came on, deviating from a straight line only for the beginning of the elliptical pass. The second gnat became a forestry service monsoon bucket hanging below. The brothers had chosen their spot carefully – high on a spur for maximum range, with concealing greenery that framed a view of the dredge and the flat sea beyond. The Bell was on the extreme left of the frame, coming in on a tightening curve.

Then, a jink in the curve as Moa realised that the soldiers were in a line parallel to the sea. He flared the curve outwards, coming straight in along the beach with the bucket a few feet above the ground.

Only Ben heard the small-arms fire. Mal was oblivious to all but bow, shaft and target. Bowshaftarget. Ben held a cigarette lighter to the fungus on the shaft and blew gently. A twist of fine smoke stood on the shaped fungus.

The Bell was hit. It trailed black smoke as it lifted to clear the dredge. Bullets pumped directly into its underside and rang on the monsoon bucket as the bucket opened. The liquid inside became rain on the dredge. In the rain was a cylindrical canister that rolled off onto the sand with much of the petrol. The Bell continued to lift, banking towards the sea, smoke billowing. The bank became 60 degrees, then 80, then it was on its side, hanging, enduring the leaden hail. The fuselage spun as if flicked by a finger. The main blades thrashed and collapsed as the machine plunged, disintegrating into the sea.

A cheer went up from the beach.

Above the dredge, mirages formed as the petrol vaporised on sun-warmed metal. Beside the dredge, unnoticed, lay the canister of LPG.

Bowshaftarget . . . one fruit from the tree . . . in a child's hands . . . dropped . . . innocent of thought . . .

The shaft was gone.

An orange spider appeared on the side of the dredge.

The dredge roared into flame that reached hundreds of feet after the escaping fumes. The explosion that followed ripped the dredge apart like wet cardboard, sending metal scything into the trees and out over the water. The blast hammered at the ears of the two brothers as they loped back into the bush, climbing higher and higher.

It took Colin some time to notice the parcel sitting on his desk. Until he did, nothing in his sight seemed connected with him in any relevant way. Outside, the helicopters came and went, going through meaningless motions of their own accord. Inside, the office was only vaguely and distastefully familiar.

He stared at the parcel until it became the only object in the office that wasn't hazy. His hand pulled it over in front of him. Two hands undid the string, pulled the paper away from a cardboard box on which the imprint of lips had been left in red lipstick.

There was no note this time. But the message was clear enough.

The gift was a geiger counter.

He thrust the box away from him, falling back, fumbling at the clasp of his greenstone watch, tearing at his shirt buttons, breaking the chain, casting both watch and pendant from him. The watch crashed on the table, but the second hand ticked on undisturbed.

'No!' He touched his scalp, running his tongue over dry lips.

But he was drawn back to the geiger counter. He pressed a switch and a small red light winked on. The speaker clicked erratically, sensing a source of radiation in the room. He brought the device closer to the watch. The frequency of clicks doubled as he brought the separation down to two feet. At four inches the clicks reached their frequency peak, a steady buzz like a blowfly. The speaker was incapable of registering more.

With a choking cry, he hurled the geiger counter at the map, where it smashed and fell. There was a blowfly blundering around in his stomach. He gagged, gagged again and vomited.

But suddenly, as he fell back in his chair, everything was calm. From an uncertain haze, everything in his office now seemed to be in focus. In fact he saw, heard, felt things with extraordinary clarity. To make certain of this, he touched things: the table top, the cardboard box, a sheaf of print-outs.

Yes. He was *aware*.

He knew, for instance, without looking, precisely how much dust lay on the window sills. He knew that the rubbish tin behind him was nearly full, he knew that there were fly spots on the naked light bulb over his head. There was a fly in the room, circling his table and legs, and at any given moment he felt its position, speed and trajectory.

Through the window, he saw the door of the grandstand open. A blowfly in a white coat came out and made its way across the grass towards his office. It moved past the window, pouring its filth and loathsomeness onto the grass like the mythical porridge that would never stop without the magic words.

The blowfly made a sound at the door.

It came in. He shot it. Blood seeped between its mandibles as it twitched its feelers on the floor. Colin stepped around the body, picked up the shotgun and metal case by the door and left.

His boots echoed in the corridor and he noticed particularly how the quality of the echo changed when he passed an open door. He knew he had killed Searle. He knew also that he was insane. That was the curious thing. How often he had imagined insanity, yet never dreamed that having achieved the state, he could view himself and his actions with such far-sighted clarity. The state of insanity was much maligned, it seemed. Better, much better to call it a state of heightened awareness.

Tents, empty. Marquees, empty. But there were men coming out of the operations room back in the guest-house, looking at him; he knew that without turning round. They would not understand, of course. They would brand him; the world would brand him. But that was only to be expected.

In the middle of the field his Iroquois waited, rotors whirring. He set out across the grass, which beat on his knees and dropped the last of its seeds on his feet. No one had ever cut the grass. It was a detail that would have irritated a lesser man.

The rotors whopped lazily overhead.

'Get out,' he said pleasantly to the patrol inside.

They were slow to comprehend.

'Get out!' he raged, pulling the nearest out to tumble onto the grass. They scrambled out.

'Get out,' he said pleasantly to the pilot and co-pilot, who looked at each other, shrugged, and did as they were told. They felt less happy about it when he rolled the doors shut behind them, strapped in and wound up the power. They scampered round to the front, making frantic gestures that Colin found intensely amusing. He laughed as they dropped out of his sight.

They were leprechauns with laryngitis and liver trouble, lost in the grass. And he laughed again at his own wit.

In two minutes he was over a lake. The water was so still in the late afternoon, it so perfectly mirrored the bush and the mountains, that its surface was invisible – a trap that had lured many a lesser pilot to his death. The music began and Colin chuckled, because he had been expecting it as one expects a friend. Chopin's 'Prelude 24' unfolded its wings and buffeted the inside of the Iroquois, trying to force him down into the lake. But nothing could touch him now; he flew on into the mountains, gaining altitude.

'Light another candle,' Wells told Dravitski.

The fire was a heap of glowing ashes. Outside, across the clearing, cicadas still chirruped, but the afternoon shadows had crept over the hut. The sun no longer lit up the webs and grime in the window; the only effective daylight came through the open door. Dravitski rose, wiping surplus brandy off his cheek.

'Yes, sir, your honour, sir.'

'Good boy. Thass what I like. Respect.'

Dravitski groped, grumbling, in the semi-dark by the cooker. A matchbox rattled and another candle spread light from its tin-can reflector. Wells reached for the cards.

'Last hand. This is for who goes first.'

'Your *ex*cellency! Now you're talkin' my language!'

'One discard and show. Highest wins, next is second, lowest is lousy last.' They heard a footfall outside.

'Smith!' Wells roared in high good humour. 'Get back in the trees. You're no bloody use out in the open.'

'Sadist!' Smith's voice grumbled and the footsteps faded away.

'Shit scared he's going to miss out.'

'He'll be missing his teeth if he doesn't keep decent watch.'

'Deal, for Chrissake!'

'Oh . . . My, my, look at Driscoll,' Foster glittered. 'That gets up my nose, that really gets up my nose.' Rosa had put her thumb in her mouth. Her lips and right eye were swollen and she stared fixedly through an obscure spot on the table's tin surface. She nursed one shoulder which was only half-covered because the front of her dress was torn to the waist.

'Cunning bitch. Never gives up, does she?'

'It's the doll gets me.'

'You shouldn't do that,' Wells told her softly. 'You can see it upsets Foz here. It ain't friendly.' His fingers flicked out, cracking Rosa's thumb away from her face. Her hand flew down past one of the jagged edges of a candle reflector, nicking the skin without tipping the candle. A red spot grew.

'It's leaking.'

'I think you've scared it, Wellsey.'

Wells looked wounded. 'It ain't my fault. It's Fozzy's fault. With a mug like that, he could be done for possession of a dangerous weapon.' Wells shifted the candle over to the edge of the table in front of Foster so that the light cast upwards on the man's sour features. Foster put on a Dracula-like expression.

'Whaddaya think of that, Rosie baby? You ever seen anything as bad as that?'

'Diabolical,' said Dravitski.

'No cards for you this time, sweetheart. Wouldn't be right.'

'That radio's been bloody quiet.'

Wells glanced at it. 'Give control a call. Then maybe they'll leave off calling us when we don't want to be disturbed.'

Foster made the call.

'Nobody at control.'

'Don't be fucking stupid. You got the right channel? Try again.'

The only answer was a gentle hiss.

Wells' face darkened. 'Can you beat that! They invited every goddamn motherfucker and his dog except us. Ring-tail bastards!'

'I want a drink,' Rosa said, gazing at the blood spot on her arm. Ladybird, ladybird, fly away home. Your house is on fire and your children are at home.

'You shoulda said.' Wells took a handful of her hair, pulled her head back and tipped brandy down her throat. As she coughed, the three men picked up their card hands and inspected them.

'You deal shit, Wellsey. Nothing but shit.'

The flush of spirit warmed Rosa low in her belly.

'I can't feel my foot,' Miska complained. Rosa inspected the foot. It had gone numb. She held the doll close to her chest, and rubbed the cloth foot to keep it warm.

'Four, dammit.'

'Two.'

'Dealer takes likewise.'

From outside came a series of grunts. Soft, guttural barks. Wells sat up.

'Hell. Venison on the hoof. Have a look, Dravitski.'

'Not now!' Dravitski looked anxious. 'Let Smitty get it.'

'Have a look!'

Dravitski went to the door. 'Nothing.'

'You call that looking?'

'Son of a bitch.' Dravitski grabbed his EWS from the wall and went out. Wells winked at Foster, inspected Dravitski's cards, made a substitution in the discard replacements.

Outside, Dravitski went two-score paces in a straight line, and scowled around. On the sunny side of the clearing there was nothing but the autumn crocuses with their illusion of spring. Nothing in the shadows round the hut. A lump in the grass under the trees. Could be anything. Nor were there any more sounds to suggest the presence of deer. Just the descending warble of a bird. That was almost the last sound Dravitski ever heard. The last was the glottal stop in his windpipe as his throat grew an arrow. Blood spurted out over the razor vanes of the hunting head and gushed from his mouth as he collapsed. He writhed, arched, and was still.

Wells and Foster waited, cards in hand.

'I can't feel my legs. I can't move them,' Miska whimpered. And Rosa huddled closer round her doll, rocking her and rubbing her all over.

'What's keeping him?' Wells said.

'It's your fault. He thinks he's on an expedition.'

'Have a look.'

'Piss off. Dravitski might have been born yesterday, but I wasn't.' But after running his eyes over Driscoll again, Foster picked up his card hand as well as the remainder of the pack and went to the doorway.

'Dravitski! Dravitski, get back in here, you cloth brain.'

He saw part of the inert shape in the grass, heard the thump, looked down at the shaft in his chest.

'Wellsey?' he said to the shaft. He buckled, falling out over the doorstop.

In one explosive movement Wells reached the wall between the door and the window, his Smith and Wesson appearing in his hands. He risked a glance at Foster and when he brought his head back his eyes were wide and his breathing fast. He cursed, his movements indecisive.

He leapt across the doorway, snatched an HK off its peg and leapt back.

'Come here,' he hissed at Rosa. When she didn't respond he dragged her to the wall, where the pain of his grip and the deadly intensity of his voice penetrated.

'Stand up!'

She came to her feet.

'Walk!'

She was half-walked, half-dragged out the door and around until Wells' back was against the outside of the wall with her body shielding him.

'Come on out in the open! Or she gets it right now!'

Nothing moved.

'I'm going to count to ten, then she's dog tucker! One . . . two . . .'

When he reached eight, a figure stepped out of the kanuka bushes at the far end of the clearing. It walked forward steadily towards Wells and Rosa. It wasn't armed. Wells looked around wildly. No one else came.

'Far enough.'

Ben slowed, but kept coming. Expressionless.

'I said far enough!' Wells dropped Rosa to bring both hands onto the HK, swung the weapon and aimed. An arrow appeared in his head, protruding from both temples. He dropped, puzzled in death.

Mal O'Hara came out from under a beech at the side of the clearing, bow in hand, next arrow nocked and ready.

'Is that all of them?' he asked. When Ben nodded, he went to Rosa as towards a mirage across the desert sands, dropping his bow and crouching with her. She touched his arm without seeing him.

'The bad girl is coming.'

'Did we win?' Ben's voice was thin with exhaustion. 'I wonder if we won?'

'Why don't you ask me?' said a pleasant voice behind him. Colin Renwick's Smith and Wesson was pointed halfway between Ben and Mal. In his other hand he held a single-barreled dart gun with a tin box under the same arm. He motioned Ben towards Mal and Rosa.

'A little togetherness, if you please.'

'Dear God . . .' Ben looked from his brother to the police commander. A strange, terrible light appeared in his eye. 'Dear God . . . We're not going through it again.'

'We'll discuss – '

Ben sprang as the revolver motioned. His hands almost connected. But Colin side-stepped as he fired and Ben curled in mid-air. As his brother hit the ground, Mal cried out as if wrenched from a deep sleep. He snatched up the bow with the string still in the notch of the shaft. But as he swung it, the revolver turned on Rosa.

'Inadvisable,' Colin said, moving to where he could easily see all three.

The bow sank to Mal's feet.

'You never really forget how,' Colin said, looking down at Ben. 'It's a bit like dancing. When you need it, it comes back.'

'We won,' Ben's lips bubbled as he breathed out. The breath wasn't replaced and Ben's eyes glazed.

'Perceptive at the point of death. I have my own theory about that.' Colin looked at Mal. 'Yes . . . you won. And with bows and arrows. I expect history is going to treat you rather glamorously, Mr O'Hara; I should think you'll feature rather prominently in children's books along with myself as the newly despicable Sheriff of Nottingham. Does that appeal to . . . ? Come right away from that bow – you dispatched those animals rather too efficiently for comfort. Now, I want you and Maid Marian to move inside. I don't want us to be disturbed for a while and it's getting chilly out here. Very carefully now, or it will cost her a set of piano fingers . . .'

Rosa's legs moved easily enough as Mal guided her. But she seemed hardly aware of him. She stopped near the door, listening for something, and had to be coaxed on.

Inside, one of the candles had died and the fire was a dull glow. Colin stood them up against the fireplace, out of reach of the weaponry. Mal brought Rosa round with one arm, holding her against his side. Not that she needed the physical support; she felt like a coiled spring. Colin laid the tin box on the table and sat comfortably on the edge, watching them.

'I congratulate you both. I confess I have a weakness for tales of derring do.'

'You think Rosa planned things? She didn't. You've got no quarrel with her.'

'No quarrel, eh?' Colin smiled. 'Please. Let's not waste time with any more pretence. Now, pay attention. For this to work properly, you have to know what's going to happen.' He opened the metal box, bringing out two bottles and a hypodermic dart.

Mal stiffened, pushing Rosa back on her own so he could keep his hands free.

'What the hell?'

'Yes. Very apt. Now look. Two bottles. This one you probably know – that's the antidote to Fentaz. We won't be needing it.' He put it back in the box. As he closed the lid he realised that Rosa was paying attention. Her gaze had focused on him. 'Ah. Feeling better, Miss Driscoll? Excellent, you'll appreciate this all the more.'

Rosa said nothing.

His glance dwelt on her a moment longer; she looked different. Something about her was changing. The feeling of déjà vu nibbled like a mouse at the edges of his thoughts; but that was an untidiness of mind, uncharacteristic of his new state. He dismissed it, holding up the bottle with no label.

'Now, this bottle is the interesting one. Usual Fentaz, but with three extra ingredients . . . namely Heliperidol, Aminazin and Triffazin. They're used by the Russians in the psychiatric hospitals they reserve for political prisoners. They cause disorientation. But above all, in the right combination, they induce a severe burning sensation.'

Mal licked dry lips.

'Crazy. You're crazy.'

'Yes, yes, yes . . . let's not get sidetracked. Now the drawback with them is that overdoses lead to shock and unconsciousness. That's where the Fentaz comes in. The anti-shock agent keeps you conscious . . .'

'Jesus God.' Mal's heart pounded in his throat. His gaze hunted the gloom of the hut, looking for some way to alter the balance. The absolute power the man held seemed to paralyse his limbs.

'. . . And it also prevents the heart from playing up. So what we have here is a little soup which should cause quite astounding levels of pain, and yet keep you in a condition to feel it until you go insane. Of course, the exact proportions of these chemicals are experimental . . .'

Nothing within reach. Better to die from a bullet. But what about Rosa? Rosa?

The shotgun came up, the revolver was laid on the table.

'It's already loaded. I brought the kit just to show you. Actually I had you and your brother in mind for this, originally, but circumstances change, time brings illumination – as does the postman.' His eyes locked on Rosa. 'Good. Excellent, Miss Driscoll. I'm glad to see you're dropping the act, I appreciate the courtesy. To show my appreciation you can have the honour of going first.'

Mal charged, skewing his body as he leapt for the revolver so that his lower half came between the shotgun and Rosa. He didn't hear the report of the gun, but felt it like a slap. Ten millilitres of liquid pumped into his stomach. The gun reversed, the butt smashed into his solar plexus, dropping him to the table. His hand reached the revolver, but sent it spinning down the table and off the other end. He slipped back, off the edge, down to his knees then on his side, curled round sobbing lungs.

'Admirable,' Colin said, looking down at him. 'But hardly realistic. Your brother's mistake didn't teach you much, did it?'

Miska slipped from Rosa's grasp and fell face down on the floor.

'Animals,' Colin said, looking at her torn dress. He opened the shotgun, removing the spent cartridge, still watching her. 'You have dropped the act, haven't you? It's hard to tell in this light. Why don't you say something?'

Mal moaned as the pain began.

'Cold, isn't it?' Colin went to the door, the dart gun still open.

'Don't close the door,' Rosa hissed.

'Well thank goodness for that. I thought I was never going to hear you.' He closed the door, pushed a table bench against it to keep it that way, and turned back.

Rosa had taken three paces forward, cat-like, to the edge of the table.

'Miska never liked you to shut the door.'

'Miska?'

Colin stopped utterly still. Slowly, his face turned the colour of spent ash. He staggered as if catching himself in the act of falling asleep, the empty gun held now in nerveless fingers. Rosa picked up the candle reflector, holding it by its base like a weapon. Wax spilled and the flame licked a jagged edge.

Outside, a fawn came into the far end of the clearing to browse.